# Humdinger

*An Irreverent Tale of Politics, Death,
and Debauchery*

*By Rick Mason*

# Contents

# About the Author

Rick Mason is a first-time writer who has a passion for exploring the world through travel and road-trips. When he's not pedaling his bike through scenic landscapes or escorting travelers to their favorite breweries or wineries all over northeast Ohio, you can find him crafting satirical mysteries that leave readers guessing until the very end. With a casual and witty writing style, Rick's stories are sure to entertain and keep you on your toes. Get ready to embark on a thrilling journey with his debut novel!

# Dedication

*This book is dedicated to all the dreamers out there that are afraid to take the first step in writing a novel. You can do it. Write what you like. You won't regret it*

# Acknowledgement

*First and foremost, I would like to dedicate this book to my wife Julie, who has always been by my side throughout many trials and tribulations. Your guidance and patience have helped me develop into the person I am today. I like to think that I am a different person now than when we first met.*

*I would also like to recognize my boys for the input that their lives have provided in my writing process. Russell, John, and Alex, you guys rock!!!*

*I would like to thank my parents and my sisters for their love and support. You all have influenced my life in such a positive way, words cannot express my gratitude.*

*I would also like to thank some friends that have provided support for this long process. John, Angie, Zach, Aimee, Jonathan, Krissy, Tim, Rob, Kevin, and I'm sure many more. You all shared a part of the inspiration for this novel.*

# Character List

**Alexander (Ace) Bancroft**-The former FBI Agent turned Private Investigator that was hired to investigate Ronald Humdinger's death. Ace was hired by Humdinger's company to investigate the death. The company board just wants to make sure that nothing nefarious occurred. The family feels that the FBI just wanted to sweep it under the rug, The FBI already determined that the death was due to natural causes but because Humdinger was a prominent politician at one time, they had to investigate. Ace is a Veteran and a former FBI agent.

**Ronald Humdinger Sr.**-Former Game Show Host of The Novice, a reality TV show where people learn the ins and outs of being on the board of his multi-million-dollar charitable company, it's called Humdinger Habitats. Like Habitat for Humanity only instead of building houses for those in need, they convert storage containers to housing for the homeless and others in need. Millionaire by inheritance, Single term elected official.

**Emilyia Humdinger**-Wife of Ronald Humdinger, former Austrian supermodel, married for the money. Detests having to see Humdinger naked after he showers. She cannot stand the sight of his spray tan lines and combover. Sleeps in a separate bedroom so that she doesn't have to be near his flabby, flatulent body.

**Ronald Humdinger Jr.**-Son of Ronald Humdinger

**Bianca Humdinger**-Daughter of Ronald Humdinger. She bears a striking resemblance to a porn star that Humdinger used to date. Ronald Sr has been known to say that he would "do her" if she wasn't his daughter.

**Vixen Humdinger**-The teenage daughter and only child between Ronald and Emilyia. Everyone is aware that Ronald Sr. was so disappointed that Vixen wasn't a boy child...Emilyia just can't bring herself to carry another child with Ronald Sr.

**Lola Aspera-Amor**-Dwarf dominatrix that works at the Tijuana brothel-prefers women but will always dominate a man if the money is right.

**Rueben Cuchillas**-Tijuana police chief, tasked with investigating the suspicious death of Ronald Humdinger. He has always tended to "look the other way" when Humdinger was involved...his co-workers assumed that there was money changing hands between the two.

**Jaime Shore**-That reporter searching for the truth...he was hated by Ronald Humdinger because he is a pit bull when he is asking questions at press conferences. Ronald Humdinger openly insulted Jaime on national TV during a press conference, saying "you are a dirty, rotten fake news reporter".

**Presley Misuse**-The Chief Operating Officer for Humdinger Habitats. He is often the target for verbal abuse from Ronald Humdinger. Everyone in the company secretly thinks that he would kill Ronald

Humdinger if he had the chance, and he thought that he could get away with it.

**Dr. Cameron Buerger, MD**-World famous Urologist known to be treating Ronald Sr. for ED and other problems concerning his sex life…being his personal physician is rough…there have been many instances where treatment with the "silver bullet", was necessary back in his porn star dating days…this has led to some scarring, warts and a host of other problems. Dr. Buerger has also been verbally abused by Humdinger when his ED meds don't work as hoped. Even going as far as telling the Dr. to prescribe higher and higher doses even though he suffers from hypertension, obesity and diabetes.

**Starletta Blaze**-The Madam at the brothel. She once had a "relationship" with Ronald Humdinger Sr. She started out as "one of the girls" and has moved up in the business. She used whatever and whomever she could to better her situation. She even had a "relationship" with Ronald Humdinger prior to his notoriety in Television and Politics. He was a doughy, pasty-faced pig of a man; even in those days but he had a never-ending supply of money that Starletta knew could come in handy for her in the future. She pretended that he was the best she ever had, and he bought it…he made sure to pay her a visit any time that he could get away.

**Joaquin Blaze**-The illegitimate love child of Ronald Sr. and Starletta. Ronald doesn't acknowledge his existence even though he bears a striking resemblance…pasty skin, reddish brown hair and freckles. Starletta has never requested a DNA test but everyone in Tijuana knows who the father is. Joaquin is forced to hide in the closet whenever Ronald Sr. comes to town.

**Dr. Francisco Bravo**-The Chief Medical Examiner in Tijuana. He comes from a long line of physicians and has been known to have a bit of a gambling problem.

# Chapter 1

Alexander (Ace) Bancroft hated Tijuana. He didn't like the sights, the smells, the scenery…yet here he was investigating the death of a former prominent politician and game show host. Most people picture Tijuana as a small, sleepy Mexican village…nothing could be farther from the truth. Tijuana is a sprawling metropolitan area with a population of nearly 2 million people. Tijuana is known for its active nightlife including strip clubs, brothels, bars, nightclubs, and wrestling venues. What most don't realize is that it is the medical device manufacturing capital of North America. It would not surprise Ace to find out that the cheap bastard was down here buying his supply of boner pills at a cut-rate cost vs. paying full price from a pharmacy in the United States.

What in the hell was Ronald Humdinger doing down here anyway? Supposedly, Humdinger had died of a heart attack in a brothel while engaging in sex games with a dominatrix. That's what Ace was here to investigate. The Federales and the FBI had already claimed it an open and shut case. Of course, the Mexican police didn't want any bad publicity from this incident, and the FBI just wanted to close the book on it, as there was no love lost between the FBI and Humdinger. He never showed any mercy when it came to appointed cabinet members, including the head of the FBI. It was well known that if you took an appointment to a chair position with Humdinger, you were expected to do whatever you were told, regardless of whether it was legal or not.

The death of any politician, current or past, under less than savory circumstances is always going to be investigated. The entire voting population will want assurances that there were no nefarious deeds committed that led to his death.

Rumor was that Humdinger was planning another run for office in the next election. His rabid followers (reminiscent of a cult following) would be out of control. Of course, sex games with a dominatrix while married to a former supermodel should be considered questionable enough. Not to his followers, though…in their eyes, he could do no wrong. If Ronald Humdinger was with a woman other than his wife, there had to be a problem with his wife. Certainly not with him. He was as close to a "supreme being" for these people as any human could be. It was scary, the things that he could say and do, and it was accepted, no questions asked.

Ace was making his way to the brothel that Humdinger had "passed away" in…in the infamous Zona Norte section of Tijuana. This part of the city was lined with bars, restaurants, strip clubs, and the occasional brothel or two.

This section of the city was not really the safest for a former FBI agent or any law enforcement officer of any type. The cartels operating in the area would love to get their hands on an FBI agent. Even a retired agent would suffice. Ace hoped that his appearance as a tourist, wearing a flowery Hawaiian shirt and khaki pants made him blend in just a bit. He knew that he had to keep a low profile here in the city, or he would be a target. Ace had considered taking a cab from his hotel room to the brothel but felt it was best to get a feel for the area by risking the 3 blocks walk up the Avienda Revolucion between the hotel and the brothel. It was broad daylight, so he felt confident that he was safe. As he approached the brothel, the first thing that he noted was the pink storefront with a donkey pictured in the windows…he was even more dismayed to see this. What in God's name was Humdinger doing at a place that had "donkey shows"? He had enough money that he wouldn't need to travel south of the border to get anything that he wanted, from donkey shows to drugs to prostitutes. The fact that the man felt it was less conspicuous for him to travel to Tijuana showed how narcissistic he really was. He was followed everywhere by his Secret Service detail. They obviously weren't known for being "invisible". The entire region was aware when Humdinger was entering the country. Roads were shut down. Entire hotels were rented, and all previous reservations were refunded without explanation.

Oh well, he might as well get this over with.

Ace entered the building and was immediately assaulted by a multitude of things. The smell of perfume and air freshener couldn't overpower the smell of body odor, urine, and marijuana. Ace was sure that all these smells were permeated throughout the walls…one smell that stood out more than others was the smell of a barn. Why would a brothel smell like a barn…then he heard the braying…the braying of a donkey? The donkey was in a room that was gated off from the rest of the building. So, this is where the famous "donkey shows" occurred. Ace was hoping to be long gone before the next show started. The last thing that he wanted to see was a "beautiful" woman having sex with a donkey. Why would anyone want to see that other than to just say that you saw it. There was truly no need to see it live. Ace was sure that things like that were available all over the internet.

# Chapter 2

Starletta Blaze saw him enter on the closed-circuit camera at the entrance. Her first thought was "cop". He just had that look. Good looking, neat haircut, trying to be inconspicuous by wearing a Hawaiian shirt and khakis. Didn't these gringos know that it made them look even more conspicuous? If they really wanted to blend in, they should try to look a bit "dirtier." Cleanliness wasn't really a thing in this part of the city.

She knew only one reason why an American cop would be in her establishment.

Why did the fat, spray-tanned bastard decide to vapor lock and die in her brothel? If he would've just done it north of the border, she wouldn't have to deal with all this bullshit. Didn't these cops understand that she had told them everything that she knew about his untimely demise? Of course, she was certain that her star "entertainer" was experiencing much more grief since she was with him when he decided to check out and move on to the big brothel in the sky.

Starletta decided to just let him stew for a few minutes in the lobby to see what he did. She thought the look on his face when he saw the donkey was priceless, and the fact that he just shook his head noticeably enough that she could see it on her tiny screen was humorous.

He appeared to be getting impatient, so she exitcd to the lobby from her shabby little office. She didn't even try to act like he was a "customer." She just came out with it and told him that she had already talked to the FBI. She had nothing more to say regarding the death of dear old Ronald Humdinger. He was fat, and he liked it rough. It wasn't her, or her employee, Lola's fault that he croaked while being dominated while wearing leather assless chaps, a leather mask, and a ball gag, not to mention the 3-inch butt plug in his ass. He could've uttered his safe word around the ball gag at any time to end the dominance, but he didn't. He just grunted and squealed like the big fat pig that he was. Ace told her that he wasn't a cop…that he was there as a representative of the family. He was just trying to gather information about what Humdinger was doing prior to his untimely demise at the hands of her "employee." Starletta exclaimed that he hadn't died at the "hands" of her employee. He was a fat pig that couldn't take the excitement that Lola was providing for him, and he just died, end of story, at least as far as Starletta was concerned.

Ace reassured her again that he wasn't a police officer and if she could just go over everything from the time Humdinger entered the brothel until he "croaked," and she notified the authorities that she had a problem, he would appreciate it. Ace told her that he was willing to pay her for her time if necessary. Starletta saw dollar signs and told him that her "going rate" was $100 per hour with a four-hour minimum. Ace peeled four $100 bills from a wad he had withdrawn from his pocket and laid it on the table. As quick as a snake, Starletta slid the money from the table and under her clothing, never to be seen again.

They entered a room off the "donkey room," which smelled of cigarette smoke, sweat, marijuana, semen and horse shit. Starletta had a seat on the small chair at the dressing table and motioned for Ace to have a seat on the strangest chair that Ace had ever seen. The "chair" looked like a barber's chair with multiple "arms or levers" attached to the sides. When Ace mentioned the oddity of the chair and the levers attached to it, Starletta went into a long description of the Kama Sutra chair and its many uses. She even told Ace that she would be more than happy to get one of her ladies, and they could give him a very detailed display of how the chair worked once they were done with their questioning. Of course, there would be an additional fee for her lady for the demonstration. While Ace was curious, he told her that he would pass. Ace was careful not to touch any of the levers…God only knew what was on them, and he was fresh out of hand sanitizer.

They had their discussion about what happened prior to the untimely demise of Humdinger. The entire exchange took about 2 minutes. Starletta took the call from Humdinger himself. He told her what he wanted and when he would be there. He expected her to set everything up and for Lola to be ready.

As Starletta finished up, Ace made a comment that he paid for four hours of information. Starletta shrugged her shoulders and said that there was really nothing more that she could provide. As an afterthought, she said it works the same way for her customers. They pay a minimum, but if they only last 30 seconds, they don't get a refund. They paid to get off…they got off…end of story. Time for you to leave.

As Ace was exiting the room, he spied a pump hand sanitizer dispenser sitting on the table, so he reached over and gave it a couple of pumps. As he started to "sanitize," he saw the amused look on Starletta's face. He instantly realized that this wasn't hand sanitizer. It was lube. Starletta cackled wildly as he stood there, dripping lube from his hands. Starletta motioned to a box of tissues as the cackling continued, and she left him to return to her office. She called over her shoulder that he should come back that evening for the show. There was a reason that they had such big jugs of lube available, and he could see why firsthand. Ace just muttered a no thanks and left the room and the jug behind, along with the big wad of lube-soaked tissues that he had just used. He called after Starletta and told her that he really needed to talk with Lola. She told him that it was her day off but that she would be back tomorrow around 10 AM so he could come and talk with her then, but he would have to pay her hourly rate. Ace just shook his head and told her that he would be back.

# Chapter 3

Starletta went into her office and shut the door. She leaned back against the door, cursing the day that she met Ronald Humdinger. Why did he have to die in her brothel? This was going to do nothing but cause her trouble. Some would think that a "famous" person dying in a business might help it…and that would normally be true, except this was a brothel, and he was a former politician. A politician who was very high up the food chain. So many hated him, but there were many who loved him and thought that he was the new Messiah.

Starletta didn't need any of his crazy, redneck supporters coming down here to her brothel looking for revenge because the big tub of lard had died here.

From what she could tell from watching American TV, he did nothing but drive a wedge between the two major political parties, nothing to unite them at all. What a fucking mess!!!

She thought back to the first time that he came into the brothel. Years before, he got involved in politics, but he was still so full of himself, even as nothing more than a businessman. A very successful businessman, for sure. At least, he was successful in his own mind. Starletta wasn't really sure how owning multiple businesses and having to file bankruptcy multiple times cquated to being a successful businessman. Apparently, things worked differently north of the border. She had to ask one of the other girls who he was…it was obvious when he entered the brothel he was full of himself. He strutted around like a rooster in the henhouse. He obviously thought that everyone should know who he was. He certainly wasn't a prime specimen of a man. Sort of dumpy, thinning hair in a combover even in those days…a fake tan, because with his lily-white skin, real sunshine would turn him into a giant blister in about 5 minutes…or a collection of about a million freckles.

Starletta wasn't a Madam back in those days, just part of the "stable" of ladies available for entertainment purposes. She was a "popular" girl back in the day. She was a full-figured lady, all-natural, a bit short in stature, but that just made her ample breasts look even more enticing to the "johns" that paid a visit to the brothel. He was a rich American, and he might be her ticket out of this hell hole…she was going to make sure she was the "chosen" one. She would use every trick that she knew to keep him coming back for more. She knew quite a few, and she was willing to share if the money was right.

He had strutted into the brothel, full of himself. All the girls sat there with their sleepy-eyed looks. Nobody even wanted to jump at this john. When she found out who he was, Starletta's brain kicked into overdrive. She could be looking at her ticket out. She hopped out of her chair and walked up to him, making sure that her ample breasts were rubbing against his arm, and asked if he was looking for a good time? He looked down at her, and then the pig moved his arm back and forth across her breasts and asked if he would be able to sample "the girls." She giggled and said they were a part of the package. If he wanted the

17

girls, he would have the girls. She dragged him towards the bar and asked him to buy her a drink. He told the bartender to give her whatever she wanted; his eyes never leaving her breasts…what a pig. She ordered the most expensive cocktail that they had in the brothel. A "Avienda Especial" which was nothing more than soda water with a lime in it. Of course, he had no idea, and it was costing him $20.00. If he ordered the same, he would get it only with a splash of tequila in it so that he wouldn't realize that he was being conned. It didn't matter, though. He didn't want a drink. He wanted to move into the "playrooms" immediately. He had things on his mind, and he needed to relieve some stress. Starletta was the perfect outlet for that.

They had an "on again/off again" business relationship for years. Humdinger would come to town and pay a visit to the brothel. He and Starletta would do "their thing." She would moan and groan. He would grunt and squeal like the pig he was and go on his way.

As time progressed, Starletta squirreled away more and more money. She also ended up pregnant, and she was positive that Humdinger was the father…she never mentioned it to him. She found out that Humdinger was into pregnant women too…the man was a pig, but he was a rich pig. When the "Madam" was injured in a shooting in the brothel, Starletta saw her chance to swoop in and acquire the business. With a little help from Humdinger, she made an offer to the Madam, and the brothel became hers. Now she was paying for her "deal with the devil"; the fat bastard died in her building, and people were looking into it. She didn't need that type of publicity.

# Chapter 4

Ace was going to walk back to the hotel and figure out his next moves, but before he did that, he thought that he would stop somewhere and grab a bit of breakfast. The one thing that he did like about Tijuana was the food. He had heard about this little place just outside of the downtown area that supposedly had the best pancakes and breakfast in all of Mexico. He wasn't really paying for this anyway. Humdinger's company was footing the bill. He might as well enjoy himself and have some great food and drink while he was here. Ace considered walking until he looked up the location on his phone and saw that it was about 3 miles away through some unsavory neighborhoods...he didn't want to end up hanging from a freeway overpass, so he started looking for a cab.

After a few short minutes, one of the local cabs pulled up to the curb, and he got in. The cabbie, Raul, asked him where he wanted to go. Ace gave him the name of the restaurant. At that point, the cabbie said that his "sister" made a much better breakfast than he would get at the restaurant, and if he wanted, he would take him to her restaurant instead. Ace decided to give it a go. If the place looked shady, he could just stick to his original plan.

Raul asked him what had brought him to Tijuana. Was he a "medical sales" person in town for one of the many medical device manufacturers? Ace didn't want to tell him the real reason he was there, so he said that he was there to view a new device that one of the companies was going to begin marketing in the USA. The cabbie seemed to believe that, so the conversation turned to other things that might be of interest to Ace.

It seemed that Raul had a lot of "relatives" in the area who owned their own businesses…his sister and her restaurant, a cousin who had a cantina, and another brother who rented scooters and motorcycles to the tourists. Raul would be a person to keep in mind for further needs if Ace had any needs that were questionable. Ace got the distinct feeling that Raul was one of those people who could get anything, anywhere.

As Raul pulled up to his sister's "restaurant" in a dusty parking lot, Ace saw a few scattered picnic tables and a food truck. When Ace started to complain, Raul assured him that he would not regret stopping here. So much so that if he was disappointed in his meal, Raul would pay for it himself, as he was going to grab a little something to eat too.

Ace walked up to the truck. After a quick introduction from Raul, he ordered the Chilaquiles and an order of sopapillas. He also asked for coffee. The stronger, the better. Bonita said that the favorite coffee was called "Coatepec coffee" and that she thought he would enjoy it. She went over to the counter in the rear of the food truck and poured him a cup, then asked about cream and sugar. Ace said to just give him a bit of cream. Bonita sat the coffee on the counter, gave him his order number, and told him that she would call his number when his breakfast was ready.

Ace went and sat at a table that was partially in the shade from the food truck. He couldn't believe how hot it was already. He took a sip of his coffee and was immediately amazed by all the flavors that he was experiencing. This coffee was like a dessert. It was like a cup of coffee with brownie batter, chocolate, hazelnut, and caramel. He was going to get some of this coffee to take home when he left. It was the best coffee that he had ever had.

Ace reached into his pocket and, pulled out a notepad, and started flipping pages. As he was flipping pages, he was watching the people coming and going from the food truck. As far as he could tell, there was no "illegal" activity going on here. People placed orders, paid, got their food, and either enjoyed it here or took it to go.

At that point, Bonita called out his number, so he sauntered up to the window to get his breakfast. When he got to the window, he saw a heaping platter of the Chilaquiles that would be enough to feed 3 men as well as another plate full of the Sopapillas. The look on his face must've been obvious because Bonita started to laugh and assured him that they had "to-go" containers if he couldn't finish it all.

Ace took both plates over to the picnic table and dug in. The Chilaquiles were amazing. A layer of fresh tortilla chips loaded with thick green salsa, topped with crumbled cotija cheese, two fried eggs, cilantro, and sliced radish. Even though Ace knew that he shouldn't do it, he cleaned his entire platter and then started on the Sopapillas. These were deep-fried pastry puffs topped with powdered sugar and drizzled with honey.

After about 30 minutes, Ace sat back and surveyed the damage that he had done. The platter with the Chilaquiles was empty other than a few crumbs and of the six Sopapillas that he started with, there were two remaining. His coffee cup was empty, and he really wanted more but knew that he needed to get busy. Sitting here enjoying one of the best breakfasts that he had ever enjoyed, he wasn't digging up any new information regarding the death of Humdinger. He walked up to the window and told Bonita that she had made the best breakfast that he had ever had and could he please get another coffee, this one in a cup to go. Raul was sitting in the back of the truck and asked if he wanted to go back to where he had been picked up or did he need to go to the factory? Ace almost slipped up and asked what factory but remembered that Raul thought that he was here for a medical device company. Ace told him that he would need a ride, but not to the factory, to the hotel that he was staying at. Raul hopped up and said that he would meet him at the cab. Ace slipped a $20 across the counter as a tip. After all, this was all being covered by the Humdinger Habitats company. He would think that they would want him to help those that were less fortunate, and Bonita was certainly appreciative.

He told Raul to take him to his hotel, the Hotel Pueblo Amigo Plaza & Casino. Raul clucked his tongue and said that was a very nice hotel, and that his company must be doing very well to put him up in such a nice place. Ace told him that they were and left it at that.

As he rode in the back of the cab, listening to Raul drone on about things to see and do in Tijuana, Ace formed a plan for the afternoon. First, before moving on to the next part of his investigation, he needed to get back to his hotel and take a nap. If this was the way that the Mexicans ate on a regular basis, he could understand the need for a daily siesta.

Raul pulled up to the main entrance of the hotel. Ace paid him in US dollars and asked him if he could give him a card so that he could contact him later if he needed a ride. Raul handed over a tattered business card and assured Ace that he would make himself available as quickly as possible when he called. Ace stood there and watched Raul drive off then entered the cool lobby of his hotel and was immediately assaulted by all the noise coming from the casino adjacent to the lobby. Ace headed to the elevators and up to his room. He was going to get a shower and then make his next moves. A plan was forming to get to the bottom of this incident. He hoped that his employers wouldn't be disappointed if they found out that there was nothing more to the death than a fat, out-of-shape American engaging in a kinky sex act, which in turn caused the heart attack. Only time and a thorough investigation would tell.

# Chapter 5

Jaime Shore watched Ace enter the lobby.

Jaime was a reporter for one of the network news channels and a frequent target of Ronald Humdinger when he was bashing the "fake news" channels that were prolific across the world, at least as far as Humdinger was concerned. What it really came down to was that if you said or asked something that didn't sit well with Humdinger, you became a target of his wrath. That wrath included attempts at public embarrassment during press conferences, name-calling, eye-rolling, and other gestures that were mocking in nature. The list of things that Humdinger would do was never-ending. He would do something outrageous like mock a person with "special needs" and you would think, it can't get any worse. But it could get worse and did every time Humdinger appeared in front of a camera. At a press conference a couple of years ago Humdinger referred to Jaime's love of animals, but it wasn't in a nice way. That outburst was due to Jaime asking about allegations from some people that Humdinger was a racist. Humdinger's retort was to ask if it was true that Shore stimulated his Great Dane manually as a form of entertainment. Fortunately for Jaime, nobody in the media liked Humdinger, even his "cronies" from one of the more "conservative" news networks. They asked the questions that he wanted them to ask, but ultimately, they all said he was a big orange blowhard who just liked to hear himself talk. Ultimately, the talk of manually stimulating his dog did hit the internet, which led to all sorts of memes with Jaime's picture and assorted Great Dane's as well as other animals and a gamut of comments to go with them. Jaime's children were exposed to this stuff all the time. Kids would bring it up at school. Some would print the pictures and tape them to their lockers. Jaime had to dig up some dirt on the circumstances that led up to Humdinger's death...he was willing to do anything to get dirt on Humdinger that would embarrass his entire family and all his loyal followers.

As Ace crossed the lobby towards the elevator, Jaime got up and entered the elevator just as the doors were closing. Jaime and Ace were the only two in the car. Ace was visibly dismayed that Jaime was there with him. He knew what was to come. Jaime started questioning him as soon as the door closed. Ace kept responding with "No comment." Jaime asked if the rumors were true that Humdinger had been in the company of a "dominatrix" when his ticker gave out?

Ace immediately responded with a simple, "Where did you get that information?" Jaime immediately responded with a comment that it must be true...since to this point, Ace had just kept spitting out "no comment". Ace could kick himself in the ass for that indiscretion. Up to this point, it was just news that Humdinger had passed away in the company of a woman who wasn't his wife.

Jaime just grinned and said, "Look, Ace, you know what kind of asshole Humdinger was," I just want the lead on the real story about his death. I won't give your name; it will be a "confidential source." Your name will never come up, and we will both get our laugh out of the story when it comes out.

The doors opened to the elevator, and Ace stepped out of the car. Jaime moved to follow, and Ace stopped him before he ever left the car with a simple, I know how to find you if I need you. Jaime stepped back, the doors closed, and headed back to the lobby. Ace turned and headed for his room. So much for a quick nap. He had to get to the bottom of what happened down here and get back to the States. He was so tired of the smell, sounds, and look of Tijuana.

Jaime made his way back to the lobby with a clear view of the elevators. If Ace came back down, he was sure to follow him wherever he went. He knew that there had to be more to the death of the big slug, Ronald Humdinger.

Why would the company hire a private investigator if it was a simple case of a heart attack while vacationing in Mexico? They wouldn't. That was the answer, plain and simple. Jaime was sure that the COO of Humdinger Habitats, Presley Misuse wanted all of this to "go away". He was set to become the CEO of the company unless one of Humdinger's children were interested in it. From what Jaime could tell, there was no interest from the children to swoop in and take over the business. All of Humdinger's children just liked living the life of the rich and famous. Not one of them was known to work hard at anything other than spending money.

Ronald Jr. was Humdinger's oldest child. He had shown some interest in politics but had not made the jump into that arena…so far. He served on multiple boards of charitable foundations; most of which paid nothing. However, he did serve on a few "boards" of less reputable companies that were known to buy influence and favoritism. When Ronald Sr. entered politics and inexplicably won his party nomination and, ultimately, the election, many companies started courting Ronald Jr. in the hopes that "favors" could be made that benefitted the companies and the "board members." Jaime had investigated the finances of Ronald Jr. as part of an investigative reporting story concerning the taxes of his father. He had found nothing amiss in Ronald Jr.'s taxes. It all appeared above board regarding his finances. The IRS saw no reason to do a "deep dive," unlike his father, Ronald Jr. willingly supplied his tax returns for the last seven years.

Bianca Humdinger, Ronald's oldest daughter, was a real treat. Jaime had an interview with her early in her father's term in office. She was beautiful, but it was obvious that she was just as vain as her father when it came to her looks. There was no question that there had been some surgical enhancement. She sat in her apartment for the interview. Her makeup and hair were perfect. Her clothing was perfect, and obviously, she had dressed to accentuate all of her "assets." When Jaime brought up her father's political career and asked her if she had any political aspirations, she droned on and on about how she was going to be the ambassador from the United States for the Island of Tahiti. When Jaime pointed out that there was no U.S. Embassy or Consulate in French Polynesia, Bianca got snarky and told him that her father would be creating the first one and that she would be the ambassador. Jaime said it wasn't just a matter of the position being "created", that there were steps that had to be taken to do something like that. Bianca didn't want to hear it. She told him that the interview was over and that he could see himself out.

Jaime was certain that Bianca had whined to her "daddy" about how mean Jaime had been to her during her interview, and that was why he had always treated Jaime worse than a person treats dogshit on their shoes.

Emilyia Humdinger…she was a wild card as far as Jaime was concerned. She was stunning, well-educated, and very independent. However, everyone knew that she came from a poor "farming" family in Austria. Ronald had spied her at a beauty pageant and promptly started the process of courting her. The consensus was that she married him for the money and the notoriety associated with the Humdinger family. She appeared to be the "Ice Queen" whenever the couple was spotted in public. She had never been observed to be the instigator when it came to any form of affection. Jaime thought back to the clips when Humdinger was in office…so many times. He reached out and took her hand. The look on her face was priceless every time that he did it. It had been rumored that holding his hand was like holding a dead fish, cold and clammy, along with a slight coating of slime. Not true slime. Everyone was aware of Ronald Humdingers propensity for sweating. It was a known fact that he owned stock in multiple antiperspirant and deodorant companies.

Would Emilyia suffer with Ronald's untimely demise? How good was the will? Did he leave anything to her, or did he leave it to his children? That information hadn't been made public yet. Jaime didn't believe that Emilyia would have done anything nefarious, but stranger things have happened. Jaime was going to find out.

# Chapter 6

Ace couldn't believe that Jaime Shore was following him around Tijuana…he had to get him out of the way if he was hoping to find out what really happened down here. Since Humdinger Habitats was paying him, he didn't feel that it was right that things leaked to the press because he was being followed around by a reporter that Ronald Humdinger had made an enemy out of. Shore had plenty of reasons to look for dirt on Humdinger. Ace decided to take a trip to the pool and "relax." Really, he was just going to see if Jaime was still hanging around. He changed into his trunks, grabbed a hotel towel, and headed down to the lobby and the pool area. Sure enough, Jaime was parked in the lobby. It appeared he was engrossed in his phone, but Ace didn't believe for one second that he wasn't observed walking through the lobby. Ace walked out to the pool area and picked a chaise lounge under an umbrella with a view of the doors from the lobby. Sure enough, he could view Jaime spying out the door to see if he was there…how was he going to shake this reporter? He did not want him hanging around while he was investigating Humdinger's death.

Ace had to be honest. He truly never cared for Humdinger. Humdinger was nothing but an egotistical ass who only thought of himself. The man was truly repulsive. Between his inability to control his mouth and his arrogance, it was all that most people could do to spend an hour conversing with him…fortunately, nobody would be subjected to his mouth any longer, other than through news clips. Ace figured that he better check into some of the people that Humdinger had humiliated too…he just found it too hard to believe that the big turd died while having sadomasochistic sex with a dwarf. While it would certainly be fitting that he went out that way, Ace didn't believe that he was going to be that lucky as he investigated this death.

Ace had to talk to the dwarf dominatrix. He had to go back to the brothel and not take "no" for an answer regarding the address for Lola. He knew that Starletta could contact her. He would do whatever it took to get Starletta to call Lola in or get him an address so that he could go and have a private conversation with her. Then it struck him. He could contact the brothel directly. He took out his cell phone and made a call to the brothel. Starletta answered on the 2$^{nd}$ ring of the phone. Ace told her that he needed to talk to Lola immediately. As he saw it, Starletta had two options: provide him with an address for Lola or wait on him to arrive with a Jaime Shore in tow. She might know him from his reporting from one of the largest news networks in the United States.

Starletta reacted just as he expected. She sounded like a roaring beast on the other end of the line. Spewing insults, all the while accusing him of blackmail and strongarm tactics. He took it all in stride. As the tirade began to slow, he asked her what it was going to be. Starletta told him to hold on. He heard the phone thump on her desk or table and then the rustling of papers. She came back on the line and spouted an address and told him that she didn't want to ever see him in her brothel again. He was not welcome, regardless of the amount of money that he might be willing to spend. At that, she disconnected the call.

Ace sat back, satisfied. Now just to figure out how to get away from the hotel without being followed by Shore.

# Chapter 7

Ace reached into his pocket and removed the business card that the cab driver had given him. He was developing a plan, and the first part of that plan was to have a car ready and wait outside when he wanted to leave. Ace gave the number a quick ring. Raul answered warily with a quick "Hola." Ace said hello and told him that he was the fare from this morning and wanted to know if he was available all afternoon for transportation duties. Raul said that he could be at the hotel in about 20 minutes. Ace said that was fine and to call when he was out front of the building. He wanted the car running and ready to go with no delays.

Ace went up to his room and grabbed his ballcap and sunglasses. He knew it wasn't much of a disguise, but it didn't really need to be. He just had to look as though he were getting ready to head out of the building again.

Ace returned to the lobby and saw Jaime immediately. As soon as he saw Ace, he was on his feet. Instead of heading for the entrance, Ace went down a hallway to the left of the registration desk. The direction sign said that the restrooms and several conference rooms were down that hallway, so Jaime assumed that Ace was heading to the bathroom. Jaime got up and went to the head of the hallway to await Ace's return and then he would just accompany him right out the door.

What Jaime didn't know was the two of the conference rooms opened onto a courtyard that led to an alley adjacent to the front entrance. Ace had ducked into one of the conference rooms and just waited on the call from Raul.

About two minutes later, Raul called. Ace told him to pull to the head of the alley and he would meet him there. Ace exited the courtyard and walked briskly to the end of the alley where Raul was waiting in his cab. It worked like a charm. Jaime had no idea that Ace was no longer on the property. Ace wondered how long he would wait before he came down the hall to check on him and realized that he was gone. Ace gave Raul the address and sat back and relaxed in the back of the cab. Raul could tell by looking at him in the back seat that he was in no mood to talk, so he just drove on.

Two blocks from the pickup location, Raul interrupted the silence and told Ace that the Policia were behind them, and it appeared that they wanted him to pull over. Ace told him to pull over but to be ready to drive off at any sign of trouble.

Raul pulled to the side of the road and placed the car in park. Ace just sat staring forward, not bothering to look behind the cab…he knew it was just a matter of time until the police found out that he was in town. Ace could hear steps approaching from the rear. Instead of going to the driver's side window, the officer stopped at his window and, gave it a couple of polite knocks and then signaled Ace to roll the window down.

Ace rolled down the window as the officer leaned over to speak to him… "Ahhh, Mr. Bancroft, we would like to talk to you at the police station. We believe that there are matters that need to be discussed regarding your visit to our fair city," the officer said in heavily accented English. Ace told the officer that he would be glad to visit the police station later that day. The officer insinuated that now would be a better option. Ace asked if he was under arrest and the officer said, "No, you are not under arrest, Senor. If you were under arrest, you would've already been removed from the car and placed in handcuffs." The patrolman then told him that he would be more than happy to "give him a ride" to the police station.

Ace declined the offer and told him that his driver would be more than adequate to take him to the station and that if the officer felt that he was being duplicitous, then he was more than happy to follow the car until they arrived at the station. Ace rolled up his window, ending any further debate, and asked Raul to drive him to the Police station. Raul nodded his head and pulled away from the curb.

Ace wondered what this visit was going to hold. Was it going to be a polite visit, or was he going to be threatened and told to leave the city? He had no idea at this point. He understood the lead detective that investigated the death of Humdinger was rumored to be on the "payroll," so to speak of Humdinger himself. There had been several occasions where it was rumored that Humdinger had gotten rough with the hookers that he utilized when he was visiting Tijuana. Rumor had it this occurred when Humdinger was having "problems" with "little Ronald," and his pills weren't working. Of course, it was always the fault of the hooker, never the fact that he was an overweight

70-something with high cholesterol, hypertension, and an enlarged prostate. His problems with his sexual prowess had to be the fault of the hooker. What a tool Humdinger had been.

While Ace was lost in thought, they had arrived at the police station. Ace told Raul to stay put, that it wouldn't take long. If he wasn't out in an hour, at the maximum, then he wouldn't be coming out anytime soon, and he was probably locked in a cell or an interrogation room. If he didn't return in an hour, Raul would have to go about his business, and Ace would call him when he was released. Raul acknowledged his understanding and told Ace that he would pull across the street to the parking area and wait for him.

Ace entered the lobby of the station and sauntered up to the front desk where a sergeant was seated and told him that he had heard that someone in the department wanted to speak with him. The sergeant asked his name. When Ace gave it, the sergeant's eyebrow went up, and he looked at him more closely, made an unintelligible comment, told Ace to have a seat, and went in the back. Ace turned to have a seat and saw that there were only two chairs, and both were currently occupied so he just continued to stand at the desk. After what seemed an interminable time, the sergeant returned and said the lead detective would be with him shortly and that he could have a seat. Ace gestured at the two occupied chairs. The sergeant just shrugged his shoulder and picked up a paperback book lying beside the computer on the desk. Ace continued to stand in front of the desk. The sergeant lowered his book and told him to go stand elsewhere, that he could not block the desk for other people that would come to the station. Ace inquired where he should stand, and the sergeant pointed at the lobby and said anywhere but here, raised his book, and ignored Ace.

Ace seriously considered moving to the side by about 12 inches but figured with all the supposed corruption in the Mexican Police establishment. It wouldn't serve in his best interest to end up in a cell because he pissed off a desk sergeant, so he moved over to the side by the doorway that appeared to lead to the back of the police station. Just as Ace made himself comfortable leaning against the wall, the door opened, and an older man called his name. He sauntered to the door and entered as it was held open for him. The clerk told him Reuben Cuchillas, the lead detective wanted to talk with him regarding the Humdinger case. Ace followed the clerk back to a dingy office at the rear of the station. He noticed the smell of old cigarette smoke and body odor before he ever entered the office, so the sloppy pig of a man sitting behind the desk was no surprise.

Reuben didn't waste any time. He immediately demanded to know why Ace was down in Mexico investigating the death of Humdinger. It was an open-and-shut case, and he didn't want him there. Ace explained that he was hired by the family to investigate further and that he didn't like being in Mexico any more than Cuchillas liked him being there.

Cuchillas immediately launched into a diatribe regarding "Money and people that feel they can do whatever they want" …Ace acknowledged the fact but said that they were paying him to investigate, so he was going to investigate, with or without Cuchillas help.

Cuchillas lifted his slovenly bulk out of a chair, which seemed to groan in relief. Ace wasn't surprised that Cuchillas was dressed like a homeless person in Tijuana. His shirt and clothes were filthy and wrinkled. Between the sweat stains under his arms and piss stains on the front of his pants, Ace was thankful that he hadn't shaken the fat slob's hand, although he was already thinking about decontaminating himself when he left the police station.

Cuchillas waddled his fat ass over to an ancient filing cabinet in the corner and pulled out a file…walked it back over to Ace, and tossed it on the desk in front of him. Ace was not surprised to see the name Humdinger on the tab. He also wasn't surprised that it was a very thin file. Ace opened the file and found a "police report" in Spanish, along with a couple of photos of Humdinger lying dead in all his naked glory. Ace asked if he could have a copy of the police report and the photos. Cuchillas balked at the suggestion, stating that he didn't want the photos of Humdinger leaked to the press. He didn't want his department to be looked upon badly because of mishandling evidence of a crime that wasn't a crime at all. Just another case of an old American dying with a hooker that was too much for him to handle.

Ace assured him that the last thing that he would do would be to share the report or photos with anyone. He also reminded Reuben that he was being paid by the family and company that Humdinger owned, so they wouldn't want anything "delicate" to be in the public either.

Ace didn't really think that the report would reveal any useful information, but he wasn't going to let Cuchillas know that he didn't speak or read a bit of Spanish.

Cuchillas took the file and came back with the copies as requested. Ace leafed through the papers and asked for an envelope to place them in as he didn't want them to be seen in public. Cuchillas opened a drawer, rattled around a bit, and slid a filthy envelope across to Ace.

Ace picked it up by the corner with some obvious disdain. Reuben just shrugged his shoulders and said that things weren't near as good in Mexico as it is in America. The poor neighbors to the south had to make do with what they had available. They couldn't go out and just purchase things willy-nilly like the wealthy people up north.

Ace rose to leave, and Cuchillas asked him where he was going. He told Ace that he had to pay for the "copies" of the report. Ace asked how much it was for the copies and wasn't surprised at all when the fat slob told him that it was $250. Ace raised an eyebrow at that, and Cuchillas just shrugged his shoulders and said that times were tough right now, and it was very hard to get toner for the copy machine. Ace told him that he would pay the clerk on the way out. At that point, Reuben leaned across the desk and said "Senor, apparently you don't understand. I need reimbursed for the copies. I am the person that chose to share them with you. Not the Tijuana Police Department. You will pay me personally."

Ace reached into his pocket and rifled through his money below that desk and eye level. Obviously, Cuchillas wouldn't be opposed to raising the price if he saw the wad of cash that Ace was carrying around. Ace made a big show of counting out the money and even made the comment that he hoped he had enough cash on him. Cuchillas assured him that if he needed to, there was a bank right down the street with an ATM that he would be willing to escort Ace to, so that he could withdraw the money. At that time, Ace tossed the cash on the desktop and said that it wouldn't be necessary to go to the ATM. Cuchillas slid the money off the desk and into his shirt pocket so quick that Ace was sure that the man must've missed his calling as a "sleight of hand" magician. Ace asked the fat slob if he was free to leave at this time? Cuchillas told him that he was always free to leave but that it would probably be best if he left, went and packed, and headed back to America where he belonged…that there was nothing for Ace to learn here in Tijuana. Ace told him that he would take it under consideration, picked up the file folder, and left the fat bastards office before Cuchillas found another reason to charge him more money. As Ace was closing the door, Cuchillas told him that he hoped to see him later on his way to the airport.

# Chapter 8

Ace left the police station and headed across the street to the parking lot where Raul said he would be waiting. He was cutting it close. He had told Raul to leave if he wasn't out in an hour. It had been about 50 minutes. Hopefully, Raul was not in a hurry to go anywhere else. As Ace entered the parking lot, he saw Raul in his car parked in the rear corner. He walked over to the car and noticed, almost immediately, that Raul was literally "asleep at the wheel." His head was back, mouth open and loud snoring was heard three rows away. Ace shook his head at the ability for people to sleep anywhere. He was truly jealous of those with that ability. Sleep has always been a problem for Ace. Maybe once he was done with this assignment, he would take a long vacation to St. John in the Virgin Islands. His uncle owned a home on the island and had told him time and time again that he could stay there if he wanted to. He might just take him up on it this time. He would love to meet the colorful character Thomas who lived in the home below his uncle's. Rumor had it that he was gay but didn't want people to know it, so he and his "partner" arranged a marriage with his partner's daughter when she was 19. It apparently didn't matter to Thomas that he was in his 50s and didn't like women. It was all about appearances.

Ace grabbed the door handle and quietly opened the door, then plopped down in the seat and slammed the door causing Raul to let out a long string of swear words in Spanish. Ace just smiled at Raul in the

42

rearview mirror and told Raul thanks for keeping an eye out for me. Raul told him that he was lucky that he hadn't gotten shot pulling a stunt like that…but he also said something about "you crazy gringos and your jokes" with a huge grin on his face. Then asked, where to "Boss" you booked me for the day.

Ace told him that it was time to pay Lola a visit and once again gave Raul the address. Raul told him to sit back and enjoy the ride. He would be there in just a few minutes.

Raul asked Ace who he really was. He didn't think that there was any way that the police in Tijuana knew "medical salespeople" by name. Ace thought about it and finally told Raul who he was and that he was in the city to investigate the death of Ronald Humdinger.

Raul appeared to accept that, slipped the car in gear, and they were off.

As Ace sat in the backseat, he was thinking about the possibility that there was truly more to the death of Humdinger than originally thought, but how was he going to uncover the truth down here in Mexico. With all the corruption and the expectation of "graft" every time that you spoke to anyone, how would you ever trust that you were getting the true story or if you were just hearing what people thought that you wanted to hear. Ace just figured he would continue to gather information and present it to Presley Misuse as necessary.

# Chapter 9

As Ace pulled up in front of Lola's residence, his first thought was, "This is not what I expected for a dominatrix." Then he thought better. He had never actually been to a dominatrix. He told Raul to wait for him and that he would be out as soon as possible.

Ace entered a gate into a small garden with lush tropical plants and went to the door at the end of the walkway. He gave the door a quick knock and waited. He heard shuffling inside and saw a small child approaching down the hallway. The door opened and he was fully ready to tell the youngster who he was there to see. He realized very quickly that "the child" was a "dwarf." He asked the dwarf to speak to Lola…she responded with a cheery, "You found her Hefe." He stood there speechless for a moment and then introduced himself. He explained that he was there to investigate the death of Ronald Humdinger. The family and company didn't want to believe that he had died of "natural causes." They knew that there had to be more to it.

Lola invited Ace in and asked if he would like something cold to drink. He said that a cool drink would certainly be welcome. Lola offered him a cerveza, iced tea, or ice water. Ace chose the iced tea as he was technically "on the clock" and he didn't want word that he was drinking getting back to Misuse or anyone else at Humdinger Habitats.

Lola left the room to get the iced tea, so Ace wandered the living area. He was amazed at the "high-end" furniture and artwork that adorned almost every square inch of space in the tiny apartment. He was looking at a Von Gogh or a very good reprint of a Van Gogh when Lola startled him when speaking to him from behind. She was as quiet as a mouse. He had never heard her approaching. She wanted to know if he liked the painting. He said that it was a very good likeness of a Van Gogh. She laughed a cheery little laugh and said, "Honey, it isn't a good likeness; it's the real thing." Ace was taken aback. How could a hooker in Tijuana have a Van Gogh...he came right out and asked her.

Lola explained that a lot of her customers provided her with "gifts." Sometimes those gifts were jewelry, sometimes cash, sometimes cars, sometimes it was artwork...like this piece. She had been given this piece by a businessman who visited her on occasion from New York City. He owned some apartments as well as a "non-profit" business that he created to help the homeless, although she thought that the business was nothing more than a way to hide money from the tax man.

Ace asked her if it was "Humdinger Habitats" by chance, and she tittered a quick laugh and said of course. Ronald was one of my best customers. He was always very generous with his cash, as well as with gifts that he sent to her after he returned to the United States.

Lola said, "Enough of that, though." What do you want to know about the day that my dear slave Ronald passed away?

Ace had a seat on the closest armchair, a leather and suede piece of furniture with mahogany trim. As he took a seat, Lola laughed and said that the chair he was sitting in was also a gift from Ronald Humdinger. He told her that it was a $2,500.00 chair and that she needed to take good care of it. She told Ace she had no idea if it really was worth that, but it was a very comfortable chair, and the leather made for easy cleanup whenever she entertained her "slaves" at home. She also asked that he be discreet and not tell Starletta about her after-hours activities as it was frowned upon. Ace reassured her that he wouldn't say anything to Starletta and asked Lola to tell her about the evening that Humdinger had died; to start from the time he got there until she realized there was a problem and contacted the paramedics.

Lola took a deep breath and started her recollection of the day. It was a day like any other day…she knew in advance that Ronald was going to be visiting as she had to clear her schedule to make room for him. When he came to town, her entire day was devoted to him and his "pleasure and pain."

She had arrived at the brothel at 3 PM to await him and his Secret Service entourage, as they always had to check things out before they would leave Ronald alone with her. Early in her relationship with Humdinger, one of the Secret Service agents had suggested that they would have to be present to ensure that she didn't do anything to "hurt" Humdinger. She laughed and told him that if her boss said it was ok for him or others to watch, that she didn't care. When the agent approached Humdinger about staying in the "chamber," she saw what his temper could be like. Humdinger went off on a rant about how these people were there to serve him and that if he was visiting a "friend" and wanted privacy that there was no way that he would maintain the Security. Humdinger was literally yelling in the agent's face about being an inbred piece of shit from Mississippi and that he could get the hell out and never come back, that he was dismissed. The agent told him that he couldn't just leave him in Tijuana. Humdinger told him to get the hell out, and he would address it when they were back in the States.

Lola said that the agent left with his tail between his legs. That was when she knew she had to be the "one in charge;" that Humdinger was a bully, and if allowed to, he would berate and belittle her, and that was certainly not the way that her services worked. She was in charge, and she made sure that all her clients knew it from the beginning. She told him to sit his pasty ass down…he spluttered, mumbled, and grumbled, telling her that nobody spoke to him like that. She told him again to sit his pasty white ass down and listen to her, only this time, she said it with a firm grip on his balls. He took a seat and started to whine about the pain. She told him that was just the tip of the iceberg. He was going to sit there and listen to the rules. If he didn't want to adhere to the rules, then there was no need to continue.

Ace interrupted and asked her to tell her what her "rules" were. Lola asked if he was interested in experiencing her services. He politely told Lola that he wasn't interested in her services, but by knowing the rules, he might be able to piece together what happened to Humdinger.

The first and most important rule was that she was in charge. The sub didn't have any choice in this. If the sub wouldn't agree, then they were dismissed.

At this point, Ace interrupted her again and asked her, "What is a "sub"? I am unfamiliar with anything about S&M".

Lola explained that a "sub" was the "submissive," and she was the "Mistress." She explained that she was the person in charge.

The second rule was that the sub was there for her pleasure as well as their own pleasure. If she demanded something from them, they must comply, or the session would end. If the sub couldn't please her, then they were dismissed. She said that there were "problems" early on in her "relationship" with Humdinger because he couldn't maintain an erection. She had told him after their second meeting that she was going to have to release him. He begged her not to do that. He told her that he "knew a guy" who could get him some medication that would help him and to please give him another chance in the next few weeks.

Ace took note of that, as he wasn't aware of Humdinger's erectile issues...he was smiling inwardly at this as he could just imagine how this must've been a problem for his supermodel wife...or was it? Maybe she had other means of receiving her needed satisfaction. He would have to check into the "person" that Humdinger knew for the meds.

The third rule was straightforward. As a submissive, he would not achieve orgasm until he was permitted to. If he couldn't control himself and got off early, then the session was complete and there were no discounts for "early release." as a matter of fact, there was a penalty charged if that occurred. The penalty was $1000, and it would be collected prior to the client leaving the room. It wasn't a huge sum of money for Humdinger but after she charged him with his first penalty, he fought to control himself after that. She said that he acted like the $1000 was going to put him in the poor house.

The final rule was the "safe word." Each client picked a safe word. If they uttered the safe word, then all "play" stopped, and the session ended. She always cautioned her clients to pick a "safe word" that wouldn't be uttered in normal sexual activity as it could slip out, and they didn't want the pain or pleasure to end.

Ace asked her what Humdinger's safe word was and if he had ever used it.

His safe word was "sheeple". Lola said that it had been uttered on a few occasions. She did ask him the meaning of the word as it was not an English word that she was aware of. He told her it was what he called his clueless followers behind their backs. She just acknowledged him and told him that would be his "safe word."

Ace asked her if Humdinger had used his safe word the night of his demise. She stated an emphatic no. He just did his normal piggish grunts, groans, and squeals as she administered his pain and pleasure. Then he quit making any noises at all. That was when she knew something was wrong, and so did the little Korean man that he had brought along to watch.

Ace asked her to hold up…"What little Korean man?" She told him that she didn't know his name, just that Ronald kept calling him "Rocket Man" and that he was a "very important" person in Korea. Ace asked her if the police were aware that there was someone else in the room during the "meeting". She told him that "Rocket Man" gave her a wad of cash to keep her mouth shut about his presence, so she did. Ace asked her why she was telling him this now. She said that he wasn't the police and that she lost one of her best "subs" and she wanted to make sure that everyone knew that she didn't do anything to harm Ronald in any way. Ace asked how he got out of the room without being seen and she told him that one of the Secret Service agents escorted him away unseen out the rear entrance. Ace asked her if any of the other agents knew that this "Korean" man was in the room with them, and she said that they were all aware. She reminded Ace that the Secret Service always inspected the "chamber" before leaving Ronald alone with her and, in this instance, with her and "Rocket Man," whoever he was. She said that the Secret Service agents tried to take Rocket Man's cell phone because they didn't want any recordings of Humdinger, and Rocket Man protested. Humdinger told them that it was fine that he kept his phone and that he knew that Rocket Man wouldn't do anything inappropriate with his phone. Rocket Man was his friend. He knew which side his bread was buttered on.

He wouldn't do anything to jeopardize the political connections with Humdinger.

This was another new development. He knew that talking to Lola was what he needed to do. He wondered if anyone at the corporate offices was aware of the Korean man's presence. He was betting that somebody knew about it, but why had they kept that information from him?

Ace asked Lola if this was the only time that Humdinger had someone "watch" during his session. She said that it was the only time that it had ever happened and that, truthfully, the Korean man seemed a bit uncomfortable with the situation. She said she looked at him a few times during the session, and he really wasn't even watching. He spent most of the time fidgeting with his clothing and staring at his cell phone. She said it was a strange cell phone, too…it had an antenna on the top that looked almost like a lens of some type. He kept moving it around like he was trying to get a signal, but he never said anything.

Ace asked her to finish telling her story without giving out too much detail. He truly didn't even want to think about Humdinger's pasty naked body strapped to a bed while she was administering his pleasure and pain, but he had to determine if the ecstasy was just too great and his old, fat heart gave out as he had been told.

She proceeded to give him some details up until the time that Humdinger quit responding. She said at that time she was using a "sound" on him, along with a metallic butt plug, and administering a low voltage electric charge that passed between the "sound" and the butt plug through his prostate. It was said to be "uncomfortable" but "pleasurable" as well, and that Humdinger loved it. He called it a "stinger to his Little Humdinger." She said that it was one of his favorite "punishments" before he was allowed his "release." Ace asked her if the device had been checked to make sure that there was nothing wrong with it that could've caused the heart attack.

She told Ace that she took it to her cousin to check the output and that it was fine. She had used it on multiple "subs" since the death of Ronald and nobody else had developed any problems other than the occasional light bleeding from the "sound" insertion. Lola said that just as Ronald reached his release, he quit moving, groaning, and grunting, which wasn't normal for him. When she looked up at his face, his eyes were open but rolled back in his head, and he was completely slack jawed. She gave him a slap across the face and told him that it was no time to take a break and he needed to "wake up." When that elicited no response, she looked closer at him and realized that he wasn't breathing. She checked his pulse and found none so she went to the door and got the agent outside of the door. She said the agent came in and checked his pulse, found none, and ordered her to remove the restraints from his wrists and ankles and to remove the sound and the butt plug as he started CPR. The lead agent told the other agent to get the other man out of the room. As he was being escorted out, he handed Lola the wad of cash and, in broken English, said to her that he was never there.

52

Ace asked her again why she told him that the little Korean man was there when he had paid her to keep her mouth shut. She said that she was hoping for some sort of "payment" from Ace, but honestly, if she didn't get paid, that was OK too, although she was missing the income that "Slave Ronald" had paid. She figured that there was no way that the little Korean man would be able to find out who told him that he was present during the death. There were many Secret Service agents who knew that Humdinger was there, and there are plenty who knew of his "fetishes" and just looked the other way, whether it be inviting a new "partner" to participate or watch, whether it was another female partner that he would bring in to "learn" what she did so that he wouldn't have to make as many trips across the border. Ultimately, Lola wasn't worried about it. She told him that she was quite capable of taking care of herself…and the first thing people did was dismiss her because of her stature. She said that was the biggest mistake that they could make because she had enough training that she could and had taken care of herself when some "patrons" had gotten angry and tried to hurt her. Apparently, some people forgot that they were paying to be "punished."

Ace had to be honest, the thought of Humdinger with a metal rod up his dick and a metal butt plug up his ass with electrodes hooked to it really made him nauseous, but knowing what kind of dickhead Humdinger could be, it was also fitting. He did tell Lola that he would like to see the device that she used and possibly take it to get it checked out. Just to make sure that it wasn't the cause of Humdinger's vapor lock.

Lola told Ace that he would have to come to the brothel to retrieve it and that he couldn't have it very long as she had many clients who liked the feel of the "electric" running through their bodies.

Ace assured her that he wouldn't have it for more than a couple of hours. Lola told him that he could pick it up at the brothel the next day as she was scheduled to work and had a couple of clients that would be in. Neither of which had any interest in the electro-stimulation therapy as a punishment.

# Chapter 10

Ace left Lola's apartment and returned to where he had left the cab and Raul was waiting right where he had left them. Ace hopped in the backseat and asked Raul if he knew anyone who could "check" an electrical device to make sure that it wasn't malfunctioning or had been tampered with in a way that it could harm someone.

Raul thought for a couple of minutes and said that he would make a couple of calls. His wife's cousin Herve might be able to do it. Raul told him that he would check that out and get back to him at the next stop…so where to "Senor"?

Ace told him to take him back to his hotel as he had to make some calls and he wasn't doing it with his cellphone. He was doing it from his room so that the charges would be covered by his client.

Raul took off towards the hotel and Ace was lost in his thoughts when he told Raul that he wanted to go to the Medical Examiner's office prior to the hotel.

Raul said that wouldn't be a problem and headed towards the center of Tijuana. Ace got out his phone and looked up the information that he had on Dr. Francisco Bravo. He wanted to see if there was any info in the file that would be helpful if he had to strong-arm Dr. Bravo to get a bit of information out of him.

# Chapter 11

Raul and Ace pulled up in front of the Medical Examiner's office, which happened to be attached to the Tijuana Police Department building. Ace was hoping that he wouldn't run into any of his "friends" from TPD. Even though they had been helpful, he felt that they were just itching to find a way to lock him up and keep him there for a few days.

As luck would have it, there were no problems at all with running into the police. They must've all been in the office out of the heat because nobody came or went from the front door.

Ace entered the Medical Examiner building and was hit immediately with the smells that emanated from an "open" body. He walked up to the counter and rang the bell. After some clanging and banging, as well as some choice swear words, a person in a surgical gown came from the back and asked if he could be of assistance.

Ace told him who he was and why he was there, and that he wanted to meet with Dr. Bravo to discuss what was found during an autopsy that he had performed on Ronald Humdinger.

The man behind the counter asked Ace if he had made an appointment to meet with Dr. Bravo? Ace told him that he had not but how busy could the Doctor really be? They couldn't have that much to do down here in sleepy little Tijuana.

The medical assistant behind the counter turned about 3 shades of purple before spouting of a long string of Spanish. Ace had no idea what he said, but he was pretty sure from the tone of it that it wasn't anything nice. Ace stood there and took the verbal bashing and finally held up his hand and said, "no hablo"...you need to speak English. This set off another tirade from him. With all the yelling going on, the person in the back opened the door to see if there was a problem. Jose said that this "Gringo" wanted to see him, and he didn't have an appointment. The Gringo also made a comment about how they couldn't be that busy down here in Mexico.

Dr. Bravo looked at Ace and asked him if he truly said that. Ace said that he had but wasn't trying to be disrespectful. He just wanted to meet with him to discuss the results of an autopsy that he had done a couple of weeks back.

Dr. Bravo motioned for Ace to come around the desk and told him that if he didn't mind talking while he worked, that he could accompany him to the back. Ace assured him that he wouldn't have any problem talking to him while he worked.

Ace followed the doctor to the back while the assistant walked in behind him. Ace had to admit, he was a bit nervous having the guy behind him. He obviously had pissed him off, and the last thing that Ace wanted was a scalpel in the back of his neck. He looked behind him a couple of times and the assistant just wiggled his fingers at him with a creepy ass smile on his face.

As they approached a double door, Dr. Bravo hit a button to the side and the doors swung open. The first thing that hit Ace was the smell of formaldehyde and bowel. The room was fairly large, with four autopsy tables in the middle. The entire back wall was covered with cooler doors, which were four high and eight rows across for a total count of 32 drawers. Ace asked the Doctor why they had so many spaces, and Dr. Bravo told him that they used to have only eight spaces but with the war between the cartels as well as with the DEA across the border, he had a need for more space. Unfortunately, this still wasn't enough space so there were two refrigerated trucks behind the building where they kept the bodies until they were claimed or, after a year, had them cremated and buried in a pauper grave at the local cemetery.

Dr. Bravo walked over to the center table and pulled the sheet back to reveal a young Hispanic man with what appeared to be multiple gunshot wounds and it also looked as though his throat had been slit, and he had his tongue hanging out of his neck.

Ace took an involuntary step back and a quick breath that was audible to the Doctor as well as the assistant in the other room.

Dr. Bravo asked if he was alright. You look a little pale, Senor. Ace told him that he was fine. He just hadn't been expecting the gruesome sight when the sheet was pulled back. Doctor Bravo chuckled and told him that a "Colombian Necktie" and bullet wounds were mild compared to some of the causes of death that they saw here in the ME office. The doctor started poking and prodding at the wounds and asked what Ace was there about.

Ace explained that he was a special investigator for the company that Ronald Humdinger owned and that he had been tasked with finding out all that he could about the unexpected death of Humdinger…especially considering that it had happened in another country and a hooker had been present when Humdinger died.

Dr. Bravo chuckled and said, "To say nothing of the concerns that he was a former politician and he was married to a former Austrian Supermodel?" Ace said that there were obvious concerns from multiple arenas, but he was there at the behest of Humdinger's company, not anyone else. Dr. Bravo asked Jose to get the file on Humdinger and bring it to him. Jose scurried over to a filing cabinet. While he was getting the file, Bravo told Ace that he could look at the file, but he couldn't copy it or remove any part of it and take it with him. If he wanted copies, he would have to go through the proper channels to get them. Dr. Bravo did say that he didn't think it was likely that he would see anything in the files that wasn't already known but he was free to look at it. Jose handed him a rather thin file folder and, directed him to a stainless-steel desk at the side of the room…and told him again that there would be no copies from the file, that included taking pictures of anything with his phone. Ace asked if it would be ok to take some notes, if necessary while looking over the file. Dr. Bravo said that would be fine, but he would have to do it the old-fashioned way, with a pen and paper, which he would find on the desk.

Ace started at the front of the folder. The first thing in the notes was the description of the deceased. Humdinger would've had a heart attack or a stroke reading just this part of the exam. He was described as an "elderly white male who suffered from moderate obesity." The entire world had been told by Humdinger himself that he was a "perfect specimen." He wasn't overweight, and his mind was as sharp as a tack. Even though he was in his mid-70s when he was a politician, he claimed that he was as healthy as a 45-year-old and was known to challenge some of his Security to arm wrestling on occasion. They found out very quickly that you didn't want to beat him, no matter what. It was known and witnessed by many the tantrums that he could throw if he was unhappy or felt that he was being mocked or embarrassed by someone. The funny thing is, he never hesitated to mock anyone. If a person didn't fit into the neat little profile that Humdinger had, they were fair game, forgetful (you were senile), handicapped (you were a cripple), Humdinger was even caught on camera mocking an individual who suffered from CP. If you were heavier than he was and you were a man, you were a "fat slob." If you were a woman, you were a "sow." He showed no mercy at all. In his mind, he was the perfect specimen.

Ace read the rest of the description of the body. There were notations regarding ligature marks on his wrists and ankles, as well as what appeared to be marks from something tied over his mouth. As Ace already knew, he was strapped and restrained to a board and had a ball gag in his mouth, so nothing of interest here. It was noted that there were no noticeable sores anywhere on the body except for some chafing around the deceased man's penis.

Blood was drawn, and toxicology results were included, as well as all the other tests that were run when someone died unexpectedly. Most of his bloodwork appeared to be normal. Of note was a cholesterol level of over 300, which was extremely elevated. The toxicology report showed traces of THC in his blood as well as ETOH. His blood alcohol was measured at .10, which was just above the legal limit. .10 had been the legal limit in most states until the 1980s when the entire country went to .08. Humdinger was a "little" drunk but not completely inebriated. However, this was an item to note. Humdinger professed to being a tea-totaler. He claimed that he never touched alcohol of any kind. Ace would have to check into that a bit further, and he made a note of it.

Ace asked Dr. Bravo if there were any blood tests done for exotic poisons. Dr. Bravo said that there had not been, as there was no thought that this was anything other than the death of an out-of-shape American who couldn't handle what the hooker was doing to him.

Ace leafed through the rest of the file, including the pictures of the body before, during, and after the autopsy was completed. Ace hoped that these photos never got into the hands of the public as they were anything but flattering. Whether the guy was a jerk or not, he didn't deserve to have his dead, naked carcass posted all over the internet.

Ace read through the notes and made note of the "clogged" arteries in the heart as well as carotid blockages of 70 percent on the left side and 81 percent in the right side. With the type of cholesterol and atherosclerosis, it was just a matter of time until his heart gave out or he threw a clot or piece of plaque and had a massive stroke. He was a walking time-bomb based on the notes from Dr. Bravo.

Ace walked over to Dr. Bravo and asked him if there was anything that "Wasn't in the notes" that he cared to share. Dr. Bravo said that everything that was found was in the autopsy notes. That he wasn't the type of person to "hide" something that might be upsetting to the family. Dr. Bravo told Ace that he was never really a fan of Humdinger when he was in office, but that certainly wouldn't keep him from "fudging" an autopsy or its findings. He was not that type of person, and if Ace thought that he was, maybe he needed to just leave.

Ace assured Dr. Bravo that he didn't think that he would leave something out of his report. He was just trying to get as much information as possible so that he could present it to the corporation and set their minds at ease that there was nothing more to come from any of this. Truthfully, Humdinger's company just wanted to make sure that they could still be trusted to conduct business around the world.

# Chapter 12

Ace left the Medical Examiner's office and headed to Raul and his car. Raul asked, "Where to Senor"?

Ace told him to just sit for a minute as he looked over his notes…Ace then asked Raul to take him back to the hotel. He needed to make some calls, and he didn't want to do it while driving around Tijuana. He wanted a drink and a nice, quiet place to think.

Raul dropped him off at the front entrance. Ace never broke stride if Jaime Shore was still on the lookout for him. He headed straight to the bar and ordered a Manhattan, neat. When the drink was delivered, he headed towards the bank of elevators and punched the floor of his room. As the door was beginning to close, a hand shot through the door and stopped it from closing. Ace groaned audibly as he was expecting it to be Jaime Shore. It wasn't. It was a short Hispanic man who seemed in a hurry to get to his room. He looked towards the buttons and didn't push any…so he must be going to the same floor as Ace was. The doors closed, and the man just remained staring at Ace, which was very unsettling. The doors opened on Ace's floor, and he exited as did the other man. As Ace was walking down the hallway, the man shouted out, "Bancroft"? Ace turned to him and told him that he was Ace Bancroft. However, he was at a disadvantage as he had no idea who this man was.

The man told Bancroft to head back to San Diego and get across the border…if he didn't stop digging into matters that didn't concern him, he would regret it.

With that statement, the man exited down the stairwell. Ace followed him, shouting all the time. Asking him what case he was talking about. The man looked up the stairwell and growled that he knew damn well what case, and this was his only warning. Backoff or pay some serious consequences.

Ace stood there dumbfounded for a few seconds. The Humdinger case had to be what the individual was talking about, but who would be concerned enough to send someone to threaten him? This threat only made his resolve to find out all that he could regarding this death. Obviously, with threats coming his way, there had to be something that people didn't want him to know.

# Chapter 13

What was he missing? So far, all indications were that Humdinger had died because he was a fat slob who couldn't handle having sex. What could be so bad that it warranted a threat to the investigator, that was only following up at the request of the company?

Who benefitted from the death of Ronald Humdinger other than the entire population of The United States of America? The entire country had been in turmoil since he lost his bid for re-election. So many people were convinced that the election had been falsified. It didn't help that Humdinger was always claiming that he had been cheated. His followers believed everything that this man said. It was truly like a cult. Ace needed to go over his notes and see if there was anything more that he could learn here in Tijuana. If not, he would do what the thug had said to do and go back north to San Diego.

Ace pulled a new legal tablet out of his briefcase and started writing the notes out and separating them into categories. He had found that writing the notes on paper vs. doing them on a laptop made him pay more attention to what he was learning during the investigation.

Ace made two columns, one for those who were interviewed and another for those yet to interview. He also made a note beside each person who had been interviewed whether they would need a follow-up interview.

So far, he would need to do a follow-up with Starletta Blaze and with Lola Aspera-Amor. He felt that they both had more to tell. He would see what he could get from them. Unfortunately, the need to talk to both again meant that he wouldn't be leaving the cartel and Tijuana behind. As he was making his lists, he had been sipping on his drink...which was now empty. Ace decided to risk the chance of running into Shore again. He was going to take his legal pad back down to the bar, sit in the back in a nice quiet booth, and enjoy a drink or two while looking over his existing notes and making new notes as necessary.

# Chapter 14

Ace needed to make a call back to the States. He had to touch base and let Presley Misuse and Humdinger Habitats know that so far, he had not made any revelations that there was anything more to the death of Humdinger other than the fact that he was an out of-shape businessman whose heart just couldn't take what Lola was doing to him.

Misuse was someone who Ace had trouble figuring out. With the first name of Presley, he was constantly being called Elvis by Humdinger, which led to many other people adopting the nickname for him. Misuse wasn't happy with the nickname at all, and he and Humdinger had become very vocal at times regarding the nickname. While the nickname, in and of itself, wasn't derogatory in nature, it was obvious that it really got on Presley's nerves when he was addressed as "Elvis" by anyone. Ace made it a point to only ever address him as Mr. Misuse when he was within earshot. Ace didn't want to make an enemy of the man who was going to be assuming the reins of Humdinger Habitats in the very near future. Misuse was the person signing his checks, so it was best for him to just stay on his good side.

Ace decided to make the call from the privacy of his hotel room instead of poolside, where you never knew who could be listening. He dialed the office number of Presley Misuse, expecting to get his administrative assistant or, at the very least, his voicemail. He was completely taken by surprise when the phone was answered by Misuse himself.

Ace got right to the point and gave Misuse his update so far. He did ask him if he was aware of an Asian friend that Humdinger might've had.

Misuse said he had no idea what nationality the hookers were that Humdinger frequented. Ace told Misuse that he had come across information that there was a small Asian man in the room watching as Lola Aspera-Amor administered her punishment and pleasure to Humdinger.

There was silence on the other end. Ace asked Misuse if he was still there. Ace then heard a chair creak, and Misuse said in barely a whisper that there was no way that the information of a small Asian man being present when Humdinger died should be mentioned to anyone. Misuse reiterated strongly that he was the person signing off on his expense checks and that information never needed to become public. Was Ace clear on that?

Ace said that he understood but didn't know what he would be able to do if he found that the little Asian man had something to do with the death of Ronald Humdinger. He would have to let the family know. Misuse didn't keep his voice down this time. He just stated, "Remember who is signing your checks!" Ace told Misuse that he would do everything that he could to keep this information confidential. Misuse said that if he could complete the investigation and the knowledge regarding the Asian man never became public knowledge; Ace could expect a very large bonus.

Ace said goodbye and hung up the phone. Well, wasn't this an interesting turn of events. Apparently, Misuse did know something about a little Asian man. Bonus or not, Ace knew that he was going to have to do some digging into this. What was the connection? How was the Asian man tied into this cluster fuck? Did he have something to do with the death of Ronald Humdinger or did the little Asian man just happen to be present at the wrong time?

# Chapter 15

Ace picked out a spot at the pool under an umbrella. He might as well enjoy the scenery while he went over his notes. The pool was quiet, but there were some very pretty young ladies frolicking about. Ace shook his head and thought maybe being here at the pool wouldn't be such a great idea. He had a mind like a squirrel when women in bikinis were around. He was more like Dug the talking dog from the kid's movie UP. The only difference is a woman in a bikini was the distraction instead of a squirrel. He decided that he would do the best he could to keep his concentration. If the women and the pool proved too much, then he would move indoors to a table at the back of the bar. Ace picked up his legal pad and started to jot down notes from his small notebook that he thought were important. He also started a list of things that he felt were of no concern.

The list of items on the list of "important" things began to grow.

He was going to dig into the background a bit more of Starletta Blaze and of Lola, the dwarf dominatrix.

He didn't think that there was anything more to be learned from Reuben Cuchillas or the police at this time. He didn't believe that they were covering anything up, but Ace wasn't ready to move him to the list of people who were of no concern. He would leave him and the Tijuana police department on the list for now.

Dr. Bravo and the Medical Examiner's office didn't appear to be hiding anything, and truly, what would they hope to gain by fudging the death certificate and autopsy results? The good doctor was moved to the other list.

Ace was so engrossed in his notes that he hadn't noticed someone sit down in the chaise lounge next to his, that is, until he heard a melodic female voice ask for a pina colada. Ace glanced to his left and took in the long, well-tanned, shapely legs, lithe body, and blonde hair slicked back with water. As Ace met the woman's eyes, he saw a smile crinkle at the corners of her lips, and she winked at him. He nodded and went back to his notes, but it was going to be very hard for him to concentrate with this beautiful woman next to him. As these thoughts were running through his mind, he heard her clear her throat slightly and asked him if he was here on business or pleasure. Ace tried to ignore her, but she persisted, clearing her throat more loudly and raising her voice a decibel or two and asked him again, "Business or pleasure?" Ace looked up from his notes, held up the notepad, and said, "Business." He thought that she might get the hint, but she didn't. She asked, "What business are you in?" Ace told her that he was in Medical Sales and that he was here for his company and their factory in the Tijuana area. His thought was that this would shut her up. Medical Sales, what could be more boring? Unfortunately, she squealed with delight and exclaimed that she was a nurse that was working for a medical manufacturer and maybe they worked for the same company. Ace couldn't believe his luck. How was he going to get out of this dilemma? He didn't have a list of companies in the area, and if she was a nurse who worked for medical companies, he didn't want to throw out a name for two reasons: he could tell her a company that wasn't in the area or two, he could name the company that she worked for.

As she was yammering on and on about working in medical sales, Ace did a quick search on his phone to find who the biggest medical manufacturer was in Tijuana. If he gave her the name of a large company, it would appear less likely that they would "cross paths" in the business. Finally, it happened. She asked him, "Who do you work for?" Medtronic was his answer. He kept his fingers crossed that it wasn't the name of her company. As luck would have it, it wasn't. She told him that she worked for Johnson & Johnson and that her specialty was wound management. She was here for training and education regarding a new colloidal silver dressing that the company was going to be introducing in the very near future. Ace pretended to know what the heck she was talking about.

The waiter showed up with her pina colada and, turned to Ace and asked him if he would like anything from the bar. Ace told him that he would enjoy an iced-tea unsweetened with a lot of ice.

As Ace turned back to his notes, the woman introduced herself as "Julie" and asked him his name. He mulled it over in his mind and told her his first name, Alexander, and didn't elaborate further. He didn't want to give her his last name. With Google, anyone could do a Google search for a name, and she would quickly realize that he wasn't what he said he was. Fortunately, she didn't ask for his last name. She just sipped her pina colada and tried to make small talk.

Ace had some experience with nurses. He knew that they were intelligent, compassionate, caring, dedicated, and usually energetic unless they were burnt out from the rigors of caring for everyone else and not so much for themselves. This young lady didn't look like she had been a nurse long enough to reach that stage in her nursing career. Of course, she was in sales, so she may have never even worked on the floor and taken care of patients, day after day after day. Her patient experience may be no more than observing as another nurse applies her products or devices as she chimes in with tips and techniques on the best way to use her product.

Ace sat his notes aside and decided that he would get back to work later. This woman was attractive and intelligent…and she was a nurse. He might be able to pick her brain about "sudden cardiac death" and what caused it, although he wasn't really thinking that would work as she was so young. Too young to have a lot of experience in Intensive Care. He figured, at the very least, she would be a pleasant distraction for the afternoon. He quickly scanned her left hand for any engagement or wedding rings and saw none. The last thing he needed was to get involved with a married woman. That hadn't worked out well for him in the past, and he didn't want a repeat.

They spent the afternoon poolside. Julie consumed another 2 or 3 pina coladas, and Ace decided to have a beer after his iced tea. Julie was exactly what Ace had expected. She was a fun person to chat with. Of course, the subject of his "business" did come up. He decided to be honest with her. He told her that he was an investigator, and he was in Mexico investigating a death.

She literally gushed with curiosity about who he was investigating, but he repeatedly told her that he couldn't divulge any personal information regarding his investigation due to privacy concerns. She told him that she would keep his secret if he would just give her a shred of information. She finally gave up and told him that she was going for a dip in the pool. As she stood and walked poolside, Ace watched her go. He shook his head to himself and wondered what he was thinking, telling her what he was there for. It didn't appear that she was likely to give up on the questions.

Julie entered the pool and began to swim through the water like an Olympic swimmer, perfect form cutting through the water, creating barely a ripple, doing a flip turn, and heading down the length of the pool again.

Ace just watched her. She was a beautiful woman, but he had work to do. He was going to have to excuse himself and leave the pool. Before that happened, though, he was hoping to get a room number here in the hotel and possibly her cell phone number. She did another turn and began doing the breaststroke, the length of the pool and back. She exited the water after the last lap and scampered to her chair and, grabbed her towel, and began to dry off just a bit.

Ace complimented her on her form. Julie told him that she had gone to Ohio State University on a swimming scholarship, and even though she was never quite good enough to get into the Olympics, she always did well enough to maintain her scholarship through four years of college. She loved to swim and took every chance that she could to keep at it and keep in shape. Ace told her that it was obvious, based on her figure, that she was in "great shape" and that swimming suited her.

Unfortunately, Ace had work to do, so he was going to have to move quickly to get her room number and cell number if she was willing. He came out and just asked her how long she was going to be in town. She told him that she would be staying at the hotel for three more days. He figured it wouldn't hurt, so he asked her if they could get together later for drinks. She was more than happy to meet him for drinks later. She snatched up his phone, looked at it, and asked his code to unlock it. He told her that he would unlock it for her, but what did she need it for? She told him that she was going to enter her number in his contacts. He unlocked his phone and handed it back to her; she pushed a few keys and handed it back. He looked at the contact that she had created. He knew that her first name was Julie, and now he knew her last name, Ritter. Ace said thanks and said, "It has been very nice to meet you, Julie Ritter. I hope to see you again later today or tomorrow".

Ace left the poolside and returned to the hotel. As he was walking across the pool deck, he was lost in thoughts of what might come out of this meeting with

Julie, so he was paying no attention to the people around him. He never even saw the tiny little Asian man sitting in the lobby, watching intently as he crossed to the elevators, so obviously, he didn't see when the little Asian man took his cell phone out of his pocket, hit a few keys on it then stood up and left the building via the front entrance.

# Chapter 16

As Ace was riding up the elevator, listening to the music overhead, he just shook his head. "Working Man" by Rush was playing on the speaker in the elevator. Rush had always been one of his favorite bands. How could such an iconic song ever be relegated to canned music in an elevator? C'mon, everyone knows that Rush was one of the best bands to ever come out of Canada. Their music certainly didn't deserve to be "elevator music."

Ace stepped off the elevator as the last notes of Working Man filtered through the speaker and headed towards his room. As he approached his room, he noticed a large envelope taped to his door. The envelope had his last name on it in a heavy scrawl and nothing else. Ace looked at it all over, and everything seemed to be ok, no obvious wires coming from it, and no white powder appeared around the rear flap, which Ace noted was not closed with the adhesive. He figured that the envelope was safe to remove from the door where a piece of clear tape was holding it. He peeled it from the door and took it into the room.

The envelope was a standard business envelope, white in color, with a peel-off adhesive strip. The type of envelope that you could purchase at almost any store in the world. The envelope was approximately ¼" thick with documents inside of it.

Ace opened the envelope carefully while wearing a pair of latex gloves so that he wouldn't disturb any fingerprints on it that may have been left by the individual who taped it to his door. As he looked in the envelope, he realized very quickly that he was looking at a stack of photographs. Ace dumped them on the desk in his room and spread them out. The first pic that he looked at was a picture of him entering the brothel where Humdinger had met his demise. Another pic showed him sitting at the picnic table the other morning, eating his breakfast at the food truck. Most of the other pics were of him arriving at the various stops that he had made, including the police station, the coroner's office, and Lola's home. Obviously, he was being followed and these pics were a message to him that he was being watched. He poked around in the envelope looking for a note or anything else that might give him a hint as to who had sent it. There was no note but there was one more photo in the envelope. Ace slid it out on the desktop. It was facedown so he flipped it over. He took a deep breath and muttered "shit" under his breath. The photo was of Ronald Humdinger strapped to the Saint Andrew's Cross that Lola had told him about. It appeared that the photo had been snapped when Lola realized that there was something wrong with Humdinger. It was obvious that she was standing in front of him, and it appeared that she was slapping his face.

Ace sat back and thought back to his interview with Lola. The only person who could've taken this photo was the little Asian man who was in the room as both Humdinger and Lola were in the pic, and per Lola, there was nobody else in the room.

Why were these pics given to him? Were they a warning? Were they a threat? Ace had to find out who the little Asian man was that was in the room. He had a nickname but nothing more. The nickname was "Rocket Man". Everyone who knew Humdinger knew that he called the leader of a small Asian country "Rocket Man," but Ace didn't see any way that Kim Lee Park could've been in the United States without every intelligence agency in the world knowing about it.

Park was an arrogant little prick who was disliked by most every leader in the world except for a handful of dictators and despots to who he was known to give money and technology to if he felt that it would benefit him in the long run. The man was a common criminal, not unlike so many before him. He lived a life of luxury while his fellow countrymen and women starved to death. Most in his country lived on the equivalent of about $1000 US per year unless you were in the chosen circle of friends and family. Then, it was common for Kim to provide them with all their needs, no matter how twisted they were. Of course, once Park helped you and provided you with something. It was expected that you would be beholden to him until he no longer felt that you were of use to him. As one of those people, you hoped that day never came. If it did, it was likely that you would be dragged from your home in the middle of the night, never to be seen again. If it was felt that you needed to be used as an example, you would be executed on state TV for everyone in the country to witness. Intimidation ran rampant, and it worked.

Ace needed to make some calls, but he felt that a trip North of the border was prudent at this point. He wasn't going to close his reservation and room out, but he didn't want to be in Mexico while he was making these calls. He wanted to be back stateside in a location where he knew nobody would be listening. As careful as Ace was, he just didn't trust the people here in this part of the world.

# Chapter 17

Ace gave the valet his ticket and stood waiting as the valet went to retrieve his vehicle from the parking garage. As Ace stood waiting, he couldn't help but glance around. He wondered if there were pictures being taken of him now. He didn't see anything out of sorts. However, he hadn't seen anything out of sorts prior to receiving the pictures on his door. He hadn't noticed the tail at all. Of course, he hadn't really been looking for a tail. He was here to investigate a death, that to all appearances appeared to be of natural causes. Of course, with the pics now being delivered, that made him think differently about Humdinger's death. Nobody would be tailing him if this were a death due to natural causes. Obviously, someone wanted to make sure that he didn't dig too deeply. Which meant that there was more to Humdinger dying while being administered to by a Mexican dwarf Dominatrix. Whoever had taken the pics and given them to Ace had just made a terrible mistake. Ace would dig until he found out what in hell was going on with this entire fiasco. When he got back to San Diego, he was going to make some calls, and some of these calls were bound to piss some people off. Oh well, Ace would find out what happened. Let them try and stop him. "They" were about to find out that Ace was not someone to mess with.

As Ace was mulling these thoughts over, the valet arrived with his car. Ace's car was nothing flashy, but as he looked at it, he realized that it screamed "cop."

It was a late model Chevy Impala, gunmetal gray in color, leather interior, not a lot of extras but there was no question that it looked like a cop's car. Maybe when this case was over, he would start shopping for a new car. As Ace thought about it, maybe he would keep this car for his "work." He really liked the car. It had some serious balls with the Police Interceptor V-8 in it, and it was comfortable. He was going to look for "another" car, though. Something that didn't look like a cop's car. Maybe a Mustang or a Camaro, maybe something vintage.

Ace took his keys from the valet, gave him a $20 tip, and hopped in the car. Ace noticed the envelope on his front passenger seat immediately, a plain white business envelope just like the one that had been taped to his door. Ace picked up the envelope and noticed that this one wasn't sealed. There was a single sheet of paper inside that had "Don't come back!!!" written on a blank sheet of paper. Ace got out of the car with the note and approached the valet, asking him what the meaning of this note was. The valet looked at it with confusion and told Ace that he didn't know where the note came from. He just went and got the car out of the garage. When he got in the car, the envelope was lying on the driver's seat. He picked it up and tossed it onto the passenger seat. He thought that Ace must've left it lay there when he got out when he checked his car into the valet stand. Ace asked him if the car was locked…he told Ace that all the cars were locked. That was the policy of the hotel. Ace wanted to know who had access to the cars. The valet told him that nobody except the valets, hotel security, and hotel management had access to the keys of the vehicles although anyone could walk by the cars as the valet parking was well marked on the second floor of the parking garage. Ace asked if there were cameras in the parking garage. The valet said that there was but that he would have to talk to security to see any of that footage. Ace told him that he would contact them when he returned in a while.

# Chapter 18

Ace got on the Alfonso Bustamante Labistida and headed north towards San Diego. Ace hadn't even cleared the city when he encountered the stop-and-go traffic associated with the border crossing. Ace wasn't a person to use credentials to get what he wanted, but he was going to make an exception and started up the berm on the left side of the freeway. He would be damned if he was going to sit for hours waiting to cross the border. He knew that he was going to take some serious shit from all the vehicles waiting to cross, but he didn't want to delay. He was like a dog with a bone. When he set his mind to something, he wasn't going to quit until he had all the answers. As Ace passed car after car and tractor-trailer after tractor-trailer with horns blaring, he thought back to the days when Humdinger was in power. He ran a huge campaign regarding all the drugs crossing our southern border on the backs of the illegals coming through the desert and across the river in Texas. Anyone who had ever worked in government knew that the bulk of illegal narcotics came across the border in vehicles. Smuggled in cars, trucks, trailers, sometimes in cars that were on trailers. The amount that the "illegals" were bringing across was minuscule. Unfortunately, most of the people who supported Humdinger believed everything that the man said, so they were all for building a wall. Hell, some had basically declared "open season" on any illegal crossing the border. Ace had friends who lived in Ohio, and there were constant complaints from them regarding all the "illegals" coming up to Ohio and stealing our jobs. Jobs that hardworking Americans could use. Most of these jobs were in poultry processing plants. Ace asked one of his friends if he would work in the chicken plant. His friend just laughed and said that there was no way that he would work there. He knew what they paid, and it wasn't near enough for him to even consider leaving his job as a police officer on the Ohio River. Ace had tried to explain to him that most of the "illegals" coming into the country were just trying to make a better life for themselves. That fell on deaf ears, though. He and many others felt that anyone here illegally should be sent back across the border. It didn't matter if they were being returned to somewhere that guaranteed their execution upon arrival. "They" didn't belong here. "They" aren't like us. Ace gave up trying to change the opinions of those who were enthralled with Humdinger and his brand of politics. Which essentially amounted to "You do what I say, or you're fired." Ace remembered the rallies that the news stations had broadcast. It was amazing to him how a pasty white, orange spray-tanned grifter could enthrall so many people with his line of bullshit.

Ace continued up the median until he got close to the checkpoint, then he nosed his Impala into the traffic to more horns blaring and a few people flipping him off and calling him a fucker and other choice words. He ignored it…the line inched forward. He finally got to the gate and handed over his passport and his old FBI ID. The person at the gate raised his eyebrows but didn't lose a beat in asking the standard question; "what was your business in Mexico, business or pleasure." Ace told him that he was there for a couple of days of relaxation. With that, the gate went up, and Ace passed into the good old US of A. It was good to be back on this side of the border. Now to, head to Humdinger Enterprises to ask some questions and make a few calls.

# Chapter 19

Ace arrived at Humdinger Enterprises in Escondido about an hour later. He pulled into the parking lot. The first thing that he noticed was that Presley Misuse's car was parked in his normal spot. That was great, because Misuse was just the person that Ace wanted to talk to. Ace entered the building and was greeted at the reception desk by a big burly, body builder type guy. Not what you would normally expect to find behind the desk as a greeter but hey, who was Ace to question who they hired. He would've hired a beautiful young lady that presented a much better looking first impression than the steroid-infused cueball sitting there now. He looked down at the nametag and said, "Tim, I would like to see Mr. Misuse." Cueball asked him if he had an appointment. When Ace told him that he did not, Cueball told him that he needed to make an appointment. Ace was losing patience with this guy, so he just blurted out, "Just tell Misuse that his investigator is here. I'm sure that he will see me!"

Tim raised his eyebrows and gave Ace a quick once-over and picked up the phone. Misuse must've answered promptly because after a few quick mumbles into the phone, the giant cueball hung up and told him that Presley Misuse would see him in his office. With a sneer, he asked Ace if he needed an escort or was he able to find the office himself. Ace assured Cueball that he could find his own way and that no escort was needed. As Ace sauntered off down the hall, the muscle-head yelled at him not to stray anywhere else, that he was just cleared to Misuse's office. Ace raised his hand in acknowledgment and continued walking down that hallway.

Ace walked up to Presley Misuse's office only to find it dark and locked up. He started back down the hall to talk to Tim and noticed that Ronald Humdinger's office door was standing open, and the lights were shining in the hallway. He just shook his head. Apparently, Misuse had already moved into the CEO's office. He walked down the hall and glanced in the office; Misuse was sitting at the big walnut desk that was reminiscent of the Resolute desk from the Oval Office. Rumor had it that Humdinger commissioned this piece after leaving politics as a reminder of how great he was when he was a politician…at least in his mind. Ace knocked and entered the room. Misuse ushered him in and told him to have a seat. Misuse started immediately with questions about the case and why was Ace back in Escondido? Did Ace have everything finalized?

Ace told him to slow down a bit. He then produced the photos that were taped to his door at the hotel in Tijuana. Misuse looked over them and asked him what they were all about. Ace told him that it was obvious that someone was following him around Tijuana. He also asked Presley if he had identified the little Asian man that he had reported to him about.

Presley said that he hadn't had any luck yet, but he was working on it. Ace then presented the last photo to Misuse; the photo with the naked Humdinger strapped to the cross and the dwarf dominatrix standing in front of him. Misuse picked up the photo and then dropped it back on the desk. He demanded to know where it had come from. Ace told him it was with the photos that were left on his door. Ace also told Misuse that he felt that the only person who could've taken the photo was the little Asian man and that Misuse needed to get moving just a bit quicker to find out who it was. Ace also told him that he felt that it was someone working for the little Asian man that had to be tailing him around Tijuana.

Misuse got up, walked across the room and poured himself a drink. He didn't even think of offering Ace a drink, not that Ace would've accepted it anyway. Ace was thinking more and more that he needed to watch his back as far as Presley Misuse was concerned. He couldn't be trusted.

Misuse paced back and forth across the enormous office several times, saying nothing. Ace was considering getting up and dismissing himself when Presley asked him if anyone else had an idea of who the "little Asian man" was. The whores, anyone? Ace told him that the only name that had been mentioned was by Lola, the dwarf dominatrix. She said that Humdinger kept calling him "Rocket Man." She also said that the man seemed a bit perturbed by the moniker.

Misuse went over to a file cabinet, entered his keycode and it unlocked. Misuse dug around in a file until he came up with a picture and handed it over to Ace. Ace took a deep breath. It appeared that Humdinger and Humdinger Habitats did do some work with Kim Lee Park.

Ace took a deep breath and asked Misuse what the hell he was doing with a snapshot of Kim Lee Park?

Misuse told him that he was mistaken, that he was not looking at a picture of Kim Lee Park. He was looking at a picture of Kim Il Soon from North Korea. He was the source for many of the shipping containers that were converted to living quarters by Humdinger Habitats. He did bear a striking resemblance to the leader of North Korea but was of no relation as far as Misuse knew. Unfortunately, Misuse was aware that Soon and Ronald Humdinger shared some fetishes.

Ace asked Misuse why Soon would've been along on the trip to Tijuana. Misuse asked him if he hadn't been listening. Ultimately, he was sure that Humdinger had invited him because Soon was a freaking pervert, just like Humdinger. Rumor had it that Soon liked to watch sex acts and that no sex acts were off limits to Soon. He liked BDSM, pedophilia, necrophilia, the list went on and on. Misuse said that there were rumors that Humdinger and Soon had both participated in sex acts with minors on a trip to the Caribbean and a famous island in the Virgin Islands. The owner of the island, known unaffectionately by the locals as "Pedophile Island," had been arrested and committed suicide several years ago while awaiting trial. There was a lot of talk that he hadn't really committed suicide. He had been silenced so that the stories of the "rich and famous" who attended parties on his island wouldn't become public. That hadn't worked out, though. The lists of people who had visited the island had been released over a period of time. The list contained names of many of the rich and famous as well as some "Royals" and businessmen who were highly placed in companies around the world. Ace had never heard Humdinger's name mentioned or Kim Il Soon's, so that was a plus. Unfortunately, Ace feared that there was going to be some serious fallout from this investigation. As Ace was lost in his thoughts, he heard Misuse say his name a bit loudly...Ace looked up from his thoughts. Misuse said, "Jesus Christ, Bancroft, are you deaf? Did you hear anything that I said?" Ace explained that he was thinking about the case and was lost in his thoughts. Could Misuse please repeat himself? Misuse shook his head, took a deep breath, and told Ace to think long and hard about digging much further into this case. He reminded Ace that it was illegal to do business with North Korea, even if it was just some shipping containers. It would be best if he just "determined" that Humdinger died from natural causes. Presley would back him up. Ace could get his paycheck for services rendered, along with a large bonus for responding so quickly and Ace could go about his business, never looking back at Humdinger Enterprises.

Ace took a couple of seconds to think, then told Misuse that he couldn't just stop his investigation. People would talk if Ace didn't interview the rest of the people involved, and there would be questions. Misuse told him not to worry about the rest of the people at Humdinger Enterprises and the Board of Directors. He would smooth it over. Ace told him thanks, but he felt that it was best if he continued for now. With that statement, he rose and left the office, never looking back at Misuse.

# Chapter 20

Ace walked back down the hall past the giant, steroid-infused dickhead at the desk without a word. As Ace was exiting, he heard the giant tell him to have a nice day. Without missing a beat, Ace flipped him off and continued out the door. He heard footsteps coming from inside and heard the door open. Ace turned and prepared to defend himself. Cueball Timmy stopped just outside of arm's length and told Ace to remember the next time he showed up. He needed to call him and make an appointment.

Ace just smirked and told the troll that he would take it under advisement, but if he needed to see someone at Humdinger Enterprises, he would be the last person that he would notify.

Ace turned and proceeded to his car, hopped in, and drove down the street to Stone Brewing Company. They had a great restaurant and patio, not to mention one of the best beers on the planet, Arrogant Bastard Ale. An ABA and some time on the patio were just what Ace needed so that he could sit and think. Ace pulled into the parking lot and was happy to see that there were just a few cars present. He should be able to get a nice seat away from anyone so that he could make a few calls in private. The hostess welcomed him and asked if he would be the only diner. Ace confirmed and asked for a seat on the patio. She told him that he could proceed to the patio and take any table that was available. She told him that Taylor would be his waitress. Ace sauntered to the patio and took a table in the back corner, with his back to the surrounding, hop-covered wall, he could watch anyone that came to the patio and could also see if anyone was getting close enough to overhear his phone calls. Ace glanced over the menu. As he was looking at the appetizers; Taylor, a cute young lady with a purple streak and a few tattoos, appeared and asked him if she could take his drink order. Ace asked for a "tall" Arrogant Bastard. Without missing a beat, the young lady spouted off the catchphrase, "It's very bitter, you probably won't like it." Ace told her that he was very familiar with the brew and there would be no question about whether he liked it or not. She smiled and told him that she would be back in just a few minutes with his beer.

Ace sat and thought about where to go from here regarding questions about the death of Humdinger. He had just decided to call Humdinger's widow when his Arrogant Bastard Ale arrived in all its bitter glory. He took a deep draught of the beer to steel himself for the upcoming call. Emilyia Humdinger was known as a real ball buster. Everyone knew that her marriage to Ronald Humdinger was a marriage of convenience. She was at least 30 years younger than her dead husband…nobody knew for sure the exact age difference because her birth certificate had never been seen. Emilyia supposedly grew up in Austria to a poor peasant family, although nobody knew if that was true, as her parents were killed in a fire on the farm when she was just 17 years old. Emilyia hadn't been home at the time. She was meeting with a Ukrainian "talent agent" who was interested in representing her as a model, or so the story goes. Rumor had it that the agent was a Russian, and she immediately became his plaything when her parents perished. No cause of the fire was ever disclosed, and Emilyia relished in her new life. She eventually started to appear on modeling runways all over Europe. She was known to have a foul mouth and an even more foul temper if she didn't get what she wanted.

Ace took out his phone and called the phone number supplied to him at the beginning of the investigation for Emilyia. The phone rang one time and went to voicemail. Emilyia's lilting voice answered and said in her heavily accented voice to leave a message after the beep. Ace left a quick message to call him back, along with his cellphone number. He knew that she would have his number, but she was notorious for not returning calls if a contact number wasn't left.

Ace took another swallow of his beer and motioned for Taylor that he was ready to order. He placed an order for Kung Pao Crunch Brussel Sprouts and also an order of Stone Wings made with Fear.Movie.Lions Imperial IPA Buffalo sauce. Taylor told him that those were two of the best appetizers at the restaurant, in her opinion. Ace thanked her as she walked away to place his order.

Ace just sat back and looked around the patio. The small lunch crowd was an eclectic mix of businessmen, yuppies, construction workers, and other assorted knots of people. Everyone was sporting a healthy tan. One of the great things about living in southern California was the fact that it was sunny almost daily, and there was no shortage of areas to get outdoors. Just as he was enjoying the people-watching, his phone rang. He glanced at the caller ID and saw that it was Emilyia Humdinger calling. He answered, and a smooth male voice told him to hold for Mrs. Humdinger. Ace shook his head. Of course, she wouldn't make a call on her own. Her assistant would have to make the call and connect her. God forbid that she dials her own phone. There were a few seconds of recorded hold music and Emilyia's voice came through loud and clear. There was no trace of her demure demeanor that was always displayed when she was appearing at Ronald's side for political events.

Emilyia asked Ace what she could do for him. He asked her if she would be available to meet with him regarding his investigation into the death of her husband. She told him that she would be more than happy to meet with him later today at her La Jolla home near Torrey Pines golf course. She said she would see him at 5 PM at home, and she would be honored if he would be her guest for dinner. Ace confirmed, and she hung up. Ace couldn't believe that she was going to meet with him this easily…and the fact that she said they could meet at "her" home in La Jolla told him that she wasn't especially upset about Humdinger's death.

With no other plans for several hours, Ace sat back and enjoyed his lunch. Taylor was correct. The Brussel sprouts and the wings were fantastic.

# Chapter 21

Ace showed up at the Humdinger estate, a grand three-floor home on a bluff overlooking the Pacific. It was rumored that Humdinger had purchased the property for a song. Unfortunately, since it was purchased by a trust, run through Humdinger Enterprises and its non-profit status, the purchased price wasn't readily available. Ace had heard about the views from the entry. You entered the home on the 3$^{rd}$ level and descended along the bluff. He had heard that there was an infinity pool overlooking the ocean at the lowest level as well.

Ace rang the doorbell and was surprised when the door was opened by Emilyia herself. He assumed that there would be staff present for such menial chores as opening doors, cooking, cleaning, etc. She looked stunning in gray yoga pants and a baggie white sweatshirt. Ace wasn't sure how anyone could look stunning without any attempt, but Emilyia could pull it off. Ace muttered "Wow". He hoped that Emilyia hadn't heard him. Emilyia said, "Pardon me?" Ace said "Wow, look at those views." When you entered, you looked through the entire open concept upper level to walls of solid glass overlooking the ocean. It was truly breathtaking, and that was the story that he was sticking with. Emilyia led the way to a walnut-lined elevator and said over her shoulder that they would be meeting on the veranda on the first level, where they would also enjoy their dinner. As the elevator descended, Emilyia asked Ace if he preferred a merlot or a cabernet with his steak? Ace said that he would leave the wine choice to her. With that, the elevator doors slid open. Ace followed Emilyia through the lower level to the veranda overlooking the pool and an expansive outdoor kitchen. Emilyia proceeded down three steps to the outdoor kitchen, opened a wine cabinet and pulled out a bottle of Opus One, handed the bottle and a corkscrew to Ace, and asked him if he would mind opening the wine while she started prepping the potatoes and steaks for the grill. Ace happily agreed to open the wine. He had never experienced Opus One but had heard great things about it. At around $500 per bottle, how bad could it be? Ace opened the wine and placed it on the table between two chairs overlooking the pool where Vixen Humdinger languished on a raft in the pool. Ace didn't want to stare too long, but Vixen was a clone of her mother. She was a beautiful young lady.

Ace returned to the kitchen area and was going to ask a few questions when Emilyia turned and asked him where the wine was. He pointed over his shoulder and said that he thought that they would enjoy it while they were talking. Emilyia bluntly informed him that he thought wrong. They were going to enjoy the wine while she prepared the steaks. She wasn't answering any questions while she was preparing dinner. Ace asked her for one question before retreating to retrieve the open bottle of wine. With a sigh of exasperation, she agreed to one question before dinner. Ace asked her what the big deal was about preparing dinner. Emilyia told him that she loved to cook but never got the chance when Ronald was alive because he felt that it was beneath her. She was to just appear at his side and look pretty. She was never to lift a finger around the house or in public. She was just there to look good for photo ops.

Ace marveled that Humdinger would treat this beautiful woman as a possession and that she would just accept it. She was stunning and was intelligent. Rumor had it that she was fluent in five languages, including Russian and Mandarin Chinese as well as English, French, and Austrian, her native language.

Ace asked her if there was anything that he could do to help her. She asked him how good he was with a knife. Ace gave her a quizzical look but told her he could manage. She pointed to a small under counter refrigerator and told him that the ingredients for a salad were in there and if he wanted to prepare the salad, he could do that. If he just wanted to sit and enjoy the view over the Pacific, that was fine, too. Ace walked over to the refrigerator, retrieved a head of romaine, some tomatoes, cucumbers, and a couple of carrots, asked where the cutting board was, and started chopping vegetables. He remarked he could enjoy the view while preparing the salad just as easily as sitting and watching her do the work. He preferred to help. She just smiled and oiled and salted the potatoes for baking.

As Ace was preparing the salad, Vixen wandered over and retrieved a Coke from the refrigerator, looked at Ace, and said, "Are you the new guy that's going to replace my daddy?" Ace was completely taken off guard and sputtered a few noises...from deep in his throat. As Ace was trying to piece together an appropriate response, Emilyia explained to her daughter that Ace was an investigator looking into the death of her father. Vixen said, "What's to look into, didn't he die with that hooker down in Tijuana?" Emilyia said a few words in what sounded like German to Vixen. Whatever was said struck a nerve with Vixen. She turned and marched inside the house.

Emilyia turned and apologized for her daughters' comments, saying that Vixen had been acting out ever since Ronald had died.

Ace assured her that all was well and continued preparing the salad. As he was chopping tomatoes, he asked Emilyia how things had been between her and Ronald prior to his death. She gave him a tsk-tsk and told him that there were going to be no more questions about Ronald until after dinner. Right now, he was to just enjoy the view and help prepare the salad, nothing else. If he insisted on asking questions, then he could leave, and no questions would be answered at all. Ace felt like a chastised child, and he didn't know why. Emilyia had never even raised her voice, yet here he was thinking about what he could do to salvage this interview.

Dinner was fantastic, a fresh salad, grilled ribeye steaks with sauteed mushrooms, and a baked potato. Ace ate every scrap while Emilyia and Vixen split a steak and a potato. Ace apologized for making a pig of himself but eating in motels and restaurants on a regular basis got very tiresome. It was nice to sit and enjoy a meal where he wasn't going to be given a check at the end of the evening.

Conversation during dinner was varied but never about Ronald. They talked about music, the arts, and

TV. The discussion about TV is what led to finding out that Vixen was a big Survivor fan. Ace had to acknowledge to both that he was a huge fan of the show and had applied on multiple occasions. This revelation seemed to swing Vixen his way. She started being civil to him. Emilyia, on the other hand, asked him why he would even want to do the show. Living in the outdoors, with no shower, bathroom, or food…why would he even consider it. Ace thought about it for a minute and told her it was truly just about the challenge. He felt that he could win the million dollars. He could get along with anyone. He recalled his high school days where he didn't fit in with any specific group of people, whether it be the "jocks" the "brains" or the "hoods" smoking across the street from the school. He could float between all groups and get along. Emilyia was plainly bored with the subject of Survivor, but it was clear that Vixen had a newfound respect for him since he had applied for the show. She asked him for advice to get on the show when she was old enough to apply. He laughed and said that he probably wasn't the best person to ask how to get on the show since he was never selected to appear, although he had been good enough to appear in a couple "in person" interviews. Vixen just giggled and said that there was still time, that he still might make it to the show.

Emilyia cleared her throat and informed Vixen that her and Ace had some things to discuss and that she could either go for another swim or go find something to watch on TV. Vixen hem hawed around a bit but finally got up from the table and said that she was going to go to her room and play video games so that they could talk about her father.

Ace just raised an eyebrow and glanced at Emilyia as Vixen walked into the home. He told Emilyia that she had her hands full with that one. She was smart, and witty, probably sneaky as well, and obviously not naïve in any way.

Ace got right down to it with Emilyia. He could tell that pussy footing around her would serve absolutely no purpose. He asked her what she thought about her husband dying while in the accompaniment of a prostitute, but not just any prostitute. Lola Aspera-Amore was a dominatrix, a dwarf dominatrix. She was the opposite of what Ronald had at home. How did it make her feel to know that Ronald was having kinky sexual relations with a dwarf in what essentially amounted to a third world country, south of the border?

Emilyia told Ace that it was no problem at all, as far as she was concerned. She hadn't had sex with the man in 12 or 13 years. That wasn't going to change. He was a blow hard braggart that couldn't even perform most times that they had been intimate. He smelled horrible, he was a flabby, spray tanned pig and if he was having sex elsewhere and leaving her alone, that was just fine with her.

Ace asked her why she stayed with him, if her disgust was so great. She motioned around her. She said, "look at this home, look at the lifestyle that I have. I wouldn't have any of this if Ronald hadn't met me at a beauty pageant in Austria". She continued, "for him, it was love at first sight. For her, not so much." She knew who he was though, and she knew that he had money, a lot of money. If he could help her get out of Austria to America, then she was all for it.

Ace asked her how she benefitted from Ronald's untimely demise since he had heard that there was a prenuptial agreement in place. Emilyia told him that there was a clause in the agreement regarding the manner of death. If Ronald died while in the presence of another woman, she inherited $100 million. That was her price for him having sexual relations outside of the marriage. Ace couldn't believe he had agreed to something like that. She just looked at Ace with a gleam in her eyes and told him that Ronald just didn't find sex with her to be enjoyable because she wasn't into all his kinks.

Ace asked Emilyia if she was aware that Ronald had a heart condition? She said that she wasn't privy to his medical information, and she never asked. She did say that it wasn't hard to figure out, just by looking at him. Even though he liked to proclaim that he was "very fit" and a slim 215 pounds and over 6 feet tall, the entire world knew that to be false. He was a pig with a huge junk food habit. He would get two or three half-pound hamburgers and two orders of fries from one of the local diners on a regular basis. With the advent of "DoorDash" he could order it, and have it delivered right to the house or his office, which is what happened most often. He thought that she didn't know about it. However, there was no hiding the reek of onions on his breath when he got home from a "late night" at the office. He also kept bags of chocolate in his office and anywhere that he went. She did say that the one thing that was true was that he didn't drink alcohol. But he did drink energy drinks by the truckload every week. She said that early in their relationship, she tried to talk to him about how unhealthy the energy drinks were, but he just shushed her and told her that he was as strong as an ox and that he was just fine.

Ace asked her if there was anyone at Humdinger's company that might have it in for him? She just laughed and said that there were any number of people at the company that benefitted from his death, but none more than Presley Misuse. She told Ace that she had heard that he had already moved into Ronald's office. As far as she was concerned, Misuse was the most likely person, if anything nefarious had caused Humdinger's death, but the coroner ruled it all as a death from natural causes, so she didn't really understand why Ace was even checking any further into the death. In her opinion, he should rule the death as natural, take his payday, and move on to the next case.

Ace mulled over whether to tell her about the incidents that had occurred in Tijuana and decided not to mention it at this time. Instead, he just told her that he believed in a thorough investigation and report and that he was just dotting all the i's and crossing all the t's before delivering his final report.

As Ace and Emilyia sat on the veranda and enjoyed the evening air, conversation lagged, and Ace felt that it was time for him to bid his farewell. While Ace had actually enjoyed Emilyia's company, he knew what kind of woman she really was, and he knew that he would never be in the same circles as her or the rest of the Humdinger clan.

Ace gave his card to Emilyia and thanked her for dinner, told her that he would show himself out but also asked her to call him if anything came to mind that she felt was pertinent to his investigation.

# Chapter 22

Ace got in his old Impala and headed back towards San Diego. He was lost in thought about who to question next and didn't notice the black SUV with tinted windows right on his bumper. As Ace slowed for the congestion on the I-5 he looked at his rearview mirror and noticed that all he could see was the grill of a large SUV. A lot of chrome and the Cadillac logo were all that was visible. Ace thought about flipping the driver of the SUV "the bird" but figured that with the amount of road rage that occurred on California highways, it wouldn't be in his best interest to do it. As Ace was halted for traffic, he felt a light tap to his bumper from the vehicle behind him. He couldn't believe that he had just been tapped by the vehicle behind him, but he chose to ignore it. Ace inched forward and came to a stop again, and again, he felt a tap to his bumper. With the $2^{nd}$ tap, Ace decided to put the car in park and ask the driver what the problem was. As Ace exited the vehicle, he tried to get a glimpse of the driver but couldn't see much inside as the windows were tinted, and there was a reflection of the clouds on the windshield. Ace walked up to the driver's side window and motioned for the driver to lower the window. The window started down and stopped with only 3 inches of space showing. Ace exclaimed that he wanted the driver to roll the window down so that he could have a talk with them. A male voice came from inside the vehicle that there was nothing to talk about. They just wanted Ace to know that they were there and that they were watching him.

He needed to be always aware that "THEY" were watching him. With that, the vehicle drove to the side of the road and drove down over the embankment to the roadway below.

Ace stood there stunned for a minute, then returned to his vehicle, noting the scratches on the bumper of his old car. He would make sure to get the vehicle into a body shop and get a quote for the repair, and you could damn well bet that he would be submitting the cost for the repair to Humdinger Enterprises. Obviously, this was connected to the case. How often does someone tell you that they are always watching you; and then drive off? Of course, since they drove off but "were always watching," did that mean that there was a tracker on his car? He was going to have to look it over thoroughly when he got to the hotel. The question for now is, was he going to go back over the border and stay in Tijuana, or was he going to find a hotel in the San Diego area. Ace decided he would head back to Tijuana. Afterall, there was a cute nurse down there at the hotel that he was staying at. He could get back down there and spend a bit of time deciding on the next steps and maybe catch up with her for drinks in the nightclub later that evening.

# Chapter 23

Ace headed south to Tijuana at a leisurely pace, arriving back at his hotel at a little past 11 PM. He decided to stop at the bar, just on the off chance that "Nurse Julie" was there. He walked up to the bar, ordered an Old-Fashioned cocktail, one of his favorites, and surveyed the room. At first glance, he didn't see Julie anywhere. He decided to finish his drink and then head up to his room and get a decent night's sleep. As Ace was leaning against the bar nursing his cocktail, he heard some female voices approaching from the lobby. He watched about a half dozen women walk in, among the group was Julie Ritter. He assumed that these were some of the other "sales" people from the medical supply company. They all giggled and wobbled over to a large table at the back of the bar. Ace turned his back on the group as the last thing that he wanted to do was to meet all her friends. Ace nursed his drink for a few more minutes and decided to head up to his room. As he was exiting the bar, he made eye contact with Julie, gave her a wink and a nod and left the room.

Ace made his way to the elevator bank at the rear of the lobby and hit the button. As he stood waiting for the carriage to arrive, he went over the day's events in his head. What had he learned? Had he learned anything of importance, or was he just spinning his wheels. Maybe Humdinger had just died of natural causes, but there was more to the story. Ace was sure of it. If it was just a simple case of natural death, why would he have been told to stay away? Why had he been followed on his return trip to the States?  Why had he been warned that he was being watched.  What was he missing?  He wasn't going to give up on this investigation right now.  He was sure that there was more to learn.  He would get a fresh start in the morning with another visit to Starletta Blaze.

# Chapter 24

When Ace got back to his room, he made sure to securely lock and bolt the door. For good measure, he placed a chair in front of the door as well. He was in Tijuana. Things could be "sketchy" down here. He didn't want to be the next occupant on Dr. Bravo's autopsy table because he wasn't using his situational awareness.

Ace took a quick look around his room. He saw no sign of anything being disturbed. He did a quick check for listening devices. If there were any in the room, they were high quality and not easily found. Ace placed his cell phone on the nightstand next to the bed and plugged it in so that it would be fully charged. Ace took a leisurely shower without fear of anyone breaking into his room, then turned in for the night. As he was dozing off, he vaguely noted that his phone had pinged…he decided that it could wait until morning, turned on his side, and drifted off to sleep. Not a deep sleep, as that is one thing he never had been was a good sleeper. He wasn't sure whether it was genetics, personality, training, or something else that allowed him to function on 5 hours of sleep on average, but he was glad that it was his "problem."

# Chapter 25

Ace slowly woke up. He looked at his phone and noted that it was just after 7 AM. A seven-hour night of sleep. Ace realized that he must've been more tired than he realized. He prepared himself for breakfast. He was going to eat in the hotel restaurant but decided that he was going to contact Raul and see if he could come and pick him up at the hotel to take him to his sister's food truck for another delicious breakfast.

Ace fished the business card from Raul out of his wallet and made the call. Raul answered on the 2nd ring. He told Ace that he would pick him up out front of the hotel in 20 minutes…or did he prefer to meet him in the alleyway like he had the other day? Ace told Raul that the front of the hotel was fine and that he would like to book him and his cab for the day. Raul said that would not be a problem and disconnected the call.

Ace descended to the lobby and had a seat while he waited for Raul. He was debating whether he wanted to enjoy the same breakfast of Chilaquiles that he had the other day or whether he was going to try something new when he felt a slight tap on his shoulder. He turned and looked up into the face of "Nurse Julie." She had a big smile on her face. She wanted to know why he hadn't ever answered her text the night before. Ace remembered the "ping" just as he was going to sleep the night before, and he mentally smacked himself for not looking at it the night before.

Ace stammered and stuttered about being tired and not hearing the notice. Julie gave a lilting laugh and told him that it was ok. She just wanted to see if he would be around the next day because she would like to get together and have dinner with him if he was up for it.

Ace told her that he would be around later that afternoon and he would give her a call or a text when he could with a time for dinner. Julie got a big smile on her face and told Ace that she couldn't wait to hear from him. She had to get to the offices for in-services, but she would see him later. Ace watched her walk away toward the front of the lobby. He had to admit, it was a pretty nice view, watching her walk away. Ace knew that he shouldn't be checking her out, but what was the harm? It wasn't like she was going to see him. She didn't have eyes in the back of her head. She really did look good in her skirt and heels. He made a mental note to compliment her on her wardrobe later in the day.

Ace's phone pinged. It was a text from Raul letting him know that he was out front. Ace told him that he would be out in just a minute and got up and headed for the front door.

# Chapter 26

Raul met Ace beside his car. He opened the rear door for Ace to enter. Ace said that he would prefer to ride in the front if Raul was ok with that? Raul said that was fine with him and opened the passenger door. Ace took a seat as Raul rounded the front of the car and hopped in. Ace told Raul that breakfast was the first thing on the list and that Ace would be buying his breakfast as well. Ace told him to stop as Raul started to protest. He told Raul that he would not take no for an answer. Raul pulled away and headed towards his sister's food truck. As they drove, Ace gave Raul an outline of his plans for the day, starting with a visit to Starletta Blaze's brothel after breakfast. The next stop would be Raul's cousin, who did electrical work to check out an electrical device, and then possibly a trip to Lola Aspera-Amor's apartment.

Raul pulled into the dusty old parking lot and there sat the food truck. The parking lot was fairly full, but that didn't stop Raul from pulling up right next to his sister's food truck. Bonita came from the side door of the truck and gave Raul a big hug, saying something in Spanish that Ace didn't understand other than the word "Gringo". He knew who she was talking about. Raul just laughed and responded in English that the Gringo was paying him better for the day than he would make if he was running his cab for the cab company.

Bonita gave a slight curtsey and said, "Welcome back, Senor Ace." She then returned to the truck and resumed taking orders from those in line. Ace took his place at the end of the line and Raul told him that wasn't necessary. His sister was going to make her best breakfast and she would call out when their food was ready. Ace enquired what he was getting for breakfast? Raul told him not to worry. He was sure that he would enjoy it.

Bonita called Raul to the truck where he returned with a tray heaping with food. Ace had no idea what he was looking at. Raul explained that there were two servings of Mexican Baked Eggs, a mixture of scrambled eggs, spinach, onions, queso cheese, jalapenos, and garlic baked to perfection. A couple of pieces of toasted sourdough bread were also present for dipping with the eggs. On another plate were a couple of pieces of bread that were slathered in what looked like refried beans and then topped with cheese, and which was melted while the bread was grilled. It was all topped with fresh Pico de Gallo. Raul explained that these were called Mexican Molletes. Ace's stomach was growling, and his mouth was watering. He could not wait to dig into this meal. Raul said, "Sit, Senor Ace, sit. We must enjoy our breakfast while it is warm." Ace wasted no time digging in. To say that the food was fabulous was an understatement. While San Diego and many other areas of the country had good Mexican food; none compared to the meal that he was having right now in a dusty old parking lot in Tijuana.

Neither man said a word until every morsel had been consumed. Ace leaned back a bit from the picnic table and told Raul that he was going to have to go back north, or he would weigh 300 pounds. Raul just laughed and told him that the heat of the summer would keep the weight off.

Ace gathered up the dishes and returned them to the truck, where he attempted to pay Bonita for the meals. She waved him off and told him that a friend of her brother's wasn't paying for breakfast. Ace told her that he had a business arrangement with Raul. She wouldn't even hear of it. She told him to shoo and went back to cleaning utensils used during the breakfast rush.

Ace returned to the picnic table and took the last swig of his coffee then told Raul that they needed to get moving. He wanted to get to Starletta Blaze's brothel before paying customers started to show up. Raul chuckled and replied that there was never a time that there weren't paying customers in the brothels in Tijuana. Between the US servicemen, the cartel, businessmen, and just horny guys, the brothels were always busy.

# Chapter 27

Ace walked into the brothel and just stood there and waited. There were a few ladies and their "johns" around, but Ace knew that there were closed-circuit cameras, and that Starletta could see him. His wait was very short-lived. Starletta came rumbling into the entry room, cursing Ace. She reminded him that the last time that he darkened her doorway, she told him that she never wanted to see him again.

Ace stood there and let Starletta wear herself out. When she finally stopped to take a breath. Ace asked her if she was done? She took a deep breath and was just getting ready to release a new tirade when Ace just told her to "knock it off." "He told her that he didn't want to disrupt her business. He just had a few more questions to ask." Starletta glowered at him and spat, "so ask." Ace said that it might be better if they spoke in private. Starletta spit and sputtered and tried to come up with an answer and finally just sputtered, "Follow me," and led him to an office at the back of the bar and brothel.

Her office was exactly what Ace expected, with one exception. It was a small room, windowless. A gray steel desk and a wooden desk chair as well as a folding chair to sit at. The exception was that it appeared that Starletta had a very good I.T. person on the payroll. She had state-of-the-art computer equipment as well as multiple monitors on the walls showing all the camera views that were available to her. Ace made note that it appeared that some of the private rooms had cameras in them as well. If he couldn't get the information that he needed from Starletta or she got difficult, he would use the fact that people were being recorded without their knowledge to his advantage. A little leverage is always a good thing to have.

Ace listened to a bit of the background music that was playing while Starletta was fiddling with her chair. Ace found it amusing that "Light My Fire" by The Doors was playing. He felt that it was time to light a fire under Starletta's ample ass. She knew more than she was letting on, and he was going to find out everything that she knew. Between the threats at the hotel and the incident on the freeway in Southern California, he knew that there was definitely something going on, and Starletta was the place to start since this was the place that Humdinger took his last breath.

Ace made a big show of taking out his leatherbound notebook and pen and then leafing through pages until he found an empty page. Then he sat back in the chair and told Starletta to start from the beginning. He wanted to know everything that had happened between her and Humdinger, from the first time that she met him up until the night that he died.

Starletta glared at him and told him that she had already told him everything and that there was nothing more to add. She met him as a working girl, they met every time that he made a trip to Tijuana. As time progressed, he provided her with some cash so that she could take over the business.

Ace asked her if he was still "utilizing" her services when she took over the business. Starletta told Ace that by then, she had become "too heavy," and he wasn't interested in her anymore in that way. Starletta told Ace that Humdinger just wasn't into pregnant women, and she was very pregnant when she approached him about money for the brothel. Ace asked her if the child was Joaquin. Starletta looked up startled, and asked him how he knew her son's name. Ace laughed and told her that in the political circles, everyone involved with politicians who rose to the level that Humdinger had, got a background check. It was at that time that Joaquin came to light. Ace asked her straight out if Ronald Humdinger was the father of Joaquin. Starletta started to hem and haw around, and Ace told her again to just knock it off. He didn't care if her and Humdinger had an illegitimate love child. He just wanted to make sure that he had the entire story. He was just "checking all the boxes, so to speak." Obviously, a child with a "Madam" could be used as blackmail.

Starletta explained that there had never been a paternity test done, but she was fairly certain that Humdinger was the father. She didn't know for sure until the boy was born. He was the fairest-skinned Mexican that she had ever seen. And he certainly bore a resemblance to Humdinger. She never made it an issue with Ronald, though. She told him that she had a child, and it was possible that he was the father. Humdinger waved her off and told her not to worry about it, that the boys needs would be taken care of. Ace asked her what she thought that he meant by that. Starletta told Ace that every month a courier appeared

117

at the brothel with an envelope of cash. The first time, the cash had come with a note stating that it was for "childcare" and it was signed RH. Ace asked her how much money was sent for "childcare." She told Ace that in the early years it was around $1,000.00 per month. Always in crisp $100 dollar bills. As Joaquin got older, the amount increased. At the time that Humdinger died, Starletta had been receiving $3,500.00 per month. Starletta had told Ronald at one time that it wasn't necessary for him to send the money, that she was doing just fine with the business. Starletta said that Ronald insisted that the money would continue so that Joaquin could live a good life, even if it was in Tijuana. Starletta said that she was glad for the money when Joaquin got older because it allowed her to hire and pay for Security for him. Most of the underworld knew that Joaquin was, more than likely, the child of Ronald Humdinger, and she was afraid that some nefarious characters from the cartels might try to take and use Joaquin as "blackmail" against Humdinger and would try to squeeze money out of him as a ransom. Starletta told Ace that she wasn't sure how Humdinger would handle it if Joaquin were taken, hurt, or killed. He had never truly "claimed" him as his son but obviously, he had cared enough to send money to help with raising him.

Ace said that the loss of the monthly stipend had to hurt now that Humdinger was gone. Starletta said that it hadn't hurt at all as the money continued to be delivered by the courier service, even after Humdinger died. Ace told Starletta that he was confused. If Humdinger was sending the money and he was dead. Who was sending the money now?

Starletta told him that she didn't know, and she truly didn't care. If the money kept coming in, that was just fine with her. She had no qualms about taking money from a dead man.

Ace made a note to check into the "money trail" for the payments. He asked Starletta if she could tell him who the courier company was. She told him that she had no idea who it was, but the courier was a big, bald, musclebound guy that looked like he was always angry. Ace's ears perked up at this information. It certainly sounded like she was describing the "receptionist" at Humdinger Habitats who he had dealt with the day before. That information pointed back to Humdinger Habitats and Presley Misuse, but it could be coincidental. It was possible that Humdinger used the cueball for various errands.

Ace moved on with his questions. How long had Ronald been utilizing the services of Lola? Starletta turned to her computer, hit a couple of keys and said that Ronald had been seeing Mistress Lola for the last 3 years. Prior to that he would "hire" any of the ladies that struck his eye. He had never really shown any interest in the "FemDom" world prior to Lola. Starletta said that she was surprised when Ronald asked her to set him up with Lola. Starletta said that Ronald had never been a "bad lover," but he wasn't a "great lover" either. He had no sense of adventure. His goal was his satisfaction, he didn't care whether the girls were satisfied or not. He paid his money, and he got off. That was what he paid for. He was always adamant that the girls be "clean." He insisted on frequent STD tests over the years, and if a "girl" ended up with something, he wouldn't ever go back to her.

Lola came to work for Starletta as a dancer. It was well known that she would run across the stage, launch herself into the air, and straddle someone in midflight. You never knew who she was going to pick as her target when she performed. It could be a guy, a girl. You just didn't know. Starletta asked Lola if she would be interested in working in the back. It was at that time that Starletta became aware of Lola's interest in "Female Domination." It was also when Starletta discovered that Lola was bisexual. She preferred women when it came right down to it, but that was just for sex. She preferred to dominate the men that she serviced, and she found out very quickly that there was a huge market for her services. Starletta told Ace that Lola was her best "working girl." Meaning that she saw more people and made more money than all the other ladies in Starletta's employ.

Ace asked Starletta if there had ever been any complaints about Lola and her services. Starletta told Ace that Ronald never complained about Lola. Ace explained that he wasn't just talking about Ronald. He wanted to know if there were any other complaints. Starletta said that there were the normal complaints from the "john's" who didn't feel that Lola lived up to her end of the bargain because they were dismissed early. This was usually because the "john" chose not to follow the orders of their Mistress, so she released them. Lola would give the "john's" three chances, if they were dismissed three times, they were not invited back. A list was kept of those that were no longer allowed to enjoy Mistress Lola and her services.

Ace remarked that obviously, Humdinger wasn't on that list. Starletta turned to her computer, hit a few keys and told Ace that Humdinger had only been dismissed early on two occasions. She didn't have specifics but assumed it was because he "finished" before Lola told him that he could. She giggled and said that "self-control" was always a problem for Ronald.

Ace asked if anyone else had ever suffered a medical emergency while being administered to by Mistress Lola. Starletta said that nobody had ever been seriously hurt by Lola. Ace asked her what she meant by that? Nobody had ever been "seriously hurt". That wasn't nobody had ever been hurt. Starletta explained that some people liked to be "hurt," whether it was being paddled, tortured, smacked, degraded, etc. The injuries associated with that type of "play" were to be expected, and there were no complaints. All of Lola's "subjects" were extremely satisfied with the services that she provided.

Ace asked about the electrical stimulation device that Lola had mentioned. Starletta told him that she was aware of the device, and it only delivered low-voltage electrical shocks, nothing that could harm a customer. Ace said that he would like to take the device and get it checked out just to make sure that there were no issues with it. Starletta said that she would have to check with Lola to see if there were any of her subjects that would be utilizing the device before she allowed Ace to take it and have it checked out. Ace told

Starletta that he would have it back to her before the evening if he could get it now. Starletta took out her cell phone and sent a text to Lola. Lola responded promptly and said that the "shocker" was not going to be used today and that it could be removed and checked but it would need to be back for the next day.

Starletta told Ace that things were getting busy, and she needed to get moving as she had other things to attend to and was there anything else that she could do for him? If not, she was going to have to show him out. Ace told her that he had just one more question and he would be on his way. He asked Starletta if she knew of anyone that would want to harm Humdinger? She told Ace that the list of people that might want to harm him was long. He wasn't the most pleasant person in the world, and he had pissed many people off on both sides of the border between his temper tantrums, his vocal disdain for "illegals" in his country which angered people here in Mexico and in the United States. His shady business dealings. Cheating on his wife who Starletta understood could be a real ballbuster when she was angry. The fact that he "mocked" many people and did it publicly, sometimes on the National and International stage. Ace told her he got the picture, thanked Starletta for her assistance, and asked her where he could get the electrical stimulator and that he would be on his way. Starletta lifted her considerable bulk out of her chair and told him that she would take him to the chamber to retrieve the device but that she would need him to sign a receipt for it. She wanted him to understand that he couldn't just walk away with it. There would be a paper trail in the event he didn't return it as he claimed he would.

Starletta led Ace up to the "rooms" upstairs and, opened a door at the end of the hallway, and walked in. Ace walked in behind her and was immediately assailed by the scent of disinfectant. It was so strong that it almost choked him as he was standing there. Ace commented about the smell and Starletta told him that every precaution was taken to thoroughly clean the chamber between customers. "After all," Starletta said, "would you want to be chained to a table or chair while sitting in someone else's body fluids?" Ace acknowledged that he wouldn't really be up for that experience…Starletta left out a little laugh and said that she was sure that her ladies could get him up for any experience that he preferred. Ace could feel his face turning a shade of red as he hadn't even thought about the innuendo that he had spoken.

Starletta approached a cabinet and removed a small black plastic device with a couple of cables attached to it and handed it to Ace, and told him that she expected the device back that evening, if possible.

Ace assured her that he would get it checked out and returned shortly. He also commented on the smallness of the device. He told her that he was expecting a large "medical type" apparatus, not this little plastic box. Starletta explained that the device was designed to stimulate muscles but had been adapted to meet the needs of Lola and her subjects.

# Chapter 28

Ace returned to the waiting car and told Raul that he wanted to go to his cousin's that he thought could check out the electrical device and make sure that it was working properly. Raul told him to hang on, pulled away from the curb into traffic and headed north up the avenue. Ace was just getting comfortable in the backseat when Raul pulled into a dingy corner lot of a gas station and told Ace that they had arrived.

Raul led the way into the gas station, then through the door in the back to a service bay. Sitting on a stool peering under the hood of an old 1972 Chevy Nova sat a chubby man, smoking a cigarette and who was busy working on the engine.

Raul called out a greeting and the man working on the car jumped and smacked his head on the hood. Letting out a string of curse words, the man turned around, say Raul and broke into a huge smile, got up and gave him a big bearhug. While this exchange was going on, Ace just stood there waiting. After a quick conversation in Spanish, the man turned to Ace and introduced himself as "Jorge, the best mechanic in all of Tijuana." Ace handed the man the black stimulator device and told him what he wanted him to do.

Jorge walked over to his workbench, wiped his hands on a greasy rag and promptly set about taking the device apart. Ace just looked on with dismay. He really was hoping that Jorge knew what he was doing.

The last thing that he wanted to do was go back to the brothel and tell Starletta that he had broken her device.

The first thing that Ace noticed was that the device was battery powered, two AA batteries. That detail alone told him that there was no way that the device had caused Humdinger to die during his session with Lola. Jorge checked a couple of electrical connections, reassembled the device and handed it to Ace and told him that all was in order. There was nothing wrong with the device other than the fact that the batteries were a bit low. Ace asked him if the device could injure an adult mail. Jorge said that any shock received wouldn't be any worse than you receive if you stick your tongue on a 9-volt battery. Jorge did say that it was possible that a person could get burnt if you had a flammable material on your body but even that was unlikely.

Ace slipped Jorge a $50 bill, thanked him for his services and he and Raul exited the car. Ace told Raul to return to the brothel so that he could return the stimulator. He didn't want to delay or have something happen to it. He had done his due diligence regarding the device, and it checked out ok. There was no need to hang on to it any longer than necessary.

# Chapter 29

Ace got back in the car after an uneventful few minutes with Starletta. She was shocked to see him back so quickly and she made a big show of checking over the device to make sure that it wasn't broken. Ace just stood there and let her make her show. When she told Ace everything looked in order and signed the receipt that she had insisted on when he took the device; she handed the receipt over to Ace and told him that he was free to go, unless he saw someone that interested him. Ace told Starletta that he was not interested. Thanked her for her time and left.

Raul asked Ace where the next stop was, and Ace told him to give him a few minutes. Ace leafed through his notebook, closed it and told Raul to take him back to the hotel.

Ace needed to make some calls and he didn't want to ride around Tijuana in the back of a cab while doing it.

# Chapter 30

Ace entered the lobby and immediately spotted Jaime Shore sitting with a perfect view of the front entrance. Ace had barely made two steps when Jaime was up and almost sprinting to catch him before he could sneak away.

Jaime stopped directly in front of Ace. Ace tried to get around him, but Shore just moved to the side to block his way. Ace finally asked him what he wanted. Shore said that Ace knew exactly what he wanted, he wanted dirt on Ronald Humdinger. Ace told Jaime that there was no "dirt" to give him. That he needed to get out of his way before he moved him out of the way. Shore backed up a couple of steps and said that there was no need to get huffy. He was just a reporter looking for a story, and if the story happened to be about Humdinger, then so be it. Ace told Shore that he would be the first to know anything that he could share after he received permission from Humdinger Habitats to release info as necessary. Jaime scoffed and said, "That meant that there would never be any information forthcoming. He knew that Presley Misuse was not going to let anything hurt the company that he was running now that Humdinger was dead."

Shore told Ace that he might want to investigate that angle further. He told Ace that Misuse wasn't to be trusted. Ace just stood there and listened, then asked Shore if he was finished? Shore said that he was and stepped aside so that Ace could get to the elevators and up to his room.

Ace entered the elevator and punched his floor. He made a mental note to find out where the hotel got their elevator music. The other day, Rush had been playing. Today it was Pink Floyd, "Money" playing. Ace thought about the coincidence of the song "Money" playing. He knew that this entire investigation was being funded because of money. Humdinger was a greedy, attention-seeking buffoon when he was alive, but he had more money than he could ever spend. Humdinger wasn't known as a generous soul. He proudly bragged that he had the first cent that he inherited when his father passed away. The entire world knew that Humdinger liked to brag about all his money, but nobody knew for certain how much money he really had. He never released his taxes to the masses when he was elected, and there was talk that all his properties were over-valued and that he had many liens against them from unpaid contractors, at home and abroad. Humdinger had properties all over the United States as well as properties in Europe and Asia. Ace was sure that much of his wealth was filtered through the Cayman Islands and Switzerland so the world would never know how much he was really worth, although he like to claim it was "billions and billions of dollars" as he motioned with his tiny little hands and told anyone that would ask that he had "huge, huge" bank accounts, and many banks handled his "huge" accounts. Humdinger truly liked to brag that many banks wouldn't even be able to be in business if it wasn't for him. The man truly thought that the world revolved around him while he was living.

The elevator doors opened, and Ace stepped into the hallway and made his way to his room. As he approached the door, he saw another envelope taped to his door. This one was not big enough to hold photographs. Ace peeled it from the door and entered his room, where he opened the envelope. It contained one sheet of paper with the words "**WHY ARE YOU STILL HERE?**" scrawled on it in what appeared to be a black marker. Ace tossed the paper onto the desk in his suite and sat down. Obviously, someone wanted him to move on and drop the investigation, at least the investigation in Tijuana. Ace was going to spend a bit more time here just because of the letter. He didn't know if he would find anything new regarding the investigation, but he wasn't going to let whoever was trying to scare him off think that they had succeeded. Ace would move on when it was time, not when they wanted him to. Ace wasn't going to be intimidated.

# Chapter 31

Ace had a seat at the desk, fished his cell phone from his pocket, and made his first call…to Presley Misuse. He had questions regarding the payments to Starletta and Misuse had to have the information that was needed.

Misuse answered on the second ring. Ace didn't beat around the bush. He asked Misuse about the payments to Starletta. Misuse explained that Humdinger had set up the fund for his "bastard child" and that the payments would continue until the money was gone. Ace asked Misuse if he thought that it was possible that someone had learned of the money and was looking into ways to cash in immediately as opposed to waiting for the cash deliveries monthly? Did someone think that if Humdinger was dead, that there would be a cash payout?

Misuse stated that the only person that would benefit immediately would be Blaze and he didn't think that she would be that stupid. Humdinger was her "sugar daddy," and he had been for some time. The cash payments didn't just start when her son was born. Humdinger had been sending her cash for a long time.

Ace didn't feel like exposing the knowledge that he had from Starletta regarding the loans and money that Humdinger had sent to her over the years. Truth be known, Ace didn't trust Misuse. He didn't want him to know everything that he knew.

Ace asked Misuse if there were any other "special accounts" that he needed to be aware of. Misuse stumbled and stuttered a couple of times and said that there were no other accounts that needed to be of concern to Ace. Misuse said that any other accounts that might exist didn't have a connection to Blaze and Humdinger.

Ace ended the call, then sat back and thought…so there were other accounts. He needed to find out what in Hell was going on. Something was being kept from him. He just didn't know what. He would do more digging, but for now, he was going to take a day or two to get to know the pretty nurse saleswoman, and then he would move operations back to Southern California.

# Chapter 32

Two days later, Ace moved his base of operations back to Southern California. He had spent two days doing nothing but relaxing by the pool. He needed to gather his thoughts and think about the case without interruption. He didn't consider the trip down to Tijuana a bust. He came away with the knowledge that Humdinger was a pervert, which wasn't "new" info. He also came back to California with the knowledge that "something" was going on. Humdinger may have died of natural causes, but there was something out there that someone or several someones didn't want him to know about. Otherwise, why were the threats, pics, and notes in his hotel room and taped to the door?

One good thing that did come out of his trip to Tijuana is that he and Julie, the nurse saleswoman hit it off well. He learned that she was from a small town in Ohio. Her mother was a nurse, and her father was the director of a radiology department in a small hospital back in her hometown when they were still living. Julie had always wanted to be a nurse so after high school, off to nursing school, she went. She spent a couple of years being a floor nurse and decided that she wanted to get into the sales end of it. She loved interacting with the trainers and the new products that they presented at the hospital. She went back to school and got her BSN, then started looking for that first sales job.

Ace talked to Julie a bit about the case without getting into specifics. Just questions about how hard it would be to make it look like someone had died of natural causes while having sex. She said that there would be ways to make it happen during the act, or it could be done by introducing some type of medication that was slow acting and that they could kick in with exertion, causing a "heart problem" during increased activity, whether it was sex or vigorous exercise. Ace explained that the "tox screens" were clear. It obviously couldn't be a poison or medication, as that would show up in the testing. Julie explained that that may not be true. If the medication was something that Humdinger took, it would show up in the screening. Unless a screening for "quantity" of the medication was done, you wouldn't know. She also explained that there were things in all of us that were found normally, but in increased dosages could cause a problem. One of her examples was potassium. Everyone had it in their body. If levels were maintained, all was good. However, if levels were too high, then there were various symptoms, from muscle weakness to heart arrhythmias that could occur. If a fatal heart arrhythmia were to occur during increased activity, the patient could drop over dead of an apparent heart attack, and nobody would be the wiser unless they look specifically for hyperkalemia.

These were all things that Ace took note of so that he could check into it further. He hoped that he could contact the coroner via phone so that he wouldn't have to go back to Tijuana. He didn't recall if potassium was on the list of tests that were done on Humdinger's blood after he expired. Ace hoped that Dr. Bravo would be willing to send him the results via email, but he wasn't holding his breath.

# Chapter 33

Ace made his first call of the day. It was to Dr. Cameron Buerger, the physician who had been prescribing the ED medication, and Ace thought that was a great place to start regarding the health of Humdinger. After all, the doctor shouldn't be prescribing the medication if his patient wasn't health enough to take it. If Dr. Buerger knew that Humdinger had a bad heart and prescribed the medication, he would be considered complicit in Humdinger's death.

Ace was routed to the doctor's answering service, so he left a message that he would like to talk to him regarding a patient and he could please call as soon as possible.

Surprisingly, Dr. Buerger called back within a couple of minutes. Ace explained what he was hired to do and asked the doctor when it would be a good time to sit down and discuss a few things about Ronald Humdinger and his untimely demise.

Dr. Buerger explained that he wouldn't release any information unless he received permission from Humdinger's wife. Ace told him to contact her and get back to him with a time to meet. Doctor Buerger told him, "You seem pretty confident that she will give me permission." Ace didn't bother telling him that he was sure that there would be no problem since it was widely known that Humdinger hadn't slept with his wife in years. Buerger didn't need to know everything that Ace knew. He wanted to keep a bit up his sleeve to surprise the doctor with when they met. Ace told him, "Just call me back when you get permission," and disconnected the call.

Ace was getting ready to call and make his next appointment when the phone rang in his hand. He looked at the caller ID and groaned audibly. "P. Misuse" was showing on the ID. He didn't have any idea why Misuse would be calling him. Ace told him to expect a final report in a few days…well, he didn't really tell him that. He emailed that info to him. Ace really didn't want to talk with the whiny little weasel, so he let it go to voicemail. Ace waited for the expectant ding of a voicemail received but the ding never materialized. Instead, there was a loud knock at his door. Ace opened the "Ring" app on his phone and was not happy by what he saw at his door. Apparently, Misuse had called from outside his apartment. Misuse and the "bald cueball" from the office were at his door.

Ace considered ignoring the knock but figured that they would just call him again, so he hit the answer button on the "Ring" camera and asked what was up? Cueball looked around like he didn't know what a "Ring" doorbell was. Misuse just explained that he wanted to discuss the case and how much more Ace felt that it would take to complete the investigation. Ace told them that he would be there in a minute and disconnected.

Ace just didn't trust the cueball. He got his "carry piece," an S&W 9mm, out of his gun safe and strapped it to his belt in the middle of his back, then he threw on a light jacket to hide it from view.

Ace opened the door, and "cueball" literally stomped into the room like the proverbial bull in a China shop. Misuse followed behind. Ace closed the door and turned to face them both. He asked, "What can I do for you, Presley?" Before Misuse could even start to answer, Cueball said that they wanted the investigation over with. Humdinger died from natural causes. Everyone knew it. Why was Ace drawing out the investigation? Was he just trying to suck more money out of Humdinger Habitats?

Ace, never missed a beat. He asked Presley why he was allowing his "pet gorilla" to answer questions that he should be answering. Ace was watching Cueball out of the corner of his eye and saw him make both hands into fists. Ace steeled himself for the lunge that was coming, but before Cueball could make the lunge, Misuse stepped between Ace and Cueball, with his back to the Cueball and told Ace that insults weren't necessary, that they could talk about this like gentlemen. Ace agreed but said that if Cueball was here, that it was unlikely to happen.

Misuse turned and told Tim to wait outside. Ace remembered…that was his name, "Tim." He liked "Cueball" better, but he kept his mouth closed while "Tim" tried to talk Misuse into allowing him to stay. Surprisingly, Misuse said again, more firmly this time, to wait outside.

Cueball retreated to the door, mumbling the entire way, and said over his shoulder that he would be waiting right outside the door and that if he needed "anything," that all he had to do was call out his name.

The door closed and it didn't go unnoticed by Ace that it didn't latch.

Ace ushered Misuse into the bedroom that Ace had converted into his office and told him to have a seat. Ace took the seat behind the desk, and Misuse sat across from him. Ace told Misuse that he didn't appreciate that Misuse had shown up at his residence and office unannounced, with his pet gorilla trailing behind him. Misuse wouldn't take the bait. He told Ace that he had tried to call prior to knocking and there had been no answer. Since Ace's car was in the parking lot, they assumed that he must be home, so he knocked. As far as Tim was concerned, he came along because he was his driver when necessary. There was no other reason than that for his presence. Ace told Misuse that Tim could stay in the car the next time that they darkened his doorstep.

With that comment, Presley Misuse said that if things went well, they wouldn't have to see much of each other after this. He just wanted to know what was going on with the investigation. He really felt that it was an open-and-shut case, and why couldn't Ace just agree that Humdinger died from natural causes because he was too old and out of shape to be playing the type of sex games that he had been playing with Lola down in Tijuana?

Ace sat back and contemplated how much to say to Misuse. Was he somehow involved in this or was he just trying to get this closed so that Humdinger Habitats could move on? Ace took a deep breath and let it out. He then told Misuse that he was "close" to finishing up the investigation, he just had a couple more things to follow up on, and he would give them his final report. Ace didn't bother telling Misuse that things were amiss. Ace knew that there was more to this situation, and he was damn well going to get to the bottom of it.

Misuse asked Ace what had to be tied up as far as loose ends and the investigation. How much could there really be to investigate at this point? As Misuse asked the question, Ace's phone started ringing in his pocket. The caller ID was blank, but Ace recognized the number as the one that he had called to speak to Dr. Buerger. Misuse told Ace that it was ok for him to answer the call if he needed to. Ace said that it was probably nothing important and that it could go to voicemail.

Ace explained to Misuse that he was awaiting results from bloodwork that was completed during the autopsy in Mexico as well as some information from some calls that he had in regarding the overall health of Humdinger. When Ace received all that information, he hoped to be able to close the case and get the report to Misuse and the Board of Humdinger Habitats.

Misuse said that was good because the Board was getting impatient about the hold-up. There were complaints about the costs associated with the investigation. He winked at Ace and said, "You wouldn't be padding your time to get a bigger payout, would you?" Ace started to interject, but Misuse continued. He looked Ace square in the eyes and asked him to name a number. Ace asked what he meant. He said, "Name a number that it would take for you to finalize this investigation right now?" Ace was a bit pissed off by the offer, and he told Misuse as much. He told Misuse that he didn't do business like that, and if that was the type of investigation that they wanted, Humdinger Habitats should've hired some fly-by-night investigator out of the Yellow Pages.

Misuse just looked at Ace and told him to finish the investigation. If he didn't hurry up and finalize his report soon, he would be "terminated" as the investigator, and they would hire someone else. Ace told him that if he wanted to terminate him, to feel free but there was a clause in his contract that he would receive a minimum of three times the billable hours if the investigation ended prematurely through no fault of his own.

# Chapter 34

After Misuse stormed out the door, Ace went to the kitchen and grabbed a cup of coffee and had a seat at the table to think. Obviously, there was a person or people that wanted this investigation to end. At that point, his phone began to ring again. Ace looked down and saw that it was Dr. Buerger calling back. Ace picked up and Dr. Buerger said that he had talked with Emilyia Humdinger, and she said that it was ok for him to speak with Ace about Humdinger's health and well-being. Ace told him that he would be happy to meet with him whenever it worked best for him and that he would be more than happy to come to his office. After all there may be medical information that Buerger needed to access in his files.

Dr. Buerger said that he would meet with Ace at 4 PM after the last patient left. He gave Ace the address. Ace just listened, not bothering to tell the good Doctor that he already had the address. Ace hung up after assuring the doctor that he would be there, and he would be on time. He also told the doctor that he would try to be as expedient as possible so as not to hold him up any longer than necessary. He understood that the life of a medical professional was all-consuming and that healthcare workers valued their time off.

Ace glanced at his phone and saw that the time was only a bit after 10AM, so he had to decide what to do until he met with Buerger.

After a bit of thought, Ace decided that he was going to check out the company where Humdinger Habitats acquired the containers for the tiny homes that they designed. After all, the owner of the company had been present at the brothel when Humdinger went to the big whorehouse in the sky. If Ace was lucky, he might even bump into Kim Il Soon.

# Chapter 35

Ace hopped into his car and headed for Chang Myung shipyards where most of the containers came from that were used for the tiny houses. Ace wasn't surprised that Chang Myung was a "South Korean" company, as doing business with North Korea was strictly prohibited by the U.S. Government. Ace was going to have to find out how a South Korean company was run by a North Korean.

Ace pulled up to the gate and was surprised that it was wide open with no guard at the gate. Apparently, security wasn't a concern. Of course, it wasn't like you could walk into the place and lug a huge storage container out with your pickup truck. Chang Myung was a legitimate shipping company. There were containers everywhere, and they were in various stages of being loaded or unloaded from tractor-trailer rigs. As Ace was driving through the freight yard, he spied what looked like a work trailer in one corner. He assumed that these must be the offices for Chang Myung. As Ace parked in front of the trailer, he noted the small sign on the side of the door with the Chang Myung logo. This was the place.

Ace approached the door and turned the knob, which he found was locked. Ace couldn't see through the blind that was drawn, so he knocked loudly on the door. He heard some commotion inside, like a chair being scooted across the floor. As Ace was getting ready to knock again, the door flew open. A small Asian woman was standing there looking as though she had been woken from a nap. Ace explained to the woman who he was and why he was there. She said that Mr. Soon was out and Ace would have to make an appointment to see him. Ace took a card from the secretary and told her that he would call later to make the appointment.

As Ace was exiting, he decided that there wouldn't be any harm in perusing through the freight yard. Maybe he would get lucky and see something nefarious happening. After 30 minutes of driving up and down aisles in the yard and seeing absolutely nothing of interest, Ace decided to leave and head back to town. As he was pulling away, he watched a man exit one of the storage containers with a hose. Ace noted that the man appeared to be wearing a gas mask or fume mask, so Ace decided to see what was going on with that particular container. Ace parked and sauntered over to the container, which was standing ajar. Ace took a quick glance inside and noted that there was nobody around so he swung the door open and got a good look at the interior. It glowed in the sunlight like new. Ace also noted the piles of a sand-like substance on the floor. It appeared that they were sandblasting the inside of the container. Why would they do that? As Ace was exiting the container, he almost knocked the worker over who had been in the container. He was as startled as Ace was. It was obvious that the man hadn't expected to run into anyone as he returned to the container. As they stood there looking at each other, Ace noted the metal seal that the worker had in his hand. Apparently, he was just coming to secure the empty container.

Ace apologized for nearly knocking the man over. He acknowledged and then asked Ace what he was doing snooping around the container yard. Ace saw no harm in telling him that he was there looking for Mr. Soon and had gotten lost while driving around the yard looking for him. The man said that he didn't have any idea where Mr. Soon was, but he would never be found working in the container yard.

Ace asked him what he was doing to the container. The man said that he was sandblasting the paint off of the interior as the container was to be sold to a company that utilized the containers to make tiny homes. Ace asked if that seemed like a bit of overkill to the man. He said that it might be because he didn't care as long as they kept paying him for every container that he sandblasted. Ace asked him why he thought that they did this to the container. He said he didn't have any idea but assumed it was just so that the containers were clean and there would be no chemical residue left that could be a problem for the purchaser of the container. Ace acknowledged that it made sense and thanked him for his assistance. As Ace was walking away, he asked him…how much do you get paid for sandblasting? The workman said that it varied by job but was usually around $50/hr. Here at Chang Myung, they paid the standard rate of $50/hr. unless the container was purchased by some non-profit group. Then the payment for his services went to $1000. This was a flat rate, so it ended up being much better than the hourly rate. He said that if the container didn't have too many layers of paint inside, he could sandblast the entire inside in two to three hours. If it was an older container, it could take six to ten hours. He said that was never the case when the container was going to the non-profit group. Whoever they were, they were very particular about the containers that they received. Most were basically new, maybe only having carried 2 or 3 shipments before Chang Myung decommissioned the container and sold it off. The worker felt that this was very odd as most shipping companies kept containers for years and years, repairing them as necessary. That was not the case here. The worker said that about one-third of all containers coming through this freight yard for Chang Myung were sold off, which was not the norm.

Ace handed the man a $50 bill and thanked him for his time and then feigned that he was still lost in the yard and could he tell him how to get back to the gate. The worker gave him quick directions, and Ace drove off. He watched the worker place the lead seal on the container and walk back toward his equipment and his truck.

What the heck was going on? Why would they sandblast the interior of the containers that were being purchased by Humdinger Habitats? Ace was at a loss. It just didn't make any sense. Ace had seen some of the tiny homes that Humdinger Habitats supplied. The insides were finished essentially like a mobile home. The insides were covered with manufactured wall coverings after they were insulated. Why would you sandblast them clean just to cover them up? Ace could think of no reason that this would be done. He also couldn't think of any reason that it was a bad thing, although he guessed that it could lead to rust if the home was placed in a humid environment.

146

Obviously, southern California didn't fit that definition at all.

# Chapter 36

Ace made his way along the crowded So-Cal highways toward Humdinger Habitats. He wasn't going to the offices this time. He wanted to go check out how things were being done in the "manufacturing" end of the business, where the containers were converted into the tiny homes destined for use in the homeless community.

As Ace was making his way to the factory, he couldn't help but think about why Humdinger had even started this business. It obviously couldn't be that profitable. It wasn't like these "homes" were high-end homes. They were shipping containers that most often had one "living space" and one bathroom with a tiny shower. The cities that these containers went to were all over the United States, with the most going right here in California.

One of the problems that Humdinger had run into when this first started was that there were many communities with "rules" regarding shipping container homes in residential neighborhoods so it wasn't like a person could get one of these containers and plop it down on an empty lot and live there. Another problem was the fact that the person or persons living in the container had to have a way to pay for the electricity and water that were needed to make it habitable. Was it possible to live in these containers as shelters? Sure, it was, but without electricity and water for the plumbing, they became sweltering, sewer-smelling ovens, and obviously, nobody wanted that parked on the lot next to their $500,000 home in Escondido or anywhere else in the country. When dealing with homelessness, there were many problems that ranged from mental illness to addiction to people who were "hiding" from something or someone. Why would Humdinger even want to be involved in this endeavor? It just didn't make sense…and where did all of the money come from for the Headquarters and all of the employees at Humdinger Habitats? Things just didn't add up. Of course, Humdinger had inherited a lot of money from his father after his passing. His father had been a glorified slumlord in the Boston area. He had bought up multiple old factory buildings and converted them to apartments which he rented to people with minimal income. He was known for renting apartments by the number of people living in the apartment, charging each tenant rent as opposed to renting at a set rate with a maximum number of people living in the apartment. Rumor had it that he had one- and two-bedroom apartments that he was renting out for $10,000 per month and that sometimes there were 15-20 people living in the apartment, all paying a monthly payment for their portion of the rent. Humdinger's father was also known for the minimal amount of maintenance that was done on these apartments. There had been numerous reports of apartments without heat due to mechanical issues. In the winter, the lack of heat led to frozen and burst pipes, so the water had to be turned off. When Humdinger, Sr. was confronted about the problems, he said that the conditions in his apartments were better than the conditions that most of his tenants would have in their home countries in Central and

South America, so his tenants were fine with the living conditions. None of his tenants ever spoke out. If they did, they would be evicted. In most areas, that would be a long, drawn-out process. Not so for Ronald Humdinger's father. He was known to have ties with organized crime, and rumor was that there were multiple judges who would do whatever was asked of them. When these judges came through, a payment was placed in a special account in the Caymans that only they were privy to. Many of these judges and other city officials were rumored to have hundreds of thousands of dollars in these offshore accounts. Even with all the allegations, no city officials or judges had ever been charged with any crimes.

Ace finally arrived at the manufacturing facility and pulled up to the gate. He gave them his name and said he was there to observe the process of converting a container into a tiny home. The guard at the gate went into the shack and, picked up the phone, and made a call. The guard returned to the car and informed Ace that he didn't have an appointment, but someone was coming from the corporate offices to show him around. Ace was told to park in the parking lot outside the gate and wait for his guide to arrive.

Ace waited patiently in his car, wondering who was going to show up as his guide. He was putting odds on Timothy, the Cueball from the front desk. He was pleasantly surprised when a young lady of about thirty years old pulled in beside his car and tapped on his window. She introduced herself as Mikki Leone and said that she would be giving Ace the tour. She did say that Mr. Misuse wanted Ace to call him afterward.

Ace told Mikki that he would take it under advisement. Mikki walked to the gate, and Ace followed along, asking her if they were going to walk all over the entire facility. She asked him if that was a problem? He told her that it wasn't, but he wasn't really wearing shoes for that type of activity, and he noted that her hi-heels wouldn't be good for any distance walking either. Mikki just laughed a light laugh and led him through the gate to a waiting golf cart. She hopped behind the wheel and motioned for Ace to have a seat on the other side. Ace hopped in the golf cart and asked Mikki to take him to the manufacturing facility for the new containers. He told her that he wanted to see the process from the start to the finished product. Mikki said that she hoped his schedule was cleared for the rest of the afternoon, as it could take a few hours to see everything that he wanted to see. As Mikki drove off towards a large building at the back of the property, Ace noted the various buildings on the property. It was a long afternoon of looking at containers in various stages of completion to their "tiny home" status, but Ace saw nothing that seemed out of place. He didn't mention that there were at least half a dozen buildings that were never visited, and he wondered what was going on in those buildings. He didn't want anyone to think that he might want to come back and pay another visit…probably an "after-hours" visit.

Ace thanked Mikki for her assistance and for being a tour guide, hopped out of the golf cart and headed toward his car. As Ace was just getting into his car, Mikki tapped him on the shoulder and told him not to forget to call Mr. Misuse. He was awaiting his call.

Ace told her that he would call from the car when he got on the freeway.

# Chapter 37

Ace figured that he might as well get the call over with and dialed Misuse's number. Misuse picked up on the second ring and, with no preamble at all, asked Ace, "What the fuck are you doing poking around the manufacturing facility"? Ace let Misuse spit and sputter another few choice adjectives and then interrupted by saying, Hey Elvis, calm down. That comment was met with a deep breath and silence for all of 10 seconds, and then Misuse started on him about being disrespectful to the person who was paying him, and maybe that arrangement would just need to come to an end.

Ace told him that was just fine, but remember, he would have to multiply his current charges by three if he ended his services without a final report.

Misuse told him to step it up and get the final report to him. He was tired of him stringing them along just trying to pad his payday. Ace assured Presley that wasn't the case at all. He was just being thorough. Ace told him that he expected to have things wrapped up in the next couple of days, and then he would come in and present the final report personally. Misuse told him to make sure that's what happened and that if there were any other Humdinger properties that he wanted to visit, they needed to be approved through him. Misuse asked him if he was clear. Ace responded that it was crystal clear.

Ace disconnected the phone and drove on. He had about an hour until he could meet with Dr. Buerger but with southern California traffic being as bad as it was, that meant that Ace would probably arrive late, so he gave the good doctor a call. He wasn't surprised when he got an answering service. He just asked them to pass on the information to Buerger that he was on his way and not to leave if he was a few minutes late.

Ace tuned the satellite radio to one of his favorite stations, one that played music from the cassette era. The song that was playing was "Who Are You" from The Who. Ace felt that was a fitting song as he drove on…he knew who he was, but he really wasn't sure who Ronald Humdinger was. Obviously, he had been the narcissistic egomaniac that everyone knew from his TV show and he career as a politician. But who was he when he wasn't acting for the cameras? Emilyia had said that he was exactly as he would expect, an arrogant officious prick who only wanted people around him who would do any and everything that he asked without hesitation. The premise behind Humdinger Habitats was providing appropriate housing for the homeless with little or no cost to them. So why would Humdinger have even considered doing something like this. Everyone knew that he was a greedy bastard. This was a business that would have no income. Granted, Humdinger had other businesses, but Ace couldn't imagine that he would even consider a business that would have zero income. Of course, the entire business could probably be a tax write-off. That still didn't answer the questions regarding where the money came from to pay all of the employees.

Ace drove on, listening to the music and thinking about his next steps. He had told Misuse that he would have his final report in a couple of days. Ace figured, worst case scenario, he could give Misuse his report, and if there was something fishy about the death, he could keep digging into it on his own dime. He didn't think that he would have all the answers in the next two days. Obviously, the company wanted him to close this case up, and they wanted to move on.

Right about that time, the lightbulb came on in Ace's brain. He knew where the money came from. It was from the TV show and the advertisers for the show, most of which were "suppliers" for the products used in the manufacture of the tiny homes. How much the companies were paying for their products and the advertising was hard to tell but Ace was sure that it was a large sum of money and the show would continue without Ronald Humdinger. Presley Misuse would probably take over as the TV personality. Ace thought that was probably a good idea. Humdinger was horrible as a speaker or an actor. He couldn't say anything that didn't come back to him. He and his tiny little hands motioning for the contestants to leave after they were terminated. Humdinger probably would've brought the ratings down, but people tuned into the show just to see what kind of fool that he could make of himself while on TV. He didn't disappoint. It was obvious that Humdinger wasn't nearly as smart as he like to portray. He claimed that he was at the top of his class in college, yet nobody had ever found a list that had Humdinger's name on it as an outstanding student. He certainly never made the "Dean's List" while he was in college, or there would be a record of it. His policies when he was in politics were about the same. No thought went into them at all. He didn't think anything through when he wanted something done. He just threw a tantrum and made it happen. If you were a cabinet member and questioned him, he fired you and replaced you with someone who would do his bidding. Humdinger had no tact when it came to dealing with dignitaries. There was a video of him literally shoving the president of a European country out of the way so that he would be in the front line for the photo op. The sad thing was people just let him get away with it. Nobody had balls enough to step up and tell him to knock it off. Ace remembered a trip that he made to England, and he made a fool of himself in front of the Queen. When people started calling his actions out, he basically told them to fuck off. The Queen was a woman; he was a man, and she knew her place. That statement is basically what kept him out of the funeral service when the Queen passed away several years after he lost his re-election bid. Of course, he blamed the current President as the reason that he was not invited. Again, it was never his fault. Everyone loved him; just ask him, and he will tell you. Ace knew that, truthfully, people just put up with Humdinger because of his clout, nothing more. He was a showman, not a great showman, but he drew a crowd, so he was "popular," even if his popularity was because he was boorish and a chauvinist. People tuned in weekly to his show to see what kind of shenanigans he would pull. When he was in politics, everything he did was under a microscope and the news reported on it mercilessly, except for Fox News. Fox News always portrayed him in a good light. The rest of the news stations were "Fake News," and Humdinger wasn't afraid to "Tweet" that on an almost daily basis. Even though Fox News had been sued due to some of the things that were reported and proved to be false, they were faithful to Humdinger. It was funny. Most of his followers echoed Humdinger's same comments. Fox News was real news. The rest of the networks were fake news, not to be believed, because they were just out to ruin Humdinger when he had been the best thing to happen to the country since Abraham Lincoln. That statement itself was comical as most of his followers were misogynists and racists who didn't think women belonged anywhere but at home in the kitchen, and unless you were a white American male, you weren't worth the time of day. It was no secret that most of Humdinger's followers thought that every "brown" person was a rapist, drug dealer, or murderer. It was statements like that from Humdinger that had led to many of his followers declaring "open season" on anyone that they thought was an "illegal." Ace had many friends that had fallen under the spell of Humdinger when he was in office and even though he had presented proof to them about falsehoods and horrible things that Humdinger had said and done, they didn't care. In their eyes, Ace was just another "bleeding heart liberal" who didn't worship God, and of course, didn't worship Humdinger, who many thought was there as a gift from God. Ace didn't believe for one second that Humdinger had been a "gift from God" …if anything, he may have been a gift from "Beelzebub" if you were into that.

# Chapter 38

Ace arrived at Dr. Buerger's office promptly at 5 PM.
He parked in the nearly empty parking lot and went to
the door…which he found locked. Dammit, had
Buerger left even though he had left a message that he
might be late, and he hadn't been late. He was there
on time. Ace banged on the door and peered in
through the tinted glass. He could see movement
behind a frosted glass window, so he banged louder.
A door to the side of the frosted glass window opened,
and a middle-aged man in a lab coat came to the door.
He asked Ace if he could help him through the
intercom. Ace told him that he had an appointment
with Dr. Buerger. The man pushed the button in the
intercom and told Ace that the Dr. had left about an
hour ago. Ace fumed. What the fuck was this all
about. Buerger knew that he was coming to see him.
Ace took his phone out of his pocket and dialed the
number of Buerger. The phone rang and rang, but
there was no answer. The man on the other side of the
door just stood there while Ace made the call. As Ace
put his phone back in his pocket, the man on the other
side of the door asked if there was anything else that
he could do for him. Ace thanked him and told him
that he would just get in touch with Dr. Buerger and
make an appointment for another day. With that, the
man said Ok, turned on his heel, and went back behind
the door next to the frosted glass window. As the door
closed, Ace noted that there were letters on the door
that said Dr. C. Buerger. Ace stood there for a
minute…if that was Dr. Buerger's office, who was

this man dressed as a doctor? As far as Ace was aware, Dr. Buerger worked in an office by himself. He had no partners. Ace banged on the door again and pushed the intercom button repeatedly to no avail. Whoever the man was, he wasn't coming back to the door. As Ace was peering through the door, he heard a car approaching from the rear of the building. He looked up and noted a black SUV but couldn't see who was driving due to the window tinting. Another black SUV, Ace, didn't believe in coincidence. Ace decided that a walk around the rear of the building was in order. As he rounded the corner, he saw that it was like any other office building: a rear door, the dumpster, and a row or mailboxes for the tenants on either side of the doctor's office, as well as a locking mailbox for the doctor and a "Samples" box that Ace assumed was for lab samples that needed to be picked up after collection.

Ace gave a tug on the door and surprisingly found it unlocked. He entered and found himself in a long, narrow hallway that led left and right to the other occupants of the building, as well as a steel door right in front of him with Dr. C. Buerger printed on the door. Ace tried that door, but he wasn't as lucky this time. It was securely locked and, from all appearances, was a fire door which sealed tightly so Ace wouldn't be able to force the door open. Ace wasn't about to give up so easily. He had a crawling sensation up his spine that there was something going on here. He decided to check with the tenants on either side of the Doctor to see if they knew of or knew who he could contact to gain access to the office suite. His first stop was at a "copy and print" shop. From the looks of the entry, there wasn't much going on with the business but there was a sleepy-looking middle-aged woman behind the counter. As Ace entered, she perked up a bit and asked him what she could help him with. When he explained that he was just looking for Dr. Buerger, she started to point him in that direction. He stopped her mid-sentence and told her that he had already talked to a lab tech or someone in the office, and they told him through the intercom that Dr. Bucrger had already left for the day. The clerk had a quizzical look on her face and asked Ace what the person looked like. Ace started to describe him, and she told him to stop. Dr. Buerger had no men who worked in his office. He had a female receptionist who was off on maternity leave, and he had a nurse who was around 60 or so. She had observed his nurse leaving about an hour and a half ago, so that only left Dr. Buerger in the office. The clerk said that wasn't unusual, as he would schedule meetings with salespeople after office hours so as not to interfere with his patients. She said that it was possible that Ace saw a salesman, but she didn't know why he would answer the intercom for Dr. Buerger.

Ace was getting an even bigger feeling that something was "hinkie" here. He asked the clerk if she knew how to get in touch with the building owner so that he could possibly gain access to the suite, just to make sure that Dr. Buerger was ok. At this point, the clerk really surprised Ace. She reached under the counter and pulled a keyring out with three keys on it. One for her office, one for the office on the other side of Dr. Buerger's office, and one for the doctor's office. She explained that all the tenants had problems with locking keys in or forgetting keys, so they each had a set of keys to access each other's spaces in the event that they got locked out.

Ace and the clerk went next door and used the key labeled Buerger to enter the office area. Ace asked her to wait out in the lobby while he checked the back. The clerk was a bit hesitant to leave him alone since she didn't really know who he was, and she told Ace that she would just go with him to the entryway to the office areas and wait at the reception desk. Ace saw no harm in that and told her to follow him. As he opened the door, Ace walked through and called out for Dr. Buerger. There was no answer, so Ace entered further into the offices and called out again. Still no answer, so Ace proceeded from room to room, searching for the doctor. After checking all the rooms, he determined that it was empty. Ace called Debbie, the clerk from next door, over and told her that, apparently, the doctor had left early and had forgotten about his appointment. Debbie was standing listening to Ace and said that it was just odd that the doctor would've left and not taken his car. Ace asked her how she knew that he hadn't taken his car? She said that it was parked in the front parking lot. She saw it when they had walked over to the office. Ace thanked her, and they left the office. She pointed out the Dr's car sitting in the lot; a late model Audi A6, gunmetal gray in color. Ace couldn't help but think that there would be no way that he would leave a car like that sitting unattended in the parking lot. Ace thanked Debbie again and, took out his phone, and called Dr. Buerger's number but got no answer.

Debbie gave Ace one of her business cards and told him to keep her in mind if he had any printing or "other" needs. She gave him a big wink and walked back to her office. Ace just shook his head and walked over to his car.

# Chapter 39

As Ace was sitting in his car deciding on his next course of action, he was unaware that he was being observed from a black SUV parked half a block away in a parking lot for an apartment complex on the other side of the street. The man behind the wheel was on the phone. He told the person that he was talking to what had happened...he then told the person on the phone that Dr. Buerger wouldn't be a problem. He was sure of it. He told whoever was on the other end of the line that he had been paid to take care of a problem, and the problem was taken care of. He reassured the person that nothing would come back to them even if the Doctor decided that he was going to cooperate with Ace. As he hung up the phone, he looked in his rearview mirror and said, "Isn't that right, Dr. Buerger? We won't have any trouble with you?" Dr. Buerger, who was handcuffed with his mouth duct taped, just shook his head. The look of fear in his eyes was palpable. It was at that point that the doctor saw Ace drive past in his Impala, and he just flopped back on the seat, tears of fear running down his cheeks.

# Chapter 40

Ace was on his way back to Humdinger Habitats main office. He figured he really needed to talk to Misuse again as much as he detested the thought, he knew it couldn't be avoided forever, and a face-to-face talk was better than trading voicemails or emails.

Surprisingly, Misuse was available to see him in about an hour, which would be just about right because of the southern California traffic. A 10-mile trip could take hours if there were problems on the multiple freeways in the area. As Ace was making his way towards the offices, he spied a large black SUV about three car lengths back. He assumed that was his tail. He had given up trying to hide and lose them. Eventually, he would find out who it was that was having him followed. He wasn't going to worry about it right now. Ace was carrying his Smith and Wesson, and if things took a turn for the worse, he was prepared to do what he had to do to protect himself. As traffic slowed to a crawl, his thoughts turned to the nurse that he had met in Tijuana. He was going to give her a call when he got a chance. She went on and on about how great it must be to live in Southern California with the weather and, the beaches, and the city. He assured her that it wasn't all that it was cracked up to be. Ace had told her that there were many times he thought about moving away and starting his investigation business anew in the Midwest. He knew that there probably wouldn't be much business in the small towns throughout the Midwest, but he assumed that there would be some towns that were close enough to larger cities that he could commute as needed to investigate whatever it was that the people that hired him wanted him to investigate. Ace figured investigating an occasional missing person who was more than likely a runaway would pay the bills. After all, the cost of living is much less expensive in the Midwest. He wouldn't need as many cases to survive or to just pay the rent like he did in Southern California. He did have a small pension from his years in the FBI and government service but it wasn't near enough to live on.

Ace exited the freeway and headed towards Humdinger Habitats. He pulled into the parking lot, entered the building, and was met by Tim, "the Cueball," as he walked up to the desk. Tim barely looked up and told Ace that Mr. Misuse was waiting in his office and he could go right down. Ace walked down the hall, wondering why "the Cueball" was being so "official" instead of the snide goon that he had dealt with the other day. Ace wasn't kidding himself that things had changed. He figured that the goon was just being polite because they might be observed by other people in and around the building as the place was bustling with people.

Ace gave a knock on Misuse's door, and he heard Presley shout, "enter!" As Ace entered he noted that the office had even more changes since the last time that he was there. Obviously, Misuse was making it his own office. There were pictures on the walls of classic cars, some with Misuse in the car, some, where he was standing beside the car, and others of just vintage cars. Ace mentioned the pictures, and Misuse started in on his "collection" of vintage automobiles. He got up from behind the desk and took Ace over to a photo on the wall of Misuse sitting behind the wheel of a shiny red corvette. Misuse explained that this car was his pride and joy. It was a 1967 Corvette with the L88 engine introduced by renowned Chevrolet engineer Zora Arkus-Duntov. The L88 allowed the Corvette to compete on the racetrack, and bolder drivers could order it at their local dealership, back in the day. However, Chevrolct was worried that average drivers couldn't handle this beast. Misuse explained that the motor produced an impressive 550 horsepower and the car had a top speed of around 170MPH. Misuse said that his car was number 100 off the line, and only around 200 were produced, which made this car very rare. He said that they currently sold at auctions in the mid-six figure range with some reaching as high as $750,000.00.

Ace told Misuse that he would love to see the car in person someday as he was a big fan of the Corvette, although if he had his choice, he would like to own a 1963 Stingray with the split-back window. Misuse gave a slight whistle and told him that those were indeed nice cars and very hard to come by. Misuse then motioned Ace to a chair and said, "I assume that you didn't just stop by to see my office décor and talk about cars." Ace nodded, took a deep breath, and proceeded to tell Misuse that he wasn't quite ready to wrap up his investigation. He thought that it would take at least another couple of weeks because he hadn't gotten to talk to everyone as of yet. Misuse asked him who he needed to talk with yet, and Ace told he that he really felt that he needed to talk to the doctor that Humdinger had been using for his E.D. medicine. If anyone knew if Humdinger had a heart condition, it would be Dr. Buerger. He explained to Misuse that he was supposed to meet the good doctor this afternoon, but he had been ghosted. He wasn't sure why. He just wanted to ask a few questions about Humdinger's health and check that off the list. He also said that there were still some questions that he wanted to talk to some people in Tijuana about.

Misuse wasn't happy. There was no question about it. The longer Ace talked, the more red Presley Misuse's face got. Finally, Misuse erupted. What more did Ace need to know? Humdinger died while having sex. He was overweight, he didn't exercise, and his diet was horrible. The one saving grace was that Humdinger didn't drink. As far as Misuse was concerned, this was an open-and-shut case. He didn't feel it was necessary for Ace to look any further. The fact that Humdinger couldn't get it up for his mistress wasn't really a causative factor in his death. The fact that he took Viagra was of no concern. A lot of men his age were assisted by pharmaceuticals.

Ace just let Misuse fume for a few more minutes. Ranting about the money that this investigation was costing and the fact that Ace would be putting Humdinger's widow in an embarrassing situation. He asked Ace if he felt that embarrassing the widow was worth it? After all, he had heard that Ace had a very nice dinner with the widow a few days ago.

Ace shouldn't have been surprised that Misuse knew about the dinner with Emilyia Humdinger, but it pissed him off a bit. He stopped Misuse in mid-sentence and told him to shut up. He didn't like the insinuation that he was doing anything other than interviewing Humdinger's wife. Then he asked Misuse how he had come by the information that he had dinner with her. He had told Misuse that he was going to meet her and ask a few questions, but he said nothing about dinner…as a matter of fact, he didn't know that he was even going to have dinner with Emilyia until he arrived at her home, and he told Misuse that.

Presley looked a bit taken aback at being told to shut up. It didn't last long. He got a sneaky grin on his face and told Ace that it was ok if he was interested in having a bit of fun with the "Merry Widow," but he told Ace to remember that she had a bit of a reputation as a real "ball-buster" and that diddling the widow didn't look good to anyone looking at this investigation from the outside, or from the board of directors. He might even think about how his reputation could be hurt if word got out that Ace did business like this. After all, he was hired to investigate an unexpected death, not look into the widow's lingerie choices.

Ace stood up and leaned across the desk, his nose just inches from Misuse's, and told him in no uncertain terms that he would not be blackmailed into submitting his report until he was damn good and ready to. He also told Misuse that if he ever accused him of impropriety again, he would quit the case unfinished and report to the board of directors that Presley Misuse didn't want the case properly investigated. He just wanted a rubberstamp that

Humdinger had died a natural death so that business could proceed as usual. Of course, with Presley at the helm instead of being one step below the CEO.

Ace turned on his heel and exited the office. He was furious that there was any question about his reputation and professionalism. Ace could put up with a lot of things, but when people accused him of inappropriate actions, he lost his cool completely.

Ace stormed from the building, got into his car, and decided that it would be best if he just headed back to his home office. With him being so pissed off, he knew that he wouldn't get anything more accomplished.

As Ace was leaving the building, Misuse was on the phone. He hung up as Ace was leaving the parking lot. Misuse had a big smile on his face. He had just talked to Tim at the front desk, and Tim told him that a tracker had been placed on Bancroft's car, so there would be no need to have someone tail him. They would always know where he was with an "app" that was on Misuse's phone.

# Chapter 41

Ace got back to his apartment, kicked off his shoes, took off his tie, and went to the fridge to get a beer. He returned to the couch with an Arrogant Bastard and took a big pull on the can. The bity bitterness of the beer helped to calm him down.

Ace decided to call Dr. Buerger again and got his answering service. He left a message for the good doctor to call him back as soon as possible. The person taking the message remarked to Ace that the doctor had been left multiple messages and as far as they could tell, he hadn't returned a single call as of yet, which was very unusual. Dr. Buerger was usually very prompt in returning calls unless he was in surgery, and since he wasn't on call, that wasn't likely. Ace explained to the clerk that he was an investigator and if he would share the doctor's cell phone number, he might be able to have the location checked. Then, there might be an idea of where he was and what he was doing.

The clerk reluctantly gave Ace the number but told him that he was not to call the number himself as that could lead to his company losing the contract with the doctor for messaging services. Ace assured her that he would do nothing to jeopardize their business with Dr. Buerger. He would have his friend at the NSA ping the phone's location, nothing more than that.

Ace hung up and dialed his old Army buddy Kevin, who transitioned to the NSA after his time in the service was up. Ace wasn't holding his breath that

Kevin would answer…after all, it was nearly 5:30 PM at Fort Detrick, Maryland, where the headquarters for the NSA was located. He was pleasantly surprised when the call was picked up on the second ring. He chatted a bit with Kevin, and Kevin finally told him to quit beating around the bush. Ace only ever called him when he needed something.

Ace told Kevin that wasn't true. He had called him last May to wish him a happy birthday. Kevin chuckled and said, yep, and the time before that it was to get a location of an ex-girlfriend, and the time before that was a phone number of a different ex-girlfriend. So, "What's the name of the ex-girlfriend this time?" Kevin inquired?

Ace gave a little snigger and told him that he couldn't be any further from the reason that he had called. He gave Kevin the cell phone number and told him that he just needed him to ping it and tell him where it was located. He didn't need to call it; Ace just needed the location. Kevin said so, "Stalking is in your repertoire now?" Ace told him that he was just trying to track down a doctor of a client, nothing to do with women…this time. As Ace was explaining he could hear the keyboard taps coming from the other end of the line. He knew that Kevin was just busting his chops and that he would do this favor for him.

Ace heard more keyboard clattering, and then Kevin said, "This is weird." The phone was not on, so he had tried to activate the phone, and it wouldn't activate, which told him that the battery was either removed from the phone or the phone was no longer functional. He did say that based on cell data; it appeared that the last was near a strip mall in San Diego. Ace told him that was where the doctor's office was located, thanked him for the info, and told Kevin that they needed to meet up the next time Ace was in the area and have a beer or two and talk about the old times when they were both in the Army. Kevin agreed but said that he would believe it when it happened and disconnected the call.

Ace sat back, took a deep draught of the beer, and decided to turn on some music. He had an extensive collection of vinyl, and he found that the process of preparing an LP for play on his Technics SL-1200M7B turntable and listening to music helped him think. He leafed through his collection and selected one of his favorite albums, Soul Time from Sharon Jones and the Dap-Kings. As the smooth, soulful voice of Sharon Jones came through his Klipsch speakers, Ace sat down, closed his eyes, leaned his head back, and started running the case through his head from the beginning. Suddenly, Ace's eyes sprang open. He had to get to Dr. Buerger. If the last place that his phone worked was his office, then Ace needed to go to Dr. Buerger's office. The doctor had to be hiding something. If he wasn't, why would he have ghosted him? With his next plan of action decided, Ace finished the beer and listened to the entire album before heading back to Dr. Buerger's office. Then Ace remembered the answering service. He called back and told them that the phone was either dead or the battery was removed, but the last location was at the doctor's office, and he said he was sorry that he couldn't help them reach the doctor. He also assured the answering service operator that he would not divulge the cell phone number to anyone and wouldn't try to contact the doctor through his cell phone. That he would only utilize the service if he needed to contact the doctor.

Ace got in his car and headed back to the doctor's office. He made sure that he had his lock-picking tools with him in case he needed them to gain entry, but he was hoping that one of the other store owners would allow him to use their key to get in. He didn't need a breaking and entering charge, and if the key was provided, he could claim that he was entering the building out of concern for the doctor. He had some friends that worked on the San Diego Police department so hopefully, it wouldn't be a problem if there was an alarm system that was activated when he entered the offices. As Ace entered the parking lot, he noted that there was no tail on him this time. Maybe Misuse had gotten the message and was backing off a bit.

Ace was happy to see that the lady was still in the office next door to Dr. Buerger's office. He entered and turned on the charm. After some chit-chat, he asked her if there was any chance that she could let him in Dr. Buerger's office so that he could check it out for himself? She was a bit hesitant, but after a bit of cajoling from Ace, she handed him the keys and told him that she would let him borrow the keys, and he could go himself. She didn't want to be there if the alarm went off and the police showed up. Ace thanked her and, went next door, and entered through the main lobby. He was relieved that the alarm apparently hadn't been activated when the doctor left for the day…although that was a bit curious to Ace as everyone knew that doctor's offices were always a concern for break-ins by people searching for drugs. Ace had experience dealing with addicts while in the FBI and while investigating a theft case a few years ago. Unfortunately, Ace had to inform the person that had a valuable family heirloom stolen that her son had stolen it and pawned it for pennies on the dollar so that he could buy "meth." She didn't want to believe it, so Ace showed her the video of her son at thc local pawn shop. Addiction caused people to do horrible things when they needed a fix. That investigation had a "happy" ending in that Ace was able to recover the stolen heirloom and then helped the woman get her son into a reputable rehabilitation program. The last Ace had heard, he was still "clean" and living a good life.

Ace walked through the office, turning on lights, checking rooms, storage areas, etc., but found no signs of foul play. He did find Dr. Buerger's phone in his private office. The phone was sitting on the desk, and it had been crushed. Ace assumed by the paperweight sitting next to it on the desk blotter. Ace had to assume that the good doctor hadn't crushed his own phone, so there was "something" going on, but how he was going to find out what that was, Ace had no idea.

Ace made his way back through the office and turned off the lights as he made his way back to the front entrance. He left himself out and shut the door behind him, walked next door and returned the keys, then went to his car. As he was sitting in his vehicle, contemplating his next move, a police cruiser pulled into the parking lot and slowly drove through, stopping in front of the doctor's office. The officer exited his cruiser and, walked up and, gave the door a pull, noted it was locked, and returned to his cruiser. The cruiser then proceeded to the rear of the building. Ace exited the car and peered around the corner. He watched the officer do the same thing to the rear door. The officer returned to his cruiser, picked up the radio, and said that someone must be jerking them around as the place was all locked up with no lights on anywhere and no sign of forced entry. Ace overheard all of this while hanging near the corner of the building. He also heard the radio response that the call had come in from a cell phone linked to Humdinger Habitats. At the mention of Humdinger Habitats, Ace's ears definitely perked up. So, someone had called the police to report that there was a break-in or something suspicious at Dr. Buerger's office. He knew he hadn't been followed, so that had to mean that they were tracking him some other way, whether it was through his phone or a tracker. Ace wasn't sure. He truly doubted that it was his phone. He hadn't left it with anyone that it could've been tampered with, and while Humdinger Habitats was forward-thinking, Ace didn't think that they had the equipment or hackers on the payroll to access the GPS on his phone. Ace assumed that there was another tracker on his car. He would have to check that out in the morning and see if he could find it. Misuse had called off the live tail but obviously was still interested in what Ace was up to. At least, that was the assumption that Misuse was the person pulling the strings. It was time for Ace to call it a night. He was going to head back home and maybe give Julie a call. It would be nice to talk to someone and not think about the case, and she was a good person to bounce theories off if they did decide to talk about his current case.

# Chapter 42

Ace arrived back at his apartment, got an Arrogant Bastard out of the fridge, turned the TV on to CNN, and sat back. Ace was amused that the current report was coming from none other than Jaime Shore. It appeared that he was still down in Tijuana. Ace listened to make sure that there was no mention of Humdinger and was relieved when he realized that Shore was reporting on reported "animal cruelty" that occurred in the area. Seriously, Ace thought. Reporting on animal cruelty in a town where it wasn't uncommon to see a dead body hanging from an overpass. If the cartel did that to another human being, why would anyone be surprised that there was animal cruelty going on in Tijuana? As Ace watched the report, he realized that Jaime was reporting just down the block from Starletta's establishment.

Jaime was rambling about the abuse of dogs and cats due to neglect in the town and surrounding area, as well as the "cock fights" and the "dog fights" that went on illegally throughout all of Mexico. Then Jaime led into another type of animal abuse. The abuse that the donkeys were exposed to when used for the "donkey shows." At this point in the report, the cameraman zoomed in on the front of Starletta Blaze's brothel, and Jaime continued about the abuse that the poor animals suffered while being used in the capacity of being a stud for a human female. Ace just sat there with his jaw hanging to the floor. He couldn't believe that Jaime Shore was reporting on "donkey shows" in Tijuana live on CNN. He knew that, somehow, this was going to come back to him. He just knew that Starletta was going to be very unhappy. As Ace sat and thought about it, Starletta didn't know that he had spoken to Shore, so maybe he would be off the hook, and really, Humdinger wasn't attending a "donkey show" when he died. A dwarf dominatrix and a small Korean man were present when he died. There was no link to the report from Shore and Bancroft. Then it happened. Shore said that he had it from a confidential informant that Ronald Humdinger had actually passed away in the brothel where there were donkey shows. There was no confirmation that Humdinger had died while at the "donkey show," but what was a former prominent politician doing in a place like this, and what was Humdinger Habitats trying to hide by not releasing that information?

Ace snatched up the remote from the coffee table and snapped off the TV. Son of a bitch, he knew he was going to hear about this, and it wasn't going to be pleasant. Ace sat back on the couch and took a big slug of his beer just as his cell phone started to ring on the table. He picked it up; "Presley Misue" was showing on the caller ID. Ace let it go to voicemail. He didn't even want to talk with Misuse at this point. He knew what was coming. There were going to be accusations about him talking to CNN and that wasn't acceptable, blah, blah, blah. Ace would deal with that in the morning. Right now, he was going to give Julie a call. Just as he reached for the fun, it began to ring again. This time, the caller ID said "Protected". He knew that there was no way he was answering that. It could be anyone from the Secret Service to the FBI to the Whitehouse, and he didn't want to deal with any of it tonight. He let that go to voicemail and then dialed Julie's number. Unfortunately, he got her voicemail, so he left her a message to give him a call when she had some time to chat and disconnected.

Ace had two messages in his voicemail. The first was from Misuse, and he was livid. Ace could picture the spit flying from his mouth as he yelled into the phone about the privacy of the investigation. Ace deleted the message and listened to the next message. This message was from someone utilizing software to hide their voice characteristics. The message was straightforward. Ace needed to end his investigation before he or someone else got hurt. There was no need to investigate any further. "Contact Humdinger Habitats in the morning and give them your report that nothing nefarious occurred and move on to his next case." The caller didn't leave a name or number, obviously, but did say that he would be in touch if things didn't proceed as suggested. Ace didn't like being threatened. He would go in and visit with Misuse in the morning and take his lumps, but he wouldn't confess to speaking with Shore at all. Ace might just "end" the investigation as far as Misuse and Humdinger Habitats was concerned, but that didn't stop him from investigating on his own. He wouldn't be paid any further from Humdinger Habitats. That might just be the plan. Give Misuse his "report" and end his affiliation with Humdinger Habitats.

The phone rang again, and Ace was pleasantly surprised to see that it was Julie returning his call. He picked up after the third ring. He didn't want to appear too "needy" and gave his smoothest "hello" that he could muster…which truly wasn't very smooth at all. Ace was never good at being a "smooth talker." He tended to be pretty matter-of-fact, which could be a good thing, but it also could hinder him in relationships.

Julie was just getting ready to turn in for the evening when she checked her phone and saw that she had missed his call. Ace kicked himself. He knew that she was in the Eastern time zone. He should've checked the time before calling her. It was almost 11 PM in Ohio. He apologized for calling so late. Ace gave her a quick rundown of what was going on with the investigation regarding Humdinger's untimely demise and the report from Jaime Shore from CNN. She asked him what more he thought that he could find about Humdinger's death. He told her that, honestly, he didn't know if there was any more to find out regarding how he died. Ace still felt that there was being hidden, but by all appearances, it looked as though Humdinger had just had a heart attack, and that was the end of it.

Julie told him to give him any medical information that he thought might be pertinent, and while they were talking, she would log into the Ohio Hospital Association website and see if there was anything that he was missing medically that may have caused the heart attack. Ace went over all the details that he had from the coroner, as well as information provided by Starletta and by Lola. Julie said that the findings from the autopsy were pretty much unremarkable. She also said that she didn't see anything that Starletta or Lola provided that added to his case. Julie did ask him if he talked with Humdinger's doctor regarding the ED medications and if Humdinger was healthy enough to handle "Femdom" sex? Ace explained that he had a meeting with Dr. Buerger, but Buerger had ghosted him and he hadn't been able to get in touch with him since the initial phone call. Julie said that was the only thing that she thought was missing. A clean bill of health from Dr. Buerger stating that Humdinger was healthy enough for vigorous sex would close the case. Julie recommended that he keep trying to contact Buerger until he got the report from him and then end the case. Get his money from Humdinger Habitats and move on to the next case. Ace said that sounded like a great idea, although he was thinking that a weeklong vacation in Ohio with his favorite nurse would be the first thing on his agenda when he turned the case over to Misuse.

Julie gave a throaty laugh and said that he was "presuming a lot. What if she had plans? She also was working since she had just returned from the sales meeting in Tijuana. Ace stuttered and stammered a bit and told her that he didn't mean it that way. Her lilting laugh told him that she was jerking his chain. Julie told him to give her a call in the next couple of days, and they could make plans.

Ace hung up the phone and turned the TV back on, but this time, he turned it to reruns of The Big Bang Theory. A sitcom was just what he needed. He put his phone on silent and sat back, enjoying his beer and the show. As the first of many episodes ended, Ace caught himself dozing off on the couch. It was only 9 PM, which was way too early for Ace to go to bed. If he went to bed this early, he would be wide awake at 2 AM.

He survived on around five hours of sleep a night. That had come in handy when he was in the Army. His parents hated it, though. There was many a morning that his father got up to find Ace downstairs sitting in front of the TV watching whatever was on…in those days, that wasn't much. Ernest Angley seemed to be on pretty much every day when Ace was young. He remembered asking his dad about Ernest Angley and what he thought of the evangelist being able to heal people with his touch. His dad just laughed and told him that it was all a show. That the people being "healed" by Angley weren't really sick or hurt, or if they were, it was a mind-over-matter thing. His father said it was amazing what the human body could talk itself into. His father basically said that Ernest Angley and other televangelists were just in it for the money. His father reminded him that they always asked for donations at the end of the show. By that time, other shows would come on so Ace would find cartoons on. His dad would leave for work and tell him to be quiet and not wake up his mother too early, and he would head out the door for his walk to work. Ace never really understood why his father never got a driver's license, but walking never seemed to bother him too much.

Rather than go to bed and be awake at 2 AM, Ace decided to go for a walk. Walking in his neighborhood in San Diego was not considered unsafe, but Ace still took his concealed carry Smith & Wesson with him. It wasn't likely that he would need it, but he would much rather have it with him than wishing that he had it if he were to get mugged. Ace started walking down the street. He just listened to the noises of the night in the San Diego area. He could hear ship's horns out on the bay, the nightbirds jumping around in the live oaks crickets, and somewhere behind him, he could hear some light footsteps. Ace didn't think that anyone would be following him but he made a beeline for the Gaslamp Quarter, just a couple of blocks away. In that area, there would be plenty of people and Ace could take a second to "window shop" so that he could see if there was truly anyone following him. Ace stopped at the windows at the front of Goorin Brother's Hat Shop. He took a quick look up and down the street and didn't see anyone trying to hide themselves in the doorways or ducking into the alleyways. Ace always liked a nice hat and there were several in the front window that caught his eye. He made a mental note to come back and check out the hats in the shop when they were open. He continued down the street to one of his favorite watering holes, the Gaslamp Tavern on 5th Avenue. The Gaslamp Tavern had a great drink menu, and the waitstaff was not skimpy when pouring the drinks. The food was also top-notch and there were seats available at the large windows so Ace could watch out the window to see if he was being followed by Misuse or anyone else.

Ace ordered a GTL Mule from the waitress. The GTL Mule was one of his favorites, it consisted of Tito's Vodka, angostura bitters, lime juice, and then topped off with ginger beer, all served in the typical Moscow Mule mug.

The waitress brought his drink and asked if he wanted to keep a tab open or close it out as he went along. Ace wasn't really planning on having more than one cocktail, so he told her he would just close his tab and handed her a $20. As Ace was sipping his drink, he was keeping an eye outside…the nice thing about this seat was that he also got a reflection in the windowpane of what was going on in the bar as well as being able to see outside. Ace saw the waitress approaching from behind him, so he turned. She handed him his $20 back and told Ace that the bartender said it was on the house. Ace told her that wasn't necessary. He didn't come in to get a free drink; he just wanted to relax and people-watch a bit. Ace looked up and was going to motion to the bartender, and that was when he saw "Tim, the Cueball" from Humdinger Habitats sitting at a booth toward the back of the bar. He was trying to stay "invisible," but with his big, shiny bald head, that was next to impossible. Ace picked up his drink and made his way towards the booth. As Ace approached, Tim tried to sink into the leather upholstery, but Ace didn't give him a chance. He slid into the booth across from him and asked him what in the Hell he was doing following Ace into a bar…why he was following Ace at all.

Tim looked as though he had swallowed a mouth full of dead flies. He told Ace that he had just stopped in for a drink. He wasn't following him. Ace leaned across the booth and told him to knock off the bullshit. He didn't know where Tim lived, but he damn well knew that he didn't live in this neighborhood and that it was very unlikely that this was a coincidental meeting. Tim finally said that he was told to follow Ace just to see what he was doing to earn all this money. Ace told him that Humdinger Habitats wasn't being billed for hours, that he wasn't working, and that sitting at a bar having a drink didn't constitute work, so he could just go tell Misuse that he would have his final report within the next two days. He didn't need to have him followed.

Tim had regained some of his bravado and told Ace that he wasn't going anywhere. He had stopped in here to have a drink, and he was going to have that drink whether Ace liked it or not. Rather than cause a scene, Ace leaned across the booth again and told Tim to enjoy his drink and hit the road. He didn't like him, and he didn't want him skulking around following him. Ace stood as Tim's drink was delivered. Tim tipped his drink to him and told him to have a nice night and that he would be seeing him soon. Ace surreptitiously rubbed his head and gave Tim the finger. Tim obviously saw it as he turned a deep shade of purple, but to his credit, he didn't acknowledge it out loud.

Ace sauntered back over to his seat by the window, sat, and enjoyed his Mule. It was delicious, then he remembered that the bartender had said that it was on the house so Ace stood again and headed towards the bar. As luck would have it, there was a barstool available that gave him a view of Tim as well as a view of the mirror behind the bar so that he could see if anyone came in that he needed to be aware of. As he had a seat, the bartender asked him how his drink was. He told her that it was good but couldn't accept the drink. He really needed to pay for it. At that time, the bartender said to Ace, "I'm hurt. You don't remember me." Ace looked at her again and told her that he was sorry, but he didn't remember her at all. She introduced herself as Amber and said that she had hired Ace a couple of years ago to basically spy on her husband because she thought that he was having an affair. After three days, Ace had given her a flash drive filled with pictures of her husband with another woman. It was obvious that they were intimate, the way that the looked at each other. Amber said that she had divorced the cheating bastard and had to start over again. As the divorce progressed, her attorney found out that her husband had been squirreling away a lot of money in a bank account that she wasn't aware of. There ended up being close to a half million dollars in the account and Amber ended up getting half of it. She put the money on a condo here in the Gaslamp Quarter and continued working here at the Tavern. She told Ace that paying for his Mule was the very least that she could do.

As Ace was chatting up the bartender, he observed Tim talking on his cell phone. Tim hung up the phone, got up and walked out of the Tavern without a look at Ace. Regardless, Ace watched his retreating figure in the mirror until he left the bar. He didn't like the guy, and he certainly didn't trust him. He could picture Tim trying to sneak up behind him and crack him over the head with a bottle or just one of his big "ham-sized" hands. Ace chatted with the bartender until 11 PM and then decided that it was a good time to head back to his apartment and get some sleep. He was going to tie up some loose ends tomorrow as far as the "report" for Misuse was concerned, but Ace wasn't kidding himself that he was done with the investigation. He was just done getting paid by Humdinger Habitats. There was something here that people wanted to hide, and he was going to find out what it was. He didn't have any other cases pending, and he was going to receive a nice payday from this investigation so he could spend some time looking into it further. He just needed to make sure that Misuse didn't find out that Ace hadn't really given up on the investigation. That wouldn't be a good thing at all.

# Chapter 43

Ace got up bright and early. He had a report to write for Misuse, but prior to that, he was going to enjoy a pot of coffee. Ace really enjoyed his mornings sitting on what passed for a patio in San Diego. It was an eight-by-ten-foot rectangle of concrete off the kitchen, looking at three sides of privacy fencing with a lawn chair and a small table. Even though it was a cramped space, it was fairly peaceful in the morning. If he leaned just right, he could see the sun rising over the Laguna mountains east of San Diego. Like most days in San Diego, this one wasn't going to be any different, sunshine and a high in the mid-70s. San Diego was truly a perfect part of the country, other than the occasional earthquake and the traffic. Ace detested the traffic. Even at this time of the morning, before 7 AM, you could expect the average speed on I-5 to be about 25MPH. Ace wasn't in any hurry to hit the road this morning, and since he had lived in the area for a significant amount of time, he knew how to get to most anywhere locally via the surface roads. If he didn't have to venture onto the freeway, that was just fine with him.

Ace made a trip into the kitchen to refill his coffee cup, a mug from the Hemingway Home in Key West. The mug was one of his favorites. He hoped to write a book someday, but for now, he was going to heat up a breakfast burrito and enjoy his coffee for a while longer.

Ace was going to write up his "final" report for Misuse. He was going to deliver it personally even though he knew that wasn't necessary. Ace wanted to make sure that Misuse couldn't claim that the report was never received via email. Ace also wanted to give Misuse a hard copy so that there was no ability to change the "electronic" report. Ace was curious how Tim would react when he arrived at Humdinger Habitats later in the day. Would he acknowledge the encounter last night, or would he go with his usual testosterone-induced meathead actions and try to act threatening? Ace had to admit, he didn't have any room for guys that were bodybuilders, especially those that obviously used growth hormones so that they would look "huge." Ace knew from past experience that even though they were big, the bulk made them slow, both physically and mentally, in his opinion.

Ace finished his breakfast, put his dirty dishes in the dishwasher, and started it, even though it was far from full. Ace hated to wash dishes; he would rather run a mostly empty dishwasher instead of washing the dishes by hand. Once the dishwasher was running, Ace hopped in the shower. What was the hurry? He should be able to type out the report for Misuse and Humdinger Habitats in about an hour, probably less.

# Chapter 44

Ace sat down at his makeshift desk and began to write out his report for Humdinger Habitats. He really felt that the best way to report this was a short and succinct report with minimal details, so that's exactly what he did, although he did state that through a "cursory" investigation, nothing nefarious could be found to indicate anything other than the fact that Humdinger had passed away while engaging in "bondage games" with a dominatrix in Tijuana.

Ace didn't mention that there was another man present when Humdinger passed away. He also didn't make mention of the fact that Humdinger had given many expensive gifts to both Lola and to Starletta over the years. Ace assumed that Misuse would be aware of that information, and it wasn't pertinent to the investigation into Humdinger's death.

Ace also didn't mention that Humdinger had a child born out of wedlock to Starletta Blaze. Why drag the kid into this investigation? The kid couldn't have had anything to do with Humdinger's death, and the press didn't need to know about his existence.

Ace quoted from the Medical Examiner's reports that all signs pointed to an obese man who was engaging in sex games that were just too much for his heart, which ultimately led to his death. Humdinger would be rolling over in his grave if he knew that the Medical Examiner called him obese in his report. Humdinger was notorious for pretending to be something he wasn't. He was quoted all of the time saying that he was 6'3" tall and weighed a slim 215 pounds. Of course, the coroner's report put him at 5'10" tall and 285 pounds so Humdinger couldn't even be honest about his height and weight. There had been rumors for years that Humdinger wore "lifts" in his shoes which is why he always seemed to be leaning forward when standing. Apparently, adding 3+ inches of height through your shoes made you stand awkwardly. Ace also noted that the medical examiner's report said that Humdinger had hardening of the arteries and partial obstructions in many of the vessels in his heart.

Ace read the "report" over one more time and decided it should suffice. He printed the hardcopy and placed it in a file folder. Ace thought about deleting the file from his computer but decided against it. After all, he wasn't done with the investigation. He was just done getting paid by Humdinger Habitats. Ace decided that his best course of action would be to "hide" the file. If Presley Misuse asked him if there was an electronic report, Ace would just tell him that he had deleted the report after he printed it due to the sensitive nature of the investigation. That should satisfy Misuse, of course, once Misuse got wind that Ace was still investigating something to do with Humdinger's death, all bets were off. Ace changed the name of the file to "Nurse Julie" and added a photo of her that he copied off her Facebook account. To anyone looking at his laptop, it would appear this was a file of a "girlfriend" and shouldn't be suspect. Just in case, Ace put an access code on the file that was required to open it. Nobody would be able to access the file without the code, and since the code was 17 digits long, it wasn't likely that anyone would figure it out in the five chances that they had before the file was locked and deleted permanently. Ace also downloaded a copy of the file to a microSD card that he stashed with the rest of the microSD cards that he used with his digital camera and his Mavic drone. There were around one hundred microSD cards, so unless someone broke in and took all of the cards, they would never find the card with his copy of the report on it. Ace wasn't sure why he was going to such lengths, but in his experience, it was always better to be safe than sorry. Access to the microSD card was also passcode protected, and Ace made sure to utilize a different passcode than the one that he had used on his laptop.

# Chapter 45

Ace's next order of business was to go over his vehicle with a fine-tooth comb. He wasn't being actively followed but it was obvious that Humdinger had an idea where he was without having him followed too closely. Ace started at the front of the car and worked his way to the rear without finding anything suspicious. Nothing looked like a tracker, so Ace decided that he would use his electronic equipment to sweep the car to see if there was any unwanted electrical or radio pulse coming from the car. As he was scanning his car, he had about decided that he was looking for something that didn't exist when the RF detector gave a single beep and stopped. Ace sat back and waited. Five minutes later, he received another beep from his RF detector. So, there was something pinging from his vehicle. It was set to ping every few minutes, which didn't really give a real-time location, but it gave a general area, and obviously, after a couple of pings without movement, his location could be pinpointed. Ace started again from the front of the car, but this time, he put the hood up and looked for anything that didn't belong under the hood. As he was looking over things, he noticed a small copper wire running from the alternator across the top of the block and up under the air filter. That obviously didn't belong there, so Ace popped the air filter cover, and there it was, a small device, not much bigger than a quarter, placed between the fins of the air filter. Ace fished the device from between the fins and looked it over carefully. It was a standard RFID transmitter, much like people used for their luggage, like an Apple Air tag, but those were battery operated. It appeared that this device worked off electricity generated by the running vehicle. The device also appeared to have a slot to plug into, and Ace assumed to program the device or to download the information contained on it. Ace left it plugged into the copper wire for now and placed it back into the air filter then closed the cover up. He would remove the device when he got to Humdinger Habitats and give it to Tim since Tim seemed to be the person who was following him most often.

Ace looked over the rest of the vehicle and found no other signs that there were any other transmitters on the car.

Ace got on the road to Humdinger Habitats with his report. Even though he was no longer going to be paid by Humdinger Habitats, he was going to continue to look into the death.

# Chapter 46

The parking lot for Humdinger Habitats was relatively empty for a weekday, but Ace spied Presley Misuse's car in the lot, so he shouldn't have a problem meeting with him even though he didn't call for an appointment, which was required per Tim, the human cueball at the desk at the entrance. Ace parked in the visitor spot and, popped his hood, pulled the air filter, and yanked the tracker from the wire. Ace strolled through the front entrance and was disappointed to see that Tim wasn't at the desk. Ace walked down the hallway towards Misuse's office and as he was walking, he heard Tim call to him from up the hall. Ace turned and told him that he didn't need an escort, that he was bringing a report to Misuse, and that he knew how to find his way. Tim began mumbling about needing to call and be announced. Ace just gave a wave over his shoulder and continued to the office of Presley Misuse. The door was closed. Ace gave a couple of sharp knocks, opened the door, and walked in. Misuse was sitting at his desk looking over paperwork in a file folder. When he looked up and saw Ace, he closed the folder and said that it would be appropriate to wait to enter after the knock was acknowledged. Ace just shrugged his shoulders and told him that he wasn't much for professional courtesy in an office setting. He tossed his file folder on Misuse's desk and said, "Here's your report." Ace grabbed a chair and had a seat as he assumed that Misuse would want to look over the report. Misuse looked at him and said, "sure, have a seat. By all means, make yourself comfortable." Ace said he was very comfortable.

Misuse opened the folder, took the single-page report out, looked up at Ace, and then back down at the report. After taking all of 30 seconds to read it, Misuse said that this was all he had to offer for a report. Ace asked him if that wasn't what he requested. Wasn't the request that he check into the cause of death just to make sure that nothing nefarious had happened to cause Humdinger's untimely demise?

Misuse said that it was, but he had expected a bit more detail. Ace told him that there was no need for details. Humdinger was too old, too fat, too out of shape, to engage in sex games with a dominatrix, and it killed him. Although the erectile dysfunction medications probably didn't help, Ace saw no need to put that information in his report.

When it came right down to it, Humdinger was just too old and fat to fuck...would Misuse prefer he used that term instead? Misuse said that vulgarity was not necessary and then he told Ace to submit his final bill, and he would send it over to accounting for processing. Ace reached into his coat pocket and pulled an itemized bill from it. He handed Misuse the invoice for almost $30,000.00 for expenses and services. Misuse glanced at the bill and told Ace that it was a bit higher than he expected, but he would run it through the board members and see if there were any questions. If not, Ace could expect payment in the next 10-14 days. Ace told Presley that was just fine, although his terms were payment in full within

24 hours of finalization of the investigation and that was in the contract that Misuse had signed when he was hired. Misuse said that he just didn't know if he would be able to get the check cut that quickly. Ace told him that there was no need to even cut a check. He had included instructions to make the transfer electronically with his invoice so there would be no delay. With the contract, Ace expected the transfer to be completed 24 hours from the time that the invoice was presented to Humdinger Habitats. Ace looked at his watch and said that he would give them until 3PM the next day. If the money wasn't transferred by then, there was a penalty of 10 percent of the bill and that was added to the bill every 24 hours after the due date.

Presley Misuse was looking more and more like he was going to have a stroke or a heart attack. He started a shade of pink on his neck and it was quickly turning to maroon on his face. He started to rant and rave about highway robbery. Ace held up a hand and told him that all of that information was included in the contract that he had signed. Ace didn't want to hear any more about it. He expected payment within 24 hours, or the clock started ticking, adding $3,000.00 the first day, to $33,000.00; the second day, $3,300.00 was added to the invoice bringing the total to $36,300.00. Ace told him, as you can see, the total due can go up very quickly. As Ace turned to leave the office, he said, "Just pay the invoice. You were the person that wanted the investigation finalized," and he walked out the door.

On his way out of the building, he saw that Tim was sitting at his desk, his bald head reflecting the lights in the ceiling above his head. Ace reached into his pocket and pulled the tracker from his pocket, laid it on the desk, and told the Cueball that his "tailing duties" were officially over and that he didn't expect to see him again. Tim started to retort. Ace held up his hand and told him to save it. He didn't have a need to respond. Just keep his mouth shut. Ace walked out the front door, hoping that he never needed to be back in this building again...unless, of course he found something in his own investigation that proved that there was something underhanded going on here that led to the death of Ronald Humdinger.

# Chapter 47

Ace climbed into the car and sat back. He didn't think that he was going to do any further investigations into the Humdinger matter today. He was going to go get a quote for repair of his car where the SUV had "tapped" him a few days ago and then decide whether to fix the car, leave it as is, and continue to drive it, or just trade it in for a new car. He really loved his Impala, but at eleven years old and over 140,000 miles on it, how much longer would he be able to trust it mechanically?

Ace left the parking lot and headed towards San Diego. He knew of a collision repair shop close to another of his favorite breweries in San Diego, Modern Times Brewing Company.

One of the nice things about Modern Times was that they also had coffee that was roasted on-site, so if you didn't want to have a beer, you had another option, coffee; which was on the list of favorite beverages for Ace. Beer, wine, bourbon, coffee, and tea were all on Ace's list, but he always joked that "water rusted your pipes" whenever it was offered to him at a restaurant or a bar. It was an old joke that went back to the early days when Ace was growing up. Ace's father Alexander, Sr. was very rarely observed drinking anything other than "mindless corporate swill" from one of the major breweries in the country in the 1980's. Miller High Life was usually his drink of choice. Ace's father never turned down a beer but would shoo a waitress who was bringing him a glass of water in about ten seconds.

Ace arrived at the body shop, sans an appointment, so the clerk at the desk said that they would have to work him in to get a look at the car. Ace said that was just fine if they weren't talking several hours. The clerk said that it would probably be no more than an hour or two. Ace ok'd the time, gave them his cell phone number, and sauntered across the street to Modern Times. It was early afternoon, so the lunch crowd was in full swing. Ace took a seat at the bar and ordered a Black House Coffee Stout. At around 5% ABV, this was a fairly "low alcohol beer," but Ace was only planning on having one while he waited for the body shop to call him and let him know that the estimate was ready. The stout tasted like chocolate-covered espresso beans. It was served at the perfect temperature, not too cold, not too warm. Ace took another deep draught of the beer and sat it down. He figured that he better get something to eat as well. As luck would have it, there was a food truck at the brewery for the day. The name on the truck was "Sublime Smoke," so Ace assumed that it was a BBQ food truck. Ace walked out to the truck and was assaulted by the delicious smells coming from the food truck and the smoker that was pulled behind it. Ace looked over the menu and decided on something called a "Mac Daddy." It was a generous helping of homemade macaroni and cheese, topped with pulled pork and your favorite BBQ sauce. Ace decided to go for the "reaper" sauce. The person behind the counter warned him that it was called "Reaper" for two reasons: one, it was made from Carolina Reaper peppers, and two, some people said that it made you think the "grim reaper" was assaulting your tastebuds, it was that hot. Ace told him that he would take the chance but asked for the sauce to be served on the side so if it was too hot, the entire dish wouldn't be unbearable. Ace could get a different choice. Zach handed Ace his food with a small container of reaper sauce and another with a sauce called "pepper trio", told him to enjoy his meal, and handed him a schedule of locations where the truck was going to be parked for the rest of the month.

Ace carried the food back to his seat at the bar, had a seat, and chowed down. He was pleasantly surprised at how good the food was. It was obvious that Zach knew what he was doing. This was some of the best BBQ that Ace had had recently. He cleaned the container to the last crumbs and drank the rest of his beer. Just as he was getting ready to walk over to the body shop and check on his quote, his cell phone rang. Ace answered it on the 2nd ring. It was the clerk at the body shop, and his quote was ready. Ace told the clerk that he would be there in just a couple of minutes.

Ace asked the bartender for a 4-pack of cans Black House Stout to go and settled up his bill. On his way to the body shop, he stopped at the food truck and told Zach that he would be looking for him this weekend out near Humphrey's by the Bay. Ace told him that he couldn't wait to try his brisket. Zach held up a finger, went over to a big slab of brisket, and carved off a piece for Ace to try. Ace took the piece and stuck it in his mouth. The brisket literally melted in his mouth. Ace told him that it was the best brisket that he ever had. Zach told him that he knew that. He (Zach) had been in the business long enough to know he had a good thing going on. He told Ace that there had been many requests for him to open a "brick and mortar" restaurant, but with property costs so high in Southern California, running the food truck worked just fine for him.

# Chapter 48

Ace crossed the street and walked into the body shop, where the clerk handed him an envelope with his quote. Ace opened it up, looked at it, and told the clerk that he would have to let them know if he was going to proceed with the repair. A repair of over $2,000.00 for what amounted to some scratches and a cracked bumper skin seemed a bit high, and Ace didn't know if he wanted to put that kind of money into a car that was 10 years old. The clerk said that he understood. He did tell Ace to check to see what his insurance company would cover and what his deductible was. Ace thanked him and headed back out to his car. It was sitting right where he left it…unlocked. Ace jumped in the driver's seat and saw the envelope lying on the seat. He assumed it was another copy of the estimate for the bodywork that the vehicle needed, so he never glanced at it again.

Ace tossed the other envelope on top of the envelope lying on the passenger seat and that was when he noticed that they were two different styles of envelopes. The envelope that was lying on the passenger seat when he got in the car was a blank envelope. The envelope that the clerk had given to him was a business envelope. However, it had the company name in the return address area. Ace picked up the other envelope and opened it. There was a single sheet of paper inside with a crudely drawn smiley face with Xs for the eyes and the words "mind your own business" scrawled underneath it.

Ace went back into the shop with the note and asked the clerk if he was aware of the note on his front seat? The clerk had a dumbfounded look on his face. The look was too real to be fake. Ace asked if he could talk to the person that had worked up the estimate and the clerk said that wasn't a problem. He called into the shop and asked to speak to Mike. A tall, lanky man in coveralls came from the back and asked if there was a problem with the estimate. Ace told him that the estimate was just fine, but did he know anything about the note left on his front seat. Mike looked at the note and said that he had never even entered the car since all the work was on the outside. He had no reason to enter the car at all. Ace held the note crumpled in his hand and, waving it around, he asked, "So you never saw this note?" Mike plucked it from Ace's hand and, with a raised eyebrow, said that he had never seen it before. He did say that apparently Ace had pissed someone off, and maybe he had better watch his back, just in case the threat was real.

Ace retorted that he was more than capable of taking care of himself, then turned on the clerk and asked him if there were any security cameras in the parking lot. The clerk, who was clearly a bit nervous due to Ace's aggressive attitude, told him that there were no cameras in the customer parking lot, only in the "yard storage" for cars awaiting work.

Ace shook his head, thanked them for their assistance and the quote, and said that he would be in touch. He left the office shaking his head. So apparently, he was still being followed. By whom? He had turned in his "final report" to Misuse. Apparently, whoever was following him hadn't got the message that he was done with the investigation, at least officially. Ace guessed it was possible that this note was unrelated to his case with Humdinger Habitats, but he wasn't sure.

Ace jumped in his car and headed back to his apartment. He was going to enjoy the afternoon without any thoughts of Humdinger and Humdinger Habitats. He just wanted, no, he needed a day to relax. Apparently, his intuition was correct. There had to be more to this entire fucking incident. What was someone trying to hide? He wouldn't give up on this investigation. He had a fairly significant chunk of change coming his way within the next 24 hours when Humdinger Habitats paid him. He didn't have to take another case right now.

As Ace made the drive home, he kept an eye out for anyone who might be following him. Low and behold, when he was just a few miles from home, he spied a black Escalade that looked just like the vehicle that he had encountered the other day when he left Emilyia Humdinger's home. Ace decided to drive around a bit. Just to see if the SUV kept on his tail or if he was overreacting. As Ace drove the side streets, he decided to make his way out to the Shelter Islands. It wasn't likely that the SUV would be going there unless they were following him, and Ace could approach the vehicle on the narrow streets near Humphrey's.

Ace crossed the bridge to the Shelter Islands and noted that the SUV was still behind him about four cars back. As Ace proceeded down the street, he pulled into Humphrey's by the Bay, parked, and went inside.

He wanted to get a schedule of the upcoming concerts anyway and then he could see if the SUV passed by. As Ace was waiting for the desk clerk to get him a copy of the schedule, he watched the front door and saw the SUV pass by. Maybe this was all a coincidence. Had Misuse and his cronies gotten to him? Was he being paranoid? The desk clerk handed him the schedule. Ace took it and thanked him, then headed for the door. Ace hopped in his car and headed towards the end of the island. There was only one road on and off of the island, and the SUV hadn't returned, so Ace would see if he could find it. There weren't many places that a vehicle could hide, so Ace was pretty sure that he would find it.

As Ace drove towards the end of the island he spied a black SUV in the parking lot of Kona Kai Marina. Ace pulled into the lot and pulled up behind the vehicle so that it couldn't be moved without hitting his car. Ace got out of the car, put his hand on his weapon and approached the vehicle, being careful to keep a direct line of sight between him and the driver's door. As Ace approached the front of the vehicle, he noted that it wasn't running, and it appeared to be empty. He got to the front and looked in as best as he could. With the deep window tint, that wasn't easy, but Ace could see well enough to be able to tell that it was empty. Ace looked all around the car, and that was when he saw the Kona Kai Marina Parking Pass in the window. So, it had been a coincidence that he had been followed. He was just paranoid. Ace shook his head and returned to the Impala. He really needed a break. He was seeing "things" everywhere. He was going back to the apartment, turn on some good music, sit and relax the rest of the day. He deserved it.

As Ace was leaving the parking lot, his phone dinged that he had a new email. He didn't risk looking at his phone while he was driving. Law Enforcement in California was very strict about distracted driving. It could wait until he got home. It was probably "spam" anyway. That seemed to be most of his emails, anyway. Ace told himself that he wouldn't look at his phone until he got back to the apartment, but he couldn't help himself. When he got to a traffic light, he glanced at his phone. The email was alerting him that there had been a new deposit in his business account in the amount of $30,112.00. Ace smiled and thought to himself, that wasn't so hard now, was it Presley? He continued home with a big smile on his face.

# Chapter 49

The next morning broke like most days do in Southern California. The sun was shining, and the temperature was a moderate 71 degrees. Ace sat at the desk in the spare bedroom, enjoying his third cup of coffee while perusing his laptop looking over the day's headlines. He also checked in on his social media sites and his business page just to see if there was anything of interest there. It was all the normal daily drivel. People discussing politics, climate change, the latest conspiracy theories, etc. Ace flipped to his Weather Underground link to check on the area's weather forecast as well as the fire risk. He was thinking of heading up to La Jolla to do a little hiking but thought it best to see if there were any wildfires in the area. He didn't want to get partway there and have to turn around due to road closures and park closures. Fortunately, it looked like there were no active events in the area, so he should have a decent day for a hike. Ace hopped in the shower, shaved and put on his hiking shoes, threw a swimming suit in a backpack along with some energy bars and jumped in his car and headed for La Jolla. He was hoping to hike to La Jolla Cove along a fairly difficult loop trail and spend a bit of time relaxing in the tide pool and the ocean near the cove. He might even read a bit. He had tossed the latest Reacher paperback in his backpack. If it wasn't too busy, he could sit and enjoy the serenity of the area and just relax.

Ace arrived at the trailhead and was happy to see that there were only two other cars in the parking lot so it shouldn't be a busy day on the trail or at the beach at the cove. Ace set out at a brisk pace towards the cove. The trail was about 2 miles each way. It was easier going to the cove than it was coming back. It was all downhill to the ocean. Unfortunately, that meant that the return trip was 2 miles uphill. Ace didn't mind. He needed to stay in shape and when he was working a case, he had little time for exercise. Today was a day that he could work at his own pace. It wasn't a race, but he wanted to push himself enough that he at least worked up a bit of a sweat. As Ace rounded the last loop in the trail until the cove, he spied the ocean. He was happy to see that there were only three people on the beach and two small boats anchored in the cove so it would be a quiet afternoon. Just what Ace needed: a day of calm and quiet. Just a good book and the sounds of the ocean and the seabirds. It was going to be a good day.

Ace picked a nice area near the edge of the cove with a couple of decent-sized rocks to sit on and lean against. He pulled out the paperback and a bottle of water, opened the book, and began to read. As he was sitting there reading, he heard a few people come and go but paid little attention to any of them. There was a couple with a small child frolicking in the water at the shoreline, but nobody was going much past their knees. Anyone who ever visited the Pacific in this area knew that while the air temperature was always moderate, the ocean was a bit chilly, normally not much warmer than 74 degrees, so unless you were a very hearty soul or wearing a wet suit, you didn't "swim" in the ocean like people did in the Gulf of Mexico or the Caribbean.

After a couple of hours of relaxing, Ace packed up his book, ate an energy bar, and headed back to the car. He had worked up quite a sweat by the time he made it back to the car, but his mind was clear, and he was relaxed. It was too late for lunch, but he could stop somewhere and grab a quick snack.

Ace had heard of a place called Dukes from a friend, and they said that the food was amazing. Ace typed the name into his phone, set his phone to direct him, and was happy to see that it was truly less than two miles from the parking lot. Ace pulled into the parking lot and felt like this was going to be a great choice. The parking lot was busy, and there was a "barefoot" bar, so the fact that Ace was still in swimming trunks, a beer t-shirt, and flip-flops wouldn't be a problem. Ace took a seat at the end of the bar so that he could overlook the ocean views and also see the front entrance. He never liked to have his back to a door. Probably something left over from his days with the FBI. The barmaid handed him a menu. He was pleasantly surprised to see that there was a beer on tap called "Duke's Blonde" that was brewed by Stone Brewing, so he ordered that as well as an order of fish tacos.

As Ace was enjoying the last crumbs of the fish tacos and the last few drops of his beer. He sat back and thought back to the last few weeks and the Humdinger case. What had he learned through his investigation into Humdinger's death?

First and foremost; apparently Humdinger was a kinky old bastard. Seriously, he had a standing "meeting" with a dominatrix, not just your run of the mill dominatrix though, a dwarf. A dwarf who by all intents and purposes seemed to be doing very well for herself. She was an intelligent woman who apparently knew what she was doing both sexually and financially. She had expensive tastes and her apartment in Tijuana showed that. She had high-end furniture, expensive artwork hanging on the walls and Ace didn't know women's clothing that well but what she had been wearing looked like designer fashion to him. She really didn't stand to benefit from the death of Humdinger, if anything it would hurt her business. Ace checked her off the list for follow-up. He didn't really think that there was anything more for her to offer as far as information regarding the death was concerned. If need be, he had all her contact information and he could follow up if necessary.

Starletta Blaze was an interesting person too. This woman, who used to have a long-term relationship with Humdinger, had finagled Humdinger into helping her acquire the brothel of which she was now the Madame. She also had an illegitimate child and Humdinger was the father. She received monthly payments from Humdinger Habitats to help with the upbringing of Joaquin Blaze. Though the child had never been mentioned during Humdinger's political career, it was obvious that he knew that he was the father. Ace had to admit, after glimpsing the boy, it would be next to impossible for Humdinger to deny that he was the father. The curious thing about the financial arrangement was that the payments hadn't stopped after Humdinger died. Starletta wasn't really affected by his untimely death either, other than some unwanted attention from the press and from local and international law enforcement but that had subsided quickly after it was determined by the local police that he died of natural causes. He was just too old and too fat to handle sex play, essentially, that was the ruling from Dr. Bravo, the coroner in Tijuana. Starletta and her financial arrangement was an enigma. Ace didn't feel comfortable removing her from the list of people that he may need to talk to in the future.

Emilyia Humdinger: it didn't appear that she had anything to do with Humdinger's death, but Ace wouldn't blame her if she did have something to do with it. He was a pig, and it was widely known that he treated women as objects and, in the case of his wife, as a piece of property. Ace thought about his meeting with Emilyia, though and what did she gain from his death? Her freedom. She could move on and maybe have a semblance of a normal life. Well, as normal of a life as an ultra-rich, beautiful woman in Southern California could have. He was sure that there were many men, and probably some women, hoping to get in her good graces so that they could live the lifestyle that she lived. She also got a nice chunk of money even though his kids from his first marriage got most of it. Her daughter would never need or want for anything unless Emilyia decided to make her daughter work for a living. Somehow, Ace didn't think that was going to happen, although if he was a betting man, he would bet that Vixen Humdinger would be shipped off to some exclusive boarding school in the next year or so, especially if her mother continued to live the lifestyle that she did when Ronald was still alive.

Ace was going to leave her on his list for now. He didn't think that there was anything there, but he just didn't feel comfortable ignoring her completely. She was obviously a good actress. She had kept Humdinger happy all this time…and had even provided him with a child.

Ace hadn't ever talked with Ronald Humdinger Jr., so he obviously wasn't going to remove him from the list at this time. Ace knew, though, that as soon as he started talking to Ronnie Jr. that Misuse was going to hear about it, and he would know that Ace was still digging around. Ace put Junior on the back burner for now but figured if there was a need to talk with him, he would just do it and face the repercussions from Misuse and Humdinger Habitats at that time.

# Chapter 50

Ace enjoyed his last couple of bites of the fish tacos and took his last swallow of beer. He figured it was time to get back on the road and head back towards San Diego. It was a pleasant drive down the Pacific Coast Highway and there was typically less traffic there than on the major freeways, so Ace headed over to the Pacific Coast Highway and made the turn to the south. As Ace entered the highway, he tuned his satellite radio to Classic Rewind and just enjoyed the music. Kristine Stone was the DJ. She was always pleasant to listen to and always added insights into the music along with her opinions…one of which was that Rush was the best band ever. Ace tended to agree with her that Rush was one of the great bands but there were so many from the 70's and 80's that were excellent, he couldn't commit to just one band. With a bit of introduction, Kristine started the next song, an oldie but a goodie, Eclipse from Pink Floyd. Talk about a mellow tune to drive to. Ace just absorbed the music, along with the scenery passing by on the west side of his car. The expanse of the Pacific, stretching away to the horizon, was definitely a sight to behold. He recalled the first time that he saw the Pacific in person. He knew that someday he would live in its proximity.

The ride was relaxing and uneventful. He was back at his apartment in less than an hour.

# Chapter 51

As Ace walked into his apartment, he knew something was wrong immediately. There was the faint scent of cologne in the air. Ace didn't wear cologne, so he knew that it didn't come from himself. Ace looked around, and everything looked OK on the surface, but obviously, someone had been in his apartment. The complex maintenance man was a young Hispanic man who usually smelled like whatever his wife was cooking for dinner, and Ace had never noticed that he wore cologne. Ace looked around more carefully. He noticed that his laptop was standing open. Ace didn't believe that he left it that way but couldn't be 100% certain. Ace ran his finger over the trackpad to start it. The screen came to his normal, password-protected start-up screen, and it didn't appear that anyone had tried to access the information on the device. There would be a warning screen if someone tried to enter the incorrect password more than three times and there was no message. Ace didn't think it was likely that his machine had been compromised. His current password was 19 digits with a mix of alpha-numeric and special symbols. The likelihood that someone could crack that in the amount of time that he was gone wasn't likely. Ditto for them to be able to put any "software" on it to see what he was doing or looking at online. The computer was heavily encrypted.

Ace looked in the bedroom and one of the drawers was slightly ajar, another sign that someone had been in his apartment. Ace was pretty anal about making sure all of his drawers were closed, as well as closet doors. It was a pet peeve of his. Drawers and doors were meant to be closed. He never left them open.

Ace went to the door and looked it over, there were no signs of forced entry, the same for the sliding glass door to the patio. So, whoever got in was a professional who had the ability to pick a lock, and they must've been good, or they would've been observed by someone passing on the street.

Ace returned to his closet and used his biometrics to access his gun safe. The door clicked open. Everything was where it should be, including the notes from the Humdinger investigation, which Ace had stashed there just in case someone came looking for them.

Misuse hadn't asked if Ace had any notes from the case. If he had, Ace had a "set" of notes all prepared to give to Misuse which just corroborated what Ace's final report showed.

That left another possibility. Had someone entered his apartment to place listening devices? It was possible that Misuse just wanted to make sure that Ace wasn't going to look any further, or it could be from another case. Ace had a friend at the local bureau who would allow him to borrow a bug-sweeping device. Of course, if Ace found anything, then he would have to decide whether he was going to remove the device or devices that would alert whoever placed them in his apartment or should he just leave them and make sure that he didn't discuss anything pertinent to the Humdinger case if he was on the phone with Julie or anyone else that would happen to call or stop by. All he had to do was say that he had concluded the case, and that should be the end of it. He would give Dean a call this afternoon from his car and ask about borrowing the bug sweeper. While he had the sweeper, he would go over his car again, just to make sure that he didn't miss anything with his search earlier. Actually, if his car was being monitored, it was possible that listening devices had been placed there as well. Maybe it would be best for Ace to go for a stroll and talk while walking. He was positive that his phone had not been corrupted by any malware.

Ace checked his S&W to make sure that there was a round chambered, placed the gun in the holster at the small of his back, pulled on a windbreaker, and headed out the door. As Ace was walking down the street talking to Dean, he noticed that there was a man about a half block back who seemed to stop whenever Ace did. Ace didn't like it, so he finished up the call with Dean. Disconnected the call and did an abrupt about-face. The man came to a complete stop when Ace turned but recovered quickly and continued walking towards Ace. He didn't even bother to give him a quick glance as he passed by. After about three steps, Ace turned again, just in time to see the man duck into a doorway. Ace walked up close to the building, reached the doorway, pulled his firearm, and jumped in front of the door, gun extended straight out and within an inch of the man's nose. He just raised his hands. He didn't say a word as Ace pointed the 9MM at his face. If the man were a typical civilian, he would be babbling by now. He just stared at Ace over the barrel with his hands up, making no move toward his belt or pockets.

Ace motioned him out of the doorway with the end of his gun. The man complied. He still hadn't said a word. Ace asked him why he was following him…to give him credit. He maintained a blank look on his face. Ace asked him again, and this time, he grabbed the man by his upper arm and steered him down the street. As Ace was holstering his weapon, the man tried to wrench free from his grip. Unfortunately for him, Ace was expecting it, so he didn't lose his grip. Ace gripped his upper arm tighter and asked him, for the third time, why he was following him. He told him that there would be no fourth time. Ace would just contact the local police department and tell them that he had captured a "mugger" who had tried to take his wallet. That would get him locked up, and they would most certainly be able to figure out who he was.

At this point, the man just snickered and said that wouldn't work out so well when the police determined that he was a fellow law enforcement officer from San Francisco. Ace asked him for ID. The man took two fingers and reached into his inside coat pocket and handed Ace a slim wallet with a badge and an ID card. The ID card identified him as Joseph Weston, Investigator for the Department of Homeland Security, San Francisco Office.

Ace asked him why he was following him; he was obviously way out of his jurisdiction. Weston told him that he had come under surveillance because of his interest in the Humdinger case. Ace said that there was no interest. He had been hired to investigate the death at the request of the Board of Directors of Humdinger Habitats because they wanted to make sure that there wouldn't be any further negative press surrounding the death of Ronald Humdinger. Ace found nothing that needed to be reported as problematic for Humdinger Habitats. With that being said, Ace asked Weston why DHS was looking into anyone who was connected to Humdinger Habitats. Weston told him that he wasn't at liberty to say anything, but if Ace wanted information, then he must not be done with his investigation. Ace told Weston that officially, he was done with the investigation, but things just didn't sit well with him. He thought that there was more to the death. At the very least, Humdinger Habitats was hiding something. Ace just didn't know what it was yet. But he would find out.

At this point, Weston told him that maybe he and Ace needed to go somewhere off the street to discuss the case. Ace told Weston that he knew just the place and it was right down the road. Ace led the way to The Rustic Root where they took a table at the back of the restaurant. They both ordered beers, Ace ordered an Arrogant Bastard, Weston a Stone IPA.

When the drinks were delivered, Ace told Weston to "spill it." Weston hesitated. Ace leaned back and just stared at him. Finally, Ace broke the silence and told Weston that he would share his information and his thoughts, but he wanted assurances that his name wouldn't be brought up if there were ever any charges levied against Humdinger Habitats or anyone connected to the company. After about 30 seconds, Weston said, "Fine," but he also wanted assurances.

219

Assurances that Ace wouldn't divulge his source for any information that Weston provided. Weston said that he could be severely disciplined if his supervisor found out that he had given a "private investigator" information. Ace reminded him that he was a former FBI agent with the highest security clearance possible, and that should be enough to convince Weston that he wouldn't divulge his source. Weston shrugged his shoulders and said that men did a lot of things for money. He didn't know Ace other than what he could find out online. For all he knew, Ace was on the take from Humdinger Habitats, and that's why he "didn't find anything."

Weston took a long draught of his beer. Set the glass down and started his story. Apparently, Humdinger Habitats and Ronald Humdinger had been on the Department of Homeland Security radar for quite some time. It started with a complaint that Humdinger Habitats hadn't paid for some shipping containers that they had acquired through a local distributor at the shipyard. When the company finally got paid for the container, Humdinger Habitats only paid about half of what the bill was, claiming that the containers were defective. Partner Trade Company contacted Ronald Humdinger himself and told him that they would have to file a lawsuit if he didn't pay for the containers in full. Apparently, Humdinger told them to go ahead and file a lawsuit. He had the biggest law firms; the best lawyers and he could drag the process out for years and Partner Trade wouldn't see a dime. Not to mention that Humdinger would slam their business practices and their company in general on his weekly television show, giving them a bad reputation in the shipping world. Being fairly new to the USA, they didn't want to lose any existing or potential business because Humdinger was known to degrade companies and people that he didn't agree with. He had been sued so many times, always with an appeal. He had yet to pay any judgements against him. Now that he was deceased, DHS was looking into the situation. DHS felt that there was a connection between Humdinger Habitats and Partner Trade Company but they weren't sure what, if any charges were that could be filed.

Ace raised an eyebrow and said that all sounded good but he didn't believe for one second that DHS had assigned an investigator to follow him around if all they were looking at was "bad debt". Sure, they might have a investigator locate someone but in this situation, everyone knew where Humdinger was. They wouldn't waste resources on this for bad debt.

Weston sat back and took a couple of deep breaths, then he said, "listen, there is some question about the containers". It is possible that illicit substances and items were being shipped in the containers. San Francisco Police Department was looking into the shipping company and into Humdinger Habitats because it was thought that there might be fentanyl being shipped in the containers, as well as "counterfeit cash". DHS felt that there was enough suspicion created by the transactions that they were just following a trail.

Ace told him that he had been in some of the containers and hadn't seen anything that led him to believe that the company was smuggling anything in them.

Weston asked where he had inspected the containers and Ace told him at the manufacturing facility for Humdinger Habitats. Weston said that they thought that there was a stop somewhere before arriving at Humdinger Habitats where the contraband was offloaded. It was Humdinger's employees that picked up the containers and transported them from San Francisco to San Diego. The odd thing is the containers never arrived the same day in San Diego that they were picked up in San Francisco. That was an anomaly. There was no reason for them to take over 24 hours to arrive. The distance was approximately 500 miles between the two cities. On a good day, it should take between 8 and 10 hours to arrive. Most containers were delivered 24-36 hours after they were picked up.

Ace asked if the containers went through customs before being turned over to Humdinger. Weston said that they were checked through customs, however there were many instances where Humdinger Habitats didn't pick them up for a week to ten days. Once the containers were cleared through customs and unloaded, they were then stored in a "yard" until they were loaded back on cargo vessels or until the trucking companies came to pick them up. The containers weren't searched again. Their numbers were just checked against the paperwork for the shipping or trucking companies to make sure that someone wasn't taking containers that didn't belong to them, whether on purpose or inadvertently.

Stranger things had been known to happen. Weston told Ace that he would amazed at the number of truck drivers that were dyslexic and couldn't get the numbers correct when picking up the containers.

Ace was doubtful and told Weston so. What did Humdinger hope to gain by smuggling illicit goods into the country? The man was a billionaire. He was always telling everyone as much when he was still alive.

Weston said he wasn't sure that Ronald Humdinger himself was involved or if it was someone in the company that was trying to pad their retirement somewhat.

Ace asked if they had ever searched any of the containers sitting in the yard prior to pick up by Humdinger Habitats. Weston said that they never had probable cause, and everyone knew that the local judges in San Francisco were in Humdinger's back pocket, as he had assigned them when he was still in politics.

Ace gave Weston the little bit of information that he had regarding the death of Humdinger. Weston told him, it seemed a bit thin. Ace said that he was hired to investigate the death, nothing else so the file would be thin.

Both gentlemen finished their beers, traded contact information, and went their separate ways.

# Chapter 52

Ace got up bright and early the next morning. He was going to take a drive to San Francisco and check out where the containers came from. As Ace was checking out the travel conditions on the local freeways, he decided that maybe taking the "Coaster" rapid rail would be a better way to go. The express train only made 4 stops between San Diego and San Francisco. This was a new service to the west coast. The first "bullet" train put into use in the Bay Area. Ace could make it to SFO in just under 5 hours and he wouldn't have to worry about the traffic and being stuck in traffic jams. He got online, checked the schedule and booked a ticket, then he showered, made himself a quick breakfast along with a big pot of coffee and relaxed until he had to leave for the train station. It would've been quicker to take a regional jet, but Ace decided the train would work just as well. The downtime on the train also gave Ace a bit of time to cobble together a plan. He needed to get into the storage yard, and it wasn't likely that he was just going to be able to walk through the main gate. Ace was already figuring that he was going to have to book a hotel when he arrived in San Francisco. He just wanted to check out the area where the storage yard was. If he was lucky, there would be an inexpensive hotel within walking distance, along with a bar or two where some of the yard workers might hang out after work. Everyone knew that a cold beer was a great way to end the workday after spending it out in the hot sun, walking and riding around a dusty gravel lot had to make you thirsty. Ace also assumed that if anything was happening with the containers that wasn't on the up and up, wouldn't be happening during normal business hours. It had to be happening late at night or very early in the morning.

Ace sent a message to Weston, asking him if the containers ear-marked for Humdinger Habitats were kept in a specific location in the yard or if they were scattered throughout. Weston sent back a quick text that said that the containers for Humdinger Habitats were kept in the northeast corner of the yard. He also wanted to know what Ace was up to. Ace told him not to worry about it. He would share any information that he found out with Weston and the Department of Homeland Security. He did tell Weston that he might need a favor if he happened to get caught and he ended up in jail for trespassing. Weston told Ace that he could let SFPD and DHS know that he was going to be snooping around. Ace told him not to do that. It was entirely possible that someone within the department was involved and knew exactly what was going on. Ace didn't want anyone else to know what he was up to other than Weston. Weston told him that he would keep his mouth shut but if he got arrested, he would not be able to say that he knew that Ace was going to do what he was planning. That would make Weston look complicit and he didn't want any part of it.

While Ace was making the trip, he made reservations at the Hilton, Union Square for three days. Ace hoped that he wouldn't be in San Fran that long, but he had the room reserved just in case things ran a bit long.

San Francisco was another of those cities that you either loved or you hated. Ace loved the city but loved the surrounding countryside even more. Muir Woods, Napa and Sonoma, Point Reyes, were just a few of the places that Ace visited when he came to the San Francisco area. He also liked the availability of gourmet quality restaurants. The food scene in the "City by the Bay" and the surrounding areas were world renowned. Hopefully Ace would be able to enjoy some of the great food in the area while he was there. Clam chowder in a sourdough bread bowl sounded pretty good right now.

# Chapter 53

Ace checked in to the hotel and was delighted to see that they had a "daily" car rental service in the hotel. That would make it much easier to get around the city. Taking a cab to a stakeout wasn't really optimal. San Francisco was a very progressive city regarding public transportation, but Ace didn't want to have to rely on the bus system or the street cars.

The container storage area on Cesar Chavez Avenue was about 3.5 miles, which wasn't a long walk in most cities but with all the hills in the Bay Area, it could be tiring. Ace recalled one time when he and a friend had visited the city; Ace and the friend had ended up walking almost ten miles that day. She was not happy about the walking. Ace would never admit it to her, but he was damn tired by the end of the day too.

Ace decided to hop on the street cars that picked up right around the corner from the hotel and take it to Fisherman's Wharf. He could grab a quick bite to eat and visit the seals at Pier 39. The storage lot was only about a mile walk from that area and it was all level walking.

As Ace was enjoying his chowder in a sourdough bread bowl, the fog started to roll in. Anyone that has ever been to San Francisco knows that it can be clear one minute and the next, you see the fog rolling over the mountains from the west. You can be in thick fog in a matter of minutes, or it may just be a light fog, and it could last for days. Ace was hoping for a fairly heavy fog bank. He obviously wouldn't stand out while he was snooping around the storage yard if he could blend into the muted shadows caused by the pervasive fog. Ace finished eating and headed out...hopefully the fog would still be with him at the storage yard.

Ace arrived at 400 Cesar Chavez Avenue and was very happy to see that the fog was still around, and it had gotten a bit thicker. The storage yard was surrounded by fence as expected but since Ace had an idea of where the containers were located for Humdinger Habitats, he could walk along the fence line and see if he could spot anything from "outside the wire" so to speak. Ace was happy to see that the storage area was surrounded by a standard chain-link fence. No razor wire on the top, not electrified. It also didn't appear that there were any dogs on site. It did appear that there were a few cameras scattered throughout the yard but overall, security seemed very lax. Ace didn't really observe anything from the other side of the fence regarding the container earmarked for Humdinger Habitats. It appeared that there were 10-12 containers sitting in the area away from the rest of the containers. Ace decided that he was going to have to make a trip back to the storage yard after hours and check things out inside, unless he could walk through the gate by claiming that he was there as an investigator for Humdinger Habitats. The only risk to that was that the Security at the yard might contact Humdinger Habitats to check on him being there. He didn't want Humdinger Habitats to be alerted that he was still looking into things. Presley Misuse wouldn't be happy at all if he found out that Ace was still looking into things. Ace would come back after nightfall. He was sure that he could get into and out of the yard unseen…and if he was spotted by cameras, they wouldn't be high enough quality to identify him. He would make sure to wear a ballcap and keep his face away from the cameras. If the fog continued, it wouldn't matter at all as everything would look like shadows anyway.

Ace started back towards Fisherman's Wharf. There were some great shops to check out and he still hadn't stopped at Pier 39 to see the sea lions…they were always good for a laugh.

When Ace arrived at Pier 39, he watched the sea lions for a bit, then made his way back to the streetcar stop so that he could get back to the hotel. Before he went back to the hotel though, he was going to make a stop at Ghirardelli Chocolate and get one of their famous hot fudge sundaes. Ace was happy to see that the line for the ice cream shop at Ghirardelli wasn't long at all. He got his sundae with hot fudge and caramel, as well as whipped cream and pecans. It was the best sundae that Ace had enjoyed in a long time.

As Ace was strolling along Fisherman's Wharf, he glanced out at Alcatraz sitting in the middle of the bay. He made a mental note to check into pricing for a tour while he was in town. He had never done a true tour of the infamous prison known as "The Rock". The closest that he had ever been to visiting the island was a "bay cruise" that took you around the island and gave you a bit of information about the island and the prison, as well as some of the protests that had taken place on the island after the closure of the prison. Ace felt that he needed to experience the island from the prison itself. As a former FBI agent, it was only fitting that Ace visit the place where Al Capone had been jailed.

Ace climbed the hill above Fort Mason to the streetcar stop and waited on the next streetcar to arrive. He would hop on and take it back to it's terminus, walk the half block back to the hotel and arrange for a car rental for the evening, through tomorrow afternoon. While Ace was waiting, he took a little time to scan the area around him, just to see if anyone was showing more interest in him than would be considered normal. He didn't see anyone, male or female, that appeared to be watching him. He didn't think that anyone would be aware that he had made a trip to San Francisco. Even if they did know, he could just say that he was enjoying a few days away now that the Humdinger investigation had ended.

Ace had an uneventful ride back to the streetcar terminus. He made the short walk to the hotel, checked into the "rental company" and rented a non-descript Prius for the next 24 hours. Ace told the rental agent that he would be back about 5PM to pick up the keys. The rental agent said that he would have the car waiting for him at the front entrance at 5PM. Ace said that wasn't necessary. He would just need the keys. He wasn't planning on going out until later that evening. The rental agent said that he would be more than happy to make sure that the parking attendant got his keys and that he would have the car transferred to the garage so that Ace could just come and pick up the car. The rental agent handed Ace a tag for the keys and just told him to present it to the parking attendant when he needed the car.

Ace decided to make his way to the "Cityscape Skybar" on the 46th floor. He could grab a cocktail, then maybe head to his room and change into his swimming trunks and spend an hour or two poolside before venturing out for the evening. The Hilton on Union Square boasted the highest bar in the city. Ace had to admit, the views were stunning. You could view Fisherman's Wharf and the Golden Gate Bridge from one side of the bar, the tables on the other side of the bar afforded you views of the "Bay Bridge" and Oakland, across the bay. Ace preferred the side overlooking Fisherman's Wharf and the Golden Gate Bridge, so he took a table, placed his order for a Buffalo Trace Old Fashioned Cocktail and just sat and relaxed. There was some light jazz playing in the background which made Ace that much more relaxed. As Ace sat and sipped his cocktail, he was forming a plan in his brain. He was going to have to find a place to "borrow" some bolt cutters. It wasn't likely that the containers would be locked, they were empty, so why would they be locked but he thought it would be best to be prepared. He was going to see if he could locate a hotel maintenance man. There should be a pair of bolt cutters here in the hospital. Afterall, sometimes people passed away with their chain locks engaged for their rooms. To get in, the hotel staff would have to cut the chain.

# Chapter 54

Ace was ready to go. It was dark outside. The fog had held so he didn't think that being seen would be a problem, but he was dressed in black jeans, a black t-shirt and a black hooded sweatshirt with a front pocket that was big enough for the small set of bolt cutters that he "borrowed" for the hotel maintenance department. Ace also put his holster and weapon on his right hip. He hoped that there would be no need to use it but again, he would rather be safe than sorry.

Ace arrived at the front desk and gave them the ticket for his rental car. The concierge asked Ace if he was heading to dinner and if he needed any recommendations. Ace thought it best to portray that he was going to dinner, that way if there were any questions asked if he were spied snooping around, it wouldn't appear that Ace was the culprit. The concierge gave Ace a couple of nice Italian restaurants that were near the hotel. At that moment, Ace saw what he assumed was his Prius pull up at the front entrance. Ace thanked him and proceeded to the vehicle where the attendant handed him his keys, opened the door and stood there waiting for his gratuity. Ace fumbled a $5 out of his pocket and told the attendant that he would give him a better gratuity when he returned later that evening.

Ace put the address for the storage lot into his phone and headed off. As he approached the storage lot, he looked around for some parking lots that were within walking distance, but not so far that he looked out of place. He lucked out, there was a little tavern across the street about a block down from the storage lot. Ace parked, locked up the car and slunk into the shadows on the other side of the street. As he approached the lot, he saw that it was very brightly lighted, but the fog was doing a great job of diffusing the light. He walked right past the gate and saw that there was nobody in the gatehouse. There was also no light, and he could dimly see a "Closed" sign hanging in the window. As Ace passed the corner of the lot, he took a sharp right and walked towards the water. The waves sloshing along the rear of the property were also a bonus because they might hide any noises that he made while checking out the yard.

Ace was well hidden in the shadows when he decided to cut the wires holding the chain link to the bottom of the fence post. It would make less noise than if he were to climb the fence and it wouldn't be likely to be noticed for days, if at all. He cut a couple of the wires, pushed the bottom of the fence out and rolled under it. The fence caught on his sweatshirt but didn't hang him up at all, he just pulled it free and proceeded to the rear of the yard where the containers that were earmarked for Humdinger Habitats were supposed to be kept. The lighting was dim due to the fog, so Ace wasn't concerned about being seen from the road running at the front of the property.

Ace arrived at the first row of containers, and he noticed that the weren't "locked" but they did have wire tamper seals on them. Ace was curious why empty containers would have a wire tamper seal on them, but he didn't try to figure it out. He knew that he had to look inside the containers, so he popped the seal on the first container, swung the door open enough to squeeze inside, the flipped on the flashlight on his phone. The first thing that he noticed was that the walls were lined with foam insulation. None of the containers that Ace had inspected at the manufacturing facility had foam insulation. They were all in various stages of being built and they were being insulated at the time of the buildout. Other than the foam insulation on the walls and ceiling, the container was empty.

Ace went to the next container and found the very same thing. The container was empty except for the foam insulation on the walls. It was white foam, and it appeared to be new. It wasn't dirty and there were very few marks in it from freight being banged into the walls. The next four containers that Ace checked were identical. Empty except for the foam insulation. Ace cut a small piece of the foam insulation from the last container and stuffed it into his pocket. He then made his way back to every container and "fixed" the wire seals so that they didn't appear to have been tampered with…at least at first glance. If he was lucky, nobody would notice, they would just come along and cut the seals off without paying close attention to them. Ace made a note of some of the container numbers as well. He didn't know if he would be able to find out what was shipped in the containers that would require insulation, but he was going to try. He made his way back to the loose section of fence, rolled under it, resecured it at the bottom, got up and proceeded along the fence to the road. As he was approaching the road, he heard a car approaching on the road, so he ducked into the shadows. As the car went past, he poked his head out and saw that it was an SFPD cruiser, it appeared to just be doing the nightly rounds, not looking for anyone or anything. Ace made his way to the road, crossed and went down the street to the tavern.

While he was there, he decided to go in and just grab a beer. If he was lucky, he might strike up a conversation with someone that worked across the street, and he might get a bit more information. The bar was mostly empty but there were a few people sitting at the bar as well as a couple at tables around the bar. There were two or three at the bar that looked like "dock workers". Maybe Ace could strike up a conversation and find out a bit more information about the containers in the yard. He had to come up with a likely scenario to broach the conversation. If any of these people were dock workers, that is…

Ace had a seat at the bar and ordered a beer. Mindless corporate swill was all that was available on tap so that's what Ace ordered. This wasn't the type of establishment to cater to the "craft beer" crowd and it showed. There were several taps, and a backbar full of the standard liquor bottles seen in dive bars all over the country. The place smelled of stale beer, sweat, and old cigarette smoke.

Ace got his beer and watched the TV behind the bar, which was tuned to a "sports channel". It was showing a deep-sea fishing program at the moment. Ace listened in on the conversations around him and couldn't determine if any of the patrons sitting at the bar possibly worked across the street at the storage yard or not. When the bartender came down his way, Ace asked him if he knew what time the yard opened? The bartender said he wasn't sure but assumed that it was around 8AM. Ace thanked him, then asked, as an afterthought, if the bartender knew if they sold the containers in the yard to private owners? The bartender had no idea, but he yelled across the bar to a table in the corner of the room; "Hey Miguel, do you know if they sell any of the containers to private owners"?

Ace turned in his seat to see four men sitting and drinking pitchers of beer at a table and it appeared that they were playing Euchre. One of the men said that there maybe a possibility to purchase a container. Ace got up and approached the table. The man that had spoken to him, looked him up and down and asked him outright if he was a cop? Ace told him that he wasn't a cop, just a guy looking to buy some containers to put on some land that he had and convert them to "cabins". There was supposed to be a large crowd of people looking for solitude and a container home had all the earmarks of an inexpensive way to get into the business.

Miguel said that it wasn't uncommon for containers to "go missing" after being damaged. Sometimes they would take parts from one container to repair another container.

Ace said that wasn't what he was looking for. He didn't want damaged containers. He wanted containers that were in decent shape so that he could do the minimum that he needed to get them into a condition where they were habitable. Ace had a "builder" who said that each cabin could be created from two containers sitting side by side.

Miguel said that it was possible that they could help him out, but Ace would have to arrange to have the containers transported out of the yard via a tractor-trailer and that depending upon the size of the container, each rig would only be able to take one or two containers at a time. Miguel also told Ace that the transactions had to be in cash with no paperwork. Miguel told Ace that the cost for each container was $1,000.00 which was a good deal. Miguel said that he knew some companies that were paying upwards of $5,000.00 per container.

Ace asked Miguel if he knew of anyone that would be willing to transfer the containers for a fee and not ask questions? Miguel said he knew a company that hauled containers around the state. Ace said that sounded like paperwork and if they were going to do this "under the table" then he didn't want paperwork to follow.

Miguel and his friends chatted in Spanish for a bit then told Ace that he could come to the yard tomorrow evening right before closing. There was a guy coming to haul a couple of containers and he was supposed to arrive about 6PM. Ace could talk to him then. Ace made the appearance of thinking about it then said that he would see them tomorrow evening and if all looked well, he would make arrangements after closing to get four containers delivered to his land in Southern California.

Ace thanked them for their help, mostly Miguel, walked over to the bar and ordered and paid for another pitcher of beer for the bar, settled his tab. Waved as he exited the bar and headed back to his car. Ace mulled over his options. He didn't know what good it would do to show up the next evening to talk to someone about transporting containers. He had no plans to purchase containers. He just needed to find out when the containers for Humdinger Habitats were being moved. He would follow the tractor-trailer and see what took so long to get the containers to Humdinger Habitats for conversion to a tiny home for the homeless.

# Chapter 55

Ace returned to the hotel and turned in the rental car. When he got to his room, he booked a rental car for a week from a local rental company that specialized in "inexpensive" rentals. He was going to have to stake out the yard and watch for containers that were taken for Humdinger Habitats and follow the rig. Ace thought about taking the train home in the morning, getting his car and returning to San Francisco but he still wasn't sure that the car wasn't being tracked. A rental car was his best option at this time. Tomorrow was Sunday, so it wasn't likely that any of the containers would be moved. He would check out Napa and Sonoma tomorrow and then be ready to "live" in the rental car until the containers started to move. Living in the car meant that Ace was going to have to go hit up a convenience store for supplies that he would need. He would be sitting from 7AM until 6PM daily. He knew that he would need some protein bars and bottled water, as well as a jug large enough to relieve himself in if it were too crowded and public to do it in a parking lot.

The car rental company was an easy bus ride away and they had Sunday hours so Ace would pick up the car in the morning around 9AM. Then he would drive up to wine country for a bit of relaxation before the stakeout.

# Chapter 56

Ace logged on to his laptop and did a quick check of emails, both in his personal and business email accounts. He saw typical spam emails in both accounts as well as an email from Julie in his personal account and an email from Presley Misuse.

The email from Julie was nothing more than the typical chit chat so Ace closed it and opened the email from Misuse. The email from Misuse was just a follow-up that payment had been made and that no further services were required from Bancroft. Misuse closed his email saying that he hoped to never use Ace and his services in the future and that he couldn't really say that it had been a pleasure doing business as Ace had made the case a much bigger deal than it needed to be. He still felt that Ace had drug it out to make his payment larger, but it was paid, and Ace could move on to his next case.

Ace began to reply but ended up deleting his response and just closed the email. Ace was going to be the bigger man. He would not glorify the email with a response…especially since he wasn't really done investigating the case. If Ace responded, then Humdinger Habitats could use that email against him if any issues arose from his own private investigation. With no response, Ace could always claim that he hadn't seen the email.

As Ace was shutting down the laptop, he got a notice that a new email was received. Ace did a quick glance and saw that it was from Dr. Buerger. Ace didn't bother opening the email. He would deal with the good doctor when he returned to San Diego. There wasn't much that he needed to talk with him about while he was in San Francisco.

Ace made his way to the rooftop bar, got a seat overlooking the skyline and ordered a beer. He was delighted to see that the bar had Pliny the Elder on tap, from Russian River Brewing. As Ace sat and enjoyed the number one IPA in the country, his thoughts drifted to Julie Ritter, RN. He really did think that getting to know her would be a good thing. After this case, he was going to put a bit more effort into that.

# Chapter 57

Ace was up bright and early, enjoying the continental breakfast and finding what the quickest way to the rental car company would be. After a bit of thought, Ace put in an online order for an Uber and went outside to await the driver. After about 10 minutes, the driver pulled up and whisked Ace off to the rental car company.

After filling out the obligatory paperwork for the rental car company, Ace left in a non-descript Toyota Corolla that appeared to have been in the rental fleet far too long. The driver's seat was ripped, and the car smelled of dampness and pizza. Ace didn't know why it would smell like pizza, but he didn't care. It was probably going to smell much worse if he had to spend more than day in it, staking out the freight yard.

When Ace woke up that morning, he had a brainstorm regarding following the containers when they left the yard. Why did he have to follow the containers. He stopped at the local Apple store and picked up some air tags. Small devices that you can track with your phone when they are activated. Ace had used them in the past when he was traveling to track his luggage. This would work the same way. Ace would just have to get to the containers and doing that while the yard was open, wouldn't be easy. It wasn't like he could just walk in and go to the containers; or could he? He could flash his ID and tell them that he was there at the behest of Humdinger Habitats, and he just wanted to check on the status of the containers that would be heading to the manufacturing facility in the next few days. It could work. It could also prompt a phone call to Humdinger Habitats and Ace wanted to avoid that, if possible. It was Sunday, maybe the area around the storage yard would be deserted and Ace could sneak in through the fence like he had the other night and place the tags, then he could just wait on the containers to be moved, and he wouldn't have to do it from the car. He could go back to the hotel and set and alert on the air tags to notify him when they were moved from their current location.

Ace made his way to the yard and was pleasantly surprised that the area surrounding the yard looked like a ghost town. There was a bit of fog rolling in off of the bay, and the parking lots surrounding the yard were largely empty except for the occasional vehicle that appeared to be abandoned, plus a couple in the tavern parking lot that must've been left by the patrons that felt that it was better to get an Uber than risk a DUI.

Ace parked in the lot adjacent to the yard and made his way along the fence to the waterfront. The air tags already registered and active on his phone and laptop, stashed in his pockets. Ace had picked up 8 air tags which left him with a couple extra as there were only six containers in the section of the lot that were earmarked for Humdinger Habitats. He could hopefully stash on air tag in each container and have a couple in reserve if there were some with malfunctions. While Apple was known to provide a quality product. It wasn't impossible that they could have a failure of a device on occasion.

Ace was delighted to see that there was nobody along the waterfront doing some fishing, other than a few seagulls. He walked back along the fence to the section that he had accessed the other night and worked his way under it. He was right next to the containers for Humdinger Habitats. He walked up to the first container and saw that his "repair" of the tamper tag was still in place, so he removed the tag, entered the first container and stood there trying to determine the best place to put an air tag so that it wouldn't be seen. First things first though. Ace dropped a tag in the middle of the floor and made his way outside, closed the container and checked his phone to see if the tag showed as active. It didn't. Damnit, the metal walls must be blocking the signal so Ace was going to have to figure out how to put them on the outside of the containers so that they wouldn't be spotted or fall off during transportation. This wasn't going to be as simple as he had hoped.

There were six containers, Ace had eight air tags, so he could experiment with a couple and still have enough to track. Anyone that had ever seen a shipping container knew that there were "holes" at the top and bottom along a corrugation, this manufacturer made their containers that way. It was supposed to strengthen the side so that they didn't collapse when other containers were stacked on top of them. Ace dropped an air tag in one of the channels and was happy to see that it was still showing up on his "tracker" as active.

Ace dropped air tags in the other containers, and then thought about putting a couple inside again. He opened one of the containers and slid the air tag behind the foam insulation and was happy to see that air tag was still showing as active. It must be close enough to the outside that its RFID frequency could penetrate the steel. He placed the last air tag, slid under the fence and returned to his car. At his car, Ace pulled his phone out and checked. All eight air tags were still showing as active. This was great news. He was not going to have to camp in the car waiting on the devices to move. He accessed the "app" and set a setting so that he would get a notification if any of the devices were moved or deactivated. Ace then headed towards Napa and Sonoma. Ace was going to cross the "Bay Bridge" and proceed up the east side of San Francisco Bay towards American Canyon and then over to Napa. His first stop, when he got to Napa, was going to be the Stone Brewing Taproom. He wanted an Arrogant Bastard Ale, after that he thought that he would make a couple of stops at some of the local wineries, Peju and Nichelini were two of his favorites in Napa. He also wanted to make a stop at Viansa and Benziger Wineries in Sonoma.

# Chapter 58

Ace's trip to Napa and Sonoma was what he would term a successful trip. He had two cases of assorted wines from some of his favorite wineries in Napa and Sonoma. He had visited the Stone Taproom in Napa and was pleasantly surprised at how nice it was. The menu at the Napa taproom was different but the beer was the same, and as always everything was top notch. Even though Stone had sold out to the corporate world, they hadn't strayed from their roots, which was making beer that smacked you in the face with the intensity of flavor.

Ace headed south out of Sonoma and decided to pay a visit to another of his favorite breweries in California. Half Moon Bay Brewing Company in Half Moon Bay before returning to the hotel. Ace made his way down California 121 to Highway 37 along San Pablo Bay. When he reached Highway 101, he went south toward San Francisco and the Golden Gate Bridge. Ace would be approaching the most famous bridge in the world from the north. Seeing the Golden Gate bridge was always a moment when driving.

Ace recalled a time, years before, when he had been stationed at the Presidio and decided that he was going to "walk the bridge", he did it, but it was at that time that he realized that he did have a slight fear of heights. Ace could feel the bridge sway as he was walking, and the only thing that he could think about was that if there was a problem and the bridge collapsed, he would die in a terrible fall to the bay. When he made it across the bridge, he called a friend and told him that he would buy him a beer if he came across to Sausalito and picked him up.

Once Ace crossed the iconic Golden Gate, he made his way along Highway 1 south towards Half Moon Bay. Many people that had never visited the San Francisco area were surprised to find out that while San Francisco sat on San Francisco Bay, South San Francisco was not truly on the coast of the Pacific Ocean.

To reach Half Moon Bay from the North, you traveled south through Pacifica and other small beach communities until you arrived at Half Moon Bay, home of the Mavericks surfing competition. If you are approaching from the east, you must cross over the Santa Cruz mountains, passing many farms that raised, of all things, pumpkins. Half Moon Bay had an annual pumpkin festival. The area was the producer for most of the pumpkins sold throughout the United States.

The trip on Highway 1 was always a sight to behold, cliffs to your right, that dropped to the Pacific, with walls of rock on your left, leading to the top of the mountains in the area. Ace loved to drive along Highway 1 but if he were to be honest, he preferred driving north along the coast, which left an entire lane between him and the cliffs. Ace didn't have a fear about his driving abilities, but other drivers were a different story, and to top it all off, this stretch of Highway 1 was popular with bicyclists, so you had to always be on the watch for the two wheeled bikes.

They were always present, regardless of conditions, fog, rain, sun...none of it mattered to the hard-core bicyclists.

Ace pulled into the parking lot for Half Moon Bay Brewing and was happy to see that their expansive patio with fire pits was open. The patio looked over the Pacific and Pillar Point Harbor. Ace grabbed an Adirondack chair by one of the firepits, ordered a Maverick's Amber Ale and an order of Crab Nacho's to snack on before returning to the hotel. While Ace was waiting for his food, he pulled out his phone and checked on the "air-tags". They hadn't moved and obviously, hadn't been discovered. Ace enjoyed his crab nachos and his ale, sat for a bit and enjoyed the views, the smells and the sound of the ocean then decided that he better get back over the mountain to the hotel before the nightly fog got too thick leading to a harrowing drive through the mountains. The drive was much easier when it wasn't foggy, Ace didn't want to risk getting into an accident with his rental car.

Ace got back to the hotel, and made arrangements with the valet to have his car readily available in case the containers started moving. The nice thing about the tags was that he didn't have to follow closely. He just needed to know when they moved and where they ended up prior to arrival at Humdinger Habitats.

# Chapter 59

Ace got up in the morning and checked the status of the air tags. All were stills showing as functional and in the storage yard, so Ace hopped in the shower, got dressed, and went to the hotel restaurant to grab some breakfast. It was very possible that today would show some movement of the containers. It was Monday, and the yard would be open. As Ace was finishing his breakfast, he got a notice on his phone that one of the tags was moving. Then he got notice that another was moving. Ace pulled up the GPS, and both tags were still showing in the yard, but they had definitely been moved. It appeared that two of the containers were being loaded onto a truck or trucks. Ace hurried to check out of the hotel and got his car.

Ace checked the location of the air-tags and saw that two of the devices were on the Embarcadero and were moving towards Highway 101. Ace assumed that the trucks would head towards the south and San Diego and wasn't surprised when that is what happened.

Ace followed at a discreet distance, checking his phone on occasion. After about six hours, both trucks exited the freeway at Camarillo. Ace exited the freeway as well. He expected the drivers to refuel the trucks, grab a bite to eat and get back on 101 heading south. That wasn't what happened. The trucks exited the freeway and stopped at a truck stop, then continued into the mountains to the east of Camarillo. The area around Camarillo had many farms and ranches. Ace sat and waited at the truck stop to see where the trucks went. He didn't have to wait long. Both containers, with their air tags still functional, were stopped at what appeared to be a ranch on the outskirts of town. Ace also got notice that the remaining containers had been loaded and were also heading this way. Why would the containers need to be taken to a ranch? This didn't make any sense. They were steel containers; nothing was special about them. It appeared that Ace was going to have to do some snooping later in the day. He was going to wait until the rest of the containers arrived on-site and then play the lost businessman and see if he could get a look at anything on the ranch. While Ace waited, he pulled up to the property where the two containers were on his laptop and looked at the satellite pics of the area. It looked like a typical California ranch. There were planted orchards around the main buildings as well as some very large buildings that appeared to be barns, storage facilities, and a couple of silos.

Ace connected to a program that he used on occasion if he needed to identify the owner of a property. This property was owned by a corporation which, on the surface, appeared to be a legitimate farming business. Everything appeared to be legitimate based on the tax information. The farm appeared to be fairly profitable. There were years where there were losses, and then there were years where there were profits. The years with profit outnumbered the years that showed a loss by at least two to one.

From what Ace could find online, this was the main farm; however, the corporation owned land all over

California, as well as in Arizona, New Mexico, Northern Mexico, and Baja California. Crop lists contained a variety of products from apples to walnuts and everything in between. Agave appeared to be the main crop in Mexico and Baja California. This wasn't surprising as it was the main ingredient in tequila. A corporate farm cashing in on the booze industry wasn't uncommon. With that being said, why would the trucks hauling the containers stop at this farm? It wasn't a necessary stop unless the containers were being loaded with something before being taken to Humdinger Habitats.

Ace pulled up a satellite map again on the laptop. He noticed a faint trail that snaked around the rear of the farm. Ace thought that he might be able to find a place to park up there and look down on the farm. Maybe he would get lucky and see what they were loading into the containers for the final trip to Humdinger Habitats. Ace slid the car in gear and made it to the road, which was what appeared to be an old "fire road." After a 10-minute drive over some of the roughest terrain, obviously not terrain that the rental car was made for, Ace was able to park in a low spot in the road. The car couldn't be seen directly from the farm. Ace made his way to a rock pile next to the road and poked his head up to see if he could see anything of importance. Lo and behold, about a half mile away sat the containers on their flatbed trucks. Both containers were open, and men were removing the Styrofoam panels and taking them into one of the many barns on the property. Obviously, the Styrofoam wasn't hazardous, yet the men were wearing respirators when they were inside the container. Ace observed the men raise the respirators to the tops of their heads when they got out in the open air. This was odd. Why would there be a need for breathing protection when removing the insulation? As Ace was watching, two more trucks with containers showed up and proceeded to the same area.

Ace checked his phone and was delighted to see that all the containers were enroute. It appeared they would arrive here this evening and if things went well, would be moved to Humdinger Habitats tomorrow.

Ace hopped in his car and made his way back to town and the local supermarket, where he picked up some necessities for an overnight stakeout in the car, then he returned to the same spot that he had been parked in earlier, climbed to the top of the rocks and observed. This time, with the help of a small set of binoculars that he had picked up at the store, he was able to get a closer look at the activity below.

The workers were definitely wearing respirators to protect their lungs as they removed the panels. They were also wearing gloves that Ace hadn't noticed before. The gloves appeared to be gloves that were typically worn by people working with caustic chemicals.

All the containers arrived before 8 PM. Ace observed the activities going on below. It was the same with every container. The Styrofoam insulation was being removed. Unfortunately, one of the air-tags, the one that had been slipped behind the insulation, was no longer showing on his tracker. Either it had been found and destroyed, or it had stopped working. The rest of the tags were still showing on his app on his phone. It also didn't appear that anyone was looking for additional tags, so Ace was hopeful that the tag had just malfunctioned.

All the activity around the trucks slowed and then ceased. The drivers were taken to what appeared to be a bunkhouse building for the night. When all activity stopped, Ace was going to see if he could make his way down to the farm and check out the containers and the building where the workers took the Styrofoam.

In the interim, Ace was going to go back to his car and get a quick nap as it appeared that it was going to be a long night. Ace was happy that this road didn't seem to get much, if any, traffic. He should be able to get a couple of hours of shut eye with no problem. Ace set the alert on his phone to notify him if any of the containers were moved, popped the hood of his car, and loosened the battery cable. If someone came along and wanted to know what he was doing, he could claim car trouble.

# Chapter 60

Ace made his way down the steep, rock-strewn hillside, being as quiet as possible. Before striking out for the farm, Ace looked to see if there were any guards patrolling the grounds and saw nobody. He also looked for dogs and didn't see any, although he had heard a dog or two barking from up on the hillside.

When Ace reached the bottom of the hill, he arrived at a plain wire fence that was not electrified and presented no problem for Ace to hop over. So far, so good, no alarm had been sounded and there didn't appear to be anyone up and about anywhere on the farm. The lights in the bunkhouse were out as well as the lights in the home on the property.

Ace approached the building where he had observed the foam insulation being moved to. He didn't want to open the main door as he was sure that it was quite noisy. He had heard the noise it made when he was up on the hillside. He knew that if he had to open and enter through that door, everyone within a mile would hear and come running. Ace rounded the corner and saw the "man door" on the south side of the building. Sticking to the shadows, Ace reached the door and turned the knob. The door was locked…shit…now he would have to pick the lock, but before he did that, he wanted to check to make sure that there were no alarms that he could trigger. As Ace was surveying the building, he did spy a camera mounted at the corner. The camera appeared to be quite old, and any hope of a clear picture from it was unlikely, due to the large spiderweb and orb weaver spider right in front of the lens. If the camera was motion activated, it was likely to have been turned off, or the alerts for movement would be happening every time the spider moved, or an unsuspecting moth got caught in the web.

Ace had the lock tripped and slowly opened the door, just waiting to bolt if an alarm sounded. Fortunately, no alarm activated. Ace entered the building, slid the door closed behind himself, and waited for his eyes to adjust to the gloom. The building was a tall steel structure with no windows at eye level, just around the top of the building. Ace didn't have to worry about the light from his phone being seen unless he played it around the ceiling of the building.

Ace found stacks of the foam insulation in one corner of the building. It appeared that all the containers had their insulation removed. Ace knew that there was no way that he would be able to find the air tag that he had stuffed behind the foam, and he knew where the containers would be going next anyway so he would just hope that the tag wasn't found. He wasn't worried about the tags that he had dropped in the holes in the containers. Those wouldn't be found unless the containers were swept for radio transmissions, which wasn't likely.

Ace found multiple 55-gallon drums of acetone in the building, which didn't fit as a chemical needed for a farm. Ace also found a large vat full of what smelled like acetone. Ace wished that he had one of the respirator masks right now, as the fumes were beginning to give him quite a headache. Ace found one of the respirators hanging on a peg near the vat full of acetone and placed it on his head. It obstructed his view somewhat, but he wouldn't have to worry about dropping over from the smell. As Ace looked around, he found a pump on the end of the vat, which had a hose running to another drum. These drums weren't labeled but obviously acetone was the main ingredient. Ace seemed to recall that acetone could be used to dissolve Styrofoam, so he went to the pile of insulation and, broke a corner off, and dropped it in the vat. The piece dissolved in a matter of seconds.

Ace figured he had pushed his luck long enough and decided to get out while he could. He hung the respirator back on the peg and made his way out of the building. After several deep breaths of fresh air, his headache from the chemicals began to abate. He made his way to the fence and hopped over then carefully picked his way back up the hillside to his car. He didn't want to encounter a dozing rattlesnake or scorpion on his way to the car.

When Ace arrived at his car, he tightened the battery cable, started it up, and made his way back into town. Once he arrived in town, he found a public parking lot and parked then fired up his laptop and hotspot. What would the reason be for dissolving the Styrofoam? Why wouldn't the containers just go directly to San Diego and Humdinger Habitats? After all, the containers had to be insulated anyway. Removing insulation to replace it with insulation was counterproductive, and it really wasn't cost efficient. Humdinger Habitats was supposed to be "non-profit" but that didn't mean that you spent money unwisely.

As Ace was searching the web for any reasonable cause to remove the insulation, he found it. Ace knew that he was going to have to go back to the farm and get a small piece of the foam insulation if he wanted to prove what he thought was going on. Ace shut down the laptop, fired up the rental car, and headed back up the dirt road to the area where he had been spying on the farm from.

Unfortunately, some lights were on in the bunkhouse and there were several people wandering around the grounds, so the likelihood of getting a sample undetected was zero. Trucks were starting. It was obvious that the containers were getting ready for the trip to San Diego. Ace took a few pictures from a distance and set out for home himself. He didn't need to stick around and follow the trucks. The air-tags were all functional, but one and Ace knew where these containers were going to end up.

# Chapter 61

Ace got home, hopped in the shower, and climbed into bed. Though the sun was rising, he hadn't had much sleep, and his brain was mush. He set his alarm for 3 hours and was soundly asleep in about 2 minutes.

When Ace finally got up around 11 AM, he checked his phone for messages and saw that he had a new voicemail from Julie as well as a message from Dr. Buerger. He would call Julie later, as far as Dr. Buerger was concerned. Ace wasn't going to return his call. Ace was going to go to his office. He was a much better "lie detector" in person, not on the phone.

Ace made a quick breakfast of protein pancakes and a fried egg smothered in enough syrup to cause a diabetic to go into a sugar-induced coma. As he was eating, he was thinking about the insulation in the containers and the fact that it was being removed prior to being delivered to Humdinger Habitats to be retrofitted as a tiny home. He was sure that the tiny homes had to be insulated when they were manufactured, so it made no sense to ship the containers with the foam insulation and then have it removed just to install new foam insulation at the manufacturing facility.

Then there was the acetone and the fact that they were dissolving the foam insulation in it. Why would they do that? Ace had found information online that some drug smugglers would mix heroin with foam insulation and then dissolve the foam and process off the acetone to recover the drugs. Was that what was happening here?  That would certainly explain how Humdinger Habitats could give the containers away to the homeless.  They were making money on the sale of illicit narcotics.  Ace needed to get a piece of insulation if he was going to prove his supposition, which meant he would have to make another trip to San Francisco. He didn't want to risk that at this time. He wasn't really on a case, so if Misuse found out that he was still investigating, it could be problematic.

Ace cleaned up the morning dishes, stacked them in the dishwasher, and ran it…even though it was empty, he had heard somewhere that it saved water to run the dishwasher vs. washing dishes by hand, and Ace hated to wash dishes by hand.  It was like making a bed. He never made his bed because it made no sense.  Make the bed, just to climb back in it that evening.  Not worth the effort.  Now, if he knew that he was going to be entertaining someone, then he would make sure that things like the bed being made were done.  He would also make sure to place a clean hand towel in the bathroom and a bottle of hand soap, not his grungy bar of soap that did the job just as well.

# Chapter 62

Ace went outside and took the device that he had borrowed so that he could check the car for trackers as well as listening devices. He checked the car everywhere, and it paid off. He located what appeared to be a "tracker" stuck to the underside of the rear bumper with a wad of some tar-like substance. Ace peeled it off the bumper. He was going to throw the tracker in the toilet and flush it but thought better of it. If someone was actively watching the location of Ace's car, maybe the best course of action was to keep the tracker "live." Although, it wasn't going to be in his car. He was going to stick it to the bumper of his neighbor's pickup truck. Josh could be a pain in the ass at times, but Ace really did like him. Ace didn't think that whoever was following him would harm Josh if they realized that Ace had switched the location of the tracker. They would probably just take the tracker off his vehicle and put it back on Ace's. Hopefully, Ace would have an idea of who it was before that happened.

Ace had to return the rental car first, so he would do that after paying a visit to Dr. Buerger. That way, nobody would be the wiser because Ace's car was still parked at his apartment.

Ace left the parking lot of his apartment complex and headed towards the good doctor's office. He knew that there would be a problem with him seeing the doctor since he didn't have an appointment, but Ace would make sure that he didn't skip out on him this time.

When Ace entered the office, he went to the window and rang the bell. An elderly woman with a name badge that said Roxanne slid the glass window open and asked if she could help him. He told her his name and said that he was there to see Dr. Buerger. She looked at her computer monitor and said that she didn't show him on the appointment list and asked him if he was sure that he had an appointment. Ace then clarified that he didn't have an appointment, but he did need to speak to the doctor if he had some time today. She asked Ace to have a seat and slid the window closed. Ace thought, not today and went out the front door to the corner of the building so that he could watch if the doctor tried to leave. Before the door even closed, Ace heard the window open, and Roxanne said, Mr. Bancroft, the doctor said that you could come right back. He is between patients right now and said that he can speak with you for a few minutes.

Ace entered the door next to the window, and Roxanne took him back to the hallway to what Ace assumed was the doctor's private office. She knocked lightly and opened the door.

Ace entered to a middle-aged man sitting behind a desk. As Ace approached the desk, he extended his hand and introduced himself. Ace shook his hand and immediately wanted to wash it. The doctor's hand was as clammy as a dead fish. Ace restrained the urge to wipe his hand on his pants and had a seat across from Doctor Buerger. As Ace sat down, he looked over the man closely, and the first thing that he noticed was that he appeared to be sporting a light black eye. He also had a rash that looked like razor burn only in the shape of a square, and it appeared to go clear across his face. Ace's first thought was that he was looking at someone who had their mouth taped shut.

Ace asked "Dr. Buerger, are you ok?" Dr. Buerger said that he was just fine and apologized for not meeting him a few days back. There had been an emergency at home, and he had to leave without notice.

Ace could tell immediately that he was being fed a line of bullshit a mile long. Dr. Buerger was obviously not a good liar. There were so many "tells" when he was telling his story. It was almost like the man had a nervous tic.

Dr. Buerger said that he had heard from Humdinger Habitats that Ace had concluded his investigation, and he didn't know why he was there to talk with him. Ace told him that the investigation was complete as far as Humdinger Habitats was concerned, but he still had a few loose ends to tie up. He also told Dr. Buerger that there was no need to tell anyone from Humdinger Habitats that he had ever talked with Ace.

With that, Ace told Dr. Buerger to cut the bullshit. He knew that there was something going on and he could rely on Ace that he wouldn't provide any info that the doctor had even talked with him.

Dr. Buerger sat back in his chair, appearing to think about what he wanted to say, then just told Ace to ask

262

his questions, and he would decide whether he wanted to answer them or not.

Ace's first question was very straightforward. Was Ronald Humdinger healthy enough to have sex? Mind you, it's not normal sex. Sex with a dominatrix. Sex that might get a little rough. Dr. Buerger said that under normal circumstances, he didn't think that there were any concerns about Humdinger engaging in sex with a dominatrix. However, he didn't feel that these were normal circumstances. Humdinger was insistent that Buerger provide him with higher and higher doses of erectile dysfunction medications. He also had asked Humdinger to provide a lidocaine gel that he could rub into his penis so that he would have better "control" when it came to sex. Apparently, Humdinger was "punished" if he completed before the dominatrix told him that he could, and Humdinger hated to lose. Everyone who watched him in politics was aware that the man hated to lose. Dr. Buerger reminded Ace of the claims of election fraud by Humdinger prior to the election even being held. Ace told him that there was no need to remind him. It was still fresh in his memory, even though it had occurred a couple of years prior.

Ace asked him, "So you think that the combination of too many meds and his overall health may have caused a heart problem that led to Humdinger's demise?"

Dr. Buerger said that was a possibility. He didn't trust Humdinger to take the required dosages of the medications.

Ace then asked the doctor what really happened the night that he was supposed to meet with Ace. Dr. Buerger stammered around and said, "I told you I had an emergency at home, and I had to leave." Ace said again, to cut the bullshit. He explained to the doctor that prior to being an Investigator, he had worked for the FBI, and he was well-trained in noticing the things that people inadvertently showed when they were lying.

Dr. Buerger looked at his watch and said that it was time for him to go. He was done answering his questions, and he stood up to escort Ace from his office. Ace never even got out of his chair. He told him to just sit down. Ace wanted to help him. He would make sure that nobody would know of these concerns. He just wanted to know what the doctor was hiding. To Ace's dismay, the doctor's bottom lip started to quiver, and he appeared as though he might vomit. The color had drained from his face so quickly. With his pallor the way it was, Ace was sure that the rash on his face was from tape across his mouth, and he said as much.

Dr. Buerger looked up at him quickly and said, "They'll hurt my family and me. I can't say anymore." Ace asked who would hurt his family. Dr. Buerger said that he couldn't tell him anymore and he needed to leave.

Ace told Dr. Buerger that he would protect him as best he could if he just cooperated and told him what happened the other night. The doctor was basically sobbing at this point. "You don't understand. They said that they would kill my wife. They would chop her up in little pieces while she was still alive and make me watch!" Ace asked again, "Who said this to you?"

Dr. Buerger took a wad of tissue from a box on his desk, wiped his nose and his eyes, and told Ace that he didn't know who they were. They had shown up at his office and busted their way into the back. They told Roxanne to go home and keep her mouth shut if she knew what was good for her, then told her her address and said that they also had her daughter's address as well.

They then took him in the back and taped his mouth and hand with adhesive tape, then made him walk to a car parked in the back, where they tossed him in the backseat. Dr. Buerger said, "I saw you nosing around" when they drove by, but you obviously couldn't see into the vehicle because of the tinted windows. The people took him to an old building and locked him in a room. After a couple of hours, a Hispanic man showed up and started by asking the doctor what he was going to tell the investigator. When he told him the things that he had just told Ace, he backhanded him and said, "NO!!!, you are going to tell the investigator that Humdinger was as healthy as any man his age." "You will say nothing about the high doses of medications that Humdinger was taking for his ED. Is that clear?" Dr. Buerger hesitated and got another smack alongside the head. The man asked again, "Is that clear?" Dr. Buerger said that was not a problem at all.

The Hispanic man left the room but not without another threat to Buerger and his family, as well as Roxanne and her family.

Buerger said he sat there for what seemed like hours but was probably only about one hour, and the men that had grabbed him at his office came back and unceremoniously tossed him in the backseat of the SUV, then took him to his home. Dr. Buerger said that he wanted to go and get his car. They just laughed and said that he could worry about that on his own…that he should be more concerned that they took him to his home and never asked him where he lived. They also told him that he might want to get inside and check on his wife.

At that point, they drug him from the backseat, cut the tape from his wrists, and kicked him in the ass to get him moving towards the door. The man almost missed the kick because Buerger was running towards the door. As he slammed through the front door, he heard the SUV pull away from the curb. He called his wife's name several times and didn't get an answer so he started looking from room to room. He found her bound and gagged in the kitchen. She was awake and tears were streaming down her face. They had also drawn a bullseye on her forehead in marker as well as a slash across her throat with a red marker. Dr. Buerger said that he removed the tape from her mouth and cut the tape from her legs and arms that were taped to the chair. His wife was sobbing.

Dr. Buerger was sobbing, telling Ace the story and Ace didn't pressure him. He told the Doctor that he wouldn't have to bother him any further and that there

266

was no need to let anyone know that he had come to visit him today. The last thing that Ace wanted to do was to put innocent people in danger. Dr. Buerger was doing what one of the most powerful men in the world wanted him to do as far as prescribing the medications. Ace may not agree with it, but he wasn't sure what he would do if he were in the same situation.

Ace asked Dr. Buerger if he had any idea who these men were or who had put them up to taking him and threatening his wife?

Dr. Buerger said that he had no idea who they were, but they obviously were well connected with someone near to Ronald Humdinger. Why else would they want to keep him quiet? Ace wasn't sure and told him as much.

Ace was just getting ready to leave when he asked Dr. Buerger one more question. He asked the doctor if he knew how to distill acetone to remove a precipitate. The doctor looked at him quizzically and said that he had no idea. The question would be more pertinent to a chemist. He told Ace that he understood that anything that was dissolved in acetone would always have some leftover toxins in it, even if it was recovered from acetone. Acetone is a toxic and highly flammable substance. You wouldn't want to ingest anything that had soaked in it. Ace told Buerger that it wasn't likely that the substance was being ingested and left it at that. He thanked Dr. Buerger for his time and reassured him that nobody would know that he had come to talk to him. Ace did tell Buerger to let the receptionist know that as well. He was never there.

# Chapter 63

Ace returned the rental car and took an Uber back to his apartment. He really needed a sample of the insulation materials in the containers. He was going to do some searching online for processes involving removing precipitates from acetone, and he might give a friend or two a call and ask for their expertise.

The containers were coming into the country on container ships from all over the world. All the containers that Humdinger Habitats purchased were from a supplier in South Korea. Was it possible that somebody in South Korea was working with Humdinger Habitats to smuggle narcotics into the country via the containers? Was the container company just a pawn being used by whomever was insulating the containers? These questions were all bouncing around in Ace's brain. If someone within Humdinger Habitats was having drugs smuggled into the country and they had hired someone in South Korea to assist, there had to be a trail, but Ace wasn't in any hurry to go to South Korea. Was Ronald Humdinger aware of what was going on? Did Ronald find out and tell them to stop? Had they worked to silence Humdinger so that they could continue. Obviously, illicit narcotics were big business in the United States. The "War on Drugs" never seemed to work. People were greedy. Humdinger had been greedy. That's why the notion behind Humdinger Habitat's providing free housing to the homeless didn't make sense. However, many of the homeless were addicts. Was it possible that Humdinger and his cronies had devised a way to smuggle large amounts of narcotics into the country undetected, then enlisted the help of "homeless" addicts by providing them with a "home" at no cost. The catch was that they (the homeless) had to help in selling and disbursing the narcotics coming into the country.

Ace sat back. He may have just figured it out. He had to get a sample of the insulation. If it contained what he thought that it contained, then it was just a matter of putting all the pieces together with all the players and figuring out if Humdinger had really died a natural death or if someone had made it look that way. Humdinger's "tox screen" had been clean for illegal drugs and poisons, but it was unlikely that there were any tests for the medications that Humdinger took on a regular basis. The more that Ace thought about it, the more that he truly believed that Humdinger had been murdered, whether since he found out about the illegal activities and told them to stop or whether it was a power grab by someone at Humdinger Habitats, Emilyia Humdinger, Kim Il Soon, Starletta Blaze, or Lola Aspera-Amor was yet to be determined.

Ace flipped through his notes and decided that he couldn't firmly rule anyone out that he had interviewed. Every single person had a reason to benefit from the death of Ronald Humdinger.

Ace went online and made a flight reservation to San Francisco for the first flight in the morning out of San Diego. He was going to go to the container yard and get a sample of the Styrofoam insulation. If he could prove that there were narcotics included in the foam, then he could really start digging into the who and why. Then, he could present his information to the police. He wasn't going to present anything to Misuse at Humdinger Habitats or anyone else. He didn't want to end up on a morgue table like Humdinger did. He had to keep this as discreet as possible. He might even enlist the help of some friends at the FBI and the local police department that he knew he could trust. He had already been warned off the case, but since he had turned in his report to Misuse, it was possible that nobody was really watching what he was doing currently. He wasn't taking any chances, though. Any further investigation that he did would be behind the scenes.

# Chapter 64

Ace made a phone call to his niece, Victoria. Most people just assumed that she was a retail store manager. What they didn't know was that she was a hacker and she did some work for intelligence agencies in the United States. Fortunately, Victoria lived in Utah, so only an hour difference in time, so Ace knew that he wouldn't be interrupting her. She answered on the third ring with a hearty, "Uncle Ace, how the Hell are ya?" This young lady was a marvel to Ace. She grew up in a small town in Ohio and then ventured off to college. She was actually the person who introduced her Uncle Ace to the glories of social media.

All her hacking skills were self-taught. She was introduced to the world of the "dark web" by some online friends and she decided that she wanted to know more about it. While Victoria had "hacked" into many web pages and businesses, she didn't do it to harm the website or business. She just had an innate curiosity about the people that she might do business with. As far as Ace knew, she had never been detected during her intrusions. Ace had actually gotten her a few jobs with the FBI that paid her very well, and it also kept her on the straight and narrow when it came to doing any damage or just snooping around the web.

Ace told her what he was looking for and gave her a list of names, then told her to check into these people's backgrounds discreetly. He wanted to know everything about them. If they were getting large electronic transfers of money into accounts that weren't public knowledge, he wanted to know. If they had any "kinks" that might be of interest, he wanted to know about it. Maybe Humdinger wasn't the only pervert in the bunch.

Ace reiterated that he didn't want any of her incursions tracked, so if there were any "government" sites, then she should steer clear of those. He didn't want anything to blow back on her if he was caught digging into information that people didn't want him to have.

They chatted for a few minutes more, and Ace told her that he had to go. Before he hung up, he provided a "private" email that people weren't aware of that she could send any information to. He loved his niece dearly, but once you got her on the phone, it was next to impossible to get off the phone. She would talk about anything and everything all day long with anyone that would listen to her.

# Chapter 65

Ace arrived at San Francisco International Airport the next morning at 8:40 AM. He didn't have any luggage, so he deboarded the plane and headed to the taxi stand.

The taxi dropped him off at the tavern across the street from the container yard. Ace had thought about his approach, and he decided that lying was in his best interest. He was there searching for a source of containers for a storage business that he was considering, and he wanted to look at the different containers to see what would best suit his needs. He wasn't sure that he would get a look at one of the Humdinger Habitats containers, but he was going to give it a hell of a try.

Ace walked up to the entrance and introduced himself as Ernest Pilar and told the guard what he wanted to do. The guard told him that he would have to clear it with the folks in the office and that he needed to wait while he made the phone call. Ace said that was no problem at all. The guard made a call, hung up, and told Ace that he could go in and look at the containers, but he would have to be accompanied. This was more as a precaution than anything else, as it wasn't likely that he was going to walk out of the yard with a container strapped to his back. Ace just chuckled and said that it was fine if he accompanied him.

Ace put on a good show of walking all around the yard looking at the different containers. After an hour or so, the guard asked him how much longer he thought he was going to be. Ace told him that he thought that he could wrap it up in the next hour or so. The guard grimaced and asked if it would be ok if he made a quick trip to the port-a-john in the corner as the 4 cups of coffee had made their way through and he needed to relieve himself. Ace said that was just fine, he would stay right where he was until the guard returned and then they could resume the inspection. The guard thought for a minute and said that he didn't see any harm in Ace wandering the yard if he didn't open any containers that had security seals on them. Ace said that wasn't a problem. He didn't know that he would need to open anymore containers. They all looked pretty much the same on the inside. The guard thanked him and hurried off to the port-a-john in the opposite corner of the lot from the Humdinger Habitats containers. Ace made a beeline for that corner and was happy to see that there were still several containers sitting in the corner. Ace went to the first and clipped the safety seal, opened it and saw the familiar Styrofoam insulation. Ace broke a small corner off and placed it in a Ziplock bag and stuffed it in his pocket. Closed the container and continued the ruse of looking at the different containers. A couple of minutes later the guard caught up to him and asked him how it was going? Ace told him that he was about finished and that he appreciated the company while he walked around the yard. Ace "looked" at a few more containers while making his way towards the gate. When they arrived at the gate, Ace thanked the security guard for his assistance and exited the gate.

Ace made his way across the street to the tavern. He was glad to see that it was open and it appeared that they offered breakfast, an actual breakfast, not a glass of grains and water as a breakfast so Ace ordered two eggs, over medium, wheat toast, and smoked sausage. He also ordered a Hamm's draft beer. Ace didn't even know that Hamm's was still available but that's what the tap handle said so he ordered it. Ace took a drink of the beer. It was a watered down as he remembered from his younger days. But it didn't really taste all that bad, and it was a great accompaniment to the breakfast when it arrived.

# Chapter 66

As Ace made his way back to the airport, he thought about the fact that he was going to have to go through Security with a sample of something that he thought contained illicit narcotics. It wouldn't matter that he was a former FBI agent or was currently a private investigator if he was caught with drugs. As much as Ace didn't want to do it, he rented a car at the airport and made the 8-hour drive back to San Diego from San Francisco. As Ace was approaching the outskirts of San Diego, his cell phone rang, he noted that it was from his niece which was very odd. He hadn't expected to hear from her for a couple of days.

Ace barely got "hello" out of his mouth and Victoria asked him what they hell he had gotten her into? She had started by looking at bank accounts of people on his list. She was absolutely sure that she wouldn't be traced but by the second account, it was obvious that someone was "watching" what she was looking at. Ace asked her if anything could be tracked back to her and she said no, but she had to really sneak around because it appeared that most of the accounts that he gave her were being watched. He asked her if she knew who was watching them and she told him that she didn't dig that far because she didn't want to alert anyone that she was looking too. If she had to guess, she said it had to be a government agency of some type, NSA, CIA, FBI, "you know, the "alphabet soup" that you used to work for before you got smart and got out, she said".

She asked Ace if he wanted her to investigate things more and he said only if she thought that she could do it without getting caught. She laughed and said that wouldn't be a problem. She did tell him that in the last few hours, she noted that whoever was looking at the accounts that he asked her to check into, the only one that appeared to be "clean" as far as being looked at was Emilyia Humdinger's accounts. Ace asked how her accounts looked, and she told him that everything looked copacetic, even her accounts in the Grand Cayman's were reported. She didn't see anything that was being hidden by Emilyia.

Ace thanked Vic and told her to continue but to be discreet and to get out if she thought that there was any chance that she would get tracked. Ace knew that his sister would never forgive him if her daughter got into legal trouble because of something that Ace had put her up to.

Ok, so it appeared that Emilyia Humdinger was going to be crossed off his list, but that still left a long list of people that may have something to hide.

# Chapter 67

On his way back to San Diego, Ace contacted a friend that was a chemist and asked him if it would be possible to meet later that evening? Ace told him what he wanted, and his chemist friend told him to stop by his house when he got back to town. He would have acetone ready, and he would take the sample into the lab and do his magic to get the "precipitate" out, if there was any and run a test to determine what it was…again, if there was any. His chemist friend felt that the only precipitate would be polystyrene and possibly some resins. When Ace asked why he thought that; he said that it didn't make sense to put illicit substances in Styrofoam just to recover them from the solution from melting them down in acetone. There were too many leftover chemicals that were toxic, and many were cancer causing agents. Ace agreed but he asked if he really thought that "drug dealers" cared if their product was contaminated with cancer causing agents? Afterall, it wouldn't kill them right away, and the life expectancy of a heroin user was very short. It was much more likely that they would die from an overdose than it was from cancer that they got from using contaminated heroin.

Ace made his next call. He called Emilyia Humdinger and asked if he would be able to meet with her in the next couple of days. He wanted to just cross a couple of t's and dot a couple of I's regarding the investigation.

Emilyia said that he could visit the next morning around 10 AM. She said that she would be home at that time but could only give him about an hour. Before she hung up, she said, "I thought that you were done with the investigation?" Ace said that he was done. He had already turned his report in to Presley Misuse. He asked her not to mention this to Misuse. She scoffed and said that wasn't a problem. Her opinion of Misuse wasn't high enough that he warranted a second thought, as far as she was concerned. If Ace wanted to meet and discuss the investigation, he didn't have to worry about her telling anyone from Humdinger Habitats. All she did was collect her "pay." She didn't owe them anything as far as she was concerned.

# Chapter 68

Ace arrived at Donovan's home around 7 PM, knocked at the door, and was greeted by the sound of a large dog barking incessantly at the door. As the door opened, he was nearly knocked over by Donovan's Great Dane, Tipsy. She was a huge dog, and she wasted no time in planting her front paws on Ace's shoulders and was looking him in the eye, tongue hanging out and slobber dripping on his shirt. Donovan told Tipsy to get down and she listened immediately, but she stood right in front of Ace, waiting to have her ears scratched. Ace gave her a quick rub, and Donovan ushered him into his house.

Ace felt bad, he hadn't visited with Donovan in a while and Donovan was quick to point it out. He wasted no time telling Ace that he felt like he only came around when he wanted something. Ace tried to interrupt but Donovan stopped him. Donovan told Ace that they needed to get together sometime and just have a beer or two…it wasn't like Donovan wanted him to go out to one of the gay nightclubs that he frequented. Donovan would be just as happy to visit one of the many breweries in the San Diego area.

Ace told Donovan that they could go visit Modern Methods as soon as they were done here if he wanted to. Donovan appeared to mull it over and then said that was fine if he wouldn't be too embarrassed to be seen in public with a "gay man." Ace told him that wasn't a problem at all. "So it's settled," Ace asked?

We are going to go have a beer or two after we finish up with the experiment with the Styrofoam?"

Donovan made a big show but finally said, "Just give me the damn Styrofoam, and we will see what we have."

Donovan took the 3" triangle of Styrofoam in the plastic bag to the kitchen, with Ace tagging along behind. There was a clear beaker with a solution in it. Ace could smell the acetone in the air. Donovan put on a pair of neoprene gloves and, removed the triangle from the bag, and placed it in the beaker of acetone. It started to dissolve immediately. Donovan used what looked like a glass cocktail stirrer and the piece of foam vanished, the acetone looking just a bit cloudy but no worse for the wear.

Donovan sat back and asked if Ace wanted to go with him and run the samples in the lab this evening or did he want to wait until Donovan went in to work tomorrow? Ace asked if it was possible to do it this evening? At least it wouldn't interfere with his normal workload that way. Ace said he would drive, and after Donovan ran the tests, they could stop and have a beer or two.

Donovan gave Ace the name of his company, West Coast Industries, and Ace plugged it into his GPS. The company was only a couple of miles away, so there was no need to get onto San Diego's congested freeways. Ace took surface streets and arrived in about 10 minutes. Donovan led the way, swiped his badge at the entrance, and stopped at the empty front desk, reached under the counter and pulled out a "visitor log," which he signed and then asked Ace to do the same. There were cameras throughout the building and if Ace wasn't signed in, Donovan could get in trouble. Donovan also told Ace that due to the amount of chemicals in the building, they would both have to wear "bunny suits, safety glasses, and neoprene gloves." Donovan told Ace that he was to touch nothing. Just sit on the chair and let him run the tests. Ace was there strictly as an observer, nothing more.

Ace watched as Donovan expertly extracted solution from the beaker and placed samples in several tubes. The first order of business was to run them through a centrifuge to drive any solids to the bottom of the tube. Those solids would then be sampled. While the centrifuge was running, Donovan took another sample and put it into a contraption that Ace didn't recognize. Donovan explained that this was a device that would be used to distill the acetone and get anything out of it that was dissolved in the solution. Donovan started to explain the entire process and Ace just waved a hand at him and told him to do what it was that he needed to do. He didn't want to learn the basics of chemistry. Ace was never a fan of Chemistry. He recalled how poorly he did in high school chemistry and just chuckled to himself…of course, he did poorly. He didn't want to take the class, but his parents were insistent.

Donovan flitted around the lab, placing samples in several machines. As he started the experiment on the last machine, the centrifuge chimed that it was done, so Donovan started removing those samples for testing in the gas chromatograph. Ace didn't see any precipitate in the bottoms of the tubes and mentioned it to Donovan. Donovan agreed that it didn't appear that there were any undissolved solids, but he pipetted the material from the bottom of the tube just to run it in case the amounts were so small that you couldn't really see them.

In the next hour, samples were gathered and all placed in the gas chromatograph to be run. Donovan told Ace that it could take a while since they didn't really know what they were looking for, so he set the specifications to determine every chemical in the acetone. The list would be lengthy, but it would be a complete list. When those results were available, Donovan would look them over and determine what, if anything, was out of place.

About 20 minutes later, the device started spitting out a list of chemicals. Ace had no idea what they were. It was a long list. Donovan went down the list, one item at a time, placing check marks beside some and circling a couple.

He slid the list to Ace and said that everything with a check mark was to be expected in acetone and Styrofoam. However, there were a couple of items that didn't belong there. The first item that was circled was diacetylmorphine, and the next item circled was N-phenyl-N-[1-(2-phenylethyl)-4-piperidinyl] propenamide.

Ace just looked at Donovan with a baffled expression on his face. Donovan asked him if he knew what he was looking at? Ace told him again that chemistry wasn't his strong suit. Could he please just tell him what it was that he was looking at? Donovan took a deep breath and then said that he was looking at residual heroin and fentanyl, along with a host of other chemicals. Ace's guess about the Styrofoam was correct. It was impregnated with heroin and fentanyl, and they were dissolving it and then retrieving the drugs.

Donovan asked Ace where he had gotten the sample, and Ace told him that it was best that he didn't know. He also told Donovan to dispose of all the solution properly and, if contamination of the machines was possible, to make sure that they were cleaned properly. Ace even suggested that if there was a way to clear the computer of the tests that were run, he should do that. Donovan said that, unfortunately, there was no way to erase the system unless you knew how to hack it, but he didn't feel that there would be a problem because he would be in first thing in the morning and would be the only person running tests on the devices. It wasn't likely that anyone else would see the information. He was, after all, the chief chemist, so nobody would question him about his activities that evening.

Donovan reiterated that this was far from pure narcotics as it would be contaminated with a host of chemicals used in the manufacture of the foam insulation as well as the chemicals in the acetone. Ace asked him if the typical dealer or user would have any idea of the contamination, and Donovan said that it wasn't likely.

Ace asked Donovan to wrap things up here, and then they could go grab that beer that Ace owed him. Ace, again, told Donovan that nobody needed to know what they had found here that evening. He told Donovan that he couldn't stress it enough that this was part of an investigation, and if someone found out that Donovan was involved, it could put him in danger. Donovan assured Ace that he would be keeping his mouth shut. He didn't need anyone coming looking for him.

# Chapter 69

Ace went and met with Emilyia. She actually appeared happy to see him…until he told her that he was still looking into the death of her husband. She asked him why and he told her that he was basically pressured into ending the investigation early and there were some things that he had found that didn't sit right with him.

Ace asked her if he could trust her not to let the board at Humdinger Habitats know that he was still looking into things? She thought about it and asked him why he felt that he could trust her? Ace thought about lying to her and just telling her that he just found her trustworthy, but he figured she would see through that line of bullshit in about 5 seconds. He told her that he had been looking into everyone at the company, including her, in regard to their finances. Ace told her that she was the only person that didn't appear to have anything to hide. Even her accounts in the Grand Caymans were reported. If she was trying to hide something, such as a large income source that she didn't want reported, it wasn't likely that she would make all of her savings known to the IRS.

She laughed at that and said that, unlike her husband. She didn't want to hide anything from the Internal Revenue Service. She paid the taxes that were required of her and reported all sources of income to her and her daughter. She was now a "citizen" of the United States, but that didn't mean that she trusted the government enough that they couldn't revoke her citizenship if she crossed them.

Ace asked her if she was familiar with the company that Humdinger had purchased the containers from and she said that she was aware of who the company was and that the reason that Humdinger had switched wasn't necessarily a financial reason. Rumor had it that the CEO of the container company liked some of the same things that Ronald had liked. She had even heard that he would accompany Humdinger to Tijuana on occasion, whether to participate or watch; she didn't know, and she didn't want to know.

Ace had to decide how much he wanted to tell Emilyia. He didn't believe for one second that she was involved in the drug smuggling operation, and he truly didn't think that she knew anything about it. However, if they were dealing with a major "cartel," whether out of Central America or Asia, Ace didn't want to put her and her daughter at risk. If they knew what was going on, it was very possible that they would become targets as well.

After some thought, Ace told Emilyia that everything he was about to tell her needed to remain confidential for her and her daughter's safety. Ace told her everything that he knew. About the drugs, about how they were getting shipped into the country, how the drugs were being recovered at a farm outside of Camarillo, then how the container, sans insulation, was shipped to San Diego and Humdinger Habitats to be retrofitted as "tiny homes" for the homeless. He told her that he had no idea how the drugs were shipped out to the dealers after being extracted from the foam at the farm. Emilyia gave a light laugh and told Ace that she was sure that there was no shortage of people that would peddle the drugs. She said that she knew for a fact that many of those hired to work at Humdinger Habitats were convicted felons who had been in trouble for drug charges. She told him that Ronald actually searched out those types of people to work for him because he thought that it made him look good to provide jobs for former felons and various other criminals. Afterall, her husband was part of the "Law and Order" party, and anything that he could do that made it appear that he was helping those types of people made him look better to the country. At least in his mind, that was the way it worked. Most people who worked for the board of Humdinger Habitats didn't share his enthusiasm when it came to hiring ex-cons with drug convictions. Too many of them had family members that suffered from addiction. Unfortunately, many people in the United States found out that addiction didn't care what type of family that you came from.

Emilyia asked Ace if he could tell her the address of the ranch/farm where the containers were taken? Ace gave her the address and she typed it in on her phone. She looked at something online and then handed the phone to Ace. Ace was looking at tax records for the property. The property was owned by a "trust" named "Joaquin Enterprises". Ace took a deep breath. Could it really be? Joaquin Blaze was the illegitimate child or Starletta Blaze and Ronald Humdinger. Had Humdinger set up this operation to provide for Joaquin? Was it just a coincidence that it was name

Joaquin Enterprises?    Ace didn't believe in coincidences.

Emilyia asked Ace if he was OK?  He said he was, why?  She said that all of the color drained from his face when he read the name of the trust.  Ace said that he was just feeling a bit under the weather and thanked her for her concern.  He told her that he would need to be heading back to his apartment, but he reiterated to her that she couldn't say anything to anyone about his visit, or if someone became aware of his visit, she couldn't tell them what he was there about.

Emilyia said that her lips were sealed, and if anyone asked about him visiting her, she would tell them that he had come to ask her out on a date.  That would keep them quiet.  She looked him right in the eyes and said that his secret was safe with her, but she did want to know if he found anything out that might blow back on her since she was married to the man for years and years.  Ace acknowledged and told her that he would keep her informed.

# Chapter 70

Ace knew what he had to do. He had to go back to Tijuana, and he was going to have to poke around Starletta and Joaquin Blaze. He did not want to go back. There was truly nothing pleasant about the brothel, the donkey shows, and the illegitimate child that had to stay in the shadows whenever Humdinger or anyone who knew Humdinger visited.

Starletta and Ronald Humdinger's relationship went back for years and years. Was it possible that he had set this up as an appeasement to Starletta? Did he set it up out of guilt? Did he do it to just keep her and Joaquin quiet? Humdinger was a creep. He had always been a creep, so Ace was leaning towards some type of blackmail coming out of Tijuana.

Humdinger didn't have much empathy, so to think that he did it out of guilt was unlikely. Humdinger was much more likely to do something like this if he felt that if it came out, it could hurt him financially. He was always all about money. As a billionaire who inherited his start from his father, he hadn't been the greatest at making money in his younger years. He had to file bankruptcy on multiple occasions, but he always came out of it smelling like a rose. Hundreds, possibly thousands of people had lost their money that had invested in Humdinger's harebrained schemes, but Ronald always had a large bank account that seemed untouchable. While many of his friends and business partners lost their life savings, he continued to rake the money in.

Humdinger was also notorious as a businessman for working on a "you scratch my back, I'll scratch yours" type of system. If he did something for you, you owed him, and you didn't have the option of questioning what he wanted in return. If you refused, he would go on social media and tear you apart. He didn't care if it was true or not. He had so many crazy followers that if he called a person or a business out about something shady, it was typically a matter of days until that business or person was no longer a problem. Most often, people just dropped whatever their beef was with Humdinger. On occasion, they would take Ronald Humdinger to court, but Humdinger had bought and paid for so many judges that it was likely that going to court wouldn't help either. There would be some legal loopholes that were "found" that allowed Humdinger to get away with whatever the crime was.

The man had owned judges, lawyers, cops, and some other businessmen. It was an impossibility that he also was a part of a cartel of some sort.

Ace was concerned that he was going to unearth more skeletons in the Humdinger closet and it could hurt him as well. Ace had to make sure that he knew what was happening. There would be no guesswork. Things were going to get ugly. If Starletta was involved with the cartel, it was likely that the Tijuana police knew it. All or most of her employees also had to be aware.

Well, it was time to pack for a trip back to Tijuana. This time, Ace would not be going unarmed. He would know soon enough if he was barking up the wrong or the right tree.

# Chapter 71

The next morning arrived, and Ace was up and moving early. He wanted to be across the border by 7 AM. About an hour before, the traffic started to back up at the crossing. Ace had made reservations at the Holiday Inn Express and Suites near the airport. Ace was driving down but it would be nice to be near the airport if he had to leave via another mode of transportation. Of course, if he had to fly out, he wouldn't be able to take his handguns back although he was pretty sure that he could turn them over to Raul for safekeeping.

Ace still had Raul's business card, and he had contacted him the night before to inquire about hiring him as his driver for the next few days? Raul said that he would be delighted to be his driver if he was as generous with his pay as the last time he was in Tijuana. Ace told Raul that he didn't have to worry about that, but he did tell Raul that they were going to have to rent a car. Ace told Raul that he didn't want anyone to associate him with Ace in case Ace pissed some people off on this trip. Raul hem hawed about the rental because he didn't have a credit card to put the car on. Ace informed him that he would be renting the car, and Raul would just be on the list as a "driver," …that was, as long as Raul had a valid driver's license. Raul said that he most definitely had a current license.

Ace made it across the border in quick order and made the drive into Tijuana. He parked his car in the "long term" parking lot at the Tijuana airport and hopped the first shuttle that came by to the terminal where he talked with a rental agent about a car. Ace was very specific regarding the type of vehicle that he was looking for. As luck would have it, the rental company had exactly what he was looking for, minus one thing: deep window tint so that he couldn't be seen inside, as well as Raul. Ace showed his license and then the photo of Raul's driver's license and added him to the list of approved drivers then waited while they brought the rental car up. The car was a late model Infiniti Q50. The vehicle was almost identical in color to Ace's Impala, a dark gunmetal gray. Ace took that as a good sign. His favorite color of car was gunmetal gray for two reasons, they typically went unnoticed, and they didn't appear dirty, even when they were covered in dust. That wasn't anything that Ace had to worry about on this trip. He wasn't planning on having to wash the vehicle before he returned it to the rental agency.

Ace called Raul and told him that he would come and pick him up. They had a full day of surveillance to do. Raul gave Ace the address, and he put it in the GPS and headed out of the airport terminal. Ace made a mental note to clear the GPS before turning the vehicle back into the rental agency so that if anyone tracked him, they wouldn't be able to see where he went by viewing the GPS history.

# Chapter 72

Ace pulled up in front of the address provided by Raul and watched Raul kiss a woman on the cheek and head towards the car. Ace got out and went to the passenger side so that Raul could drive. Raul whistled as he got in. He said that it was a very nice car, much nicer than his own car. Ace said there was nothing wrong with his car but explained that he didn't want anything to come back to him if Ace upset some people on this trip to Tijuana.

Ace asked Raul to take him to the nearest window tinting company. Raul said that he had a cousin who did window tinting. Ace just chuckled and said, "of course you do". It really seemed that Ace had lucked out when he had hopped into Raul's cab so many days ago. Raul knew the city like the back of his hand, and he either knew or was related to everyone in town.

They arrived at the window tinting shop. Raul went in and talked to his "cousin." When he returned to the car, he told Ace that his cousin was able to squeeze him in right now, but it would cost an extra $50 because they didn't have an appointment. Ace agreed, and Raul pulled the car around to the back of the shop, where his cousin met them. He introduced himself to Ace and held out his hand. Ace looked at it and raised an eyebrow. Raul told Ace that he had to pay before the work was done. This wasn't like America, where you paid for things when the work was done. They wanted the money upfront because it wasn't an easy job to remove the tint if the customer decided that they didn't want to pay for it.

Raul talked with his cousin in Spanish, and after a couple of back-and-forth conversations, Raul turned to Ace and said that his cousin agreed to do the tinting for $250, but he didn't think that the rental company would be happy when he took it back with the windows being tinted. Ace told Raul to tell him that it was not his concern; that Ace would deal with the rental company when the time came to return the car.

Raul's cousin said to return in 2 hours, and the job would be done. Raul explained that they would just wait in the building while the work was done. Ace liked that they were going to be out of sight of any prying eyes for the next couple of hours. He wanted to think about what he was going to ask Starletta about, as well as having a conversation with Joaquin. Ace felt that he also needed to have another conversation with Lola as well.

# Chapter 73

The vehicle window tinting was completed, and Ace had to admit, it was a good job. Ace hopped in the front passenger seat, and Raul got behind the wheel, and they headed to Starletta Blaze's brothel.

As Ace entered the brothel, he walked directly to Starletta's office. The door was closed, so he knocked loudly. He heard curses coming from the room in both Spanish and English, and then the door was thrown open, and there stood Starletta Blaze in all her glory, flowery muumuu, and the stench of patchouli emanating from every pore of her body.

She looked Ace up and down and uttered a few derogatory remarks in Spanish, and then asked him what the fuck he was doing back in her brothel. She had been told that the investigation was over.

Ace asked her who had told her that he was done with the investigation. Starletta realized that she may have messed up and said that nobody had actually told her that it was over. She just assumed it was since she had heard that Ace had left the country and hadn't been back for a couple of weeks. Ace looked at her with a smirk on his face and said, "you know what happens when you assume, right?"

Starletta just looked at him and gave him the finger.

Ace said since it appeared that she was through being nice to him, that he just wanted to talk to her about a couple of things that had come up during his investigation. She told him that he would have to pay her for her time. She was done dealing with "gringos" that thought they could get what they wanted from her for free. Ace asked her how much, and she told him her rate was $500/hour. Ace told her that it was steep since he wasn't getting anything but information. She just held out her hand and said, "Cash only," or I am going back into my office and closing the door. Ace reached for his wallet and took out five crisp $100 bills, counted them off, and placed them in her sweaty hand. Ace couldn't be certain, but he thought he noticed a tremor in her hand. Was she really this upset that he was here? She was getting $500 whether she told him anything or not. Why would she be nervous? He followed her into her office and closed the door as she motioned him to a chair across the desk from her. She took some papers that were lying on top of her desk and, gathered them up, and put them in a drawer. Then she sat back, crossed her arms, and just stared at him. After about 20 seconds, she said, "times a wasting. In 59 minutes, you will owe me another $500 if we aren't done.

Ace took a deep breath and started. His first question was about her pregnancy and Joaquin. She turned purple, she was so angry. She told him that there was nothing more that he needed to know. Ronald Humdinger was an easy source of money. She happened to get pregnant by him and nine months later, Joaquin was born. She and Ronald had talked about the fact that he had a son with her, and Ronald said that nobody could know about this. If the information got out, it could ruin his political chances, and they had arrived at a dollar amount that he would have to continue to pay to keep the information private. Starletta said that she knew that it was essentially "blackmail" that she was demanding money for his silence, but he had plenty of money and he also had his dignity. She didn't pretend that he would be proud if the information got out that he had been sleeping with a hooker in Tijuana and had been stupid enough to get her pregnant. He had even asked her about ending the pregnancy, but she told him that wasn't an option. As a Catholic, she would never, ever end a pregnancy. It was a sure-fire ticket to Hell if she did that. Humdinger had tried to pressure her into it, but she would not relent. He finally just gave up on that option and started sending her money on a monthly basis, even prior to the birth of the baby.

When their son was born, she had a bit of hope that Ronald would be so happy to have a son that he would become a part of the boy's life. That wasn't to be. Whenever Ronald came to visit, she literally had to lock the boy in a closet so that he would not have to see him. When he got older, she just told him to stay in his room until she told him that it was ok for him to come out.

Starletta said that it hurt her so much that Ronald wouldn't even acknowledge the boy when he was in town. She wasn't deluding herself into thinking that he would ever be a real part of Joaquin's life, but it would be nice if he would just acknowledge his existence and treat him like a human being. It wasn't that Ronald treated him poorly. Ronald just pretended that he didn't exist. When Starletta took over the brothel, and Ronald had tired of her and moved on to

Lola, she wasn't really disappointed. When he was elected to political office, she was ecstatic. She assumed that she wouldn't ever have to see Ronald again. She thought that it would be too problematic for him to visit with the Secret Service in tow. The first time that he called and made an appointment at the brothel to visit with Lola after he became the "prominent" politician, Starletta couldn't believe it. She asked him what he was going to do about his security. He told her not to worry about it that they would be right outside the door. She started to complain to him about that and how bad it would look with American "police officers" standing in the hallways of her brothel, and he told her to just shut her fat trap. He paid her and he paid her a lot of money for her bastard son as well as the amount of money that he spent when he visited. He didn't give a shit if every customer in the place left when he visited. He said that he actually preferred it that way. He told her that was the way it was going to be from the second visit forward. He would visit, and she would dismiss all the girls and close the brothel. Lola would be available, and he would pay her what the tab would be for all the business that was being missed by sending the ladies home, and he didn't care if he shared the money with the hookers or not. He told her that he didn't want to hear another word about it.

Ace asked her how the Tijuana police reacted when he came to visit the brothel. She looked at him for a second, then said that the Chief of Police was known to accept bribes from people with a lot of money. Obviously, Ronald Humdinger was a person with a lot of money. Reuben Cuchillas met with Ronald on his first visit to the brothel after being made Chief detective. Starletta said that there was talk of money needed for the "special detail" that the police would have to put in place when Humdinger visited the brothel, and Cuchillas told Humdinger that anytime he was coming to the brothel, he needed to notify him. There was no need for Ronald to contact Starletta; Reuben said that he would take care of notifying her and making sure that the area was secure prior to his arrival with his Secret Service. Reuben also told Ronald that he expected a briefcase containing $10,000 every time he came to visit, or it could be very bad for him. Starletta said that Ronald nearly had a stroke, and he threatened Cuchillas, exclaiming that he wouldn't be blackmailed. Cuchillas said that it wasn't blackmail; it was a business transaction for his security, nothing more, but everyone knew how dangerous Tijuana could be, so there might need to be money changing hands to appease the cartel members in the area. After a bit of haggling, Humdinger acquiesced and accepted the $10,000 payment per visit. Of course, Humdinger told Cuchillas that no word of this could ever get out, and Cuchillas reassured him that as long as the money kept flowing, there would be no leak.

Interestingly, Ace didn't know anything about the payments to Cuchillas, although there had always been an assumption that some money had changed hands in the past. Ace had no idea that there were such large sums of money changing hands, but the fact that there was no record of the payments coming from Humdinger Habitats and the transactions appeared to be cash, it was most likely some type of money laundering scheme. The "drug dealing" was making more and more sense at this point.

Ace looked at his watch and saw that he had about 10 minutes left before he was going to give Starletta another $500, and he didn't want to do that, so he decided to hurry and wrap this end up.

He asked Starletta if Joaquin had any idea who his father was. Starletta looked down at her desk, and when she looked up, she actually had tears in her eyes. She told Ace that Joaquin absolutely knew who his father was. She said that it hurt her so much that Ronald never acknowledged the boy, and as Joaquin had got older, she told him who his father was and why he couldn't see or meet him. The anguish that she showed while talking about this was visible. Ace was pretty sure that if he asked her if she was glad that Humdinger was dead, she would tell him that it was a blessing to her and to her son…although she was surprised that the money kept coming in even after Humdinger had died. She had assumed that the money would cease the day that he kicked the bucket in her brothel. Joaquin knew that his father was dead and that Ronald Humdinger hadn't wanted him, so Joaquin was unfazed when his mother told him that he had died.

Ace looked at his watch and said to Starletta. It looks like I have a little time to spare. She told him that there would be no "credit" for him leaving early. He looked at her and told her that he never figured that there would be. Ace got up and turned to leave. As he was leaving, Starletta yelled that she hoped to never see him again. Ace turned and told her that he hoped to never have to bother her about this again, but he couldn't guarantee it because he still wanted to talk with Lola before he headed back across the border.

Starletta told Ace that he could probably still find Lola at home because she wasn't scheduled for the day. Ace tipped his hat and headed out the door.

# Chapter 74

Ace hopped in the car and gave Raul the address for Lola Aspera-Amor's home. Ace hoped she was home. He just had a feeling that Starletta and Lola knew more than they were saying. He had just got some information from Starletta, and she didn't even know that she had given him anything. The money for Cuchillas wasn't in the books and it had to be coming from somewhere or someone. Ten-thousand dollars every time that Humdinger came to town wasn't a drop in the bucket. Ace just knew that the money had to be coming from the illegal drug operation in Camarillo. He just needed to figure out how and who was involved.

They arrived at Lola's, and Raul pulled his cap down and told Ace that he would see him in a bit. He was going to take his afternoon siesta. Ace shook his head. He truly envied people who had the ability to sleep anywhere and anytime. Raul was obviously one of those people.

Ace rang the old-fashioned bell on Lola's door. He heard movement inside, but nobody came to the door, so Ace rang the bell again. This time, Ace heard a call from inside to espera un minuto, which Ace took to mean be there in a minute. The door swung open and there was Lola, only this time she wasn't wearing normal street clothing. She was wearing a black leather bustier and black leather hotpants with black fishnet stockings and stiletto heels. Even with the 4-inch heels, she was still barely waist-high to Ace. Her face lit up in a big smile, and she greeted him as "Senor Bancroft." She then asked him if her "sub" was expecting him? He asked, "pardon me?"

Lola then said that she was with a client and the client hadn't said that she was expecting anyone else that would be joining them. Lola had a very firm rule that when she was being assisted or was dominating more than one "sub" at a time, she needed to be made aware prior to the appointment. Typically, she would end her session if something like this happened, but she would be willing to make an exception if Ace was going to be joining them.

Ace assured Lola that he wasn't there to join in the fun. He was trying to wrap up his investigation and he had a couple of questions yet. He didn't think that he would be interrupting her day since she wasn't working at the brothel. Lola reminded him that she did some of her BDSM work on her own; not all her services went through the brothel.

Ace asked when it would be a good time to sit and chat with her. She said that now would work; she would just have to go back into her chamber and place the "ball gag" back in her "subs" mouth and let them know that she would be along shortly, maybe give them a quick swipe with her crop and tell her to behave while she was gone. Ace said that was ok, that he didn't want to intrude. Lola assured him that he wasn't intruding at all. She was sure that her subject would be more than happy to wait. Sometimes the anticipation is a real aphrodisiac for her "subs."

She ushered Ace into her living room and motioned toward a chair, then she excused herself and went to the back of the building. Ace heard some talking and then a sharp smack and a squeal that certainly didn't sound like the person was in pain, although it was obvious that it was a woman with Lola, not a man.

Lola flitted into the living room and had a seat herself. So, what can I do for you, she asked?

Ace was a bit uncomfortable thinking that there was a woman restrained at the back of the building and he was sitting here chatting with Lola, but she had said that the anticipation was an aphrodisiac for some people, so he got right to it.

He chatted with Lola about how they met...again...and then asked her if she had ever been involved with the local police or the Secret Service when "Slave Ronald" came to visit. Lola said that she always made it a point to chat with the Secret Service agents that accompanied Humdinger. Lola also said that she always made it a point to converse with the local policeman who came and cleared out the brothel when Humdinger was coming to the brothel. Ace asked her if she knew the name of the police officer. He wasn't surprised when she said that his last name was Cuchillas. She never knew his first name but knew that it started with an R. because it was on his identification that he flashed around when he cleared out the brothel. Lola said that he always made it a big deal to show her his ID when he came in, even though he knew that she was the person that Ronald was coming to see. Afterall, she was the only "dwarf dominatrix" working at the brothel, so who else would Humdinger see other than Madam Starletta?

Ace asked her if Ronald saw Starletta on a regular basis when he came to Tijuana. Lola said that Ronald always spent at least half an hour with her prior to Ronald coming to her chamber. Ace asked her why Ronald would be with her, and Lola shrugged and said she had no idea. It wasn't for her to question the Madam of the brothel if she wanted to keep her job.

Ace asked Lola if she was aware of Starletta's son Joaquin? Lola said, "Of course, why wouldn't I be aware of Joaquin?" Ace explained that he had been told that Joaquin wasn't allowed to be seen when Humdinger came to town. Lola laughed a light titter and said that it may be true when Ronald was in town, but Joaquin was a regular at the brothel every other day of the week. His mother used him to help clean and do maintenance at the brothel on a very regular basis. She said that when Starletta wasn't watching, all Joaquin did was lean on his broom and ogle the working girls. He was a teenage boy after all, so he is going to look at pretty girls that are scantily clad in see-thru lingerie that left little to the imagination.

Ace asked Lola if she had ever received "extra" pay for an extremely satisfying session with Ronald, and she said that hadn't happened, although Ronald would send her "gifts" occasionally, such as the artwork that he noticed on his last visit to her home. She preferred "gifts" instead of cash, and Ronald knew that.

Ace asked her if she had ever witnessed Ronald using any illicit drugs? She said that she had not. However, she had observed him taking a double dose of his "boner pills" because he was always afraid of disappointing his mistress by not being able to maintain an erection. She said that she had told him several times that it wasn't good to take too many of those pills because of the side effects. He told her that he would take the risk to make sure that she was satisfied. With that comment, she rolled her eyes and laughed and said that she had never been "satisfied" when Ronald left but he didn't know that. It was part of her job to make the submissive believe that the Mistress was so happy with them and how they had controlled themselves.

Ace asked if she wasn't "satisfied" because Humdinger couldn't control himself? She said that wasn't it. She had yet to find a "submissive male" that satisfied her. She preferred submissive women, but money was money, so she would take it from whoever wanted to pay her, whether they were male or female.

Lola looked at the clock on the wall and asked if there was anything else, as she really did need to get back to her client. Ace told her that was all he wanted to know for now, but he would call if he had any other questions that came up. Ace thanked Lola and told her that he would see himself out.

As Ace was walking to the SUV, he was disappointed to see that there was a Tijuana Police SUV parked behind his SUV. As he approached, the door of the cruiser opened, and out stepped one of the scruffy police officers that Ace had seen on his last visit to the station. The man sauntered up to Ace and told him that Chief Cuchillas wanted to see him back at the station.  Ace told the man that he would stop by later. He looked Ace up and down and said, "You misunderstand. This isn't a request. I am to take you to see him right now." Ace wasn't going to give in to this lackey and ride in the cruiser with him.  He looked straight at him and told him that he could follow his SUV to the station, but he would not be riding in the back of his smelly cruiser unless, of course, Cuchillas wanted a national incident on his hands by arresting him.  If that was the case, then he would make a call to the embassy, and he could talk with a representative from the US federal government, or he could just wait and talk to Ace when he made it to the station.  With that, Ace turned on his heel and, hopped in the passenger seat and told Raul to drive.

Raul pulled away from the curb and asked where to go.  Ace said that it didn't matter; just drive and see if the cop was going to follow him or not.  The cruiser sat firmly at the curb as they turned the corner.  It appeared that the cruiser wasn't going to follow him. Ace was sure that the police officer had notified Cuchillas as to what was said.  Ace was sure that Cuchillas would not want an international incident.

Ace told Raul to go back to Lola's house.  He just remembered something else that he wanted to ask her. Raul said Ok turned at the next corner, and started weaving his way back to Lola's.  When he got there, the police cruiser was no longer parked there.

Ace got out of the car and knocked at Lola's door again.  He heard nothing, so he knocked louder.  When there was still no answer, Ace opened the door and yelled for Lola, but he could barely hear himself yell as the thrash metal music coming from the rear of the building was so loud. Ace marveled at how soundproof Lola's building was. He hadn't heard the music outside when the door was closed at all.

Ace made his way back to the "chamber," calling Lola's name the entire way back. He didn't want to get shot by her because she thought that there was an intruder in her home. When he got to the rear of the apartment and the closed door at the end of the hallway, Ace put his ear close to the door, but all he could hear was music. He opened the door slowly for two reasons, the first being that he didn't really know what he would see when he opened the door, and he wanted to prepare his brain for it. The second came back to Lola taking a shot at him or hitting him with something because she didn't know who was in her house.

As the door creaked open, the first thing Ace noticed was the St. Andrew's Cross with a naked woman strapped to it with a leather mask over her face and a ball gag in her mouth. Ace shouted again for Lola, but she didn't appear to be anywhere in the room, so he turned to search and damn near ran her over. She was standing behind him with a whip of some sort and a glazed look in her eyes. He asked her if she was ok? She said that she was fine, but she had to go freshen up before resuming her dominance over her subject. He said he had just one more question that he had thought of after he left, and could she answer it for him very quickly? She sighed and said to make it quick as she really wanted to get back to her "sub." Ace was positive that she was high on something.

Ace asked her if Ronald had ever mentioned Joaquin Enterprises or a ranch outside of Camarillo? Lola thought for a minute and then said that he hadn't ever mentioned it, but she said that a courier came to make a delivery to her on one occasion, and his truck had a label on the side that had J.E. Ranch on it. She didn't know what J.E. stood for, but it would make sense that it stood for Joaquin Enterprises. Ace asked her what kind of delivery that they had brought her, and she said that it was the antique chair in her sitting room that he had sat in. From what she understood from Ronald, it was a very rare antique chair that was worth a lot of money, and he wanted her to have it.

Ace turned to leave but then stopped mid-stride and asked Lola if she knew any of Ronald's company employees? She waived her finger at him and said, "I protect my client's information at all times. I will not tell you which men or women associated with "Slave Ronald" that I have met for my pleasure or theirs. That is not the information that I am willing to provide." With that, Lola told Ace to show himself out, and to lock the door this time when he left. She turned on her stiletto heels and went into the chamber.

As Ace was leaving, he heard the crack of a whip and a whimper that was either pleasure or pain. He wasn't sure…if he had to guess, he would have to say that it sounded like a pleasureful whimper, but he didn't know for certain.

# Chapter 75

Ace hopped back in the SUV and told Raul to head to the County Coroner's office and the morgue. He would meet with the chief medical examiner if he was available and then walk next door to the police station to see what Cuchillas wanted with him.

Ace entered the building where the coroner and the morgue were housed and asked to see Dr. Bravo. The clerk eyed him up and down and asked if he had an appointment. Ace told him that he did not however, if he would relay to Dr. Bravo that Ace Bancroft was there to see him and he didn't have a problem meeting while he worked, he would appreciate it. The clerk got up and entered a door to the morgue. A few minutes later, he returned and ushered Ace through the door to the back and escorted him to an autopsy table where Dr. Bravo was elbow-deep in the chest of a Hispanic male. At least Ace assumed he was Hispanic, based on his skin tone...unfortunately, the poor man's head was missing.

Dr. Bravo looked up at Ace and asked him what he could do for him. Ace looked at him and said that he could save him the trouble of determining what the man died from. It was obvious that his head was missing. Dr. Bravo gave a light laugh and asked Ace if he thought that he was funny. Ace said that he wasn't trying to be funny. It was just that the man's head wasn't there, so wouldn't it be easy to just list the cause of death as "decapitation" and move on?

Dr. Bravo told Ace that was the problem. Too many people would do just what Ace suggested but Dr. Bravo said that wasn't the way that he worked. He did a thorough exam even if the cause of death was simple to identify, such as being decapitated. However, Dr. Bravo said that this man's head had been removed after he was dead. Why? He had no idea because it appeared that the man had bled out from a perforated ulcer. His abdomen was full of blood when he did the post-mortem. Had he been alive when he was decapitated, blood would've sprayed out of him like a geyser. This man's blood had already coagulated in his gut, so there was very little blood around the wounds to the neck, which Dr. Bravo took great pleasure in showing to Ace. He then showed Ace, the man's arms, and they were covered with 'track marks" from IV drug abuse, which was not really a common occurrence in the local population. Dr. Bravo said that he was certain that this man had made his way to Mexico through Central America or possibly even the Caribbean. Dr. Bravo said that they had not identified this man yet and it wasn't likely that they would. He would end up being cremated and placed in the mass grave at the local cemetery where most of the homeless and unidentified ended up.

Dr. Bravo stripped off his gloves and went to the sink to wash his hands. He said to Ace, that's enough on this poor man. I'm sure he isn't why you are here to talk with me.

Ace just blurted out the question. Was Dr. Bravo aware of Joaquin Blaze and his relationship to Ronald Humdinger? Dr. Bravo looked at him and said that he most certainly knew who Joaquin Blaze was, but he didn't know anything about his relationship to Ronald Humdinger. Ace said, "Come now, Doctor. Everyone in town must know that Joaquin is the son of Ronald Humdinger." Dr. Bravo said that he didn't care if Joaquin was the son of Ronald Humdinger or the son of Prince Harry who his relatives were, made no difference to him. He had run into the boy in town on occasion. He was always very polite and respectful, something that was hard to find these days. Why was Ace here asking about Joaquin? He couldn't think that Joaquin had anything to do with the death of Ronald Humdinger. To think that would be ludicrous, the doctor said.

Ace said that was enough about Joaquin for now, but he wanted to know if Dr. Bravo had ever heard of Joaquin Enterprises from Camarillo, California? Dr. Bravo thought for a moment and said that he had a man come through his office, obviously deceased, and he was wearing a shirt from JE Ranch in Camarillo, California. That was the only place that he had ever heard of, and he only remembered it because he thought that Camarillo sounded like a nice place, and he thought that he might go there for a visit someday as it wasn't that far north of the border so it could be visited as a day trip, or maybe a long weekend.

Ace asked him if he could look the man up and tell him a name or what he had died from. The doctor said that he was one of the many unidentified bodies that appeared in and around Tijuana. As far as the doctor could remember, the cause of death appeared to be some type of poisoning. He could find more information if Ace could wait to get the information, as the doctor would have to go through his files and try to locate it. He didn't recall the exact date that the body had appeared on his table, just the JE Ranch shirt. Ace asked him why he thought that it was poison that had killed the man. He said that it appeared that the man was an addict and had maybe gotten some bad drugs because he had bled out like he had injected rat poison. At that comment, the doctor stood up and looked over at the table of the man that he had just been doing the autopsy on and said, you know, this man may have died the same way. I need to do a tox screen to see if there are any poisons present.

Ace told the doctor he only had one more question. Did he think that Ronald Humdinger had taken any illicit drugs prior to his death. Dr. Bravo said that his tox screen was negative for illegal drugs. However, it did appear that he had taken a large dose of sildenafil, but Ace already knew that because he had seen his report when he had been here a few weeks ago. Ace asked him if the sildenafil could've assisted in his death. The doctor thought for a minute and said that it was possible but not likely unless Humdinger was taking much more than he was supposed to take and taking them more often than he should. He said that too much could depress Humdinger's breathing, and he would just drift off if he took too much, but since he had been having sex, it wasn't likely that his breathing had been depressed.

Ace asked him if Humdinger, having been tied to a cross, arms above his head, a leather mask on, and had a ball gag in his mouth if that would interfere with his breathing. Dr. Bravo said that it obviously would, but he hadn't been given any information like that when he performed the autopsy on Humdinger. He was told that he collapsed at the brothel while being attended to by a prostitute. He just assumed that he was having sex when he collapsed due to his underlying heart condition as well as living the slovenly lifestyle, which included eating food that was horrible for him, leading to clogged and hardening of the arteries, weighing almost 300 pounds hadn't helped him either. Ultimately, Dr. Bravo reiterated his findings. The reason Humdinger had died was due to natural causes. Although there may've been some underlying circumstances that hastened his death, it was still death by natural causes.

Ace thanked the doctor for the additional information and asked if it would be ok to get back in touch with him if he had any further questions. Dr. Bravo said that would be just fine as Ace showed himself out of the autopsy room.

# Chapter 76

Ace left the Coroner's office and made the short walk around the building to the Police Department. As he walked past the SUV, he gave Raul a quick wave and told him that he should be back in a few minutes. If he wasn't out in an hour, he needed to go to the U.S. Embassy and tell them that Ace was being held illegally. Raul nodded his understanding, and Ace proceeded to the entrance.

As Ace entered the station, he took one last look around to see if anyone appeared to be following him. He walked up to the desk and told the clerk that he was there to see Reuben Cuchillas. The clerk didn't even look up. He just asked if he had an appointment. Ace had had enough of the bullshit, and it was obvious by the tone of his voice when he told the clerk that Cuchillas had sent a man to collect him and bring him back, and Ace had refused, "so enough of the bullshit, go tell Cuchillas that I'm here or I am walking out that door and he won't see me again unless I have the press from CNN in tow, and he would just show them how corrupt the police in Tijuana were!"

The threat seemed to work. The desk clerk got up from his stool and slunk into the back. A few minutes later, he returned and motioned Ace to a door beside the desk and told Ace that he could go back to Cuchillas office.

Ace strode to the door, waited for it to buzz open, and he entered the dimly lit staff room. He saw Cuchillas standing at his doorway, and Ace made a beeline for his door.  Ace walked into his office and Cuchillas shut his door and motioned for Ace to have a seat.

Cuchillas walked around his desk and had a seat.  He had a stupid-looking smile on his face as he asked what brought Ace back to his lovely community?  Ace didn't take the bait.  He just looked at Reuben Cuchillas and asked him what he wanted with him.  Obviously, it must be important if his name is being flagged at the border when he crossed into the country.  After all, that would be the only way that Cuchillas knew that he was in the country.  He also must've put his name out at the rental companies because he couldn't have known that Ace was going to rent a car ahead of time.

Cuchillas still had the slimy smile on his face.  He looked straight at Ace and told him that it was very common to alert the border for individuals who could disrupt the way of life in Tijuana.  He told Ace that he must've done something while he was here on his last visit that made the "Federales" uncomfortable.  A lowly police chief didn't have the kind of power to put a U.S. citizen on what constituted a "watch list."  That was something that the Mexican federal government controlled.  Ace told him that he could smell bullshit from miles away, and he was getting a really strong smell of it right now.  Ace told him that he knew if enough money was provided to someone at the border, they would slip a name onto the list just as easily as they would take a name off the list if enough money changed hands.  Ace then told him to get on with it.  He knew he was there for something; he just didn't know what it was yet, and he really needed to get moving if Cuchillas just wanted to see his shining face.

Cuchillas leaned back, steepling his fingers in front of him, took a deep breath, and said, "I get the impression that you don't like me, Mr. Bancroft. I don't understand why. I am a very likable man. Just ask your employers at Humdinger Habitats. They always enjoyed my assistance when their "dear leader" made his trips south of the border."

Ace asked him what he meant by "assistance?" As far as Ace was concerned, the people at Humdinger Habitats didn't have any need to even know when Ronald Humdinger was making a trip across the border. That was information that was handled by the Secret Service, not that Security at Humdinger Habitats and he told Cuchillas as much.

Cuchillas just gave a short laugh and said that it was true that the Secret Service worked with the Federal government of Mexico, but the Federal government of Mexico tasked the local authorities with ensuring that Humdinger was safe while he was visiting Tijuana. Cuchillas saw to it personally. He worked closely with the Secret Service, Humdinger Habitats internal security people, and the Mexican cartels, which all did business with Humdinger in one way or another.

Ace asked him what type of business Humdinger Habitats would have with the cartels in Tijuana. Cuchillas raised an eyebrow and asked him who he thought it was that ran the brothel that Humdinger frequented. He laughed and said, "You don't really think that whore Starletta Blaze could manage her business on her own, do you?" Ace said that from what he understood, there was a time when Humdinger had propped up her business with some extra cash until she got on her feet and no longer needed him. Then he moved on to a new prostitute in the building, and Starletta continued to run the business. Ace said that from what he could tell, it appeared that she was pretty successful, considering what she did for a living years ago, and now she was running the business.

Cuchillas just chuckled and shook his head. He muttered almost unheard by Ace, "Stupid Americans." Ace did hear him, though, and asked him what made him a "stupid American." Cuchillas asked Ace if he really thought that a hooker was smart enough to run a business like a brothel. All her business was, was a place for the Cartels and any other business that chose to use it as a place to launder their dirty money. Ace asked him why he was telling him this? Obviously, Cuchillas telling Ace that the cartel and Humdinger Habitats were laundering money through the brothel would put him at risk. Cuchillas laughed again and said it wasn't a risk to him. He told Ace that he needed to retreat to the other side of the border or risk becoming a streetcorner display hanging from a streetlight in the middle of an intersection if he was lucky. If he was unlucky, they might never find a trace of him again if he didn't drop this foolishness and just go live his life. Cuchillas said, consider this your last warning. You do not want to investigate this any further. If you do, something bad could happen to your friend Raul and his family members. Did Ace really want to bring harm to these people?  If Ace truly didn't care about them, then by all means, keep nosing around things that no longer concern you.  Unfortunately, Ace could expect a call from Raul's wife that he was missing in the next 24 hours if Ace didn't stop.  Ace asked him if he was giving him 24 hours or if he was telling him to leave now?  Cuchillas said that he would leave now if he were Ace, but he didn't think that any harm would befall Ace or anyone else connected with the investigation if Ace was out of the country by noon the next day.  Ace looked at Cuchillas and told him that he would take it under advisement.  He also said that no harm was to come to Raul or his family if Cuchillas knew what was good for him.

As Cuchillas spit and sputtered, trying to form a response, Ace rose and left the office without a look back.  He was going to return to the car and have Raul go back to his home.  He didn't want any harm to come to him or his family just because Ace had hired him as a driver.  Unfortunately, Ace knew that it was not beyond the realm of possibility that Raul would be murdered because he had "helped" the American investigator.

# Chapter 77

Raul wasn't happy that Ace had him go home. He told Ace that he wasn't afraid of Cuchillas or the cartels in the area. He had done nothing wrong by driving an American around, and he wasn't afraid. Ace told Raul that he didn't doubt his "machismo" at all, but now wasn't the time to push his luck. Ace told Raul that he wouldn't ever be able to forgive himself if something were to happen to Raul or his family. Ace handed Raul $1,000 cash and thanked Raul for his services. He also told Raul that he and his immediate family might be approached by someone from the U.S. Consulate in the next few days. If they were approached, they would have to make a decision, and not an easy decision.

Raul said that there was no decision to be made. He would live here in Mexico until he took his last breath on this Earth, then he would be off to meet his maker, and he would do it with no regrets.

Ace left Raul and went to the consulate and asked to meet with the Consul General. The Marine at the desk said that it wasn't normal to just walk in and request a meeting with the Consul General. There was a certain protocol that needed to be followed to meet with a sitting Consul General. Ace listened to everything that the Marine had to say, then said to the Marine that if he would just let him know that a former FBI agent was asking to meet with him, that he was there to ask a personal favor and, he could verify who he was by giving the FBI a call, he was sure that they would verify his identity. The Marine told Ace to go have a seat and he would make some calls.

Ace went and sat within sight of the desk and waited. After about twenty minutes, the Marine called "Agent Bancroft". Ace rose and approached the desk, and said that he was no longer an agent with the FBI. The Marine just smiled and said that as he understood it, the FBI was a lot like the Marines: once an agent, always an agent, once a Marine, always a Marine. The Marine said that the Consul General could give him ten minutes but that then he was off to another meeting. At that, the Marine came around the desk and instructed Ace to follow him. After a short walk, the Marine knocked on a door and opened it for Ace to enter. Ace walked in, and the Marine closed the door behind him. Ace heard the lock click in place as the door closed. Obviously, security was of utmost importance here in Tijuana. That was a good thing in this part of the world. The Consul General of the Tijuana office, Thomas Rhett, a career member of the Senior Foreign Service, arose and reached across his desk and gave Ace's hand a nice firm handshake, then motioned towards a chair and told Ace to have a seat.

Ace sat and said that he wouldn't beat around the bush, that he understood that he was a very busy man and that he had just a few minutes before he needed to head to another meeting. Rhett raised an eyebrow and said that Ace's seniors said that he was a no-nonsense agent and was basically the same in his personal life, so he motioned him to proceed but not to worry about the time. The next meeting wasn't a matter of huge importance, more of a "fluff" meeting with some

323

locals regarding new business here in the area. A meet and greet with handshaking and polite conversations.

Ace thanked him and proceeded to tell his story from beginning to end. Rhett sat back and said that he wouldn't be at all surprised to find out that Humdinger and the cartel were working hand in hand, but he didn't know what this information had to do with the consulate here in Tijuana. Ace then explained the threats that he had been given in regard to Raul and his family. Ace asked if there was any way that there could be a man or two put on extra security for the next few days just to keep an eye on them. He didn't think that there would be any problems as Ace had relieved Raul of his duties and explained to him why. Rhett picked up a phone and asked the Marine that Ace had spoken with to come back to his office.

The Marine, a gunnery sergeant with Hartmann on his name tag, knocked and entered, then stood at attention on the same side of the desk as Ace. Thomas Rhett said, relax "Gunny" have a seat. The sergeant looked at Ace, raised an eyebrow, and had a seat. Rhett asked Ace to explain the situation with Raul and his family to Sergeant Hartmann. Hartmann listened to the story, asked where Raul lived, and asked what he would like. Ace said just a couple of guys to keep an eye on the family for the next few days until Ace was north of the border again. He didn't think that there would be any problems, but he didn't want Raul or his family hurt. Ace said that he would be more than happy to hire these men privately and pay them a significant fee to make sure everyone was ok.

Sergeant Hartmann said that payment wasn't necessary, as Raul had been assisting some people in the Consulate for some time. He wouldn't be harmed; he was sure of it. He then asked Ace if he thought that Raul had been a chance meeting when Ace entered the country weeks ago. Ace said he had thought that it was. The Consul general said that it had been set up from the beginning. Anytime a person of some importance in the US government entered the country, they were notified. While Ace was no longer an FBI agent, he could still be a valuable target to the local cartel, and he was watched while he was in the country. The US didn't want an international incident with the cartel and a former FBI agent who was investigating the death of a former politician. Even if the politician wasn't highly respected within the international community or the US government, he was still a former politician who had access to a ton of information, as did Ace.

Rhett and Hartmann assured Ace again that Raul and his family would be just fine. Rhett dismissed Hartmann and then turned to Ace and asked him what he planned to do while he was still in Mexico. Ace told him that he wanted to meet with Lola Aspera-Amor again and ask her a couple more questions, and he might also want to meet with Joaquin and Starletta Blaze before heading north across the border. Rhett handed him a card and told him that it was a direct number to Security here at the consulate, and all he needed to do was call and give them his name and where he needed assistance, and help would be dispatched to that location.

Ace thanked the Consul General for everything and said that he would get moving. He was going to his hotel and call it a day, then he would get a fresh start in the morning. Hopefully winding everything up by the end of the day tomorrow and he would head back to San Diego.

Thomas Rhett told him to be safe, shook his hand and, escorted Ace to the door, clapped him on the shoulder and told him to watch his back.

# Chapter 78

Ace was up bright and early the next morning. He went to the hotel lobby and grabbed a couple of donuts from the "continental breakfast," as well as a large cup of black coffee. Ace noted that it poured like tar when he used the carafe. Ace didn't care at this point. He wanted to be alert. A jolt of caffeine and sugar would definitely help with that. Apparently, he was no longer welcome in Tijuana and even though the Chief told him he had 24 hours, Ace didn't feel that he could rest on his laurels regarding his personal safety. He was now carrying two weapons, his S&W 9MM as well as his model 1911 .45. If he got into a gunfight with the cartel, he wasn't going out easily, that was for sure. He guaranteed he would be leaving some big-ass holes in some people. Ace kept up his marksmanship skills. He was just as good a shot as he was the day that he left the FBI. That was a skill that he always planned on maintaining. He hoped someday that it wouldn't be necessary to worry about being shot, but as an FBI agent and now a private investigator, it was always a possibility.

Ace's first stop was going to be Lola's. He wanted to talk with her about the insinuations that there was a cartel connection. He hoped that Lola wasn't in that deep. He didn't necessarily agree with her way of life, but Ace knew that anyone who worked for the cartel always had a threat of death over their heads. There were expectations to meet, whether it was the amount of money that you brought in, the amount of drugs that you sold, the people that you smuggled across the border, etc. Ace didn't want to see any harm come to the dwarf. While she wasn't his cup of tea, she actually seemed like a very nice person. He didn't think that she would truly hurt anyone. Ace knew what the cartel would do to her if she crossed them, though. He hoped that Cuchillas was full of shit and was just trying to intimidate him to get him out of Tijuana.

As Ace pulled up in front of Lola's house, he couldn't help but notice that Heroes by Peter Gabriel was playing on his satellite radio. While Ace didn't dwell on superstitions, he thought that this was a fitting song. He hoped that he would be a "hero" when this was all over with…a live hero, not a dead hero. He needed to get this investigation over with. He knew that he could just walk away from it. It really wasn't his concern now that he had given Misuse his final report, but Ace just didn't feel right about leaving the investigation incomplete. That was not the way that he worked.

Ace knocked at Lola's door and waited. After a minute or two, the door swung open, and there stood Lola in all her glory, sweatpants, and a baggy t-shirt, no makeup, and certainly no sign of her "dominatrix" outfit.

She gushed out, "Mister Bancroft, what brings you to my door this early morning? Have you re-thought my offer of showing you what my services are really like?" Ace told her that was not why he was there, but she would be his first call if he ever changed his mind…Lola tittered a little laugh and asked him to come in. Ace entered and had a seat in the "art deco" chair that had apparently been a gift from Humdinger, and Lola hopped up on the sofa on the other side of the room, then hopped back down and said, "Where are my manners? Would you like something to drink? Coffee, tea, lemonade?" Ace said that a cup of coffee would be great. The cup of tar from the hotel was still sitting in the SUV at the curb. While Ace liked his coffee strong, he didn't like it so strong that it ate his stomach lining when he drank it.

Lola returned from her kitchen with a cup of coffee and some cream. Ace thanked her and said that black was fine and took a sip of the steaming brew. He told her the coffee was wonderful, but that wasn't why he was here.

Ace didn't beat around the bush. He told Lola that he had been informed that Starletta was in the back pocket of the cartel, as were her ladies at the brothel. He asked Lola if she worked for the cartel in Tijuana or anywhere in Mexico. Lola gave him an emphatic answer. She was not involved with the cartel, and as far as she knew, Starletta Blaze wasn't either. That didn't mean that some cartel members didn't visit the establishment on occasion, but that was purely for "business purposes" if Ace knew what she meant.

Ace asked her if she had ever been approached by anyone from the cartel. She said that there had been some communication when she first showed up in the area, but Starletta took care of it. Ace asked her what she meant by that. She said that Starletta had a friend in the Tijuana Police Department who had some connections and that she spoke with him about getting the cartel to leave her "ladies" alone. She didn't want any trouble with the cartel, but she also didn't want to be involved with them as business partners. After talking with Starletta, she was never approached again by the cartel. Ace asked her if she knew who Starletta's contact was at the PD. She said she wasn't sure, but she had seen Reuben Cuchillas in the brothel many, many times. If she were to hazard a guess, it would be Cuchillas that Starletta was connected to.

Ace then asked her if she was aware of any illicit drugs being passed through the brothel? Lola said that there were definitely some "prescription ED meds" that were passed around, but she had never seen anything like cocaine, heroin, crack, or even marijuana in the brothel. Starletta was emphatic that substances like that were not to be used or brought into the brothel at any time. If a customer was observed with illicit substances, they were asked to leave. When Ace asked her why that was, Lola said that she thought it was because of Joaquin being in and out of the brothel on a regular basis. She thought that Starletta feared that Joaquin could come into contact with something like that when cleaning, and it could hurt or kill him if it were fentanyl, and she would not risk it.

Ace sat and made small talk while he drained the last of his coffee, then thanked Lola for her info and for being so helpful and excused himself.

# Chapter 79

Ace made his way to the brothel via the congested streets of Tijuana, making sure that he wasn't being followed. If he was being followed, they were good. He saw no sign of a tail at all. Ace was surprised that he could park right in front of the brothel. While it was early, the streets of Tijuana were always congested, and finding a parking spot close to your destination was rare.

Ace entered the lobby and spotted Joaquin sweeping the floors in the back of the area where the donkey shows were held. There were a couple of "ladies" lounging about, but the establishment seemed "slow." Ace was hopeful that meant that Starletta would have some time to talk with him, although knowing how much Starletta liked him, he was sure it would be an inconvenience to her, no matter what she had going on.

Ace just stood there as he knew that there were many cameras on him and Starletta would acknowledge his presence soon enough. Within thirty seconds, she stormed into the main room cursing and cussing him as she approached. Ace just stood there and let her vent. When she ran out of breath, Ace asked her if she was done?

She just muttered "pendejo" and asked him what the fuck he was doing back in her business. He told her that he had just a couple of questions and he would be on his way. Hopefully, never darken her doorstep again. She just scoffed and said that she would believe that when it happened. Then she turned and started to walk away from him. Ace stood there, and she turned and asked him if he was coming or just going to stand there like an idiot? Ace followed along but made a beeline for Joaquin instead.

As Ace approached Joaquin, he leaned the broom he was pushing against one of the tables and just stood his ground. Ace asked him how he was doing, and the boy just stared at him. At that point, Starletta's shrill voice, like nails on a chalkboard, screamed for Ace to get away from her son, or she would have him removed from the building, and there would be no more answers to any of his asinine questions.

Ace turned and walked to Starletta at her office door, where she stepped aside and ushered him in. When she entered the room, she slammed the door and proceeded to tear Ace a new asshole about approaching her son. He was off limits. Nobody talked to Joaquin unless she gave permission. She asked him if she was making herself clear enough for him or if she needed to speak slower so that he could understand?

Ace noted that Starletta seemed even more hostile towards him than usual, and he figured he would ask her about it...what could it hurt. Starletta told him that she was tired of seeing him around. She just wanted to get her business back to normal, and as long as he was poking around, she couldn't do that. Ace sat for a minute, then said to Starletta that he hadn't really been around that much and didn't understand how his presence could affect her business anyway. Starletta told Ace that every time he showed up, she had a follow-up visit from Reuben Cuchillas from the Tijuana police, and the clientele, as well as her ladies, didn't like the police hanging around the brothel. Ace said that he was sorry that Cuchillas was pestering her, but Cuchillas was one of the questions that he had.

Ace asked her if Cuchillas was on the take from the cartel? Starletta asked him how she would even know that? Ace then said that he had heard that the cartel had a hand in running her brothel and that the brothel was laundering money through her business as well as running illegal drugs through the business.

As Ace finished up, he noticed that Starletta was turning a shade of purple that he hadn't seen in a human. Then she blew up; she literally stood and, with her hands shaking, pointed at the door and told him to get out. She would not stand in her business and be accused of helping the cartel. She didn't approve of illegal substances being used in her business, and if any of her ladies were caught using or giving illicit drugs to the clients, they were dismissed. She didn't put up with that type of activity. Ace sat and let her vent after it appeared that she had run out of steam and finished with a short-of-breath, "Why are you still sitting here?" comment. Ace asked her if it was possible that these things were being done without her noticing it. She took another deep breath, and Ace thought she was going to start screaming again, but she didn't. She very calmly looked him in the eye and said that she was not associated with the cartel in any way, shape, or form, and she did not allow the use or distribution of illicit substances in her business.

Ace asked her what her relationship with Cuchillas was. She looked at Ace and said that she had no relationship with him. He would visit and have a drink or two occasionally, he never utilized any of the ladies, and he very seldom had any guests with him when he did show up in her building. The few times that he had showed up with guests, it was usually a new police officer with the department. She assumed that he would bring them to her business to show them that this was a place that they could come to and not worry about getting in trouble if word got out that they were there.

Ace told her that someone told him that she was indebted to the local cartel, and that's what kept her afloat. She started to turn that odd shade of purple again, so Ace worked to defuse the situation before she erupted in shouts again. He told her that he didn't believe the source but felt that he had to check it out, especially if Humdinger had a vested interest in the business as well. She told Ace that Humdinger had no interest in the business. She had paid him off years ago. He had just been a customer, nothing more than that, for the last 10 years or so. He paid for services and drinks that he received while in the building. He got nothing for free when he visited.

Ace asked her how she managed to do the fiscal part of the business. Had she taken some accounting classes, or did she have someone on her payroll who took care of all the accounting issues that came with owning a business? She gave a light little laugh and said that there was no way that she would do her own accounting. Humdinger had set her up with an accountant who was paid well to do her books and other accounting needs. She trusted him completely. Ace asked her if she would mind telling him who it was that did her books. She looked at him and said that he knew damn well who did her books. Ace assured her that he had no idea who handled her accounting. She said that Presley Misuse had been doing her accounting for over 10 years, and prior to that she had done them on her own. She said that Misuse never gave her a reason to mistrust him. He was always prompt, polite, and responsive when she had questions or concerns about her finances. Of course, the fact that he received 5 percent of her profits as payment helped, she was sure.

Ace then went out on a limb and asked her if she knew anything about a place called Joaquin Enterprises in California? She said that she had never heard of it.

Ace thanked her for her time and was just getting ready to leave, and he said, did you say that Cuchillas comes to visit you every time that I visit? She said that was absolutely true. She fully expected Cuchillas to show up within 10 minutes of Ace leaving the building. Ace asked her how Cuchillas would even know that he had been there unless her business was being watched? She thought about it for a moment and then said that it was possible that one of her workers contacted him when Ace left the building.

Ace asked her to keep their information from him if possible. If she would just tell Cuchillas that he was there to wind a few things up as he was heading back to the airport to fly back to San Diego, he would appreciate it. At this point, Starletta told him that she didn't do anything for free. If he wanted her to lie to the police, it was going to cost him $500. Ace took his wallet out and handed her five $$100 bills, and headed out the door.

# Chapter 80

Ace got back in the rental vehicle. As he was heading to the vehicle, he noticed three cars with people sitting in them within sight of the entrance to the brothel. One was a cabbie who appeared to be sleeping, the two other vehicles could well be police vehicles that were unmarked. They were beat up, but both appeared to have been kept in good condition considering that they were in Tijuana, which was notorious for vehicles being damaged by passing cars, motorcycles, and scooters, not to mention the occasional stray bullet or two. Ace didn't think that it was likely that these two were cartel members. In his experience, the cartel very seldom traveled as singles in cars, the cartel worked like animals, they worked in packs. If these cars were carrying cartel members, there would be at least two but up to four occupants in each car, not one.

Ace started the SUV and drove off; he wasn't surprised to see both vehicles fall in behind him as he headed to the airport and the car rental where he had rented the vehicle the day before. Ace just hoped that someone would be able to give him a ride back to the hotel where his car was so that he could check out and head north to San Diego. Ace kept watch, and both cars followed behind him. Whoever they were, they were making no attempts to keep from being seen. Ace pulled up to the car rental return and watched as both vehicles that were following him stopped at the curb right up the street and just waited. Ace turned in the rental and asked about a ride to his hotel. The clerk asked which hotel he was staying at. When Ace told him the Holiday Inn Express near the airport, he picked up a phone, dialed a number then, said a few words in Spanish then, hung up, and told Ace that the hotel was sending their shuttle to pick him up and that he was welcome to wait here inside or he could sit out front and wait, whichever he preferred. Ace thought about it for a minute. He could wait inside and just hop on the shuttle when it arrived out front, and then he could see if the two vehicles were going to follow him on the shuttle, or he could go outside and sit on the bench and keep an eye on the two vehicles and their occupants. He might even get a glimpse of them and see if it was anyone that he recognized. He decided on the latter and went out and sat on the bench to wait. Before he sat down, he took his phone out and put it to his ear as though he was on a call and walked towards the first car. When he got within about 20 yards of the car, he could get a glimpse of the driver and was delighted to see that it was the desk clerk from the police station. It wasn't the cartel which made Ace breathe a little easier. Apparently, Cuchillas wanted to keep tabs on him, so he had sent a couple of lackeys from the department to tail him. Ace figured that he would go into the hotel on his arrival and check out, then hop in his car and head north. If he were doing the tailing, he would follow as far as the border and then turn back and report that the American had left the country. Only time would tell if that's what was going to happen.

As Ace walked back to the bench, he saw the shuttle arriving via the service road, so he dashed to the shuttle and boarded it, but not before giving the first car a quick wave and a motion that he was rolling.

Ace said hello to the driver, a pleasant old man who spoke a little broken English, and then took a seat directly behind and to the right of the driver so that he could talk with him as they drove. Ace told him that it was likely that he would be followed by two vehicles and described them to the driver. The driver peered in his rearview mirror and responded that they, indeed, were following him. In broken English, the driver asked if Ace wanted him to try and lose them. Ace told him that wasn't necessary and that he could just take him directly back to the hotel. With that, he sat back for the 10-minute ride, closed his eyes, and tried to think about his next steps.

# Chapter 81

Ace was rolling towards the border, just one of the two vehicles that had been following him in tow. The other driver had apparently returned to the police department or Cuchillas felt that only one was needed since Ace was making no attempt to keep from being followed. He wasn't concerned about being stopped at the border. He still had enough contacts with DHS that he wouldn't be held up, and if he was, he knew who to call.

Ace looked, and the tail was still behind him, two cars back. The closer that Ace got to the border with California, the slower and more congested the traffic got. Ace could be a real dickhead and drive up the shoulder. With his retirement FBI ID, there would be no problem when he nudged his way into the front of the line. However, it would be foolish for his tail to do the same as it was unlikely that they were prepared to cross the border and deal with DHS or ICE agents at the crossing. They just wanted him out of Mexico, and he was happy to oblige them, so he just kept moving forward in the slow lane. Let them waste their day following him until they gave up and turned around. He didn't care.

When Ace was just half a dozen cars from the border, he saw the vehicle that was following executed a U-turn and head back south. Ace was glad that he didn't have to worry about them following him across the border. It wasn't likely that they knew where he lived, and he wanted to keep it that way. Obviously, there was no reason to trust the Mexican police in Tijuana. Ace was sure that Cuchillas was dirty, and that meant that the people who were following him probably were, too.

Ace knew that he was going to have to talk to Presley Misuse and that it was not going to be a pleasant conversation. Ace had told him that he was done with the investigation, and he obviously had continued digging into things that Misuse felt were of no concern to him. Ace was sure that the question of whether any of this additional information caused the death of Ronald Humdinger or not would be an issue. Ace didn't know if there was a direct correlation to the death of Humdinger and the apparent illicit activities being done at the ranch in Camarillo, but if it looked like a duck and quacked like a duck, it was most likely a duck.

Ace was going to do a bit more digging regarding the ranch before he approached Misuse. It was very likely that he would get a "cease and desist" order if he went to Misuse first. Even though Humdinger was dead and buried, there were still many corrupt judges that he had appointed who would be more than willing to do whatever was asked of them by Humdinger Habitats. The nice thing about the digging that he was going to do was that it was all electronic, so he could sit in the comfort of his apartment and do everything from his computer or his phone.

Ace arrived back at his apartment just in time to watch the sunset. The traffic was horrible as usual, a 20-mile drive took him over 2 hours to make the trip back to his apartment.

Ace made his way inside and the first thing that he noticed was that his security system wasn't on. Ace was sure that he had activated the system when he left. Ace took out his gun and did a quick search of the apartment. All appeared normal, but Ace knew he was going to have to do a more thorough search for "bugs." If someone had the ability to break into his apartment and turn off his alarm system, he was certain that they would be tech-savvy enough to place some listening device, possibly even some micro-cameras. One thing for certain was that there had been no attempt to access his computer since it was with him in Tijuana.

# Chapter 82

Ace got out his "sweeper" that he had borrowed and had so far neglected to return and checked over his apartment. He found four listening devices as well as three cameras that had been installed. He left them in place for the time being and, packed up his laptop, and headed to the local pub where he could sit in the back and work on his laptop without fear of being observed. He wouldn't be using their public Wi-Fi, though. Ace was friendly enough with the owner of the establishment that he had the password to their secure Wi-Fi and from what Ace knew about computers and computer systems, was that the system had a 17-digit password with letters, numbers, and special characters. It wasn't likely that anyone would be able to sit and crack their system in the amount of time that Ace was going to be there. If someone was following him who was that good at breaking into computer systems, Ace knew he didn't have a chance anyway. He was hoping that wasn't the case.

Ace fired up the laptop and connected, then he sent a quick "message" to his niece and asked her if she could dial into his laptop and give him some of her access? She messaged back almost immediately and said that wasn't a problem, but good old "Uncle Ace" was going to owe her. She also told him that there would be no way left to track back to her if he happened to get caught going to places that he shouldn't. She wasn't risking her ass for him, no matter how much she loved him.

Ace told her that he understood and that all he really needed was access to Joaquin Enterprises' systems and records. She told him that wouldn't be a problem at all, took control of his device, and redirected it to where it needed to go while Ace just sat there with his hands in his lap and watched her do her work. He truly was amazed that anyone could do what she was doing. He watched and was lost in about 2 minutes. Victoria told him that he was all set up and she already had him in their system. All he had to do was scroll, just like being on the internet, and he could look at all the files that they kept on the mainframe. She gave him a quick tutorial and disconnected after wishing him luck.

Ace started with "board members". He was surprised that all the board members appeared to be aliases. There was a "John Smith," a "John T. Doe," a "Jane Doe," and various other names that were obviously not real. Somebody was keeping secrets, for sure. Ace expected that what he didn't expect to find, and he did, was account numbers for various bank accounts around the world. There were accounts in Mexico, the Caymans, Switzerland, Italy, and the Bahamas, not to mention multiple accounts all over the United States, including banks in California, Texas, Florida, Ohio, New York, Michigan, and Illinois. Most of the accounts were in the major banks, but there were some accounts in "small banks" in what appeared to be small rural towns, mostly in Ohio and Michigan.

As Ace perused the accounts while enjoying a cold beer, he started to notice a trend. Most of the transactions taking place in large banks were just under the reportable limit of $10,000.00. The transactions were also placed in various accounts throughout the day. It appeared that an average day saw between thirty and forty transfers daily from Joaquin Enterprises. The average amount being transferred daily per transaction was $9,500.00. With an average of 35 transactions per day, that was just shy of $350,000 per day, and there were electronic transactions every day. Ace looked back over 90 days, and there wasn't a single day that was skipped. That equated to approximately $30 million dollars being transferred every 90 days. Transactions in the smaller banks in Ohio and Michigan didn't adhere to the smaller transactions, but there were many fewer transactions in these banks. It appeared that the small banks in Ohio and Michigan may very well be legal transactions for services, supplies, etc.

After an hour of looking through Joaquin Enterprises' systems, Ace knew what he had to do. He needed to see who these transfers were going to. He knew that "hacking" a bank wasn't as simple as hacking Joaquin Enterprises' computer system, and he really hated to ask, but he was going to have to call his niece and ask her if she had any suggestions. He knew that he couldn't ask her to hack into the banking systems because it was likely that it would be tracked back to her, and he wouldn't put her at risk.

Ace picked up his cell phone and called Victoria again; she answered on the 2nd ring with a hearty laugh and asked Ace if he had already gotten kicked off their system? He said that wasn't the problem. Then he told her what he had found.  She said that there was no way that she would access banking systems.  Ace told her that he figured that, but he wanted to pick her brain to see if she had any ideas on how he could find out who the transfers were going to, as they all appeared to be to "numerical" accounts, not to a named account.  Victoria thought for a minute and then asked Ace if he had a Venmo or Zell account.  Ace confirmed that he did have a Venmo account.  She said, there's your answer. You have account numbers. Go to the send money option and choose to send money using your account ID.  Enter the account number in a specific format that she provided, then click proceed.  You should see the account holder's name as it is set up on the bank servers.  The app tells you the beneficiary's name so you can confirm who you are sending money to.   Then just cancel the transaction and you are done.  You have the name or names on the account.  Depending on the number of different accounts, it could take a while, but Ace would get the information that he wanted without alerting anyone that he was snooping around and that he wasn't breaking any laws.  Ace told Victoria thanks and told her that at some point in the next few years, he hoped to make it out to pay her a visit…she just said, "Yeah, yeah, you have been saying that for years. I will believe it when you are knocking on my door," with a giggle, she disconnected the call.

Ace started to do his "Venmo" transactions with the account numbers and noticed a pattern very quickly: all the large transactions were going to a bank in Tijuana under the same account name, Joaquin Enterprises.  The smaller transactions were just what they appeared to be: transactions for true business needs. Payment for parts, chemicals (acetone), some farming equipment, etc. Ace discounted the smaller transactions because he found nothing out of the ordinary other than the large amounts of acetone, and he knew what that was being used for. So, Joaquin Enterprises was based out of Tijuana yet the ranch was in Camarillo, California. Obviously, businesses on both sides of the border were common, especially in states that bordered Mexico. That in itself wasn't unusual. The fact that the business was named after Ronald Humdinger's illegitimate son was unusual, though. There had to be a connection. Either Humdinger himself had set up the business and the account or someone else in the know at Humdinger Habitat's or someone in Ronald Humdinger's personal life knew enough to set up the business with the name of Joaquin Blaze.

Ace decided to check on the Business Entities site for the California Secretary of State. The webpage had a search option, so Ace typed in Joaquin Enterprises and was surprised when the address for the ranch in Camarillo showed up in the results. Joaquin Enterprises was registered with the state of California, so there had to be some legitimate business dealings. It appeared that the founding member was Ronald Humdinger, along with Starletta Blaze of Tijuana, Mexico.

Starletta had been lying to him. She did know about Joaquin Enterprises even though she claimed no knowledge of it, but here, her name was on the "charter" for the business, plainly visible on the

347

website from the state. Why would she lie about it? She wouldn't if she thought that it was a "real" business that was helping her with funds to raise Joaquin. If she was aware that they were processing narcotics through the business, she would obviously deny, deny, deny. Ace wasn't going to bother with a trip back south of the border. He was going to call Starletta and just ask her straight out why her name was on the very business that she denied any knowledge of.

Ace dialed Starletta's phone number and was surprised when she picked it up on the 2nd ring. When Ace told her who it was, she let out a string of expletives in Spanish, finishing with pendejo. Ace just let her vent and then asked her again about Joaquin Enterprises. Starletta asked him if he was just stupid? She had already told him that she didn't know anything about the business. Ace stopped her and said that it was funny because he was looking at the company charter on the California Business Entities website, and she was named one of the founding partners along with Ronald Humdinger. Ace heard nothing but static through the line and had actually thought the call had dropped when he heard a deep breath and Starletta said that Ronald Humdinger told her that he had a business venture that he started, and he had named her as a partner so that Joaquin would always be taken care of. She didn't know any more than that. She assumed that was where the monthly delivery of cash came from that helped with raising Joaquin but other than that, she was in the dark. She said that Humdinger told her that while it couldn't be known that he was Joaquin's father, he didn't want his son living as a poor Mexican in Tijuana. He wanted to make sure that when he was old enough, that there was a business for him to step into that would keep him solvent and rich for the rest of his life.

Ace asked her about the account for Joaquin Enterprises in the Tijuana bank. She claimed to know nothing about it. Ace knew that he wouldn't be able to get into the transactions at the bank, but his thought was that if Starletta was aware of the account that was receiving around $30,000,000.00 every ninety days, it wasn't likely that she would be running a brothel in Tijuana. She would be living the rich lifestyle on the coast with a large home and a staff to wait on her and her son for all their needs. She wouldn't be hawking hookers to soldiers and perverts and cleaning up after the donkey shows.

Ace was inclined to believe that she didn't know how much money was going in the account and that she probably wasn't even aware of the account in Tijuana. After all, all the deliveries for Joaquin were made by courier, and it was a cash transaction so there was no way to trace it back to Humdinger Habitats or to Joaquin Enterprises. Plausible deniability was a good thing for Starletta in this situation.

Ace asked Starletta if she had any idea who would be running the account in Tijuana, and she said she had no idea, but she would be willing to go in and ask for a balance and a transaction statement. If she was on the list of founding partners for Joaquin Enterprises, she should certainly be able to see what was in the account. The only thing that she thought she would need would be the account number.

Ace thought about it for a minute and gave her the account number. He told Starletta not to poke around too much because it might alert someone who was watching over the account. She assured Ace that all she was going to do was get a balance sheet and a transaction summary for the last 90 days. She said that she also needed to make a quick trip to Tijuana for some specialty food for her donkey so she could just meet him north of the border with the information that she got from the bank. Starletta told him that she would call him the next morning and let him know how things had went and when she was going to be arriving in San Diego. Ace told her that it would be in her best interest to tell nobody about this until he found out what was going on with the account and that she had to be discreet. If there was a problem with the bank providing the information to her, she should, under no circumstances, make a scene and draw attention to herself.

Starletta assured Ace that she would be fine, her cousin Jorge worked at the bank in the accounting area, and he would help her without notifying anyone. He owed her anyway because he frequented her brothel, and he didn't want his mother to know. She would just use a bit of "blackmail" to get him to look the info up. Ace just chuckled and said, "Of course, you have a relative working in the bank." Starletta asked him what he meant by that, and he explained that he had found that his driver had a lot of "relatives" when he had been down in Tijuana, and now Starletta was doing the same thing. He told her that he was surprised at the number of relatives considering the size of Tijuana. Starletta told him that "familia" was everything to the Mexican people and that Americans could learn a lot from that. Ace didn't disagree.

Ace thanked Starletta and said his goodbyes. She said that she would talk to him in the morning and disconnected the call.

Ace sat back and thought about this situation. Everything seemed to come back to Ronald Humdinger and Humdinger Habitats, along with Starletta's brothel and her son Joaquin. What was he missing? There was obviously a piece of the puzzle that he didn't have. What could it be?

# Chapter 83

It was time for Ace to go through his notes again. He had to figure out what he was missing. There had to be something that he had overlooked.

Ace pulled out his notes and, pulled up the additional notes on his laptop, and started checking things off.

- Humdinger died in a brothel.

- Autopsy didn't show any reason for his death other than natural causes. (although not sure how much "testing" for illicit substances was done)

- The coroner, Dr. Francisco Bravo, had a gambling problem but didn't appear to be on the take. He had no reason to fake the findings of the autopsy, as far as Ace could tell.

- The lead investigator, Rueben Cuchillas, was most likely dirty and working with the cartel or cartels in Tijuana.

- Starletta Blaze appeared to be innocent of any wrongdoing, although there were still questions about Joaquin Enterprises.

- Lola Apera-Amor, the dwarf dominatrix, didn't benefit by the death of Humdinger; if anything, it would hurt her business as far as her bottom line was concerned. Ace didn't really feel that she warranted further investigation.

- Emilyia Humdinger, the grieving widow, didn't appear to have any malice toward Humdinger other than the fact that she didn't want to have sex with him, hence the reason that she allowed him to visit the brothel on occasion. If he was getting his rocks off with all his weird kinks in Tijuana, he wasn't bothering her.

- Presley Misuse, Ace sat back and closed his eyes to think about Misuse. Misuse was a "tool". He wasted no time sweeping in and becoming the primary operating officer at Humdinger Habitats. He appeared to benefit the most from the death of Humdinger. Ace couldn't put his finger on one particular reason, but he didn't trust Misuse. He wanted Ace to rush the investigation. It was obvious that Misuse didn't like Ace digging too deep into how things worked at Humdinger Habitats and the other businesses that Humdinger had been involved in.

- The "threats" that he had received regarding the investigation here in San Diego and in Tijuana, along with the pics, were concerning. Who had arranged the intimidation tactic with the pictures?

- Dr. Cameron Buerger was another loose end. He had avoided meeting with Ace for days, then out of the blue calls and is able to meet with him...after he had given Misuse his final report. Buerger had to be hiding something, but what? Ace circled his notes regarding Buerger for further follow-up.

- Kim Il Soon, the man who had been in the room with Humdinger when he died, was another loose end. Ace knew that he was a source for a lot of the containers that were used and that he was North Korean but was now living outside of North Korea. Ace was concerned that the drugs were coming through the containers that Soon provided, but he would have to talk with Soon if he were going to find out any more info regarding the containers. Ace was sure that as soon as he approached Soon, Misuse would be called, and Ace would be in deep shit. Ace put Soon on the back burner and would return to him if he couldn't find any other links.

Ace wrapped things up for the day and decided it would be a good day to sit and relax, maybe listen to a bit of music, then turn in for the night and get a fresh start in the morning after Starletta called with what she had found out at the bank. Ace walked over to his turntable, flipped through his extensive collection of vinyl records, and picked one of his favorites, Styx, The Grand Illusion, and placed it on the turntable. There was something cathartic about the process of cleaning the vinyl records, placing them on the turntable, and lowering the stylus to the record. Ace had a seat, kicked back the recliner, closed his eyes, and just listened to the music. In a matter of minutes, he was sound asleep.

# Chapter 84

Ace woke up stiff and sore. Sleeping in a recliner was not his ideal night, but he must've been worn out. He never heard the turntable turn off. Thinking about it, he wasn't sure if he had even heard the $2^{nd}$ song on the album before he was sound asleep.

Ace got out of the chair with bones cracking and joints creaking. He decided to go for a quick walk to loosen his joints up and then come back and grab a quick bite to eat. Maybe Starletta will have called by then.

Ace grabbed a cup of coffee and set off on his walk. He had only gone about a block, and his phone rang. Ace knew that it wouldn't be Starletta yet, as it was a bit early for the banks to be open in Tijuana.

He was surprised when he looked at his phone and saw that it was "Nurse Julie" calling him at this early hour. Of course, she lived in the Eastern time zone, so it wasn't that early for her. He answered with a cheery hello. She said he certainly sounded chipper this early in the morning, and he told her that her voice was enough to cheer up the grumpiest of men. She laughed lightly, and they exchanged small talk. Ace could tell that she was in her car, probably on her way to an appointment or an in-service at one of the many hospitals in northeast Ohio. As they chatted while he was walking, he talked to her a bit about the case. He told her that he was stumped and just wasn't sure where this was leading other than the fact that there were drugs coming through the country in the containers being used by Humdinger Habitats to house the homeless in the area. Obviously, there was at least one person at Humdinger Habitats that was dirty, if not more. He told her about the banking issues and how Starletta Blaze was checking into it with a relative who worked at the bank.

Julie asked him if he thought that was a good idea. It sounded to her like there would definitely be some cartel connections, and Starletta could get hurt if she dug too deep. Ace told Julie that she was just trying to find out who was on the account where the large sums of money were being transferred to, and since it appeared that her son's name was on the account, it shouldn't trigger any warnings. At least, that was his hope. While he personally found Starletta a bit repugnant, he was starting to like her just a little bit. She wasn't stupid by any means and had made the most out of using her feminine wiles to further her into the business world in Tijuana.

Ace and Julie chatted a bit more about this and that. Julie asked Ace if he was considering a vacation when he was done with his case. Ace asked her if she was asking him to go on vacation with her? She said no, but if he wanted to visit Ohio, she was pretty sure that he would enjoy himself. There was a ton to do there, and she knew a lot of people, including this guy who did brewery tours. She was sure that he would have a great time. There were many microbreweries in the area, and she knew how much he enjoyed them. Ace told her that he would think about it and he would most certainly follow up with her when he had this case settled.

Ace told Julie goodbye as he was walking back up to his apartment. He disconnected and walked in.

# Chapter 85

Just as he was getting ready to jump in the shower, his cell phone started ringing again. He assumed that it would be Starletta calling him, but his stomach lurched when he saw the caller ID, and it said Presley Misuse. Ace considered not answering the call but figured that would just lead to Misuse and his "driver" showing up at his doorstep and he didn't want or need that headache, so he answered.

Misuse was in rare form, he had a call from Tijuana that Ace was still investigating, and he was basically bitching and moaning about the fact that Ace had ended that investigation, and he wasn't going to be paid anymore. He had already taken the company for $30,000.00, and that was where it was going to end. When Misuse stopped screaming to take a breath, Ace asked him if he was done or if he should just set the phone down and let him continue to berate him like a five-year-old. Ace figured that he didn't have to hold back since Misuse was no longer employing him to investigate the Humdinger case. What was the worst that he could do? Not much, really. Ace could investigate anything that he chose to. After all, his service was a hired service. If he chose to do parts of his investigation at no charge to the client, who would complain? And since Humdinger Habitats was no longer a client, there was no need to listen to Misuse harangue him. Ace told Misuse that he wasn't going to listen to him bitch. If he had some questions that he could ask in a civil manner, Ace would be more than happy to listen and possibly answer those questions if he felt that they deserved an answer.

Ace could hear Misuse grinding his teeth through the phone. Misuse started to respond a couple of times, but Ace could hear him taking some deep breaths to calm himself. Misuse knew that Ace wasn't a pushover and that he would have no problem disconnecting the call. After a few seconds, it appeared that Misuse had calmed himself enough to maintain his composure.

Misuse said, "Let's start over then." "Why am I getting reports that you are still investigating the death of Ronald Humdinger?" Ace told Misuse that he was just tying up a few loose ends that he felt needed to be resolved, that they had nothing to do with the cause of Humdinger's death, which most certainly appeared to be from natural causes, which is exactly what was in the report that he had provided. Misuse asked him, "Why he was investigating anything other than the cause of death, as that was what he had been hired for in the first place?"

Ace took the time to explain that some anomalies had come up in his investigation that he felt it was needed to be addressed from his standpoint but again, it was nothing that would affect the report that he had given to Misuse.

Misuse was losing his temper again; Ace could hear the angst in his voice. He told Ace that he was done with his investigation and that there would be no further digging into Humdinger Habitats or Ronald Humdinger, or he would notify the FBI. Ace just laughed and asked him how well he thought that would work out since he was a retired FBI agent with a lot of friends still at the Bureau? Ace told him to stop with the hollow threats. Ace told him that there was no reason for Misuse to be involved in any further investigation…unless there was a reason why he was concerned. Misuse sputtered out a retort that this was ridiculous, but if Ace wanted to spend his own time pissing off the cartel and law enforcement in Mexico, it was his head on the chopping block. Misuse said he had nothing to worry about, that he wouldn't be swinging from a light post in Tijuana because he was poking around where he shouldn't. Ace was the person that needed to worry about that…

Ace went to hop in the shower again, and again the phone rang. He was going to give Misuse the ass-chewing of his life, but he saw that it was Starletta calling him, so Ace once again turned off the water for the shower and answered. Starletta was bubbling with excitement, so much so that most of her conversation was in Spanish. Ace got her to stop talking for a minute and reminded her that he didn't speak Spanish and that she needed to talk to him in English. She called him a "pendejo" again...obviously, a term that she was fond of as she had called him that at least 50 times over the last several weeks.

Starletta started her story over, this time talking very slowly like she would a child. Ace told her that she could converse at a normal pace. While he didn't speak Spanish, he had no trouble understanding her accented English. Starletta rattled off a few more words in Spanish. Ace was sure that they weren't flattery, but he didn't care. Starletta said that her cousin at the bank had checked into the account, and it appeared to be a legitimate business with transactions occurring on an almost daily basis. He did say that the amounts of money in the transactions were questionable, but when he checked into the company, for all intents and purposes, they were a "real" business with crops that varied by the season and that the income appeared to be highest during the harvest seasons.

Her cousin also told her that the board of directors was listed as Ronald Humdinger, Rueben Cuchillas, Cameron Buerger, and Kim Il Soon. It appeared that Humdinger and Kim Il Soon were each 30% shareholders, while Cameron Buerger and Rueben Cuchillas each maintained 20% ownership.

Starletta's cousin told her that most of the transactions that occurred were electronic, and they were transfers from the account in Tijuana to another account in Switzerland, which meant that there would be no finding out where the money went once it arrived in Switzerland. The Swiss were very proud of their banking privacy laws. This was a truly multi-national consortium, two people from the United States, one from Mexico and one from North Korea, although he was now considered a citizen of South Korea.

Ace thanked Starletta for the information and told her not to push anymore about the account and to make sure that her cousin knew not to say anything to anyone as he didn't want to draw attention to it. Starletta assured him that nobody would say a word and hung up.

Ace finally got his shower. While he was showering, he was planning how to approach Dr. Buerger about this development. Ace knew that Buerger would ghost him again if he thought that there was a chance that he was going to get into trouble about something. Ace couldn't understand why a respected doctor would be involved in something that appeared to be illegal, but greed made people change.

# Chapter 86

Ace pulled into the parking lot for Dr. Buerger, then thought twice about parking around the front, so he drove his car around the back and blocked the good doctor's car in the parking spot so that he wouldn't be able to leave by sneaking out the back door. He could sneak out the back, but he wouldn't be able to go anywhere in his car. Ace was going to go in and tell the receptionist that he needed to see Dr. Buerger. When she left the front desk to go talk to the doctor, Ace was going to go out and around the corner of the building and see if he tried to leave via the rear entrance.

Ace entered the building, and everything went as he expected. Doctor Buerger did try to leave via the rear entrance of the building, but Ace was standing there when he came out. The doctor tried to retreat back inside the building, but Ace stood in front of the entrance and told Buerger that he just wanted to talk to him, and he couldn't understand why he would try to leave if he hadn't done anything wrong or illegal.

Dr. Buerger hemmed and hawed a bit. Ace finally just told him to shut up. He didn't want to hear any excuses. He wasn't in the mood to deal with a liar. He just wanted some answers to a few questions, and then he would be on his way. Dr. Buerger was sweating profusely and was obviously very nervous, but he finally relented and told Ace that he could spare a couple of minutes, but then he would have to go as he had patients to see. Ace just laughed and said that he just witnessed the doctor trying to leave the building, regardless of the patients that he claimed he had to see so he could save that line of bullshit for another day.

Doctor Buerger led Ace to his private office in the back of the building, then stepped aside to allow Ace to enter first. Ace just laughed and said that he wasn't falling for that trick. He pointed, and Dr. Buerger entered with Ace close behind. The office was like any other office in any other strip mall in the country: metal desk, wooden desk chair, mismatched chairs for visitors to sit in, with walls painted beige and a green commercial-grade carpet on the floor. As Dr. Buerger rounded the desk to have a seat, Ace came behind him and pulled out each drawer. He wasn't surprised to see a small, nickel-plated handgun in the right top drawer. Ace told the doctor that he would just hold onto the pistol until he was done talking to him; then, he would be more than happy to hand it over. Of course, while Ace was sitting there, he was emptying the gun and putting the bullets in his pocket. It was possible that the doctor had more bullets in his desk, but until he got it loaded, Ace would be long gone.

Ace finished with the bullets and leaned across the desk. He looked right at the doctor and asked him to tell him about Joaquin Enterprises.

The color drained from Cameron Buerger's face instantly. The light sheen of sweat was now pouring down his face like he had been standing in a rain shower. Buerger started to claim that he didn't know what Ace was talking about, and Ace told him to save it. He knew that Buerger was a 20% owner of the business and that his partners were Ronald Humdinger, Kim Il Soon, and Rueben Cuchillas. Obviously, Humdinger was out of the picture, so it was a matter of determining how the "ownership" was going to be divided up. There was thirty percent of the ownership hanging out there. Was his share going to be divided equally to each remaining member, making Kim Il Soon the majority owner or were Buerger and Cuchillas trying to manufacture a coup of sorts so that one of them would be the majority shareholder? Was there someone else vying for the thirty percent and becoming a new partner? Ace told Buerger to start talking, or he was going to turn what information he had over to the FBI and let them handle it, although it was likely that was going to happen anyway with the information that Ace had so far.

Dr. Buerger took a deep breath and said that he was just an investor in Joaquin Enterprises. Afterall it was a working ranch that produced food products throughout the year, as well as the portion that was a dairy farm.

Ace said that was all well and good, but he wanted to know more about the drugs that were coming into the country via the containers. Dr. Buerger tried to be convincing when he said he had no idea what Ace was talking about. Ace just took out his phone and said that he would make a call to the FBI. While he might not have all the answers, Buerger would be locked up for a while, and Joaquin Enterprises would cease to exist. He could expect to see Kim Il Soon and Rueben Cuchillas picked up in a sweep although Cuchillas would be a bit more difficult since he was a police officer in Mexico, but Ace was sure that it could be done. Then Ace asked Buerger how long he thought that he could last in prison. He was sure that Cuchillas and Soon both would have contacts that would end his life very quickly. After all, fights in prison were common. A pasty-faced doctor wouldn't have much of a chance against the hardened criminals in Lompoc or any of the other federal prisons throughout the state of California.

Ace told Buerger that maybe it was time to come clean about what was going on and maybe he could get some leniency during sentencing. He told Buerger that there was no way that he was leaving the office without information. He had been hired to find out what had happened to Humdinger, and this was part of the investigation. Albeit not the report that had been given to Misuse at Humdinger Habitats but, if there was any chance that Misuse or anyone else was involved, they would all be swept up and held for trial.

Buerger sat across the desk from Ace, wringing his hands, and then he started sniffling like he was about to cry. Ace just sat there and stared at the doctor, finally raising his hands and saying, "I'm waiting. I told you I am not leaving until I get the information that I came for."

Buerger finally looked up at Ace and said that he wanted assurances regarding his and his family's safety if he told him what he knew.

Ace told him that he couldn't guarantee anything as he wasn't a law enforcement or a court officer. Any plea bargain would have to come through the prosecutor's office, but Ace would put in a good word for him if he was helpful now.

Buerger started talking. Two hours later, Ace was leaving the office and his head was swimming. Before Ace left the office, he contacted the local FBI and waited for them to arrive to take Buerger into custody. The SAC also gathered Buerger's family and put them into protective custody. Ace was sure that once word got out that Buerger had talked, there would be many moves made, and Ace expected a lot of fallout from what he had just given to the FBI. The SAC told Ace to watch his back, that powerful people would be coming for him, and not just criminals. Ace could expect people who worked in the federal government to be out to get him. These were people that didn't care whether he lived or died, and if they found him, it wasn't likely that the FBI would ever find his body.

# Chapter 87

Ace met with the assistant director of the FBI that afternoon and spelled everything out as Buerger had explained it to him.

Apparently, Humdinger had been approached several years ago by Kim Il Soon, a North Korean who now lived in South Korea but had homes in the United States and Mexico as well. Soon, he told Humdinger that he could make him an even richer man than he was and would be able to turn Humdinger Habitats into a "profitable" business even though it had to maintain its non-profit status. All Ronald Humdinger had to do was allow the containers used for the homes to be shipped in with "foam insulation" that had been impregnated with illicit narcotics. Soon would provide the expertise and all the equipment necessary to recover the drugs if Humdinger could give him an out-of-the-way location where it could be done. Humdinger told him that he had just the place, a ranch that he owned outside of Camarillo. It was out of town, and it was a functional ranch, so trucks coming and going shouldn't be a concern. If any concerns arose regarding the increased truck traffic, Humdinger would just "donate" a large sum of money to the Mayor's re-election campaign. There would be no record of the transaction, though, so if the Mayor decided to "hide" the donation and look the other way regarding the trucks, Humdinger wouldn't say a word. After all, Humdinger had been known to pay many people off that he thought could be a detriment to his political aspirations. The people that he had paid off were numerous, although the common denominator was that most all of those paid off to keep quiet were women, porn stars, beauty queens, authors, actresses. The list was long.

Humdinger came up with the name of Joaquin Enterprises. As Dr. Buerger put it, any money that he paid to the whore mother of his bastard child could come from these funds, and they would be cash. The only people aware of the cash exchange would be those involved with Joaquin Enterprises, the courier that was used, and Starletta Blaze, although she would know nothing of the business. She would just know that she was getting cash money every month from Humdinger to help raise her son. As payment, she had to keep her mouth shut regarding who his father was.

Kim Il Soon oversaw the process of the drug recovery. He then worked with Rueben Cuchillas as a contact for the Mexican Cartel to get the drugs into Mexico just to be smuggled back across the border into the United States. The deputy director asked Ace why they would do that? Ace said that it was all a part of Humdinger's plan to make the "illegal" immigrants look bad. He was notorious about claiming that they were all rapists, murderers, thugs, and drug mules, and they were what was wrong with this country. Essentially, it came down to someone to blame. Nobody looked for contraband leaving the United States. Customs is always looking for contraband coming into the country. If people got caught smuggling into the country, it just gave Humdinger more credibility with his cult following. They all wanted all the "brown" people out of the country.

Humdinger had talked about securing the border, and if his followers wanted them out, so be it. He would do what he could to make them all look like criminals.

Cuchillas was on the take to the local cartel in Tijuana as Ace had suspected all along. He also got a lot of cash from Humdinger to look the other way in regard to Starletta Blaze, her business, and her son. If anyone started to poke around, it was up to Cuchillas to make sure that the poking stopped or the people were silenced. Since the cartels were intimidating people daily with torture as well as murders, it wasn't hard to keep people away from Starletta. It truly appeared that Humdinger did care a bit for her and their son but not enough to admit that he had the child. He just wanted them safe and unharmed and well cared for. While Humdinger was a pig, he seemed to always take care of his family. Even after his many divorces, he took care of his ex-wives and his children. It was always assumed that Humdinger "had" to take care of his ex-wives because of court orders however, it appeared that he never questioned any settlements and spousal support and child support requests.

As Ace was finishing up his meeting with the Deputy Director, he told Ace that he might want to lay low until all parties were rounded up, including Cuchillas in Mexico. He was likely to be the hardest person to arrest unless there was a way to get him to come to the United States, where he could be taken into custody. Ace thought about it for a minute and told the Deputy Director that he had a plan to get Cuchillas across the border and when he set it in motion, he would notify the FBI so that they could make the arrest. The

Deputy Director raised an eyebrow and told Ace to be safe. He recalled how he never put his own safety as a priority which had led to some close calls in the field. Ace assured him that he would be as safe as possible when dealing with a cartel. Ace just wanted assurances that there would be a team ready when he gave the call that things were moving forward. The DD said that wouldn't be a problem.

# Chapter 88

Ace called Cuchillas and told him that he wanted to meet with him in regard to Humdinger and his death, as it appeared that he hadn't died of "natural causes" after all.

Cuchillas asked Ace what information that he had to point to something other than a natural death, and Ace told him that he didn't want to discuss it over the phone. He felt that it could be best explained in person. He wanted Cuchillas to know that it appeared that Starletta and Lola were both involved and as a private investigator, he had no say over who was arrested in Mexico. Ace told Cuchillas that this would go a long way in helping him to earn the respect and admiration of the US law enforcement community. If he were the person to take people into custody for the untimely death of Ronald Humdinger, he would be a hero. Ace knew that throwing out "hero" to Cuchillas would hook him. His arrogance wouldn't allow him to say no. Just as Ace expected, Cuchillas agreed, and Ace gave Cuchillas a place and time the next morning, just across from the Mexican border near the San Ysidro crossing.

They were going to meet at this little restaurant that was known for the great breakfasts that they served; Morning Glory was the name of the restaurant. The restaurant did a booming business, what was not common knowledge was that it was run by the Department of Homeland Security and was regularly used to meet with "contacts" from the Mexican side of the border. The place was wired for eavesdropping with microphones and hidden cameras everywhere. You couldn't go anywhere inside the restaurant, including the bathroom, where you weren't recorded. It was also fixed so that cell phones didn't work while inside the building. Overall, this was a perfect spot to take Cuchillas into custody.

# Chapter 89

It was another bright and sunny day in Southern California. Ace was sitting at a table just inside the entrance at Morning Glory. He had actually arrived about an hour early so that he could get an order of their souffle pancakes, which were to die for. He wanted to have something to eat because as soon as Cuchillas entered the door, he was going to be taken into custody, and Ace wouldn't have any time to enjoy his breakfast. He had agreed to accompany Cuchillas to the FBI office for interrogation, and with the bureaucracy of the FBI, it could be hours and hours before Ace had a chance to eat. Ace didn't care one bit that Cuchillas wasn't going to get any breakfast. Ace hated crooked cops. Cuchillas was crooked. Ace was sure that when it was all said and done, there would be many more charges levied against Cuchillas than just the things surrounding the Humdinger case. Cuchillas was going to go to prison for a very long time, and that suited Ace just fine.

Ace heard the bell above the door ring, in sauntered Cuchillas with a big grin on his face. Ace raised his hand to motion him over. Cuchillas had only taken about three steps when a man in the first booth stood up and grabbed Cuchillas from behind, bent him over the booth table, and handcuffed him, all while giving him his rights.

Ace stood up, walked up to Cuchillas, looked him in the eye, and said, "Welcome to America. We hope you enjoy your stay. It's going to be a long one." Ace smiled and followed them out the door, where Cuchillas was unceremoniously tossed into the backseat of a black SUV that had materialized out of thin air. The SUV left the parking lot at a high rate of speed. As Ace was walking to his car, his cell phone began to ring in his pocket. He pulled it out and answered, telling the Deputy Director that he had nothing to worry about, that he was on his way and would be there for the questioning.

The Deputy Director told him that he appreciated that, but he had called for another reason. There had been a report of a disturbance that had come across his desk. The disturbance was at Ace's apartment. When police arrived, they had found his door kicked in, and his apartment had been trashed. There was also a large baggie of a "white substance" sitting on the table in the kitchen. The police had taken custody of the substance and tested it, and it tested positive for fentanyl. The local police knew that Ace was a former FBI, so they had called the local office to let them know what had happened. The FBI told them to keep a lid on it and that there was no way that he had been involved in something like this. The police agreed, and even agreed to turn over the fentanyl to the FBI, which they were in custody of now. The Deputy Director said that it was being tested in the lab as they spoke, but they would have more info by the time that he arrived at the office. Ace said thanks and disconnected the call, then got the report from his chemist friend out of his glovebox. Ace wasn't a betting man, but he would bet a million dollars that the chemical composition would match what had been found at Joaquin Enterprises.

Ace made a call to a locksmith on his way back to his apartment. He wanted to make sure that everything was secured and not open for anyone to walk in off the street. The locksmith agreed to meet him in an hour, so Ace just headed home, notifying the director that he would be there in just a bit and if they could hold off questioning of Cuchillas until he got there, he would appreciate it.

# Chapter 90

Ace was pissed; his door was trashed. The locksmith took one look and said that there was nothing that he could do to secure it until Ace got a new door installed. Ace was fuming. He had to get to the FBI office. Where was he going to find someone to install a new door this quickly? The locksmith, who Ace didn't know, said that he could call a construction company that might be able to do the install, but Ace would need to provide the door. Ace just looked at him and said, "I don't know a damn thing about a door. I have no idea what I should order." The locksmith laughed and said that it was a very simple way to get this resolved. There was this place called Home Depot that would walk him through the process of measuring the door while he was on the phone, and for a little extra cash, the locksmith would go and pick up the door and wait for the construction company to install it before he installed the locks.

So, after a quick phone call and $2000.00 later, Ace had a door on its way to be delivered. The locksmith reminded Ace that the cost didn't cover the knobs and locks that he was going to install, so there would be an additional bill of at least $500 for the locks and his time. Ace just shook his head. It was a good thing that he had received a large payday from Humdinger Habitats for his services. He was bleeding money like water with his "follow-up" investigation. Ace might talk with Misuse about an additional payment since it appeared that Humdinger Habitats was in the clear as far as illegal activity was concerned. Ace wasn't really optimistic that Humdinger Habitats would send any more money his way, but it didn't hurt to ask.

Ace arrived at the FBI field office and went in…he was greeted enthusiastically by everyone as he entered. He loved that he still had these connections even though he left the Bureau; these were lifetime connections, and they had proven handy many times. He wanted this type of cooperation to continue. To do that, he had to make sure that he kept his old employers in the loop when it came to investigations that were "Federal" in nature, just like this one had been.

Deputy Director Laughlin met him at the door and asked him how his apartment was. Ace gave him a quick rundown and said that it appeared that his door had been broken down just to plant the drugs. Nothing else appeared to have been touched. Laughlin shook his head and asked him what he had gotten into. Ace raised an eyebrow and said that he was about to find out, when they started questioning Cuchillas. Laughlin clapped him on the back and said that it was great to see him back in the office, but it was nice when he was gone because there weren't near as many headaches now as when Ace was "working" at the bureau. He said that it was nice now that the younger agents were all strictly by the book. He told Ace it was nice that they didn't know how to skirt "the book," but it sucked at times because it made it harder to capture and prosecute criminals.

Unfortunately, this wasn't something that was just happening here, it was happening nationwide ever since Humdinger had been in office and was always claiming that the FBI and the DOJ were out to get him. Of course, it didn't seem to matter that if Humdinger and his cohorts weren't breaking the law, they wouldn't have these issues anyway.

Ace agreed. He felt that Humdinger had done more harm than good when he was in politics. Ace understood that a lot of voters felt that it was a good time to try a person that wasn't a "politician," but that experiment had failed. Mainly since Humdinger felt that the rules and laws just didn't apply to him. He felt that he should have immunity. If he broke the law, it was ok because he had been elected. He was the leader of the greatest country in the free world, and he felt that this afforded him the right to do whatever he wanted, no matter how illegal the activity was.

This investigation was a primary example of the arrogance that was shown by Humdinger. He felt that doing business with people who were considered the "enemy of the state" was ok if it benefitted him. He was in cahoots with a crooked cop who worked for the cartel. He was getting drugs through a North Korean, and he had Dr. Buerger in his back pocket as well. There were large sums of money being sent electronically all over the world. Humdinger didn't need the money. What moved men who had the kind of power he had to get involved in something like this? Ace was sure it was ego and arrogance. The ability to do and get away with things that most of us couldn't. If they got caught, they just bought their way out of it. That was typical of all politicians, and that's where the grand experiment failed because as soon as Humdinger got in office, he became exactly what he was trying to change…a part of the swamp. He was going to drain the swamp, and all he succeeded in doing was making the swamp even larger because all of the folks in the "billionaire boys club" now knew that they could get away with almost anything, and nobody could stop them.

# Chapter 91

The questioning of Cuchillas wasn't going well. It actually wasn't going at all. He refused to say anything other than "lawyer," which didn't really work for him because the FBI was linking him to terrorism. They told him that he could cooperate or go to Guantanamo Bay. The choice was his. He just looked at the interrogator and said lawyer.

Deputy Director Laughlin said that he wasn't worried, that they would leave him to sit for a while and then come back to him. He would talk eventually. Ace could go home and check on his door and apartment, and they would let Ace know if they found any trace of Kim Il Soon. They truly believed that he had left the country and was either in Mexico or South Korea.

Ace asked the Deputy Director if they raided the ranch yet. He confirmed that it hadn't happened yet. They were watching and at this time, no new containers had arrived. Ace said it was entirely possible that Kim Il Soon didn't even know that things were crumbling around him, and he might still show up here in California. Ace asked the Deputy Director to just keep an eye on the ranch for now and give Ace a bit of time to locate Soon. D.D. Laughlin said that he wouldn't raid the ranch until the next batch of containers showed up. When they showed up, all bets were off. The FBI had to catch them in the process of melting down the Styrofoam and obtaining the narcotics from the residue. Ace agreed and headed home. As Ace was leaving, the D.D. again told him to watch his back and they would let him know if there were any new developments.

Ace got back to his apartment just in time to see the locksmith finish installing the new locks on the new door. The locksmith told him that he had put his best-quality deadbolt on the door. The lock was nearly impossible to pick, and it had an extra long deadbolt that prevented the door from being kicked in so easily. He turned the keys over to Ace and handed him the bill. Over $1,000.00 for a lock, doorknob, and installation, but it was clear that what was installed was top-of-the-line. Ace gave the locksmith his credit card to process the charge and waited. The locksmith thanked Ace for his business, gave him his receipt, and turned to leave, then he turned back and said that he almost forgot to tell Ace, but a friend of his came looking for him, but he told her that he didn't know where he was or when he would be back. Ace asked him if he got a name or if he could describe her. He said that he didn't get a name, but describing her wouldn't be a problem. She was a dwarf, and she was dressed in black leather. Ace thanked him again and entered his apartment.

Lola had paid him a visit? What was that about? Ace wasn't sure how she even knew where he lived. He didn't ever recall providing her with his address, just his cellphone number. Although he figured that there were "apps" out there that you could use to find an address if you had a number, or a name. It was probably even easier if you had both and possibly a city to search online.

He searched through his notes and found a phone number for Lola and made the call. She answered on the 2$^{nd}$ ring, with a breathy hello Senor Ace, how are you doing? Ace told her that he was just fine. He was just curious why she had stopped to visit him today while he was out. Lola said that she had some information regarding the Asian man who was with Ronald Humdinger, and she just wanted to talk to him. She had to make a couple of stops at some S&M Boutiques in the San Diego area, and she though it would be nice to visit, after all he had been to her home a couple of times, but she had never got to see what type of life that he lived, and she was curious. Ace assured her that his was a boring life and nothing exciting for her to see. She said, based on the door that had been broken in at his apartment, she didn't believe him. Either he had a bad temper, or someone else had broken into his apartment…that seemed far from boring to her.

Ace asked her what she recalled about the Asian man. She sounded miffed on the phone. She told Ace that she thought that it would be nice to just sit and chat with him and not just talk about the man who accompanied Slave Ronald to his sessions. She really was interested in "getting to know" Ace better. She wanted to get to know him more personally.

Ace stopped her there. He told her that he had zero interest in ever using her or her services. It just wasn't his thing. He could tell by her tone of voice that he had hurt her feelings, but there was no way that he was becoming involved with a dominatrix. Whether she was a dwarf or not, he wasn't into giving up his "control," whether it was in his personal or professional life. Ace asked her again what she could tell him about the Asian man.

She was pouting and asked Ace why she should tell him anything if he couldn't even take the time to have a drink with her. He said to her, "Lola, you initiated the contact with me today, not the other way around. If you don't want to tell me anything, that's ok. I don't know if there is anything more that you can tell me about him anyway. I have his name, I have his business address, and I have three physical addresses of his homes." Lola said that was all good, but did Ace know that he had supplied Humdinger with a "new" brand of ED medication that isn't available on the market yet in the United States? Ace said that he didn't know that information but wasn't sure how it was relevant. She tittered and said, I think it's relevant because the first time that he ever took it was the night that he died in the brothel.

Ace had to close his mouth. Was it possible that Kim Il Soon had murdered Humdinger, thinking that he would acquire the remaining 30% and would be the majority shareholder of Joaquin Enterprises? Ace thanked Lola for the information and told her that if he were ever back down in Tijuana, that he would stop and visit her, not in a professional manner, but as a friend, not a client. After a bit more chit-chat, Ace disconnected and started packing a carry-on. He was heading back to San Francisco to check on the "shipping company" and the whereabouts of Kim Il Soon.

# Chapter 92

Ace arrived at SFO at 750PM and headed to the rental car counter, secured a small Toyota Corolla, and headed off to the container storage yard. Ace parked in the bar parking lot, skirted alongside the fence and was happy to see about a half dozen containers in the section of yard that was for Humdinger Habitats. There would be some movement in the next couple of days, if not tomorrow, which meant that Ace needed to locate Kim Il Soon before the raid at the ranch, or he would be gone. It was hard to say where he would go, not back to North Korea, but the rest of Asia was a possibility. Where best for a man of Asian descent to blend in, than anywhere in Asia.

Ace made his way from the container yard to Partner Trade Limited, the company that the containers came from and what appeared to be a front for the illegal drug trade set up by Kim Il Soon, Ronald Humdinger, Rueben Cuchillas, and Cameron Buerger.

Ace still couldn't figure out why Buerger was in on this but, at this point, didn't really care. He was in protective custody as was his family. It wasn't really up to Ace to know why people did what they did.

Partner Trade Limited was closed. At least, that was the appearance. There were very few lights on in the building, and the front entrance was locked. Ace parked his car and started walking the perimeter of the building. As he made his way around the corner, he ran into Kim Il Soon exiting from a back door. He appeared as shocked to see Ace as Ace was to see him, then Soon reached into his jacket and pulled a gun, fired a snap shot at Ace, which missed his head by about a hair and ran to his car. Ace reached for his weapon, out of habit but recalled that he had flown up and didn't hassle with the paperwork of carrying a weapon on a flight.

Ace dropped over the edge of the culvert at the back of the property and waited. He heard a car pass by, and he risked a peek as it rounded the corner. It was a silver Jaguar, and Ace had enough time to get the license plate. As Ace was crawling out of the ditch, he heard two more shots, so he took off running toward the front parking lot, where he saw his rental car sitting on two flat tires. Obviously, Soon didn't want him to follow. Ace wasn't concerned. He was going to call his old Deputy Director and give him the license plate of the Jaguar. The car was a high-end luxury vehicle that would definitely have a GPS in it. The FBI could track the movements and descend on Soon and make the arrest.

Ace fished his phone out of his pocket and made the call the Deputy Director Laughlin, who told Ace that they would get someone on it and have Soon picked up in a short while.

Ace figured, what the Hell? It was going to be hours until someone could get to the building to repair his flat tires, he might as well check out the building. With that, he walked to the rear door, found a nice stout rock, tossed it through the window in the door, reached in, and unlocked it. He was surprised when he opened the door that no alarm sounded. It was possible that it was a silent alarm, but it looked as though Soon had not activated the alarm system based on the panel on the wall next to the door. It said that the system was idle, so Ace would have as much time as he needed to check out the building.

Ace found the office for Soon, which was conveniently labeled with Kim Il Soon beside the door. Ace turned the knob and entered a luxurious office. Standing and taking it all in, Ace decided to look for anything in regard to Ronald Humdinger and Humdinger Habitats. He was disappointed when he found files that were all in Korean. He just took everything under the letter H in the file cabinet. While he didn't read Korean, the file dividers were in alphabetical order, so Ace assumed that anything pertaining to Humdinger and Humdinger Habitats would be in the H's.

Ace left the building the same way he entered and called the rental company and told them that his vehicle had two flat tires. Could they please send someone with a replacement vehicle to the address as quickly as possible as he had a flight that he needed to catch. The rental clerk said that someone would be out within 30 minutes. Ace leafed through the files and hit paydirt. While he didn't speak Korean, he found pictures of Humdinger Habitats in a file, as well as what looked like "notes" regarding the company. There was also an aerial view of the Ranch that was now Joaquin Enterprises in the same folder.

# Chapter 93

Ace had the rental clerk just take him to the airport rather than rent another car. He wanted to catch the next flight to San Diego and if he was lucky, there would be an empty seat on it. Ace looked at the board and saw that there was a flight boarding in 10 minutes for San Diego, he went to the ticket counter and checked to see if there was a seat available. The clerk said that he was lucky, there was one seat available in business class and that he could purchase the seat for just $2,149.00. Ace just shook his head and handed over his credit card. The clerk processed everything and handed him his boarding pass, then directed him to the gate. Ace took off at a trot, and he didn't care whether he was first on or last on, just as long as he made the flight. Ace boarded just as they were getting ready to close the door at the gate and had his seat. It was a short flight, so there was no need for a drink, a meal, or in-flight entertainment. Within ninety minutes Ace would be disembarking in San Diego, and he would be home. He would turn the files in his possession over to the FBI and be done with this investigation. He had had enough of the entire Humdinger fiasco. He wanted to go home, take a shower, listen to some good music and have a drink or two, then sleep the night away. He knew that Deputy Director Lauglin would keep him informed as to what was found out about the drug smuggling, Cuchillas, Soon, and Buerger.

# Chapter 94

Three days later, Ace was planning his trip to Ohio to visit Julie when his phone rang. It was Deputy Director Lauglin. He just wanted to give Ace an update. Apparently, Humdinger had gotten cold feet or felt that he had made enough money off the illicit drug trade and wanted to end the arrangement. Humdinger was also planning for another foray into the world of politics and knew that there would be too much to hide if the arrangement continued. Dr. Buerger was also in agreement with ending the arrangement, but Cuchillas and Soon both had other things in mind.

The paperwork that Ace had "found" in the parking lot of Soon's business was fairly detailed as to the business dealings. It provided dates, times, dollar amounts, that had traded hands as well as several accounts that the money was transferred to. Apparently, the brothel that Starletta owned was being used to launder money as well as other businesses around Tijuana, San Francisco, and San Diego. It didn't appear that Starletta was involved at all other than taking money from her "clients," many of which paid more than was requested. Obviously, that wasn't a problem for her or her ladies. They all wanted to make as much money with as little "work" as possible. Hence the "hourly" rate whether the "johns" were there for an hour or for ten minutes. Cuchillas ran the operation out of Tijuana and Soon ran the operation out of San Francisco as well as running the shipping operations from Korea to a small island in the

Philippines where the impregnated foam was installed in the containers, but only the containers that were earmarked for Humdinger Habitats, it appeared that the rest of the containers were actually filled with products being shipped to the United States, the empty containers were explained away as being purchased empty by Humdinger Habitats because Ronald Humdinger didn't want them to be "dirty," he wanted them to always look nice for the TV and dirty and dingy containers weren't TV friendly.

Cuchillas had finally spilled his guts when the FBI was loading him up on a C130 bound for Cuba. He explained how the drugs got into the country and how Humdinger wanted it smuggled back in with "illegal immigrants" crossing the border. He didn't care if some of them got caught, it just made him look better to his following. The "coyotes" were paid large sums of money to get their "cargo" to carry a backpack full of fentanyl across the border. The cartel didn't care whether it made it across the border or not. They had already been paid, the coyotes had been paid, Cuchillas had been paid, any drugs that made it across was just cash for the drug dealers throughout the states, and the fact that the drugs were contaminated with cancer-causing agents from the foam and the acetone was of no concern either. Humdinger, Soon, Cuchillas, and Buerger all knew that the likelihood of an addict living long enough to contract cancer was extremely thin. Most addicts that used drugs cut from fentanyl didn't live to see the ripe old age of 40, let alone live long enough to get cancer.

Soon was arrested at the San Ysidro border as he was trying to leave the country. He also wasn't talking until the interrogation team started reading from the paperwork that Ace had found. When he was accused of killing Humdinger, he turned on Dr. Buerger, who had prescribed the ED medication for Humdinger; however, he slipped up when he said that he replaced the medication in his bottle with medication that he had when he was with the hooker in Tijuana. The medication was basically Viagra, but soon had mixed a bit of a stimulant into the pills that would elevate Humdinger's heart rate and blood pressure to unsafe levels. The hope was that Humdinger would just quit frequenting the brothel because Cuchillas was hoping to blackmail Blaze into giving it up, and they all knew that would never happen as long as Humdinger was visiting the brothel. Soon claimed that he hadn't meant for Humdinger to die but it was what it was.

When asked about the Secret Service agents that had been there when Humdinger had died, and they smuggled him out, Soon was more than happy to provide names of the agents involved as they had both requested large sums of money to keep their mouths shut. Kim Il Soon had paid them, and from what he understood, they were both still part of the Secret Service. Laughlin assured Ace that was not the case. Both agents had been arrested in the middle of the night. Neither was married, so there would be no leaks from a spouse. If a parent contacted the Secret Service about their missing son, they would be given the run around (basically told that they were on special assignment) until a time and place that all of the information regarding "corrupt" Secret Service agents being arrested and charged would be released to the press. Of course, both men will have already been tried and sentenced.

Deputy Director Laughlin told Ace that he had performed admirably and he could always come back to the bureau. If nothing else, he could come back and do training for the new agents. Ace thanked him for the offer but said that he was content running his own business and reporting only to himself.

The Deputy Director asked him what his plans were for now. Ace said that he might take a little vacation. He had heard Ohio was nice and thought he would check it out. Laughlin laughed and said, watch out for those nurses. I hear they are freaks, but in a good way, and then he hung up.

Ace stared at his phone; how did Laughlin know about Julie Ritter? Well, it was the FBI, and he was a former agent. He had to assume that they kept close tabs on their agents, whether they were active or retired.

Ace made one more call. It was to Jaime Shore, the news reporter who hated Ronald Humdinger. He told him that he would be sending him a "file," but that his source would have to be an "unnamed" source.

The End

Made in United States
North Haven, CT
24 January 2025

64905880R00238